P9-DVN-666

THE WIZARD LORD

TOR BOOKS BY LAWRENCE WATT-EVANS

THE OBSIDIAN CHRONICLES

Dragon Weather

The Dragon Society

Dragon Venom

LEGENDS OF ETHSHAR

Night of Madness

Ithanalin's Restoration

Touched by the Gods

Split Heirs (with Esther Friesner)

THE ANNALS OF THE CHOSEN

The Wizard Lord

THE WIZARD LORD

VOLUME ONE OF THE
ANNALS OF THE CHOSEN

LAWRENCE WATT-EVANS

A TOM DOHERTY ASSOCIATES BOOK
New York

TOR®

This is a work of fiction. All the characters and events portrayed in this novel are either fictitious or are used fictitiously.

THE WIZARD LORD: VOLUME ONE OF THE ANNALS OF THE CHOSEN

This book is printed on acid-free paper.

Edited by Brian Thomsen

A Tor Book
Published by Tom Doherty Associates, LLC
175 Fifth Avenue
New York, NY 10010

www.tor.com

Library of Congress Cataloging-in-Publication Data

Watt-Evans, Lawrence, 1954–
The wizard lord / Lawrence Watt-Evans.—1st ed.
p. cm.—(The annals of the chosen ; v. 1)
"A Tom Doherty Associates book."
ISBN-13: 978-0-765-31026-2 (acid-free paper)
ISBN-10: 0-765-31026-0 (acid-free paper)
I. Title.

PS3573.A859W59 2006
813'.54—dc22

2005044636

First Edition: March 2006

Printed in the United States of America

0 9 8 7 6 5 4 3 2 1

Dedicated to my friend Kurt Busiek

ACKNOWLEDGMENTS

My thanks to Timothy S. O'Brien for essential aid in creating the world of this story.

THE BALLAD OF THE CHOSEN

When day turns dark and shadows fall
Across the broken lands
And madness turns to taloned claws
Our gentle ruler's hands

Then eight are called by whims of fate
To save us from our doom;
The Chosen come to guard us all
And lay evil in its tomb

[chorus]
If a Wizard Lord should turn
Against the common man
These Chosen eight shall bring him down,
Bring peace to Barokan!

The Leader shows his bold resolve
Confronting every foe
His words will guide the Chosen as
He tells them how to go

The Seer seeks the comrades out
And gathers them to fight
Nor can their foeman hide from him;
He has the second sight
[chorus]

The Swordsman's blade is swift and sure
His skill is unsurpassed
If any stands against him, then
That fight shall be their last

A lovely face the Beauty has,
And shapely legs and arms
She distracts the evil men
And lures them with her charms
[chorus]

There is no lock nor guarded door
That can stop the Thief
He penetrates the fortress dark
To bring the land relief

Every song and story told,
The Scholar knows them all
He knows the wizard's weaknesses
To hasten evil's fall
[chorus]

The Archer's missiles never miss;
His arrows find their mark
He strikes at evil from afar
To drive away the dark

The Speaker harks to every tongue,
Of stone and beast and man
He finds the Dark Lord's secrets out
So no defense can stand

If a Wizard Lord should turn
Against the common man
These Chosen eight shall bring him down,
Bring peace to Barokan—
Yes, the Chosen guard us all,
Bring peace to Barokan!

THE WIZARD LORD

[1]

The youth leaned over the wooden rail, one hand on the shutters, looking down into the valley.

The sun had dropped below the western ridge, plunging fields and groves into shadow, and an evening mist was thickening, further obscuring the still-green trees below the pavilion. Sparkles of colored light flickered through the mist and the leaves as some of the *ler* went about their mysterious business, bright and sharp against the blue-green dimness.

The sky above was still ablaze with color, orange in the west, indigo above the distant cliffs in the east, in stark contrast to the mist-shrouded depths. The pavilion seemed suspended between two worlds, the clear emptiness above, the soft thicknesses below. It was beautiful, and the youth gave the *ler* and the Wizard Lord silent thanks for such fine weather.

"Hey, Breaker!" someone called from somewhere in the pavilion behind him, breaking the spell. "If you aren't going to drink your share of the beer, I will!"

"Oh, no, you won't," the youth said, turning. "I'd rather leave it for the *ler* than waste it on the likes of you!"

That got a laugh from the dozen young men clustered around the village brewmaster, and a path opened for Breaker to stride up and take his heavy mug of ale from the old man's hand. He took a swig, swallowed, and looked around to see whether anyone else was still waiting a turn.

He had apparently been the last; he gulped more beer, then stepped away to leave room for anyone who needed a refill.

Inside the pavilion was neither the misty dimness of the valley nor the vivid color of the sky, but a third world, a world of wood and stone and candlelight. The air was clear, but daylight was fading, shadows beginning to appear despite the yellow glow of a hundred lanterns set on the handful of tables and hung from the beams overhead. The familiar faces of his friends and fellow villagers surrounded him; close at hand, clustered around the brewmaster, were the young men who had just finished bringing in the barley harvest—a job of which he had done his share and more. Over in the back of the big room a few other villagers, his elder sister among them, were tuning their instruments for the evening's planned entertainment. Three old women sat in rockers by the big central hearth, talking quietly.

Most of the rest of the local population would probably stop in later to help celebrate the harvest—and not incidentally, to drink up the few remaining kegs of last summer's stock of beer and make room in the cellars for the new batch that would see them through the coming winter. For now, though, most of the pavilion's hall stood open and empty beneath the lantern-hung beams, tables folded and benches stacked against the stone wall at the back.

Five people were sitting on a bench at the far end of the terrace rail, Breaker noticed, by the door to the outside road. One was the village's elder priestess, the sigil of office glowing faintly upon her forehead, while the other four were cloaked, and three of them were elaborately adorned with protective *ara* feathers. Breaker was fairly sure he recognized one of the feathered ones as the Greenwater Guide, the man who worked the southwestern road out of Mad Oak, past the eponymous tree itself, but the others were unfamiliar—presumably travelers the guide had led, probably on their way to Ashgrove and perhaps beyond, since Breaker could think of no reason strangers would be stopping in Mad Oak.

Or perhaps they had just come from Ashgrove and were bound for Greenwater. That was actually a little more likely; from Greenwater one could travel on to the Midlands and the southern hills and all the wide world to the south of Longvale, while beyond Ashgrove were just half a dozen towns in Longvale and Shadowvale before the safe routes ended.

Whatever their destination they clearly were travelers, since two of them wore *ara* feathers, and even cloaked, Breaker doubted there was a man in Mad Oak he wouldn't have recognized. He wondered why the travelers weren't claiming their share of the beer; they were certainly watching the harvesters drink, and Elder Priestess would have let them know they were welcome to share in the land's bounty.

And why did one traveler not have *ara* plumes on his cloak to ward off the hostile magic of the wilds between towns?

"Hey, Breaker!" called one of the young man's companions. "If you keep staring at those people, we may just have to throw you over the rail to the *ler* to apologize for your rudeness!"

The other young men laughed as Breaker turned around angrily. "I wasn't staring!" he said. "At least, no more than *they* were staring at *us.*"

"All the same, you don't seem to be paying attention to the rest of *us*—or to the beer, and that's an insult to all the work we did today to earn it. Maybe we should heave you over just on general principles."

"You think you could throw me over the rail, Joker?" Breaker demanded.

"Oh, not by myself," Joker retorted. "But I'm sure some of these other fine fellows would be happy to help."

Breaker's momentary annoyance was already spent; he smiled. "Now, why would they want to help *you,* Joker? There isn't a one of us you haven't tormented this summer!"

"But at least I do the beer justice!" He turned and held out his mug. "Brewer, another round!" The brewmaster obliged him, opening the tap as Joker thrust the mug into position.

"They *are* staring at us, aren't they?" remarked Elbows, another of the group, looking past Breaker at the strangers.

Breaker turned again. He was almost beginning to get dizzy, looking around at everything like this, and he frowned at himself. This was supposed to be a celebration with his friends—it had been a good year and a good harvest, thanks to the *ler* and the Wizard Lord and plenty of hard work, and they had the summer beer to drink up to make room for the brewer's next batch. In an hour or so they would be dancing with the village girls, begging kisses and maybe something more than kisses, and here he was looking at the sky and the *ler* and the travelers and everywhere but at his companions and the beer. He felt somehow detached from his surroundings, as if he were a mere observer rather than a participant, and he didn't know why; it certainly wasn't a common sensation for him. It was as if the *ler* were trying to tell him something, but he couldn't imagine what.

He gulped the rest of his mug, but did not immediately turn back to refill it.

The strangers really were watching the harvesters with an intensity that seemed out of place.

"If you want some beer, come ahead," Breaker called to them. "We can spare you a few pints."

The travelers glanced at one another, exchanged a few words Breaker could not hear; the priestess leaned over and whispered something equally inaudible. The guide—Breaker was sure now that that man was the guide who worked the roads to Ashgrove and Greenwater—threw up his hands, rose from the bench, and stepped away, clearly dissociating himself from whatever the others were discussing.

Then the strangers rose, all three of them, and began walking toward the party of harvesters. The priestess hesitated, then arose and followed them.

Breaker watched their approach with interest. He set his empty mug down on the nearer of the two tables the brewmaster had set up, and put his hands on his hips.

The two of the strangers who wore feathers, a man and a woman, also carried staves—not simple walking sticks, but elaborately carved and decorated things as tall as their bearers, with assorted trinkets dangling from them here and there. The third figure was a big man, bigger than Breaker himself, and as he walked his featherless cloak fell open to reveal a heavy leather belt with a scabbard and hilt slung on one hip—a large scabbard, though the cloak still hid its actual length, and an unusually large and fine hilt.

And all three of them, Breaker saw now that their faces sometimes caught the lanternlight as they moved, were old, easily as old as the grandmothers chattering by the hearth. That was odd; travel was usually considered too dangerous for the elderly.

But then, Breaker was already fairly certain these three weren't just traders or wanderers; he had a thought or two as to who they might be, though it was hard to believe. He stepped aside, to let them at the keg of beer, but the old man with the staff spoke.

"We didn't come here for beer, I'm afraid."

"Though we do appreciate the offer," the old woman added hastily. She glanced around. "We are grateful to the *ler* of this place for making us welcome, and would not spurn any hospitality they might see fit to give us."

"If you want to talk to the *ler*, you want to talk to the priestess," said one of Breaker's companions, with a nod at the woman behind them. "We're just honest working men with beer to drink up."

"And it's honest men we seek," said the man with the scabbard.

Breaker and his fellows glanced at one another.

"If you're looking for workers, we've already done our share," Brokenose said. "Filled the storehouses to the rafters, we did."

"And how do you propose to tell whether we're honest?" Joker asked. "Take our word for it?"

The man with the staff held up a hand. "We aren't looking for workers—not the sort you mean, at any rate. We just need *one* man, in all Barokan."

Joker grinned. "Is your granddaughter *that* ugly, old man, that you need to go searching from town to town to find her a man?"

"Why don't you keep your wit to yourself, lackbeard?" the man with the scabbard replied. "It's not as if you have much to spare."

That got a better laugh than either of Joker's sallies, to the local youth's annoyance. Breaker smiled, but did not actually laugh; instead he said, "Why don't you save us all some time, and just tell us what you want of us?"

The man with the staff glanced at the old woman, but before either of them could speak the man with the scabbard said, "All right, then—how would one of you like to be the world's greatest swordsman?"

The laughter stopped abruptly, and smiles faded. The young men all stared at the old fellow with the scabbard—with, as Breaker had already realized, the sword. That wasn't just a big knife on his belt; it was a *sword.*

And those staves—the other strangers weren't just travelers carrying protective charms, were they? If this was the Swordsman, then these two were probably either others of the Chosen, or they were wizards—and the staves implied wizards. Breaker had never seen a wizard before. Oh, he had heard stories, but so far as he knew, no wizard had set foot in Mad Oak in more than fifty years.

Not that anyone particularly *wanted* a wizard here—wizards usually meant trouble. The one who had passed through when his grandparents were children had been harmless enough, but there was still a dead patch at the north edge of town where nothing would grow, and where anyone who set foot felt chills and nausea, that was said to be a relic of where a Wizard Lord had slain a rogue wizard centuries ago, rescuing three kidnapped maidens in the process. Wizards brought plague and fire—or at least, the stories said they had in the old days, before the Wizard Lords tamed them.

"Are you serious?" Brokenose asked, breaking the silence.

Elbows looked past the three strangers and asked Elder Priestess, "Is he really the Swordsman?"

She held up empty hands. "It could be illusions and trickery, but so far as I know, they are what they claim to be."

The Swordsman opened his cloak and pulled it back to display the entire scabbard he wore. The sheath was almost three feet long, and if the blade matched, then the weapon he bore was unquestionably a sword.

Breaker had never seen a real sword before. He and his friends had fought duels with sticks as children, of course, despite maternal demands that they not do anything so dangerous as waving sharp sticks near each other's eyes, but the longest steel blade he had ever seen was Skinner's knife, the length of his forearm. He stared at the brass-and-leather hilt.

"I am indeed the Chosen Swordsman," the Swordsman said, "and I have come here to find my successor. So, does any of you care to claim the title?"

The little crowd fell silent once again; Breaker sensed his friends moving away from the strangers, backing off from this outrageous intrusion on their celebration. He glanced around.

Brewer had stepped behind the table that held the beer kegs, separating himself from the entire conversation. The musicians on the far side of the pavilion were staring; the grandmothers had stopped rocking their chairs to watch. The harvesters had formed up into a tight group, a closed barrier against the strangers.

And Breaker had somehow wound up a little to one side, outside the group.

Joker was front and center, with Brokenose and Elbows on his left, Spitter and Digger at his right, and the rest of the party behind, while Breaker stood off to the left, toward the rail overlooking the valley.

That odd sense of detachment, of being separate from the others, welled up again, and again Breaker wondered whether it might be a message from some *ler*. None had ever taken any interest in him before, and no one had ever suggested he might have any priestly talents, but they were everywhere, and saw everything, and guided the townsfolk's lives; perhaps one was trying to guide him now.

And whether a *ler* was involved or not, the idea of spending the rest of his life here in Mad Oak in Longvale, growing barley and beans and watching the seasons wheel around until his soul finally fled into the night, never seeing what lay beyond the horizon, suddenly seemed horrific beyond imagining.

And surely, if he were the Chosen Swordsman, one of the eight designated heroes, he could travel wherever in Barokan he pleased, and do more than tend crops until he died. He could go anywhere, speak to anyone, even the Wizard Lord himself.

"I'll do it," he said.

For a moment the pavilion fell silent, as a smile spread across the Swordsman's face and the two wizards glanced at one another. Then a familiar voice muttered, "And they call *me* 'Joker'!"

Breaker half-turned and growled, "And they call me 'Breaker.' Shall I demonstrate why?"

"Now, there's no need for that," the male wizard said quickly.

"But he's never even *seen* a sword before!" Joker protested.

"Neither have you," Breaker retorted. "Neither has any of us. What's that have to do with it? It's *magic,* isn't it?"

"That doesn't mean there's no effort involved," the male wizard said hastily.

"What, you need to talk to the *ler*?" Brokenose asked.

"Oh, a little more than that," the male wizard replied. "After all . . ."

"You have to practice every day," the Swordsman interrupted. "One hour every day, rain or shine, summer or winter, sick or well. If you don't have a sword, you practice the movements without it. If you're too sick to move, you review it in your head, moving whatever you can, even if it's just your eyes. And you do it *every day,* or the *ler* won't let you sleep, or eat, until you do." He frowned. "I'm an old man, and I'm sick of it—I want some *rest.* That's why I'm offering you a chance to replace me."

"I never heard that, about daily exercise," Spitter said.

"Why would you?" the Swordsman said. He glanced at the male wizard. "You think the Council of Immortals goes about spreading every little detail of their methods to any farmer who might ask?"

"What happens if you just fast for a day, and don't sleep, and wait it out?" Digger asked.

The Swordsman grimaced, but before he could speak the wizard said, "You really wouldn't want to do that."

"That would break the Swordsman's oath to the Council of Immortals," the female wizard added.

"An oath that binds some very powerful *ler,*" her companion confirmed.

"I was never fool enough to try it," the Swordsman said. "I had enough problems without angering wizards and spirits."

"What of it?" Breaker asked. "Practice every day—that's no problem. We haul water every day, tend the crops every day . . ."

"Not in winter," Spitter interjected.

"We do *some* sort of work every day of our lives; this wouldn't be so different. I'll do it—or is there more to it?"

"Well, of course there's the whole bargain," the male wizard said. "The whole reason the Chosen are Chosen."

"To kill the Wizard Lord," Breaker said. He looked the Swordsman in the eye. "How many Wizard Lords have *you* killed?"

"None," the Swordsman snapped. "Even here, you must know that! I've been the Chosen Swordsman for forty-four years, since I wasn't much older than you are, and I've seen three Wizard Lords hold power, and they've all served honorably and well so far—the weather has been good, the wizards well-behaved, criminals captured, the beasts held at bay. No one needed to remove them. And the Swordsman before me served for thirty-eight years and was never called, and the man before *him* . . . well . . ."

"The man before him slew the Dark Lord of Goln Vleys," the male wizard said. "But he lived happily for another twenty years afterward."

"So it's been a hundred years or more since the Swordsman was summoned to kill a Wizard Lord," Breaker said. "I don't think I need to worry so very much about that part of the job."

"But the whole purpose of the magic is to defend against a corrupted Wizard Lord," the female wizard reminded him. "You mustn't forget that."

"Breaker, are you seriously considering this?" Joker asked quietly, all humor gone from his voice.

Breaker turned. "What if I am?" he asked.

"I think you should take your time about anything this important," Joker said, still utterly serious. "Talk it over with your parents, with people you trust. Talk to the priestess, maybe consult some *ler*. This is . . . If this is true, if these people are who they claim to be, this is *big*, the biggest thing to ever happen here. Don't let them ruin your life by dragging you into things too big for you."

"Too *big* for me?" Breaker snorted. "You think I can't handle it?" But then he calmed, and said, "But you're right—I don't need to rush into it."

"You couldn't rush into it in any case," the male wizard said. "There's a great deal to be done before the title can be handed on—you must be trained and prepared, the *ler* summoned and constrained, a sword found for you. And it may be you won't be able to take the role; it requires natural ability, as well as magic, to be chosen as the world's greatest swordsman."

"But you look like you're capable enough," the Swordsman said. "Don't let old Islander here put you off."

Breaker looked at the Swordsman, then at the two wizards, and finally turned to Elder Priestess, who had been standing silently throughout the discussion. He half-expected her to tell him why he could not consider the strangers' offer.

"It's your decision," she said.

"Then I'll think about it," Breaker said. "And I'll have another beer." He turned and held his mug out toward Brewer, who obliged.

[2]

Breaker woke up in his own bed, which was a pleasant surprise; he had no memory of returning home from the pavilion.

He did remember most of the evening, though. He remembered the wizards and the old Swordsman, and his sister Harp chastising him, during a break in the dancing, for even *considering* their offer. He remembered Brewer rapping his knuckles on the last keg to demonstrate that the summer beer was indeed gone. He remembered Joker being surprisingly subdued the whole evening. He remembered singing along with "The Ballad of the Chosen," or at least the verses he knew, and he had joined in the chorus for that old song about the Wizard Lord of the High Redoubt hunting down the three murderers. He remembered dancing with Curly and Little Weaver and even young Mudpie, and having the distinct feeling that Elder Priestess was watching him as he danced.

But what had happened after the dancing ended was lost, drowned in the summer beer.

Breaker sat up warily; sometimes the day after such a night found his head aching and his guts troubled. This time, though, the *ler* had been kind—he felt fine. The morning sun spilling in the window was still tinged with gold and slanting from low in the east, so he had not slept particularly late despite the beer and the dancing.

And the barley harvest was in. Brewer's boys would be busy for the next several days, starting the next batch of malt, and there were undoubtedly people cleaning the pavilion, but Breaker was in neither group. He could take a day or two to do nothing before starting preparations for winter.

Or he could find those travelers, and ask if they had been serious in suggesting he might become the world's greatest swordsman, one of the Chosen, the eight heroes designated to keep the Wizard Lord in check.

Not that the present Wizard Lord was in any obvious need of restraint; he had been in power for a few years, and Breaker had heard not the slightest rumor of impropriety. The weather had been as well regulated as ever—sunny days relieved by scattered clouds and cool breezes, the gentle rain falling only late at night, and so on. No rogue wizards had been reported anywhere in Longvale. The wild beasts stayed in their caves and forests, and no travelers had been set upon and eaten. All was right in Barokan.

Breaker glanced at the sunlit window, trying to remember just how long the present Wizard Lord had been in power. When had news of his predecessor's resignation and the incumbent's ascension reached Mad Oak?

Breaker knew he had been old enough to understand the news, and to ask questions until his parents got annoyed enough to send him to bother Elder Priestess instead. It had been spring, he remembered; she had been walking the fields, talking to the *ler,* asking them to help the crops grow, and he had walked alongside, badgering her with pointless questions about wizards and true names and Chosen Heroes—except then the conversation had drifted to when he would be ready to work in the fields himself, doing more than running errands or gleaning.

He must have been a few months short of his twelfth birthday, then, so that was almost eight years ago.

If the Wizard Lord had behaved himself and ruled wisely for eight years, it seemed unlikely he would turn evil now.

Not that Breaker understood why *any* Wizard Lord would ever go bad and need to be removed. After all, when all Barokan's wizards appoint you to hold the power of life and death over them, when you are master of half the magic in the world, when you can control wild animals and even the weather itself, when you can go anywhere and do almost anything, why would you risk it all by breaking the rules?

He knew from the stories that sometimes a Wizard Lord *did* go mad, or turn bad, so that the Chosen were summoned to slay him, but it seemed amazingly stupid. Maybe the first one, all those centuries ago, had thought he could somehow get away with it, but the others since then must have been fools.

In most of the stories about Wizard Lords, of course, the Wizard Lord was the hero, protecting people from monsters or evil wizards, or tracking down criminals who fled beyond the boundaries where the priests couldn't reach them, but there were those few Wizard Lords who had gone bad and been slain by the Chosen. Just a few, a handful, out of the dozens of wizards who had held the title.

And of course, as the Swordsman had pointed out, none of them had done anything of the sort in more than a hundred years. The Chosen were still needed, just in case, but they didn't need to *do* anything. They were like the guard on the cellars—as long as he was there no one tried to sneak in, even though all he did was stand ready.

So becoming the Chosen Swordsman, or any of the others, wouldn't mean he would actually need to kill a Wizard Lord; he would just need to be *ready,* and knowing that he was would keep the Wizard Lord from abusing his power.

Would being the Swordsman mean he would meet all the other Chosen? Not that he particularly wanted to meet the Leader, or the Thief, but meeting the Beauty . . . he wouldn't mind that. Or the Seer, who was privy to so many secrets.

But unless they were summoned to slay a Wizard Lord, he supposed they would remain scattered across Barokan.

How were they summoned, if they were needed? Elder hadn't known, when he asked her all those years ago; she had just said she supposed it was magic.

Those wizards would undoubtedly know, or the present Swordsman—and Breaker had the perfect excuse to ask them all the questions he wanted, if he was considering becoming the Swordsman's replacement.

Breaker wasn't sure how serious he was about taking the job, but he definitely wanted to talk to those three again, preferably with less of an audience this time.

He rose and found his drawers and his trews, and a moment later he ambled out to the kitchen to inquire about breakfast.

His mother was rolling out dough, and did not look up as he entered, nor did she say a word. Breaker paused in the doorway. He knew she had heard him; her ears were sharp, and the occasional thump of the rolling pin would hardly disguise the thump of his footsteps. On any ordinary morning she would have looked up and wished him a good morning.

His two younger sisters, Fidget and Spider, were sitting silently at the table, staring at him.

He sighed.

"What did I do?" he asked. "Or not do, if that's the case."

The rolling pin stopped. "Harp told me about the strangers," his mother replied.

That stirred a few memories. His parents had not come to the harvest celebration; his father had reportedly felt ill, as he often did, and his mother had stayed home to make sure it was nothing serious. Fidget had brought the news, and had asked Elder Priestess to look in on Father on her way home, and maybe talk to the *ler*.

"Is Father all right?" he asked.

His mother snapped, "Don't change the subject!"

"I'm not . . . well, maybe I am, but I'd like to know."

"Elder says he ate something he shouldn't have, as usual, but he'll be fine. *You,* on the other hand, seem determined to ruin your life."

"I'm not determined to do anything, but yes, I'm considering the possibility of becoming the Chosen Swordsman. How would that ruin my life?"

"You could get called away at any moment to traipse halfway across the world to kill the Wizard Lord! You'd kill the man who lets the crops grow, who sends the spring rain and hunts down killers. And if the call came in the middle of the harvest, or of planting, it wouldn't matter—you'd have to go all the same, even if it meant losing the entire crop. And he might kill *you,* instead—it's happened, you know. The Chosen don't always all survive. The first Dark Lord killed something like *half* of them, my grandmother told me."

"That was what, a thousand years ago? Things are different now, Mother."

"Six or seven hundred, I think—less than a thousand, at any rate. And who says everything's changed for the better? Maybe the Wizard Lords have gotten smarter again, and found ways around all the precautions!"

"Mother, there hasn't been a Dark Lord in a hundred years. The current Swordsman has never seen one, and the Swordsman before him didn't, either. The wizards who *choose* the Wizard Lords have gotten smarter, and they don't pick bad men anymore."

"How can you be sure of that? And if it's true, then why do they need *anyone* to be Chosen?"

"It's just a precaution. A tradition. And I think I'd like being part of the tradition."

"They don't pay you anything, do they? You'd still need to make your living in the barley fields or some other ordinary place, *and* do this sword nonsense in your spare time."

"I suppose," Breaker said. He hadn't really thought about that part—so few people in Mad Oak ever used money that it hadn't occurred to him to worry about it.

"So why would you want to do it, then? It's extra work and danger, and what do you get in return?"

"I don't know," Breaker admitted. "It's just . . . well, I'd be famous.

I could travel. And it ought to impress the girls, don't you think? Don't you want me to find a good wife, and sire some grandchildren for you?"

His mother snorted derisively. "I don't know what sort of girl would be impressed by foolishness like that."

Breaker thought that a good many girls would be, but he didn't say that. Instead he said, "It's a needed role, Mother. *Someone* has to do it."

"Even if that's true, which I am not convinced of, why should that someone be *you*?"

"Because I think it . . . oh, I don't know. Because I want to, that's all."

His mother stared at him for a moment, put down the rolling pin, crossed her arms on her chest, and then said, in her flattest and most deadly voice, "You want to be a killer?"

"No, I do *not* want to be a killer," Breaker replied. "What are you talking about?"

"The Swordsman's *job*, his whole purpose among the Chosen, is to kill the Dark Lord, and anyone else who tries to stop the Chosen from killing the Dark Lord. If you become the Chosen Swordsman, you'll be accepting that role. You'll be agreeing to kill people. You'll be promising to stick a great big knife through someone's chest. Is that what you want?"

"But I won't *need* to kill anyone! There aren't any more Dark Lords!"

"But you'll have agreed to do it if a Dark Lord happens."

"I suppose, but . . ."

"You'll be a killer."

"I'll be a Chosen Hero, and yes, that might mean killing someone, but only those who deserve to die. What's wrong with that?"

His mother stared at him for another moment, then threw up her hands with an exasperated "Oooohhhh!" and stamped out of the room.

Breaker watched her go, genuinely puzzled. Yes, the Swordsman and the other Chosen killed people, when it became necessary, but they were *heroes;* it was part of the job. His mother knew that; she had certainly told him enough stories about heroes who slew men and monsters right and left. She had told stories about the horrible vengeance Wizard Lords enacted on rogue wizards and other fugitives with great relish, including plenty of gruesome details, and she never seemed to think there was anything wrong with *that.*

How was it any different if her son became the Swordsman?

Then his gaze fell, and he saw that Fidget and Spider were staring at him.

"Oh, shut up," he said.

"I didn't say a word!" Fidget protested.

"I didn't, either," Spider said. "It wasn't us. Are *ler* talking to you?"

"No," Breaker snapped. "I'm not a priest or a wizard."

"Will you be if you become the Swordsman?"

Breaker started to say no, then stopped. "I don't know," he admitted.

"Would you really kill people?"

"Only bad wizards," Breaker assured her. "Not *real* people. No one from Mad Oak."

Spider nodded a solemn acceptance of this; Fidget looked less certain, but Breaker left the subject at that as he began rummaging through the cupboards for something to break his fast.

Spider and Fidget managed to maintain a surprising and atypical silence while they ate; their mother did not return, and when Breaker had taken the edge off his appetite he decided that she wasn't *going* to return while he was there.

He still did not entirely understand the reasons for her anger, but he knew better than to try to dissuade her; he had never been able to talk her out of one of her moods. His father or Harp sometimes could, but Breaker had never quite figured out how. As far as Breaker was concerned, the best thing to do was to simply be somewhere else until his mother had worked through her anger on her own. Accordingly, as soon as his stomach stopped growling he waved a quick farewell to his sisters and headed out of the house and up the slope toward the pavilion.

The Wizard Lord had provided a dry night and a pleasantly cool day, and the sun was still low above the distant eastern cliffs; wisps of morning mist lingered in the trees and fields. Breaker found no reason to hurry. He ambled past the smithy and the carpenters' shops, then took the middle path under the pavilion terrace, stretching his legs to skip every second stone. He called a greeting to the brewmaster and Younger Priestess as he passed the shadowy door to the cellars; he could hear rattling and sloshing, and the priestess speaking to *ler* in their own language, presumably negotiating with them for all to go well with this new batch of beer.

No one returned his call, but that was no surprise; they were busy. He emerged from the shadows into the slanting sun and turned to mount the southern steps. At the top he turned again, and slouched into the pavilion itself.

Last night's debris had largely been cleared away, the floor swept, and he wondered whether some of the villagers had risen early to deal with this, or whether Elder had talked some of the *ler* into taking care of it.

Then he noticed the old woman seated by the flickering hearthfire, and wondered instead whether the wizards had used their magic.

But a wizard's magic, like a priest's, still depended on the cooperation of *ler*—wizards just used different *ler, ler* not tied to a specific place. A priest could call on the spirits of earth and tree, field and stream, root and branch, spirits bound to their own corner of the world, while a wizard controlled spirits of wind and fire, light and darkness, spirits that could roam freely wherever their fancy—or the wizard's orders—might take them.

And of course, priests generally *asked* the *ler* for favors, and bargained with them, where wizards were said to bind them and compel them.

Elder might have summoned the pavilion's own *ler,* the spirits of plank and stone that dwelt in the structure itself, or the *ler* of the surrounding trees, or of the mice and insects and other creatures that undoubtedly lived beneath the building; the wizards could have summoned a wind from halfway across the world to blow away the dust and spilled beer. Either way, the floor was swept.

As he stood there considering this the old woman, the female wizard, looked up and saw him.

"Ah, boy," she said. "Come here, would you?"

Breaker hesitated—like most villagers he avoided strangers, and this woman was not merely a stranger, but a wizard. Not only might she unwittingly anger the local *ler* through ignorance of their ways or her mere presence, but she had *ler* of her own at her beck and call, strange *ler* not bound to Mad Oak or its surroundings.

But that was all the more reason not to be rude to her, and if he was to become the world's greatest swordsman, one of the Chosen, one of the assigned heroes who would defend Barokan should the Wizard Lord go mad, then he would presumably need to deal with strangers, and even with wizards, regularly. He would need to get over his reluctance. He squared his shoulders and marched across the room to her.

She gestured at an empty chair, and he sat down beside her.

For a moment the two of them sat silently, looking at one another while trying not to stare rudely; then she asked, "I know you don't use true names here in Mad Oak, but what do they call you?"

"Breaker," he said.

She grimaced. "And what do you break?" she asked. "Not heads, I hope."

Breaker smiled. "No," he said. "My mother's dishes, the poles for the beans, that sort of thing. I was clumsy as a child; my father said it was because I was growing so fast that my body had to keep relearning how to move."

"I'm not sure that's much better," the wizard said. "A head-breaking temper would be a bad thing in a swordsman, but a *clumsy* swordsman might be even worse."

"I'm not clumsy now," Breaker said. "Ask Little Weaver, or Curly."

"Who are they?"

"The girls I danced with last night. They'll tell you that I've caught up with my growth."

"So you remember last night, then?"

"Most of it."

"The beer hasn't washed it all away? You remember the dancing—do you remember what you spoke of with my companions before the music began?"

"You mean about becoming the Swordsman? Yes, I remember."

"And do you still want to take on the role?"

Breaker hesitated, remembering his mother's words, her hostile face. "I'm not sure," he said. "I don't want to be a killer."

"Well, that's all right, then," the wizard said. "We don't want you running off and putting a blade through the Wizard Lord on a whim; killing a man is serious business, killing a wizard even more so, killing the Wizard Lord most of all. We want a swordsman who is reluctant to act, who will give even the darkest Lord a fair chance to depart in peace—but who is ready to do what is necessary if the Lord will not yield."

Breaker blinked at her. "Depart in peace?" he said. "Is that possible?"

"Certainly!" She smiled at him, and he noticed a tooth was missing on one side. "As long as a corrupt Wizard Lord is removed from power, why would anyone care how? In all the centuries of the Wizard Lords' rule, there have been five slain by the Chosen—and three who left of their own free will rather than face the Chosen, giving their talismans and oaths over to the Council of Immortals and allowing a new Wizard Lord to take power."

Breaker gazed silently at her for a long moment, then said, "I'm sorry; I thought I understood the system and knew about the Dark Lords, but it seems I was mistaken. *Eight* Dark Lords? I had only heard of four, I think. And who or what is the Council of Immortals? I heard it mentioned last night, but I admit I don't know what it is." He grimaced. "I begin to think I was far too hasty in saying I might want to be one of the Chosen."

The smile vanished, and the wizard sighed.

"There is a great deal of history involved," she said. "And far too many complicated rules have accumulated. It all started out very simple, but of course it couldn't *stay* simple."

"But why not?"

"Because it's done by people," the wizard said. "We can never leave anything alone; we always meddle, and adjust, and repair." She straightened in her chair. "So then, Breaker," she said, "what *do* you know of the Wizard Lords, and the Chosen Heroes?"

Breaker hesitated. He had heard the stories as a child, but told in childish terms, and he did not want to sound childish to this woman. She seemed to be treating him as an adult, and he did not want to lose that respect. He would tell the story as he remembered it, but not necessarily in the same words.

"More than six hundred years ago," he began, "a group of wizards decided that Barokan would be a happier land if a single person ruled it all, from the Eastern Cliffs to the Western Isles, to put an end to destructive disputes between wizards—wicked wizards and magical duels had laid waste to large areas and killed many innocent people, and everyone agreed it had to be stopped, and these wizards thought that setting up a single ruler was the best way to stop it. They chose one of their number to be this ruler, the first Wizard Lord, and bestowed upon him much of their combined magic, binding to him the most powerful *ler* known to humanity, including mastery of the skies and wind.

"With so much magic at his disposal none could stand against the Wizard Lord, and he brought peace to all the lands from cliffs to sea, and reigned well for many years. He hunted down and slew any wizard who preyed on the innocent, and arbitrated disputes to prevent magical duels. In time he grew old and tired, and he gave up his power and withdrew from the world, and named another wizard his successor as Wizard Lord. He, too, reigned long and well before going peacefully into retirement.

"But the third Wizard Lord, although he had feigned otherwise, had an evil heart, and once he was in power he began to kill his enemies and to steal whatever he saw that caught his fancy, and to hunt down and slaughter *all* other wizards so that they could not threaten his rule, rather than just the few who made trouble. But a few of the surviving wizards, although they could not face the Wizard Lord's overwhelming magic directly, devised a scheme to bring him down. They chose a few ordinary people and granted them magical abilities that the evil Lord could not counter, and these Chosen Heroes were able to confront and slay the Wizard Lord, though most of them died in the process. And when it was all over, a new Wizard Lord was chosen—but the surviving heroes also found successors, for themselves and their slain comrades, and let it be known that henceforth any Wizard Lord who violated the trust of the people of Barokan would be slain, as the third one, now called the Dark Lord of the Midlands, was.

"Nonetheless, every so often a Wizard Lord has thought he found a way to defeat the Chosen, or was simply overcome by madness or evil, so that three more times the Chosen had to leave their ordinary lives and find their way into the Wizard Lord's stronghold, wherever it might be, and kill the corrupt ruler. The most recent was a little over a hundred years ago, when the Dark Lord of Goln Vleys was defeated, and the eight Chosen—the Swordsman, the Beauty, the Leader, the Scholar, the Thief, the Seer, and . . . I don't remember the others just now."

"The Archer and the Speaker."

"Oh, that's right. Anyway, the eight are still Chosen, but don't really need to do anything but stand ready, since our modern Wizard Lords are good, well-chosen rulers—"

"Well, that's what we always hope for, certainly."

"I don't know of any Council of Immortals, though."

"Oh, but you do! You mentioned us. You just don't know the name."

Breaker frowned. "What are you talking about?" he asked.

"The group of wizards who set up the Wizard Lords in the first place. That's us, the Council of Immortals."

Breaker stared at her for a moment. "Are you claiming to be six hundred years old?" he said. He knew priests and wizards could do amazing things, but he was not sure whether he was willing to believe that—she was obviously elderly, but *six hundred years*?

"No, no," she said. "We aren't *literally* immortals. And I certainly wasn't born until centuries after the first Wizard Lord was appointed. But the group of wizards that set him up in power, and that created the Chosen, didn't disband; they admitted new members as the old died off, including any Wizard Lord who retired honorably, and continued on, keeping an eye on matters from behind the scenes. It's the Council of Immortals that chooses each new Wizard Lord, and that picks the Chosen, and sometimes it's the Council of Immortals that tells the Chosen when the time has come to remove a Wizard Lord who has become a danger and refused to resign willingly. You see?"

Breaker thought about that for a moment, then said, "So the Wizard Lord does not actually rule Barokan? He's merely a figurehead for this council?"

"No, no, no," the wizard said, shaking her head vigorously. "We don't rule anything; the Wizard Lord does. He has the magic, the eight Great Talismans. He controls the weather and the wild beasts. He has the authority to hunt down and kill rogue wizards—any wizard who disturbs the peace, even if he's a member of the Council. All we do is choose who will be given the power, and decide if and when it must be removed. And giving the command to the Chosen, as we have just a handful of times over the past seven hundred years, requires a nearly unanimous vote—if just three of us believe the Wizard Lord's misbehavior does not require his death, then the Chosen are not called."

"But you *could* decide to remove him at any time."

"Well . . . yes."

"So you really have the final authority."

"Collectively, I suppose we do. But we don't use it."

Breaker considered that for a long moment, then asked, "Why not? Why bother with this system of controlling the Wizard Lord? Why doesn't the Council rule directly?"

The wizard grimaced. "We don't control him. I just told you that."

"You have the power to kill him . . ."

"Only if we almost all agree! And believe me, lad, we don't often agree on *anything.*"

"But why did you—or your ancestors—set this up? Why didn't you just rule Barokan yourselves? Why don't you now?"

"Because we don't *want* to—don't you understand? We're the descendants of the rogue wizards you hear horror stories of at your mother's knee—and most of the stories are *true,* Breaker; have you ever heard about the Siege of Blueflower?"

"I know the song . . ."

"The song is *true,* Breaker. That really happened. If there's no greater power to rein us in we wizards run rampant across Barokan, pillaging and plundering and smashing anything we please, and fighting among ourselves. You must have heard how the old wizard wars laid waste to entire areas—you just *said* it happened, so I *know* you heard about it! Well, the only thing that prevents that sort of chaos now is the Wizard Lord, the one man with the power to smash us all. There's a *reason* we vested the means to destroy him in ordinary men and women, rather than keeping it for ourselves and our fellow wizards—we know we can't be trusted with it."

Breaker thought about that for a moment. He thought about the Siege of Blueflower, famed in song and story, where according to legend three rogue wizards had joined forces to enslave an entire town, and had ordered the men of the town to defend them against the Wizard Lord, on pain of seeing their wives and daughters tortured to death should they fail to do their utmost.

The men had done their best, for the most part, and out of pity the Wizard Lord had done his best to see that neither they nor their loved ones died—but the song's last three verses were a mournful recitation, horrifyingly detailed, of how the victorious Wizard Lord and the freed townsfolk had found the mangled remains of a dozen young women in the dead wizards' stronghold, and how the Wizard Lord had grieved over his failure to save them all.

That had been five hundred years ago—but this wizard was acknowledging that she was one of the heirs to those three rogues.

"But then why doesn't the Wizard Lord just kill you all, so you can't go rogue? And then you couldn't unleash the Chosen."

"Because that *would* unleash the Chosen—the Chosen have instructions to kill the Wizard Lord if the Council fails to reassure them every year or so that everything is running smoothly. Our ancestors weren't suicidal—we *like* being wizards, even if we know we can't be trusted."

"So the Wizard Lord is required to defend Barokan against the wizards, *and* defend the wizards against themselves, without killing you all? And the Chosen are there to ensure that works?"

"Yes."

"It sounds complicated."

"It is. I told you earlier that it was. We don't claim it's a perfect system; it's just the best our ancestors could come up with, and it's worked well enough since then that we haven't tried to change it much. If anything, we've made it even more complicated, adding new rules and more Chosen over the years—and we haven't had to kill a Dark Lord in over a century, so it seems to be about right."

"I suppose."

"And now you have a chance to be a vital part of it all."

"By promising to kill the Wizard Lord if he . . . what? If he displeases this Council of yours? His fellow wizards?"

The wizard let out an exasperated sigh.

"More than displeases us," she said. "He has to start killing or raping or robbing innocent people—and not just one or two, either—before we'll summon the Chosen. Either that, or breaking the rules."

"See? If he breaks your rules!"

"Breaker, the rules are all there to make sure he's not trying to destroy the system and make himself invulnerable. The rules mostly say that he can't kill the Chosen, that he can't interfere with them or with anything else that's designed to keep him in check, that he can't try to acquire magic that would let him defeat the Chosen. That's all. He can do what he pleases otherwise; he can kill members of the Council and we probably won't try to stop him—past Wizard Lords have done just that.

After all, the whole *point* of the Wizard Lord is to keep all the other wizards under control, and that includes us. And remember that we don't *control* the Chosen; we can tell them we want the Wizard Lord dead, and why, but if they think our reasons insufficient, they won't go."

Breaker blinked in surprise. "You can't *make* them do it?"

"The whole point of the Chosen is to dispose of Wizard Lords gone bad; of course wizards can't control them!"

Up to that point Breaker had been convincing himself that the whole system was corrupt, that he and everyone he knew had been deceived about how Barokan was ruled, that the Chosen and the Wizard Lord were just tools of this mysterious Council of Immortals, and that his mother was right and he should take no part in it, but this suddenly changed everything . . .

If it was true.

But if it *was* true, then in a way the Chosen were the ultimate power in all Barokan. He wasn't just being offered a ceremonial position that would give him magical abilities with weapons that he could use to impress girls; in a way, he was being entrusted with the final authority over . . . well, over *everything. He* would be the one to decide whether the Wizard Lord lived or died. Yes, the Swordsman was supposed to obey the Leader, and listen to the other Chosen, and apparently to this Council of Immortals that he had never heard of by name until yesterday, but it was the Swordsman who was ultimately expected to kill any Wizard Lord who might turn to evil—and he could make up his own mind about it. *He* could decide! He, Breaker of Mad Oak, could determine the course of history.

"What if the Chosen decided to act without your Council's urging?"

The wizard shrugged. "Then they would act. They have that right, indeed, that obligation, as part of their role—and sometimes the Seer knows things the rest of us don't; it's part of his or her magic to know certain things about the Wizard Lord without being told, so it might well happen. If the Seer and the Leader decide the Wizard Lord must be removed, then the Wizard Lord must be removed."

"Even if the Council didn't agree?"

She shrugged again. "We couldn't stop them. At least, I don't think we could. But why would that happen? If the Wizard Lord is bad enough to make the Chosen risk their lives to slay him, then the Council should be happy to see him removed, and probably *would* be urging them on."

"But what if you weren't? What if the Wizard Lord subverted your Council somehow?"

"Well, that's another reason we don't control the Chosen. Yes, they could act on their own."

"Then I'll do it," Breaker said, rising from his chair. "Go ahead and cast your spell."

The wizard blinked at him, and brushed at the *ara* feather she wore in her hair.

"It's not that simple," she said.

Breaker sighed. "Nothing ever is," he said. "What do I have to do?"

"Talk to the Swordsman," the wizard told him. "At least, that's how you begin."

Breaker tried to coax more from her without success, and at last, with a bow to the wizard and another to the *ler* of the pavilion, he took his leave.

[3]

The world's greatest swordsman, chosen defender of Barokan, was not an early riser; he did not emerge from Elder Priestess's guest room until the sun was halfway up the eastern sky. Breaker had been waiting impatiently, eager to talk over what the wizard had told him—and to find out just what was actually involved in accepting a role among the Chosen, if not just a wizard's spell. The wizard had refused to explain, saying it would be better to hear it from the man who knew it all firsthand.

Elder had let him into the house, but then gone about her own business; she knew no one in Mad Oak would touch anything in her home without her permission. When at last the Swordsman ambled out into Elder's parlor he found Breaker standing there, almost bouncing with anticipation.

The man blinked at the youth, then said, "I take it you've decided to give it a try."

"I think so," Breaker said. "It depends." He tried not to stare, but he could not help noticing that the Swordsman, apparently fresh from his bed, the laces of his shirt and trousers awry, nonetheless had his sword on his belt. Breaker wondered if the man slept with it.

"Depends on what?"

"On exactly what's involved. I *think* I want to do it, but . . . well, you've been the Swordsman a long time. Do you ever regret it?"

The Swordsman snorted as he wandered past Breaker toward the pantry. "Lad, I don't know that there's much of anything worthwhile a man can do that he'll *never* regret. You'll always wonder how it might have been if you'd done otherwise. All in all, though, I've been glad I chose to be what I am."

Breaker followed as far as the kitchen doorway. "The hour's practice?"

"It's no great hardship. One gets accustomed to it quickly enough." The Swordsman opened the pantry door, then hesitated. "I am an invited guest in this home," he announced to no one in particular, "and a stranger to this town. If I am violating any customs or edicts, I am unaware of it." He waited.

"I think Elder would have told the *ler* you're her guest," Breaker said.

"It never hurts to speak up," the Swordsman said, leaning into the pantry to look around. "What's custom in one village is a crime in the next. You've got a few things here—this thing about *never* using *any* of a person's true name is unusual, for example."

"Is it?"

"Well, I won't say this is the only place that does it, but yes, it's unusual. There are villages where it's an insult to *not* use part of a true name."

"I've never been in another village," Breaker said.

"No?" The Swordsman pulled his head out of the pantry and glanced at the youth. "No surprise, really. Well, if you take the role, that'll change. You'll be expected to travel to keep up on the news, so you'll know if the Wizard Lord is misbehaving."

"All the time?"

"No, no—just occasionally. Where *is* the priestess, anyway? I don't feel right opening her jars and boxes when she's not here." He thrust his head back into the pantry.

"She's out in the fields talking to the *ler,* hearing what they have to say."

"Keeping up with the gossip, is she?" Breaker heard the rattle of an earthenware lid.

"Asking about the weather and the crops, I think."

"Ah, that would make sense. I'm sure she knows the *ler* of her land better than anyone else, and knows what they want. What's in . . . oh, raisins! Excellent." Pottery rattled, and the Swordsman emerged from the pantry a moment later with both hands dripping raisins and his mouth too full to speak. He crossed the kitchen, gesturing for Breaker to accompany him out to the yard.

Breaker followed, and the two seated themselves on a wooden bench beneath a graceful willow; the shade was hardly necessary on so cool a day, but it was pleasant enough. Breaker could see flickering shadows among the leaves, too faint to be birds, and knew some of the more visible *ler* were watching them. He waited politely while the Swordsman chewed and swallowed.

"Like some?" the older man said, holding out a still-full hand.

"No, thank you," Breaker said. He wondered slightly at the audacity of the man, grabbing great wallowing handfuls of Elder's goods that way—but then, not only was he an invited guest, he was the Swordsman, one of the Chosen. Presumably his position allowed him certain liberties and privileges.

"They're good."

"No." Breaker didn't have any special privileges—at least, not yet.

The Swordsman shrugged, and said, "Tell me what else you need to know," before stuffing more raisins in his mouth.

"What exactly is involved? I mean, what do I need to do? What will my life be like?"

"Well, we told you about the daily exercises," the Swordsman said thoughtfully, licking raisin residue from his fingers. "And every so often you'll travel to either the home of one of the other Chosen, or some predetermined meeting place, to discuss whatever rumors the two of you might have heard about the Wizard Lord. Sometimes someone will drop in on you, too, or meet you somewhere while you're traveling. You'll get messages from the other wizards every so often—the Council of Immortals, they call themselves, though that's just bragging."

"Messages? What sort of messages?"

"Oh, mostly just checking up to make sure you're paying attention. They . . ." He suddenly stopped and threw Breaker a sideways glance. "Can you read, lad?"

"A little. My sister learned it to help with her music, and she taught me the letters."

"Well, you'll need to read and write sometimes. Not much. Let's see, what else?" He looked up at the luminous green of the willow leaves, and Breaker noticed light and shadow flitting across the greenery in ways that had nothing to do with sun or wind, but only with the movement of the *ler*. The Swordsman's presence seemed to have disturbed them somewhat.

"You need to keep a sword handy, of course," the Swordsman said. "And you need to carry certain talismans when you travel, and have them nearby when you do your practice."

That explained why the man had his sword with him here in Elder Priestess's home, where no one was going to attack him. "What else?"

The Swordsman pursed his lips thoughtfully, then blew out a puff of air. "Nothing else. That's all of it, as long as the Wizard Lord behaves himself."

Breaker hesitated, then said, "And if he doesn't, you kill him."

"In theory, yes. The Chosen would gather, discuss whether the misbehavior is bad enough to call for removal, and if it is we would devise a plan, then go and deal with him. But it hasn't happened for a century, remember. My father used to say they should have disposed of the Lord of the Golden Hand, but apparently the Chosen at the time didn't think so. My father thought he made the winters much too cold, but that wasn't really a crime, was it?"

"So you've never killed a wizard?"

"No."

"Have you ever killed *anyone*? I mean, if you're the world's greatest swordsman, then you must fight other swordsmen sometimes . . ."

The Swordsman snorted. "Who'd be stupid enough to fight me to the death? Everyone *knows* that I'm the best in the world, that the *ler* of steel and flesh make sure I can't be beaten. Oh, sometimes people want to duel me just for fun, I've fought any number of duels, but it's always just until I disarm them, or at most to first blood. No, I've never killed anyone, and I fervently hope to keep it that way. If you're thinking taking my role means you can go out and slaughter anyone who annoys you, then you're wrong—being one of the Chosen doesn't exempt you from the law, and we can be hanged or otherwise punished just as effectively as anyone else. And if you *are* thinking along those lines, then we've all misjudged you."

"No! No, I don't want to kill anyone. I just wanted to be sure I wouldn't need to."

"Not unless a Wizard Lord goes bad."

"And that hasn't happened for a hundred years."

"That's right." For a moment he looked as if he intended to say more, and Breaker waited, but nothing more came.

After a brief silence, Breaker asked, "What's it *like*? How do people treat you? Do women . . . Are you married?"

"I was married once," the Swordsman said. He frowned. "She died in childbed. So did the babe."

"I'm sorry."

The Swordsman shrugged. "It was a long time ago."

"But . . . well, what is it *like*, being one of the Chosen?"

The Swordsman had been looking off down the valley; now he turned his attention to Breaker and met the youth's gaze.

"I ought to tell you it's wonderful," he said. "I want you to take the job, so I can retire and rest and just forget about practicing and listening to all the nasty gossip and the rest of it, so I ought to tell you whatever will make it sound good to you. I should say that everyone loves you, and women throw themselves at your feet, and all that—but I won't, because not only do I have too much respect for you, for myself, and for the truth, but if I *did* lie to you like that, and you took the job and found I'd lied, you might hunt me down and kill me, and there wouldn't be much I could do to stop you, and I might well deserve it."

"Then it's . . . it's that bad?" Breaker's visions of a lifetime of glory shattered. He swallowed.

"No, it isn't. Honestly, it isn't. But it's not that wonderful, either. It's a job. People don't treat you as a hero; you're just someone with a strange occupation, like a fletcher or a well-digger. You get respect, but no more than that, and sometimes people forget that you've got just the one promise to keep and expect you to be a hero in other ways, not just in keeping the Wizard Lord in line. You get teased for *not* killing the Wizard Lord, sometimes by people who've just been talking about what a nice master he is, how safe and calm everything is and how well-behaved the weather is, or even about how he tracked down some ghastly criminal who had fled the village—yes, the Wizard Lord himself sent bears to drag that nasty rapist back before the priest magistrate, and that was wonderful, he's such a great man, why haven't you killed him?" He shook his head. "People can be so odd sometimes. And of course, it doesn't pay anything, being one of the Chosen—you still need to earn your living somehow. I've got an acre and a half of rice back in Dazet Saltmarsh, and I sometimes work as a courier when I travel, to pay my way. But there are good points. Sword tricks do impress people, even when they know it's as much magic as skill, and yes, they impress women at least as much as men. I don't regret choosing to take the job—I was a few years older than you are, but only a few, when I started, and I could have been making a stupid choice, but I don't think I did. I've had a good life. Still, I'm getting old and tired and it's time to hand it on to someone else. Do you *want* to be that someone?"

"Yes," Breaker said. The Swordsman's honesty had decided him, at least for the moment—but then, he had thought he had decided before, and had kept having second thoughts.

For now, though, he wanted the role. If the older man had claimed it was all fame and fortune Breaker might have balked, thinking it too good to be true, but the description was well within believable bounds. It wasn't perfect—but it sounded like a worthy role, one he thought he could fill, one that would please him more than a lifetime raising barley and beans.

And he wouldn't have to kill anyone, his mother's doubts notwithstanding. The current Swordsman never had . . .

Or at least so he said, and Breaker believed him.

"Yes, I do," he repeated.

"Then let's see if you have what it takes," the Swordsman said, getting to his feet and brushing the last few bits of raisin from his beard and shirt.

"I don't understand," Breaker said, also rising.

The Swordsman sighed. "Son, if you're going to be the world's greatest swordsman, then you have to *demonstrate* that you're better than the other candidates. You need to show the *ler* that you're trying. You need to give the magic something to work with."

"I don't think . . ."

"You need to learn to *use a sword,* boy. Then you need to beat me in a duel. Fortunately for both of us, we need only fight to first blood, and I don't need to try my hardest—but you still have to have *some* idea what you're doing."

"Oh," Breaker said.

He hadn't expected this; he had been assuming it would all be done instantly, by magic—that the Swordsman or a wizard would wave a hand or chant an invocation to the appropriate *ler* or hand him a talisman, and he would simply become the world's greatest swordsman, *knowing* how to use a blade.

He felt foolish; that was never how anything worked. The priestess didn't just ask the *ler* for the crops, and have them magically appear, after all—they still had to be planted and tended and harvested, and it took months. Why, then, would this far less common magic be any easier or quicker?

"That's why I haven't started my daily hour of practice yet," the Swordsman said, drawing his sword. "You're going to practice *with* me."

"But I don't have a sword!" Breaker protested.

"I have another in my baggage, but no, I'm not going to trust you with it yet. You'll start with a stick—something that isn't sharp. If you show promise after a few days we'll get you a real blade."

"Oh." This sounded much more likely than transformation with a word and a wave, but also worse than he might have hoped—days before he even picked up the tool he was supposed to master? Just how long an apprenticeship was he beginning—assuming he *was* beginning it, and the whole thing didn't fall apart? Breaker eyed the bare steel of the sword, noticing how it shone dully in the morning sun. "And you'll use that?"

The Swordsman shrugged. "Maybe. Or maybe not; it depends what we're doing. Right now, though, I want to teach you the very basics, beginning with what a sword is." He held out the blade and pointed.

"This is the blade. The point, the edge, the back—much like a big knife. But see these grooves?"

Breaker looked.

"They're called blood gutters," the Swordsman said.

Breaker swallowed uncomfortably at this reminder of the weapon's nature. "Oh. To let the blood flow more freely from the wound?"

The Swordsman snorted. "That's why they're *called* that," he said, "because people think that's what they're for. Actually, though, they're just to save weight, making the blade thinner without weakening it. That's important, much more important than any tricks with blood flow—a sword doesn't weigh much, but move it around long enough and every ounce matters. After an hour waving this about, you'll be glad of those gutters even if you never draw a drop of blood."

Breaker ventured an uneasy smile.

"Now, here's the guard—and it's called that because it guards your hand, of course; no tricks with the name there. The crosspiece here is the quillons. The base of the blade that extends through the hilt is the tang, just as it is in a knife, but it's narrow—I can't show you, but take my word for it. That goes through the wooden hilt, with the leather grip bound to it with wire, and here at the end is the pommel. Know what that's for?"

Breaker blinked at the little metal knob. "To keep your hand from slipping off?" he guessed.

"To keep the *hilt* from slipping off, more nearly—but it wouldn't need to be so large for that. No, it's a counterweight, to balance the sword."

"A weight? But I thought you just said . . ."

"I did. I said you don't want any extra weight in the *blade*. This isn't in the blade." He held out the first two fingers of his left hand and laid the sword across them; it balanced neatly an inch or so from the quillons. "A good sword will balance just there. Too much weight in the blade and you'll tire quickly, you'll have trouble controlling it, it will turn in your hand; too much weight in the hilt and your blows will have no force behind them. It needs to balance. Hold out your hand."

Reluctantly, Breaker obeyed, and watched nervously as the Swordsman laid the blade across his palm.

"Feel how it balances?"

Breaker almost trembled at the touch of the cold metal; he had never seen or felt such fine steel before, and he could sense the *ler* within it—hard, fierce *ler,* kin to those he had felt in knives and arrows, but more intense, more alien, far more powerful, and most especially *colder.* He had never before encountered anything that felt as coldhearted, even though he knew the physical metal was no colder than any ordinary implement.

Quite aside from the blade's spirit, though, it was immediately obvious what the Swordsman had meant about balance; the sword did indeed balance perfectly at the point he had indicated. It took no effort at all to hold it steady on his open hand.

It didn't seem quite natural—but of course, it *wasn't* natural. Swords were the product of technology and magic working together.

"Pick it up."

Breaker hesitated, then closed his other hand on the worn black leather of the grip.

It fit perfectly into his hand, as if it had been made for him, or as if he had used it every day for a season. He turned his wrist and the blade flashed upward like a startled bird—still cold, but now alive and eager.

"It's so light!" he exclaimed.

"It's a good sword," the Swordsman replied. "It feels lighter than it is."

Breaker essayed a few cautious moves with the sword, turning it this way and that, as the Swordsman watched. Breaker glanced at the older man, who gestured for him to continue.

Still hesitant, Breaker took a few swings at an imaginary foe, and could sense the sword's chill pleasure in being used this way. He closed both hands on the hilt for a long swooping chop at the air.

He was vaguely aware as he did that the Swordsman was moving away. The traveler bent down as Breaker clove the air with a wild swing. . . .

And then the Swordsman was in front of him, a long willow twig in hand, and the stick was thrusting toward Breaker's eyes. Instinctively he swung the sword around, chopping at the green stick, but somehow the twig moved around his blade and still came at him, as if it had writhed like a snake.

And then the tip of it touched the tip of his nose and pulled away, and he stepped back, trying to gather his wits. The sword in his hand wanted him to do something, but he did not know how to respond.

The willow twig slashed at the back of his hand, a stinging blow, but Breaker held on to the sword and twisted it around to face this attack.

"Oh, excellent!" the Swordsman said, stepping back and raising his stick to vertical. "You didn't drop it, you didn't try to use your empty hand—for a barley farmer who never held a sword before, nor saw anyone wield one, that was *excellent*!"

"What?" Breaker said, feeling very stupid. The weapon he held seemed suddenly ordinary, just another metal tool.

"My dear lad, you do have a swordsman's instincts. You have a natural talent. The wizards' *ler* who guided me to you have served us both well."

"I don't understand."

"I am *telling* you, my boy," the Swordsman said patiently, "that you have the inborn ability you need. You have the instincts to work with the sword's *ler*. With my training and the necessary magic, by spring *you* will be the world's greatest swordsman—and *I* can go home and live out my life in peace!"

Breaker looked at the Swordsman, then down at the sword in his hand.

"Oh," he said.

It had never really occurred to him that he might not have the ability. What he had doubted was whether he truly *wanted* to be one of the Chosen.

And he still wasn't entirely certain of that, but at this point, after being told that he was indeed chosen by *ler* and not simply a random volunteer, he was not about to admit it.

[4]

An hour later Breaker was exhausted, sweating despite the coolness of the air, and very unsure of his own abilities, despite the old man's praise. The Swordsman had taken the sword from his hand—without asking, and without Breaker intentionally releasing it—and had then sheathed the blade and given the youth a willow twig, so that they were evenly matched.

The twig's *ler* was warm and green and soft, completely unlike the sword's, but still, it fit his hand and was about the right length.

The old man had then demonstrated that he could do things with his hands and a willow stick that Breaker would never have thought possible. He could move it with a degree of speed and precision more reminiscent of Harp's hands plucking strings in one of her fastest reels than of anything else Breaker could think of; he could put the point on any portion of Breaker's body in seconds, no matter how Breaker might dodge or twist or struggle, or how fiercely he might wave his own willow twig about trying to ward off the touch.

An hour of waving a willow twig left Breaker shaken and shivering, as tired as if he had been hauling heavy loads uphill.

And at the end of it the Swordsman looked at him, nodded, and said, "That was good. Be here again tomorrow, and we'll work on it some more." Then he turned and marched back into Elder Priestess's house.

Breaker wordlessly watched him go, then angrily flung the willow twig aside and stalked around the house to the village square. He wiped the sweat from his brow with his sleeve, then rubbed at the spot on his chest, right over his heart, where the Swordsman's stick had jabbed him repeatedly.

"Breaker," someone said.

He turned to see his sister Harp standing in the break between Priest's house and the village shrine, and for an instant he wondered what she might have been asking the *ler;* then he remembered that that passage could be used as a shortcut down to the blacksmith's forge and the smith's adjoining house, a house that was also home to the old blacksmith's youngest son, Harp's friend and perhaps future husband Smudge. A visit there was far more likely than consulting priests or *ler*.

"Hello, Harp," Breaker said.

"Are you on your way home?"

"Yes. You?"

She didn't bother to answer, but fell in beside him as they walked up the winding lane.

It was a beautiful day, a gentle breeze rippling leaves that were just beginning to turn to red or brown or gold. The sky above was richly blue, arching from the pavilion atop the ridge in the southwest to the distant cliffs in the east. The fields at the foot of the slope were bare and dark, and some of the village children were picking through the debris left by the harvest, looking for barleycorns to chew or scraps they could incorporate into toys or games. The trees beyond the farthest field hid the river and docks from sight, but Breaker knew they were there, marking the boundary of Mad Oak, the edge of his family's world.

The weather and Harp's presence swiftly eased his temper, and the view down the ridge reminded him of his place in Mad Oak, and that becoming one of the Chosen would mean a place in the wider world beyond.

"So," Harp said, as they left the square, "are you serious about this?"

"About what?" He didn't really need to ask, but he wanted to hear her say it.

"About becoming the next Swordsman."

He didn't answer immediately, but rubbed absently at the bruise on his chest.

"I'm not sure," he said at last, as they passed the house adjoining their own. "I thought I was, but I keep changing my mind."

"It's a big decision," Harp agreed.

Breaker nodded.

They stopped in front of the family home by silent mutual consent, and stood for a moment. Then Breaker said, "I don't want to be just a barley farmer all my life. I don't want to be just the kid who broke things."

"You don't have to be," Harp said. "I was called Spiller when I was little, you know, and everyone thought I'd just be a farmwife like our mother, raising beans and children, canning and sewing and cooking."

"And you think you won't be? You won't just marry Smudge and grow beans and barley, and bear his children?"

"Oh, I might—but when was the last time anyone called me Spiller?" She smiled.

"That's different. You've been playing the harp since . . . well, since . . ."

"Since I was ten, and you were six," Harp finished. "Thirteen years. And no one's called me Spiller since I was twelve."

"It's a little late for me to take up anything like that, then. I never had your ear for music."

"You never tried."

"I never wanted to."

"But you want to wield a sword?"

"I don't . . . well, I . . ." He frowned, remembering the cold ferocity of the blade when he first held it, and the exhausting hour with the willow branch. "I don't know," he admitted.

"Erren," she said, "tell me what you *do* know. What *do* you want? Not just what you *don't* want, but what you *do.*"

Startled by the almost-forbidden use of a piece of his true name, which demonstrated just how seriously Harp took this question, Breaker hesitated a moment longer to gather his thoughts. Hearing that bit of his real identity spoken aloud seemed to help, and at last he said, "I want to be a part of something bigger than Mad Oak. I want to *see* more than Mad Oak. Sometimes it feels as if I'm closed in here, trapped in this place, caught between the ridge and the river, as if the *ler* are holding me here against my will, and I need to escape. But I don't want to just wander aimlessly around Barokan, like a rogue wizard—I have roots here, I know that, my true name tells me as much. I want to stay here, but at the same time I want to see more, to *be* more. I want to see the ocean, and the Midlands, and the salt marshes, and to stand at the foot of the Eastern Cliffs to see how high they truly are—but not as a stranger; as someone who belongs there, just as I belong here. I want a role, a place in the world, but a *bigger* one than growing barley in Mad Oak. It's not enough, being here. I see Joker and Brokenose and the rest, and they're fine here, they're happy, they don't want anything more, but I *do.*

"But I don't know *what.*"

"Just more, huh?"

"Yes. And becoming one of the Chosen—how much more could there be? I would be a part of all of Barokan, not just Mad Oak or Longvale."

"So that's why you agreed to be the Swordsman?"

"Yes. But then—there's the whole thing about killing. A sword is made for killing—I was holding a sword earlier, and I could feel how cold and hungry it was, how ready to kill. It's not like a hunter's arrows, where the prey's *ler* surrenders itself to feed us—the sword is meant to *take* that which no one wants to give, and that frightens me a little. I don't want to kill anyone. And if I don't, if I'm not ready to use the sword as I'm meant to, then what am I really accomplishing by being one of the Chosen? Killing the Wizard Lord is what they're chosen *for,* after all. And that means they're useless, really—the Chosen don't *do* anything."

"They will if there's another Dark Lord."

"But there *won't* be."

"Because the Chosen are there. It's like some of the priests you hear about, in other towns—they do things to *stop* the *ler* from doing things. They offer prayers and sacrifices and rituals not to make the crops grow or the game come close, but so the *ler won't* carry off the children or blight the land. If they weren't there, the towns would be just as uninhabitable as any wilderness. And if the Chosen weren't there, the Wizard Lord could turn dark in an instant, and no one would stop him."

"But why would he turn dark?" He waved a hand at the sky. "Look at the weather he gives us! It's beautiful. He's doing fine. Why would that ever change? Most people don't go about stealing and raping and murdering, even if they have the chance."

"The wizards did, though, in the old stories. Maybe it's something about being a wizard, about binding *ler* with talismans. Or maybe it's just that some people are like that, even if *we* aren't, and they *would* go stealing and raping and murdering if they had the chance. A few do, you know, despite everything, and the Wizard Lord hunts them down to bring them to justice, so we know such people still exist. Perhaps there are many more of them, but knowing that the priests and the Wizard Lord would catch them keeps most of them from doing anything bad—but if one of them *were* the Wizard Lord . . ."

"So don't choose people like that to be Wizard Lord."

She shrugged. "Maybe you can't tell them in advance, even with magic."

"It still seems . . ." He groped for a word, and finally said, ". . . clumsy."

"The system's worked for hundreds of years. So the question is, do you want to be part of it? Or would you rather not have the responsibility? If you don't want to be a farmer or a musician, there are still plenty of other choices besides being the world's greatest swordsman. You could become a guide, maybe, or a bargeman, if you want to travel."

Breaker nodded. He had sometimes thought about exactly those options.

"The Swordsman says I have the ability, though," he said, remembering the feel of the sword in his hand. It had felt strange, but somehow right.

"Did he?"

Breaker nodded. "He tested me this morning. In fact, we practiced for an hour. With sticks." He grimaced. "He hit me a lot."

"Well, after all, he's not just *a* swordsman, but the world's *greatest* swordsman. He can defeat anyone. But he said you have the ability you need?"

"He did."

"Then maybe the *ler* led him here deliberately. Maybe you're *meant* to be the next Swordsman."

"Or maybe he's lying—he wants to retire and will take the first willing candidate, no matter how inept I am."

"Maybe. But he's one of the Chosen. He's supposed to be a potential hero. Would he lie and shirk his duty?"

"He might," Breaker said, without much conviction.

"I suppose he might. So what it comes down to, baby brother, is whether you trust him, and whether you trust yourself to be one of the Chosen, and whether you *want* to be the Swordsman. If you'd be satisfied being a guide—well, the Greenwater Guide has no heir that I know of, and they don't ever have to kill anyone."

"Well, maybe if some fool of a traveler wandered off and offended the wrong *ler* . . ."

"Even then, it wouldn't be the guide's job—he'd just let nature take its course. So which would you rather carry—*ara* feathers, or a sword?"

"Most guides only ever learn and work one or two routes. The Chosen protect all of Barokan."

"Yes. It's quite a responsibility."

Breaker stood silently for a moment, considering, and remembering the morning's experiences; then he smiled and shrugged.

"*Someone* has to do it," he said. "It might as well be me."

Harp smiled back, and the two entered the house.

Perhaps an hour later their mother, known in Mad Oak as White Rose, returned and saw Breaker seated at the kitchen table.

"So you've given up on that foolishness?" she demanded, without preamble.

Breaker did not pretend to misunderstand her. "On the contrary," he said. "I'll be practicing with the Swordsman for an hour every day until he feels I'm ready, and then a wizard will transfer the magic to me, and I'll be one of the Chosen."

She started to open her mouth to argue, then saw the expression on his face.

"You're sure, then," she said.

"I am."

"Even if it means killing a man."

Breaker had had time to prepare for this. "If the Chosen are ever sent to kill the Wizard Lord, Mother, I think we can all be sure he deserves it. It hasn't happened in a century, and it probably won't happen in my lifetime—but if it does, then yes, I'll kill him if I must. This is a good role, an important role."

She stared at him for a moment, and he gazed steadily back.

"Well," she said at last, "you're nineteen, you're a man—I can't stop you. But I think you're being a fool."

"Someone has to do it," Breaker said, as he had to Harp. "It might as well be me. And if that makes me a fool, then so be it—I'm a fool. But remember, we live in peace, untroubled by rogues or bad weather, because the Wizard Lord watches over us—and we can trust him to do that because the Chosen watch over *him*. I learned that from *you,* Mother. Am I a fool to do my part to maintain that peace?"

White Rose sighed.

"I hope not," she said. "By all the *ler,* I hope not!"

[5]

Breaker's mother was the last to reconcile herself to her son's new calling, but by midwinter even she had finally accepted it, at least to the extent of allowing the Swordsman to move into the family home, so that his trudging through the snow would not delay the daily practices—and so the town's unexpected long-term guest would not impose on Elder Priestess any more than he already had. White Rose knew better than to needlessly aggravate the town's senior interlocutor with *ler*.

The two wizards who had accompanied the Swordsman had left after just three days in Mad Oak. Once they were certain that the Swordsman had found his successor they had no further business in town, and Mad Oak had little to entertain visitors.

"Call us when the time comes," the woman had said, handing the Swordsman a talisman, which he quickly pocketed. Then she turned to the guide and said, "To Greenwater, then!"

For the first month after the wizards departed half the village expected Breaker to give up; it became a popular amusement among the townsfolk of all ages to come watch the practice sessions and see an old man with a blunt stick repeatedly embarrass big strong Breaker, regardless of whether the youth was wielding a similar stick, a real sword, or almost anything else that came to hand. Time after time, when the two of them squared off after the day's lessons, the Swordsman demonstrated that he could hit Breaker anywhere he chose, at any time he chose, with either a stick or a sword.

By the end of that first month, however, it sometimes took him two or three tries before he connected, and the townsfolk had largely stopped speculating on how soon Breaker would abandon his pursuit of a role among the Chosen.

In the first few days some of the other young people of Mad Oak had challenged Breaker to mock duels after seeing his poor showing against the old traveler; most of them were startled to discover that in fact Breaker was not slow or clumsy at all, and could match or better most of his opponents from the very first. After a month Breaker could usually fetch any challenger a sound blow on the side of the head within the first minute of combat, and the impromptu stickfights ceased. Some of the village wits began to mockingly call Breaker "the Young Swordsman," rather than using the nickname he had borne for a dozen years.

But as the practice sessions continued, the mockery faded. By midwinter, when White Rose invited the visitor to sleep in the loft, calling her son the Young Swordsman was no longer a joke at all.

The Old Swordsman could still reliably defeat the Young, though. The young man who still thought of himself as Breaker could put up a good fight, and hold off his more experienced foe for several minutes, but inevitably every bout still ended with a rap across the back of his hand, a tap on his heart, or some other blow indicating his defeat. No weapon the Young Swordsman might wield ever touched the older man.

That irritated Breaker, but there seemed little he could do about it, and he *was* definitely improving—just not enough to matter, yet.

In his more optimistic moments, though, he could imagine a day when he could beat the Old Swordsman and claim a role among the Chosen. He tried to imagine what that would be like, but failed.

He spent many evenings, after his household chores were done, asking the Old Swordsman about his life as one of the Chosen, getting answers that varied according to the old man's moods. He discovered that the more specific a question, the more likely it was to get a consistent and useful answer—which was hardly a surprise, since that was almost always true everywhere, regardless of the topic of discussion.

He tried to think of useful, specific questions, but it wasn't always easy.

"When you travel," he asked, "do people just give you food and shelter, wherever you go, just because you're the Swordsman?"

The Swordsman laughed at that. "No," he said, and because he was in a good mood that night—dinner had been roast ham and chestnut gravy—he went on to explain that sometimes he was treated as an honored guest, sometimes he had to work for his keep, sometimes he had to pay with coin, and there were a few towns where he was shunned no matter what he did.

"Sometimes," he said, "a little display of fancy bladework and passing the hat will cover my expenses nicely; you'll want to learn some tricks, like slicing through lit candles without blowing them out, for such occasions."

"Like *what*?"

The Swordsman snorted, fetched his blade, and demonstrated his ability to slice a good beeswax candle in two while leaving the top half still in place and burning, if a little wobbly.

"More!" Fidget called.

"Tomorrow," the old man replied, and from then on it became a household tradition for him to perform one such trick every evening, to the great amusement of Spider and Fidget—such as slicing a tossed apple into thirds in midair, or spearing the only red grape from among half a dozen green ones flung at him, or first swinging his blade above a cloth spread on a table so fast that the wind of its passage stirred the fabric, then once the cloth moved, passing the blade beneath it without scratching the table, cutting the cloth, or letting the cloth entangle the sword . . .

His repertoire was impressive, but Breaker ceased to find it amusing fairly quickly, as in each case he was set to attempting to imitate the stunt the next morning. Some such tricks were much easier than they looked; most were not. Breaker failed to master most of them—which did not discourage the Old Swordsman at all, but it did discourage Breaker.

"You have no magic helping you," the old man said, after one such failure.

"Could you do it without the magic?" Breaker countered.

"I don't know," the Swordsman said. "I might; I've been practicing a long, long time."

Breaker grimaced silently in reply.

He continued to ask questions, though.

"What are the other Chosen like?" he asked one very cold night, as the family huddled by the hearth, as much to silence his father's grumbling about the weather the Wizard Lord had sent them as because he really wanted to talk.

"I haven't met all of them," the old man said.

That startled Breaker, and he turned his attention from the fire to the Old Swordsman. "You haven't?"

"No," the old man said, rubbing his hands together. "I've never met the current Beauty or the current Thief, so far as I know. They keep to themselves."

All three of Breaker's sisters had turned to listen now, while their parents kept their faces toward the fire.

"Why?" Fidget asked.

"I can't say for certain," the Swordsman said, "but if you think about it, thieves don't generally like advertising themselves. And the new Beauty lives in Winterhome, where the women keep themselves secluded—I've only been there once, and I didn't meet her. I didn't like it much—it's right under the cliffs, you know, and it feels closed in and unbalanced, as if half the sky is ready to fall on you. And the whole society there is strange, with the division between Host People and Uplanders; half the year it's too crowded, and half the year it's half-empty. It's not comfortable. Or at least, I didn't find it so."

"You said the *new* Beauty lives there," Breaker said.

The Swordsman snorted. "I did, didn't I? Foolish of me. She's been the Beauty for more than twenty years now—in fact, I wonder how much longer she can last at it. That's hardly new. But what I meant was that I did know *a* Beauty, who retired in favor of the present one because her husband-to-be got jealous and she decided having a family was more important than serving the Council of Immortals. And yet another held the post when I first joined the Chosen, though only for a year or two; I never met her, either."

"Tell me about all of them!"

And to Breaker's surprise, the old man obliged—though not immediately. He waited until the younger girls had been sent to bed before continuing.

The Beauty was a role intended as a distraction more than anything else, he explained; just as the Chosen Swordsman was by definition the greatest swordsman in Barokan, the Beauty was by definition the most beautiful woman in Barokan, which meant that her mere appearance was often enough to make grown men forget whatever they were supposed to be doing. Her original purpose among the Chosen had been simply to make the Wizard Lord's servants and guards—and perhaps even the Wizard Lord himself—abandon their duties, so that the other Chosen would meet less resistance.

The Beauty did not need to practice anything, as the Swordsman did, nor do anything special to preserve her beauty; *ler* took care of her appearance with no effort on her part. This did not mean that her role came without a price, though; she was constantly barraged with the attentions of men, and inevitably drew the envy of other women. How the Chosen Beauty handled this varied from one to the next, but for all of them it was wearing. The Swordsman had held his role for forty-four years; no Beauty had ever lasted that long, and he doubted any ever would. Whether even magic could keep a woman supernally beautiful for several decades was an open question, and one that showed no sign of being answered any time soon.

"I don't know much about the woman who was the Beauty when I was first chosen," the old man said. "She had held the post about a dozen years, I think, and had had enough of it. She did no traveling anymore, and resigned the role before I had gotten around to meeting her. Her successor made a point of finding me, though—and bedding me, as I was young and handsome then, not the battered ruin you see now."

"Bedding you?" Harp asked, startled.

"Oh, yes. And if you're thinking that might have become complicated, such a relationship between two of the Chosen, you should consider that human nature is such that the woman universally acknowledged to be the most beautiful in the world cannot be visibly pregnant; therefore, the *ler* of her talisman would not allow her to conceive. That was a part of her magic. That was one reason she gave up the role later."

"But . . . She tracked you down in order to bed you?" Harp persisted. "But she didn't *know* you."

"Yes, well, she was . . . a little odd, perhaps. But also, she wanted a man her magic didn't affect. I think she wanted to prove she could seduce a man without magic. Not that that was at all difficult in my case, back then."

"Her magic didn't affect you?" Breaker asked.

"No, of course not—haven't I told you about that?"

"No."

"Oh." The old man looked slightly embarrassed, for the first time since Breaker had met him in the pavilion the night of the harvest dance. "That's part of being Chosen. We're . . . well, not immune to magic, exactly, but almost. None of us are affected by each other's magic, nor can the Wizard Lord's magic harm us directly. In general, the *ler* bound to us protect us—didn't you notice I had no *ara* feathers on my cloak when I arrived?"

"I did," Breaker admitted. "I had heard that the Chosen had magical protections of their own, stronger than *ara* feathers, but I hadn't known you were immune to each other's magic."

"We are. So Boss is persuasive but can't order us to do something suicidal, and the Beauty is beautiful but not irresistible, and so on."

"Boss?"

"The Leader. The other nicknames change, but I think the Leader is always called Boss. Certainly the two I've known were both called Boss."

"You've known two?"

The old man sighed. "Breaker, I've known at least two of *all* the Chosen—I'm the oldest of the eight by more than a decade. Seer is next, then Lore . . ."

"Lore?"

"The current Scholar. His predecessor was an old man called Tales—I'm not sure what happened to him after he retired, but he must be long dead by now. But you know, I'm wrong—Lore wasn't next after Seer, the Beauty was. Since I've never met her, I forgot for a moment. So it was Seer, Beauty, Lore, and then I think it must have been the Thief."

"Does he have a nickname, like Boss and Lore?"

"The Thief? I don't know—I told you, I've never met her."

"Her?"

"Yes. This time. The one before was a man."

Breaker nodded. "How long has she been the Thief, then?"

"A long time, but she was very young when she took the role." He sighed. "The Speaker would be next—poor little Babble! And then the new Boss, and finally Bow, taking over from Arrow as the Archer. I only met Bow once—he made a point of coming to find me and introduce himself, and show me some of his archery. That was just a few years ago. He could do amazing things, just as I can with a sword, but I can't say I was impressed with *him.*"

"Tell me about all of them!"

The old man sighed again, and kept talking.

For some time after that, every night after Spider and Fidget had retired the Old Swordsman told Breaker and sometimes Harp a great deal of what amounted to gossip about the Chosen, and later about some of the wizards he had known in his dealings with the Council of Immortals, and even the Wizard Lords themselves that the old man had known, the present one and his two immediate predecessors. The old man seemed to think this chatter was foolishness, but Breaker justified it to himself by saying that he might someday need to work closely with the seven other Chosen, and to consult with the Council, and perhaps to confront the Wizard Lord, so the more he knew about them in advance, the better the chances for harmonious cooperation.

Harp didn't bother trying to justify her curiosity; she simply shrugged and said there was little else to do on nights when her fingers were too cold to play the harp decently.

Breaker took a special interest in the descriptions of the current Wizard Lord, looking for reassurance that the man was sane and good, and there would be no call for the Chosen to remove him. Alas, the present holder of the office was apparently something of a hermit; the Swordsman had only met him once, years before. No one seemed to know much about him. He came from the south, and was reported to spend all his time in a lonely tower in the Galbek Hills, well away from the nearest village, though the old man did not know whether this was because he did not wish to trouble anyone, or because he sought privacy to work his magic, or what. The previous Wizard Lord, a friendly and well-liked man, had done well enough living in a mansion amid the hustle and bustle of Spilled Basket, one of the trading towns in the Midlands, and the Old Swordsman had anecdotes about him that kept Breaker and Harp entertained for a night or two. The Lord of Spilled Basket had apparently had a sense of humor, as well as justice, and some of the punishments he visited on fleeing criminals had been amusing—rapists receiving the unwanted attention of amorous hogs, thieves having their clothes stolen by raccoons, and the like.

That was the evenings; by day there were still household chores to be performed, ice to be fetched for melting, wood brought in for burning, cleaning and cooking to be done, and of course at least an hour every day of practice in swordsmanship.

And every day, Breaker spent that hour being hit, and growing ever more frustrated by his inability to hit the old man in return.

One chilly, overcast day, when the Young Swordsman had taken a whack on the ear as well as a jab in the chest in quick succession, he flung his stick down in the trampled snow and exclaimed, "I still haven't ever beaten you! Not even once!"

"Well, no," the older man said, mildly surprised by his outburst. "And you won't, until you're ready to take on my role. Lest you forget,

I am not merely a very good swordsman; I am the *world's greatest* swordsman, magically guaranteed by all the *ler* of muscle and steel. By definition, I can't be beaten in a fair fight."

"Then what's the *use* of these endless practice bouts?"

"I need to practice for an hour a day," the Old Swordsman said calmly. "You know that. You'll have to do the same, once I'm free of it. You might as well get in the habit. Believe me, practicing against a live opponent is far more entertaining than thrashing a dummy or a tree. Furthermore, lad, you *will* beat me eventually—and when you do, when you draw first blood with a real blade, the magic can then be passed from me to you, and it will be too late to change your mind. You're learning quickly, and improving steadily, whether you know it or not—so quickly I suspect some magic at work, though whether it's the doing of the wizards, or your town's *ler,* or something in yourself, I couldn't say."

"But if you're the world's greatest, how can I ever defeat you? The magic won't allow it!"

"But *I* will. I said I can't be beaten in a fair fight; who ever said we would always fight fairly?"

"Then why don't we just do it now, and get it over with? I'm tired of being publicly humiliated."

The Old Swordsman cocked his head and gazed thoughtfully at his student; then he took a moment to look around. The surrounding yard and the village streets were empty of life, since anyone with any sense was staying inside, out of the cold wind.

"Whether it's done publicly, you can judge for yourself," he said. "As for humiliation, I don't think anyone considers you to be humiliated—not after they saw what you could do against someone who *isn't* the world's greatest swordsman."

"*I* consider myself humiliated," the Young Swordsman replied. "I'm not as concerned with the opinions of others as I am with my own self-respect, and that's taken a beating with every unanswered blow you've laid on my skin these past three months."

The Old Swordsman once again gazed at Breaker thoughtfully.

"You may have a point," he said.

"You say it's the magic that makes you unbeatable, and that we'll cheat to let me defeat you," Breaker said. "Then why do we need to wait? Why continue these practice bouts? Let me win, get it over with, and you can have the rest you say you want."

The Old Swordsman took his time before replying. "The simple answer to that is that you need to be good enough to make your victory convincing; the *ler* must believe my defeat is genuine. When I first came, you couldn't have fooled them for a moment. But the simple answer isn't always the best. You still aren't one-tenth the swordsman I am, or that you might someday be even without magic—it takes years to master the blade—but you have come a surprisingly long way in a short time. Perhaps you *are* good enough."

"I think I am."

The older man snorted. "Of course you do," he said. "Then shall we summon the wizards, and say you are ready to challenge me for the title of world's greatest swordsman?"

"Yes!" the Young Swordsman said, but then his enthusiasm faltered. "That is, I think . . . Just how were you planning to cheat?"

"The easiest way would be to slip or stumble, giving you an opening. Or I might contrive to break my blade at an inopportune moment. We'll be fighting with blades, not sticks—we can use either wood or steel, but they must have points and edges. The magic requires the fight be to first blood—well, or worse, but I am not interested in a fight to the death, and since I would not care to lose such a battle, I assume you would be at least equally reluctant. It's easier to draw blood with steel, but of course it's also easier to slip and do some serious damage."

"Oh," the younger man said.

"I'll need to beseech the *ler* of blades and steel not to aid me, but that can be done easily enough, especially since we'll have a wizard or two present."

"Do we really need an audience?"

The Old Swordsman hesitated. "You know, I'm not entirely sure," he said. "It's traditional, certainly; there was an audience when I took the title, quite a large one. We'll need a wizard afterward, to transfer the binding upon the talisman, but I'm not . . ."

"The what?"

"The binding of the talisman."

The Young Swordsman did not repeat the question, but his expression made it clear that he wanted further explanation.

"Haven't I explained this? Or didn't the wizards, while they were here?"

"Not that I recall just now."

"Well, of course, there's a talisman. All the magic that makes me the Chosen Swordsman is bound up in it."

"I knew that part, that there are talismans."

"Yes, well, there's one essential talisman, the one that holds the *ler* of swordsmanship, and then I have a few others that help out in lesser ways. That first one, though, is bound to my soul, and that binding will need to be broken, and a new one made to *your* soul. And the wizards will want to make sure that the link to the corresponding Great Talisman is transferred securely."

"That's a part I don't quite understand. What link?"

"The link that keeps the Wizard Lord from just killing me if I go up against him; my talisman, the Talisman of Blades, is bound to one of his, the Talisman of Strength—it's one of the eight Great Talismans that provide most of his magic. If I die, if the Wizard Lord kills me, the link between my soul and my talisman will break, and the *ler* of my talisman will know, and because they know the *ler* of the Great Talisman will know, and the knowledge will free them of the oaths that hold them, and the Wizard Lord will lose one-eighth of his power. We eight Chosen each have one. If he kills four of the Chosen, then half his magic would be lost, and so on. If he were to kill all eight he would be nothing but an ordinary wizard, if that, and the Council or perhaps even just local priests would be able to deal with him."

Breaker considered this for a long moment, then said, "Perhaps I am not as ready as I thought. I knew there was a talisman and that I would need to take ownership of it by some magical means, but I hadn't realized that would mean binding my *soul,* or tying me to the Wizard Lord through a series of talismans . . ." He shuddered.

"Are you thinking you might not want the job at all, then?"

Breaker took a deep breath, then said, "No. I want it. I just want to absorb all this. If you call the wizards, though, how long until they arrive?"

The Old Swordsman shrugged. "Who knows? They're wizards."

"Call them," the young man said. "I'll be ready soon, probably by the time they get here."

"Good," the older man said. "Very good." He cast an oddly troubled look at the younger man, then clapped him on the shoulder. "Enough for today," he said. "Let us go find someplace warm!"

[6]

The first wizard came flying down out of the gray winter clouds just two days later. He dropped down into the middle of the village at midday, but stopped abruptly a few inches above the ground and hung awkwardly in the air at the center of a small whirlwind. Mad Oak's own *ler* were not making him welcome.

Naturally, this apparition caused quite a commotion. The weather was cold and overcast, so most of the townspeople were indoors, but a few children had been throwing snowballs at one another in the square. They ran screaming when the wizard arrived, calling for their parents, the priests, and the village *ler*. Breaker, who still thought of himself by that name even though most of his neighbors now called him Young Swordsman, or just Sword, had been moving firewood from the shed to the hearth when the commotion began, and did not hear it immediately; when he did realize something out of the ordinary was happening he still took the time to stack the wood in its proper place before following his sisters down the sloping street.

The Old Swordsman had been cleaning a sword, and did not rush the job; he finished his task, then carefully sheathed the blade and put away his cloths and polishes before finding his coat and joining the crowd.

Almost the entire village stood in a circle, leaving a broad open area around the wizard, when the Young Swordsman arrived; only the three clerics—Elder Priestess, Priest, and Younger Priestess—had dared approach closely. As the young man strode up he could hear the wizard speaking.

". . . no harm; flying was simply the fastest way to get here."

Breaker looked over the shoulders of his neighbors, and marveled at this wizard—and quite aside from the fact that he was hanging in midair, supported only by wind-spirits, his appearance left no doubt that he was a wizard.

The two wizards who had accompanied the Old Swordsman three months before had looked like ordinary travelers, for the most part. Oh, they had had their staves and talismans, and the *ara* feathers any traveler would have, but their clothing had been plain woolen cloaks over the same garb anyone might have worn. This new arrival, though, was far more flamboyant. He wore a bright red robe trimmed with elaborate embroidery in gold and green; the patterned hem flapped around his ankles, and the wide sleeves fluttered. His unbound black hair would have reached halfway down his back had it not been whipping wildly in the unnatural wind that held him aloft. A dozen talismans rattled and gleamed on a cord around his neck, and gold rings the size of a circled thumb and forefinger hung from his ears. The carved and enameled staff in his hands was capped and shod in gold, and held a score of additional talismans.

"And why were you in such a hurry to visit Mad Oak?" Elder Priestess asked.

"Because the opportunity to see the world's greatest swordsman in formal combat does not come along often, and I didn't want to miss it!"

The Young Swordsman stiffened as several dozen pairs of eyes turned toward him, including the eyes of all three of his sisters.

The wizard saw the direction of those gazes, and turned his own attention that way, as well. Elder took her time before she, too, turned.

"Formal combat?" she said.

"Yes," the Young Swordsman admitted. "But it won't . . . I mean, we aren't . . ."

"To first blood," the Old Swordsman said from behind him. "I believe the young man is ready to attempt it." He strode up and clapped Breaker on the shoulder.

"You *said* he was," the wizard called.

"And we will find out soon whether I was right. I believe certain magic must be involved, though, for the match to have its intended effect of transferring the title—magic requiring a wizard's attention. That was why I sent word to all of you."

"I'd have been just as happy if no one watched," Breaker said, to no one in particular.

"When will it be?" the wizard asked. "The message was vague—you know how poor a sense of time some *ler* have."

"We hadn't set an exact time," the Old Swordsman replied. "We needed to know just what's required in the way of wizards' magic."

"Oh, it's a simple partial release and fresh binding—very easy, the sort of thing even an apprentice could probably do," the wizard said. "I could certainly manage it, if you like—you could hold the match this very afternoon."

The two swordsmen looked at each other.

"If it's all the same, I'd prefer to . . ." the younger began.

"We wait," the elder interrupted. "No offense, Red Wizard, to you or your *ler,* but I'd be happier with more than one experienced magician involved. Just to be safe."

"Of course, of course." The wizard attempted a bow of acknowledgment, but the magical vortex held him upright, turning the bow into more of a wiggle. "You can demand half the Council, if you like—I think we'll all be eager to see it."

"I was going to say, I would rather wait," Breaker said, glaring at his teacher.

"Then might I ask, my esteemed priest and priestesses, that you petition the *ler* of your lands to let me set foot in Mad Oak?" the wizard asked, turning to the clerics. "I assure you, I mean no ill to any person or spirit here, and will keep my own immaterial servants in check."

"And I suppose you'll want lodging, as well," Elder Priestess said.

"Oh, I would not wish to intrude on your privacy; I will be happy to sleep in the pavilion on the ridge, if that might be permitted."

"I thought wizards were supposed to be arrogant," Spider whispered in Breaker's ear as the clerics conferred. "He doesn't seem arrogant to me!"

"He *looks* fancy enough, though, with all his bright colors and things!" Fidget whispered in reply.

"Wizards are just people," their brother replied. "The Old Swordsman's told me all about them—some are arrogant, some are humble. Like anyone."

A murmur of chanting came from the circle, and abruptly, the whirlwind vanished; the wizard stumbled as he dropped the last few inches onto the frozen mud of the square, but caught himself without falling.

"Thank you," he said, essaying a proper bow this time.

"Our *ler* prefer human beings to arrive on foot," Priest said, apologetically. "They have a very strong sense of how things ought to be."

"Of course," the wizard said, brushing off his robes and shaking his hair into place. "I meant no offense. Every town's *ler* have their own little whims; I just hadn't realized yours had that particular preference. Naturally, I'll do everything I can to oblige them."

"Come on," Elder Priestess said. "I'll show you where you can sleep." She beckoned for the wizard to follow her as she led the way toward her home. Apparently she had no intention of making the town's guest sleep in the drafty, poorly heated pavilion, despite his offer.

Thinking of the cold, Breaker wondered idly, not for the first time, why the Wizard Lord allowed winter to still happen; was his command of the weather not enough to prevent it? The Old Swordsman had claimed not to know any answer to that one.

"Well, that's *one* wizard," the Old Swordsman said, smiling at Harp, Fidget, Spider, and their brother as they all turned toward home, eager to get out of the cold. "Two or three will be enough. Then we'll put on our show, give you the talisman and bind the *ler*, and I'll be done with it all, ready to leave as soon as the roads are open in the spring."

"And you'll be the Chosen Swordsman," Fidget said, looking up at her brother. "Who'd have ever thought *that* would happen?"

The Old Swordsman laughed, but Breaker just batted a hand at his sister, who ducked the blow easily. He did not laugh.

And, he noticed, neither did his other sisters.

Other wizards were not long in coming. With the river frozen over and snow blocking the paths only those who had captured wind elementals or found other ways to fly were able to come, so the first wizard's flamboyant arrival was repeated, with minor variations, three more times over a period of five days. All these wizards, two men and a woman, were strangers; apparently the two who had brought the Swordsman to Mad Oak in the first place either had not received the message, had decided not to attend, or were unable to fly.

And four wizards, the Old Swordsman decided, was plenty; with this fourth and last arrival the wizards now outnumbered the priests hosting them, and waiting for more would be an imposition on Mad Oak's hospitality. Furthermore, he and Breaker had gone over their plans carefully, and both felt ready to perform their little exhibition. They could not rehearse it move for move, as that would make it impossible to fool the *ler,* and trying to set out specific moves in words did not seem entirely practical, but they agreed on what areas the Old Swordsman would try to leave exposed to Breaker's blade, and discussed just how the performance could be kept spontaneous and convincing while still yielding the desired result.

Thus prepared, the Old Swordsman sent Spider and Fidget to tell the assorted magicians that the formal challenge would be made the next day, and on the afternoon following the fourth wizard's arrival the Old Swordsman strode into the town square and proclaimed loudly to no one in particular, "I am the world's greatest swordsman! No one in Barokan can defeat me with a blade!"

Breaker had been waiting in a convenient doorway, feeling the tension in the air that meant *ler* were listening and watching; he thought he had even glimpsed light and movement in some of the winter shadows. Now he straightened up, flung back his hood, and marched out to face his teacher.

"I can defeat you, you old fraud," he said, "if you forgo magical assistance!"

Wind stirred, and shadows moved; a wave of glitter seemed to glide across a nearby snowdrift, as if something were refracting the watery sunlight. The air almost seemed to vibrate; the former Breaker had never before felt such a concentration of *ler,* not even during the spring planting rites.

"I need no magic to beat the likes of you," the elder sneered.

"The empty words of a windbag!"

"The simple truth."

The younger raised his hand in challenge. "Then prove it—send away your captive *ler,* put down your talismans, and face me on even terms!"

Now he could feel dozens of eyes on him, as well as the presence of the *ler.* He resisted the temptation to look around at the hidden audience, peering through shutters or door cracks, or around corners—but even Priest's old cat, curled on a windowsill, seemed to be staring at him.

All four wizards were unquestionably in the surrounding houses, watching through the shutters to be certain that the challenge was properly made.

"I will!" the old man called happily. "Tomorrow, when the sun tops the eastern cliff, we will meet here with our swords. I will order my *ler* not to interfere, and we will see that my title is no brag, but mere fact!"

"Tomorrow, then, old man!"

And with that, the two turned on their respective heels and marched off.

Behind them the air shimmered, and the cat's gaze followed the Young Swordsman's departure.

[7]

The sky overhead was already blue and brightening when Breaker arrived in the town square, well before the sun cleared the looming clifftops to the east. He wore a white woolen coat he had borrowed; he hoped it would make him harder to see against the snowy surroundings. Yes, the Old Swordsman intended to lose the fight, but the youth wanted to make it easy for him—and, more importantly, believable for those watching, both human and *ler. Ler* responded to human beliefs and emotions, as Elder Priestess had told him often enough, so the fight had to look as convincing as possible to everyone and everything watching.

And yes, the audience was already there. Priest was standing in his doorway, watching somberly, wrapped in the red cloak he wore when acting as magistrate. To one side the two priestesses, Elder and Younger, were waiting, both wearing the green of their office. Joker and Brokenose and Spitter were leaning against a nearby wall, hands in the pockets of their long winter coats, their expressions surprisingly serious.

Breaker's family had followed him to the square, and his parents and younger siblings stood clustered at one edge of the square. Harp, followed by Smudge, had joined the other musicians in a corner, though of course none of them had brought their instruments. Digger had joined them, though he had never shown any interest in music; noticing Smudge's annoyed expression, Breaker guessed that his friend had been a little too obvious in showing that his interest lay in the harpist, rather than the harp.

The Red Wizard and two of the others, the woman known in Mad Oak simply as the Wizard Woman and the man called Greybeard, stood gathered at one side; the fourth wizard, Black Coat, had not yet appeared.

Dozens of other townsfolk stood waiting, as well—none of them had ever seen a real swordfight, unless the last few months of practice might be counted.

And the air shimmered with the presence of *ler;* colored light sparkled in every shadow. Breaker looked around, trying to gauge their mood, as he drew his sword and took a practice swing.

That was how he came to notice the rabbit, and the hawk, and Priest's cat, all staring at him.

The cat—well, cats were inexplicable creatures, and might stare for any reason, or none at all. The hawk might conceivably have been attracted by the presence of so many *ler,* thinking they might guide it to its prey.

But what was a rabbit in its long white winter coat doing in the middle of town, sitting unafraid among so many humans, and staring so intently at one of them? He stared back.

Some of the observers noticed his intent gaze, and they, too, saw the rabbit in the square.

The rabbit noticed them, as well, but did not react in anything like normal rabbit fashion; it did not freeze, or flee, but looked casually around.

"Yes," it said, in a high-pitched, inhuman voice, "it's magic."

Someone in the audience screamed, and several others murmured; feet shuffled in the snow, and someone tumbled on a slick spot and caught herself against a wall. The so-called Young Swordsman, feeling very young indeed, closed his eyes and swallowed.

He had heard of talking animals, but he had never seen one before—

well, not one *he* could understand; he knew that the priests could sometimes speak to the *ler* of ordinary beasts and birds, just as they spoke to other *ler*. An animal speaking aloud in a human tongue was an entirely different matter; he had never really believed in them, even though the Old Swordsman had told him that the Wizard Lord used them as messengers.

And believing or not, he had certainly never imagined they might sound like this; he had assumed they would have human voices, but the rabbit spoke human words in a rabbit's voice, to very disconcerting and unnatural effect.

He opened his eyes again and focused on the rabbit, which looked calmly back. He asked, "What sort of magic? What are you?"

"I am a rabbit, of course—but at the moment I serve as the eyes, ears, and voice of the Wizard Lord."

The voice was almost a squeal, some of the words hard to make out, but Breaker understood perfectly—presumably, he thought, because that was part of the magic.

"Did you think I wouldn't take an interest in the identity of the Chosen Swordsman?" the rabbit asked. "The Chosen are of rather obvious importance to me—I want to know they are all people of good sense and goodwill, and not glory-seekers who might declare me evil so that they can make themselves a name by slaying me."

"It hadn't occurred to me," Breaker admitted. "You're so far away . . ." He shuddered as a thought struck him. "You *are* far away, aren't you?"

"I am," the rabbit said. "I am in my tower in the Galbek Hills; I couldn't spare the time to come in person, and would not wish to impose on Mad Oak's hospitality in the depths of winter in any case."

"Thank you," the youth said, though he was not sure what he meant by it. "We are honored, of course." He bowed. "I'll try my best to show good sense—if I win, I mean. I certainly mean you no ill."

"I can see that."

Breaker jerked upright at that. Could the Wizard Lord see into his heart, hear his thoughts? Accounts of just what the magical overlord of Barokan might be capable of were wildly inconsistent and universally considered unreliable—even the Old Swordsman said he was unsure just what was true and what was mere legend.

This whole business of becoming one of the Chosen suddenly seemed like a mistake. Setting himself up as one of the judges and executioners over someone who could make a rabbit speak from more than a hundred miles away was surely unspeakably foolhardy; how could anyone in his right mind accept such a role?

"Is there . . . I mean . . ."

"I'm hurting the rabbit's throat," the rabbit said. "No more." Then it turned and hopped away a foot or so before turning back to watch.

The youth hesitated—but then the Old Swordsman arrived, Black Coat at his side, just as the sun's light flared golden above the cliffs, and the air buzzed with sudden tension. The Young Swordsman turned to face him.

In turning he noticed the hawk perched on a convenient rooftop, still watching him. Was that another vantage point for the Wizard Lord? Was it another wizard using similar magic to observe the duel? And the priest's cat really did seem unnaturally intent.

Were there others? Mice under the shutters, spiders in the eaves?

The Old Swordsman seemed to have missed the excitement of the talking rabbit, and he was ignoring the murmuring of the crowd, the muttered questions, the nervous edge, the tinge of near-panic in the air. His attention was entirely on his opponent, and he seemed more determined, more *there,* than Breaker had ever seen him.

"Are you ready, boy?" the Old Swordsman said, drawing his sword. Breaker raised his own blade.

"Forswear the aid of your *ler*!" he called, remembering his role.

"With the *ler*'s consent, I have left my talismans on my bed," the elder man said, "and this man beside me has driven away other *ler* that might have aided me. You face nothing but my own skills—which will be more than enough, I have no doubt! I think it will be spring, at the very least, before you are ready to take my title!"

Breaker hesitated, but then he reminded himself that the old man was trying to make it look good, trying to make everyone believe the fight was honest. He had promised to give Breaker an easy opening, an opportunity to show what he could do and prick the older man's upper arm.

Just draw first blood, and he would be declared the world's greatest swordsman, one of the Chosen, with the magic to make the claim true.

He fell into the stance he had been taught, left foot back, right foot forward, left knee straight, right knee bent.

"A moment," the wizard Black Coat said, stepping forward, hands raised. "If this is to be done, let it be done properly."

The Young Swordsman relaxed slightly, lowering his weapon.

The wizard stood between the two combatants, and gestured to them to indicate the starting positions they should take. Then he announced, "We are here today to see whether this young man, a scion of the town of Mad Oak in the central region of Longvale, son of the man called Grumbler and the woman known as the White Rose, can prevail in armed combat against the man reputed for many years to be the greatest swordsman in all Barokan. By the request of both participants, I and my fellow wizards, as members of the Council of Immortals charged with overseeing the choosing of Barokan's defenders, and all the priests of Mad Oak, as representatives of the place of this combat, have called upon the *ler* of earth and sky, of blade and bone and blood, of steel and fire, to refrain from all interference—let this battle be settled only by the strengths and skills of mortal men! Is it so agreed?"

The answer was not spoken but felt, as if a great wave had rolled through the air, carrying the word *yes.*

"And do the combatants agree that this bout is to be decided by the first drop of blood shed, and that no further proof will be asked in determining the victor?"

"We do," the Old Swordsman said; Breaker hastily agreed.

"And is it understood by all that the victor shall be proclaimed the greatest swordsman of Barokan, and shall become the possessor of the talisman and powers granted to the holder of that title by the Council of Immortals, and shall accept the role of one of the Chosen Defenders of Barokan, and swear by his true name to fulfill the duties of that role?"

"Yes." This time the word was spoken aloud by both men—and the rabbit.

"Then when I lower my arm, let the bout begin." Black Coat stepped back and raised one arm high, while the two swordsmen raised their swords and assumed fighting stance.

Then the wizard's hand dropped, and the Old Swordsman's blade came jabbing at him, and Breaker focused all his attention on his sword and his opponent, forgetting about rabbits and wizards and everything except defending himself.

The old man had said he intended to make it look good, and he had obviously meant it; he was pressing the youth harder than he ever had in training or practice, and the former Breaker gave ground, stepping back. He did not drop his defense for an instant, though; steel clashed and whickered, but neither point nor edge touched him.

Breaker had not expected so fierce an assault. He wanted it to "look good," yes, but the way the old man was pressing him a single slip might send the old man's sword through his arm, or put a gash in his cheek. For several seconds he could do nothing but defend; he had no time to consider an attack of his own, as he was far too busy remembering the lessons he had been taught over the preceding months, and putting everything he had learned about defense to the test.

Keep the blade high, never overextend, always be aware of his surroundings so as not to stumble and so no unexpected second foe could take him by surprise, anticipate the blows rather than reacting to them, if possible move to the side and not back when dodging, trust his reflexes . . . there was so much to keep in mind! He focused himself on using it all.

It was enough, but just barely; several of the old man's blows were close enough that Breaker could feel the wind of their passage, and he was fairly sure one cut a lock of hair from his head—it was a good thing hair couldn't bleed.

At last, though, the assault seemed to falter, and Breaker ventured a quick jab.

The Old Swordsman turned it easily.

Breaker was puzzled—and somewhat frightened. Hadn't the Old Swordsman set all this up so he could lose, and give up his duties as one of the Chosen? Why, then, was he fighting so hard? He was attacking as fiercely as he did in practice, if not more so—had he changed his mind?

Or had the whole thing been a ruse, perhaps? Was Breaker to be a blood sacrifice to the *ler* of swordsmanship, so that the Old Swordsman could carry on? He had heard of such magic, of how some *ler* required such sacrifices. Maybe this was a requirement of the role, like the daily hour of practice—perhaps every so often, every five or ten years or whatever, the Swordsman must prove his worth by slaying a worthy foe.

Breaker's arm almost shook at that thought, and the tip of his blade wavered; it seemed far too likely. He had believed everything the old man had told him, but what if it had all been a pack of lies, meant to lure him into this fight, where he could die in ritual combat?

If that was what was happening, then Breaker knew he was doomed, but he had no intention of making it easy for the old man—and maybe he was worrying about nothing, maybe the wily Chosen was really just making it look very, very good. He shifted his grip slightly, to keep sweat from affecting his hold on the weapon; despite the cold his hands were damp. Even as he kept his eyes on his opponent's wrist and shoulder, he tried to think of tricks he had learned, anything he might use to win this fight.

Or just to *survive* it, if the Old Swordsman really had betrayed him and meant to kill him.

The older combatant lunged. The tip of the Old Swordsman's blade missed the younger's ear by no more than an inch, and the Young Swordsman told himself to stop worrying about such things and concentrate on the matter at hand—the duel. Whether his opponent was fighting to the death or to first blood didn't really matter at this point; against so superior an opponent Breaker had to fight as if he were fighting for his life. He countered the thrust, only to have his blade knocked aside once again. He brought it back in line in time to parry an attack.

"Well done," the rabbit called loudly, in its squealing, inhuman voice.

The Old Swordsman started and glanced aside, and the Young Swordsman lunged, and the point of his sword jabbed through the old man's leather coat and into the flesh of his shoulder.

The crowd gasped.

Startled, both fighters froze for an instant, and then, as if at an agreed-upon signal, simultaneously stepped back, pulling the blade from the older man's shoulder.

The tip of the sword gleamed red in the morning sun, plain for all to see. The air hummed with the magic of waiting *ler*.

"I believe I've won," Breaker said, his voice unsteady. He felt slightly ill. He had not intended to strike the shoulder; such a wound could be far worse than the pinprick in the arm that he and the old man had discussed.

But he hadn't had much choice—and even now, he remained wary, afraid that the old man might resume the fight.

Why had the Old Swordsman fought so determinedly? Why hadn't he left a better opening? Breaker felt himself starting to tremble in reaction; his stomach was churning.

At least the wound did not seem *too* serious; blood was seeping through the leather, and undoubtedly there was a great deal more beneath, but the Old Swordsman clearly still had the use of his arm and was neither screaming in pain nor writhing in agony.

"Yes, I believe you have," the old man said unhappily, clapping his left hand to his bleeding shoulder.

"You don't sound pleased," Black Coat said, stepping forward. "Having second thoughts?"

"I might be, at that," the old man said, glancing at the rabbit.

The Young Swordsman's eyes followed the elder's gaze in time to see the animal turn and hop away.

There was clearly something going on here he didn't understand, but he did not want to admit that and ask about it in front of half the village. "Now what?" he said.

"Now," the wizard said, stepping forward and throwing an arm around the youth's shoulders, "we must bind you to the talismans and their *ler*. You are now the greatest swordsman in Barokan, as demonstrated by your victory, and must therefore be one of our Chosen Defenders—let us now confirm that with the spirits of blood and steel." He turned Breaker toward his parents' house. "How much of your true name do you know?"

"A few dozen syllables, perhaps."

"We will need it for the magic, as much of it as you can remember—the *ler* care nothing for the names we humans give each other."

"I know that," Breaker said, allowing himself to be set in motion, his bloodied sword still in his hand. He looked at his defeated opponent, who was stripping off his pierced coat to allow Younger Priestess access to the wound, and at his own family, who were stepping aside wordlessly to allow him past.

His parents' expressions were unreadable, while Spider and Fidget were staring at him with frank openmouthed awe. Harp had vanished, fled somewhere during the fight, though Breaker—the Swordsman, now—had not seen her go and was unsure why she had left. Smudge and Digger were gone, as well.

No one had rushed forward to congratulate him—not his parents, nor his sisters, nor Little Weaver nor Curly, nor Joker nor Brokenose nor any of his other friends. All but Harp and Digger were there in the crowd, watching, but none of them had said a word, no one had applauded his victory. They were just staring at him silently as the black-coated wizard led him away.

He wasn't sure exactly what he had expected, but he thought there ought to be more enthusiasm than *this*.

"So tell me as much of your true name as you can," the wizard said. "I will need to recite it, so I had best start learning it."

"Erren Zal Tuyo," the new Swordsman began; then he stopped.

The wizard glanced at him, startled. "You must know more of it than *that*!"

"Of course I do, but . . ." He gestured at the silent audience they were passing.

"Ah, I see," the wizard admitted. "We'll wait, then."

Ten minutes later they were in the loft bedroom where the Old Swordsman—now the former Swordsman—had been staying, a room that had been Harp's when the family had no houseguest. The wizard closed the trapdoor and pushed a chest over onto it, since there was no lock.

"Now," he said, turning to the Swordsman, "what was that name again?"

"Erren Zal Tuyo kam Darig seveth Tirinsir abek Du po Wirei Shash-Dubar hyn Silzorivad," the young man replied. The air seemed to shimmer as he spoke, and he felt the sounds tugging at something inside him, even though he did not know what they really meant or even what language they were. He had not spoken the names aloud in well over a year, not since Elder Priestess had last renewed his ties to the land and soil of Mad Oak, and while any true name attracted the attention of the *ler* he did not remember the effects ever being anywhere near so strong before.

"Ah," the wizard said, nodding and apparently untroubled by any untoward phenomena. "If I interpret that correctly, you have a destiny, though I can't say what it might be—perhaps merely the one you achieved today by establishing yourself as one of the Chosen. And then I suppose we have the four cardinal *ler* that attended your birth, while

Silzorivad must have been the spirit present in your mother's womb at the moment of conception. Shash-Dubar . . . I don't know that. A local spirit, perhaps? Some connection to your father?"

"My mother says Elder Priestess told her it has to do with the months she was pregnant with me."

"She may be right. Do you know any more?"

"No. Just that. Elder Priestess might . . ."

The wizard held up a hand. "It should serve. Your destiny and the four *ler* are the essential parts." He leaned his staff against a table and opened a large purse that hung from his belt; Breaker noticed that the drawstring writhed unnaturally. The wizard paid no attention to the animated cord as he began drawing out talismans.

When he had brought forth a dozen of his own he turned and added them to the collection already lying on the narrow bed. There were tiny carved figures in wood and stone, baked-clay tokens in a dozen assorted shapes, things of beads and wire, waxed feathers and vials of precious oils—at least a score in all.

And at the center was a tiny triangular silver blade, no more than three inches long, that shone with a fierce intensity, as if catching a flash of summer sun—but this was winter, and the sun still hung low above the Eastern Cliffs, and the room in which they stood had only a single window, facing north.

"That's the one you'll need to carry, Erren Zal Tuyo," the wizard said, pointing to the blade. "That's the core around which the magic will be wrapped."

"What if I lose it?" Breaker asked, gazing uneasily at the gleaming device.

"Oh, I don't think you can," the wizard replied. "The *ler* will see to that." He adjusted the arrangement on the bed, then stepped back and looked it over.

"That should do," he said. "Now, stand here, and look at the blade." He gestured to indicate the spot he meant.

Breaker obeyed, and stood staring down at the bed as the wizard began to chant incomprehensible words in an unfamiliar language.

The surge of power was immediate; the air hummed with magic, and colored light shimmered across the talisman-covered bed, gold and red and blue. Breaker felt suddenly dizzy, and started to step back, but when his attention shifted from the little silver blade a wrenching, stabbing pain thrust up from his spine and through his head. His eyes watered, and his vision blurred, so that the only thing he could see was that talisman.

He focused on it again, and the pain vanished as abruptly as it had appeared, but his vision was not restored; all he could see was the shiny bit of metal there on the brown blanket. He locked his gaze grimly on to it as the wizard's voice droned on.

He heard his own true name, the name the *ler* knew him by, the name that described his soul and defined his place in the world of spirit, in the chant, and he felt something happen; now it was not merely the threat of pain that kept him staring intently at the talisman, but a sudden inability to imagine ever again seeing anything else. This was where he *belonged,* and what he was meant to be, meant to do—staring at the talisman was what his entire life had led up to, what he was *for.* The glowing silver filled his vision, as big as the world and everything in it, and the wizard's voice had become a chorus filling his ears, the one human voice accompanied by a thousand that were definitely *not* human.

His hands and feet were numb; the skin of his face felt burning hot. Time ceased to pass in any rational way; every second was an infinity. He was a part of the talisman, no longer aware of any other existence.

And then he was no longer aware of anything at all.

[8]

The new Swordsman did not so much awaken as gradually become aware of his surroundings.

He was lying in his own bed, fully dressed—in fact, he still had his boots on, though his coat had been removed. He was lying on his back, staring up at the blue flowers his mother had long ago painted on the plaster ceiling of his room. His hands were at his sides, and both were clutching something; his right hand was closed on something hard and cold, while his left held something sharp and hot. He had no memory of how he had gotten down from the loft and into his own room at the back of the house.

And all through him he could feel the rushing of . . . of *something*. He didn't have a name for it. It wasn't heat or cold or raw magic, nor was it any of the natural emotions or physical sensations he was familiar with. It was something numinous, something of *ler,* but he could not give it a name.

He blinked, his first conscious movement since he had lost himself in the wizard's chant, and that seemed to break some small part of the spell; he could still feel the rushing, and his hands still held whatever they held, but he was once again entirely himself, the young man called Breaker—or the Young Swordsman.

He raised himself up on his elbows and looked around.

The thing in his right hand was the hilt of a sword, one of the two the Old Swordsman had brought—hardly a surprise, since they were the only swords in Mad Oak. He raised the blade and looked at it, then let it fall at his side.

He opened his left hand to find the silver talisman clutched to his palm; he closed the hand again.

He was not alone in the room; his mother was sitting on his one chair, watching him. She had that familiar worried expression she wore whenever one of her children was ill, whether from eating too many sweets or angering the *ler* or whatever other causes might put a child to bed with aches and fever.

He glanced at the window and asked, "What time is it?" Then he reconsidered, and without waiting for a reply asked, "What *day* is it?"

"It's still the same day," his mother said. "It's a little after noon."

"Oh, good," he said, sitting up. "That's not bad."

"Not *bad*? You were unconscious for *hours*! Even when that black-coated wizard and the Old Swordsman and your father hauled you down the steps you didn't so much as stir!"

"I wasn't exactly . . . well, I was unconscious, I suppose, but it . . . I can't explain. It's magic."

"Of course it's magic!" she snapped. "You've gone and gotten yourself involved in things you shouldn't, you have wizards putting spells on you and Elder Priestess arguing with half the *ler* in Mad Oak about you,

you defeated the world's greatest swordsman in battle—of *course* it's magic! It's a wonder you're still alive and have your own soul!"

He grinned, and asked, "How do you *know* I still have my own soul?"

"Erren Zal Tuyo, do you think I don't know my own son?"

The sound of the first three elements of his true name was a shock; he could not recall ever having heard his mother say all three of them aloud before. People in Mad Oak didn't *do* that. The mysterious rushing seemed to swirl and eddy at the psychic impact.

"I suppose you do," he admitted, still smiling. "Though I'm not entirely sure *I* do anymore! That spell—it connected me to the *ler,* to everything, and it took me a while to remember who I was and find my way back. I wouldn't have been surprised if it had taken a few days, or even months."

"So it's all worked, then?"

"I think so."

"And you're the Swordsman? The world's greatest swordsman? One of the Chosen?"

"I *think* so."

"And now you're ready to go kill the Wizard Lord if someone asks you to?"

Breaker's cheerful mood dimmed at that question. "I suppose I am," he said—but as he spoke he remembered the talking rabbit, and how the Wizard Lord had been reluctant to hurt the creature's throat by forcing it to continue its unnatural speech. That was hardly the act of a cruel or thoughtless man; Breaker could not easily imagine why he might be called upon to kill such a man.

But as he remembered the fight he was reminded of other questions. Why had the Old Swordsman fought so fiercely, when he had come to Mad Oak and spent months in preparation specifically to lose that very duel? Why had the Wizard Lord's rabbit spoken up when it did, startling the Old Swordsman and giving Breaker the opening he needed?

Why did the Wizard Lord live virtually alone, out in the wilderness? He had not dared ask that before, but now . . .

"Where's the Old Swordsman?" he asked. "I need to talk to him . . ." He belatedly remembered thrusting a sword point into the man's shoulder. "Is he all right?" He glanced down at the sword in his right hand, and saw that yes, it was the same weapon, and a bit of his opponent's blood was still streaked on the tip, though someone had wiped away the worst of it.

"He's packing up," White Rose said. "Younger Priestess cleaned the wound and started it healing, and one of those awful wizards used her magic to call a guide, who said the southeastern road should be passable at least as far as Greenwater; he's on his way here from Ashgrove now. He and the old man should be ready to go first thing in the morning."

"He's leaving? Just like that?"

"He got what he came for. You're the one with the magical job now, one of the Chosen; he doesn't belong here anymore. He's just an old man going home to his family."

"I didn't think he had any family."

"Well, he's going *somewhere,*" his mother said angrily. "He's not staying here in Mad Oak; we've had quite enough of him."

"I thought . . . the roads . . . I mean, I still have more to learn . . ." Breaker's voice trailed off as he realized he wasn't sure of the truth of his own words.

"Not from him, you don't. He's leaving."

"I need to talk to him." Breaker sprang to his feet and flung the sword onto the bed, then marched past his mother and out the door of the room.

The steps to the loft were on the line between stairs and a ladder, very steep but not quite vertical; Breaker scrambled up them as his mother called after him worriedly, "Is it safe to leave your sword down here?"

Breaker ignored the question as he clambered up through the open trap and looked around.

The Old Swordsman—the *former* Swordsman—was sitting on the edge of the bed, studying something he held in his hand. He looked up at Breaker's entrance. "I suppose you have more questions about how it all works, now that you know what it feels like," he said, before his replacement could speak.

"Those, too," Breaker agreed, as he closed the trap behind him. "But first I need to know something else—why did you . . ." He broke off in midsentence as he noticed the lump under the old man's shirt. "Are you all right?"

The former Swordsman glanced down at the hidden bandages. "Oh, I'm fine," he said. "Your pretty little priestess fixed me right up; there's hardly even blood on the gauze."

"I'm sorry."

"Oh, I hope not. It's a little late to undo any of it."

"No, I just meant that I hadn't wanted to hurt you that badly. A little cut on the arm would have been plenty, wouldn't it? But you kept your guard up, you pressed me hard; I never had an opening for your arm."

"I know," the old man said. He grimaced. "Believe me, I know."

Breaker hesitated; now that he was here and had a perfect opportunity, it was surprisingly hard to get the words out. At last, though, he said, "Why did you fight so well?"

"So *well*? I *lost,* didn't I? There I was, the world's greatest swordsman, and some overconfident kid . . ."

Breaker cut him off. "You were supposed to give me an opening. You were supposed to let me win."

"I *did* let you win."

"The rabbit startled you."

"I suppose it did." He set aside the thing he had held, then turned his attention back to Breaker. "And remember, boy, that the Wizard Lord isn't limited to rabbits. He can see and hear and speak with *other* animals, as well. Rats or mice, for example—well, I'm not sure he can make a mouse speak, there may not be enough breath there to work with, but he can see through their eyes and hear with their ears."

"I suppose he can," Breaker said, unsure where this was leading.

"I know he can—I've spoken with him that way plenty of times over the years."

"All right, then."

"And is there any reason to think that he can't do as well with insects, or spiders?" He pointed at a web between two rafters. "That little eight-legged dot up there might be listening to our every word, sending it all to the Wizard Lord in his hilltop tower. For all I know, the air itself might carry our words to him."

"So he could be listening to us right now?"

"Indeed he might. Quite a powerful magician, our Wizard Lord. Master of all Barokan, from the Eastern Cliffs to the Western Isles, and most likely able to see and hear anything he chooses that takes place anywhere in his realm."

"But he can't be everywhere at once."

"No, he's still more or less human, he's not a *ler.*"

"So he probably *isn't* listening to us."

"But he could be. After all, he did take an interest in our duel. If the Seer were here, she could tell us—she always knows when the Wizard Lord is listening or watching, it's part of her magic. But *I* can't tell, and the Seer isn't here." He grimaced. "I didn't want her here, for fear she would talk me out of . . . well, out of something."

Puzzled, Breaker asked, "Would she? Talk you out of dueling me, I mean?"

"I don't know, any more than I know whether the Wizard Lord is listening."

"And what if he *is* listening? Does it matter?"

"Perhaps not; I just wanted you to realize that you may have somewhat less privacy than you are accustomed to, now that you have come to the Wizard Lord's attention."

Breaker considered this, and then nodded. "I see," he said. "This is something you hadn't really mentioned."

"That's right. I didn't."

"Are there *other* drawbacks to being Chosen that you neglected to mention?"

"Almost certainly."

"And might they have something to do with your unexpected resistance in our duel?"

The old man sighed. "They might, or they might not. Perhaps I was simply overcome by pride when it came to the event, and I couldn't bring myself to do *too* much less than my best—and even without the talisman and its *ler,* I still had more than forty years of practice. Maybe I wanted to see if I *could* beat you without my magic."

"But didn't you *want* to give up the role?"

"Perhaps not as much as we thought."

"Even after all you had done to arrange it?"

"Even then." He glanced up at the spiderweb, then said, "Or perhaps I was having second thoughts about what I was doing. Perhaps I began to doubt the wisdom of my actions."

Breaker frowned. "You don't think I'm good enough to replace you?"

"Oh, no—you were good enough, no question about it. The magic was blocked, but I still had all my years of practice and experience to draw on, and while I was not necessarily doing my very best, while I was hesitating, I was still trying to defend myself, and you beat me without a deliberate invitation on my part. To do that after so little training, not even a full season—you're definitely good enough to suit the role, and can only get better. No, that's not it."

"Then what is?"

The old man sighed. "The fact is, I *was* having second thoughts—not about *you,* but about whether it was fair to burden you with the role when you know so little of the world. I did not intend to give you your chance until I had made peace with myself that it was the right thing to do."

"And did you find that peace, then?"

"No. You and the Wizard Lord's rabbit took matters out of my hands, and I was presented with the accomplished fact, and no way to reverse it. I have no choice but to accept my defeat and go home to my niece and her husband, and hope they'll take in a useless old man."

"And I must take up your burden. Is it really so onerous, though?"

The former Swordsman hesitated, once again throwing a glance at the spider.

"For more than thirty years, I didn't think so," he said. "Of late, I am less certain."

"Is it just the years, then? I . . ." Breaker caught himself. "Thirty?" he asked.

"Yes."

"But you have been the Swordsman for forty?"

"Forty-four."

"Then something changed, a few years back?"

"I have seen three Wizard Lords during my term. The first two I trusted."

Breaker took his meaning immediately, and this time both men glanced at the spider. For a moment neither spoke; then Breaker said, "If he *is* listening, and is what you think him to be, then you now stand already condemned by your own words, wouldn't you think?"

"Quite possibly, yes."

"And you lied to me, didn't you, when we first met, in the pavilion after the barley harvest?"

"Did I?"

"You said the Wizard Lord was an honorable man."

"And he may well be; I may be mistaken. I have no proof, no real evidence at all, that he is anything less than the honest and just ruler he claims to be. I believe what I said was that he has served well thus far, and to the best of my knowledge he has—but there is something about him that I find uncomfortable. He has more of a temper than the other two, he seems less predictable, less rational; he worries me. Where the other Wizard Lords lived in elegant homes convenient to friends and family and tradesmen, and where people could easily petition them, this one insists on living in his ramshackle tower out in the Galbek Hills, more than a mile from the nearest village. Instead of a proper staff he's served only by half a dozen maids—no men or boys. He has no wife nor even, so far as I know, a favorite among his maids, and his background is a mystery to me, where the others often spoke of their roots. It may be that he's just a harmless eccentric, and I cannot point to any evil he has done, but neither do I feel certain that he has done none, or that he will not do something terrible in the future."

The full significance of this was gradually sinking in.

"You think the Chosen may be called upon to kill him."

"Possibly, yes. And I'm an old man; I did not feel I was still fit for the job. I am old enough to retire in any case, but this uncertainty made it more urgent, so last summer I began seeking my successor, and at harvest time I found him." He smiled humorlessly. "I found *you.*"

Breaker frowned in response. "You found me, and trained me, but in all the months you've been here you did not see fit to mention *why*. In fact, you did everything you could to reassure me that I would not be called upon to kill anyone. I trusted you, and you have deceived me from the first. I don't . . . I don't even know where to begin . . ."

The old man held up a hand. "You don't need to," he said. "Do you think it hasn't eaten away at me all these months? I like you well enough, lad—oh, I don't say we'd ever be the best of friends, but you've a good heart and good sense, certainly more than most of your friends here, like that Joker, or that skirt-chasing Digger, or the drooling ninny you call Spitter. Half a dozen times I thought of walking away, telling you the *ler* had told me you weren't suitable—but if one of us does have to face an angry Wizard Lord in a battle to the death, I would rather it be you, not only because I value my own life, but because I *am* old and tired, not just in body but in spirit, and I think you would stand a better chance of defeating him. Oh, when I was young I would have gone bravely enough, and fought him however I could, but now I fear I would hesitate when resolution was needed, guard when I should attack, question when I should obey. Remember, I am the oldest of the Chosen."

"No longer," Breaker corrected him.

"Ah, too true. Well, I *was* the eldest. The Leader is half my age; even the Scholar is twenty years my junior. I would not fit well in such a company, should we be called upon to perform our assigned task; age and caution do not befit the Swordsman."

"So you coaxed me to succeed you, without warning me of your doubts about our present master."

"Yes. I'm not proud of it—but you were eager, and I had no solid basis for my concerns, and who knows, perhaps I'm wrong and you won't be called, perhaps the Wizard Lord is a fine man who happens to have odd tastes. Or perhaps he'll trip on a stone and break his neck tomorrow, and the Council's next appointee will transform Barokan into a paradise. So I kept silent and we carried on."

"And then at the last moment your conscience troubled you, and you thought better of it?"

"Oh, not my conscience, boy—not entirely, at any rate. I was still ready to let you take the job without knowing what you might be getting into. It wasn't my conscience. It was that rabbit."

"What?"

"The Wizard Lord's rabbit. I supposed he would know what was happening, but to appear so openly, and speak as he did? It troubled me all the more, and I began to doubt the wisdom of handing on the title of Swordsman."

"You thought the Chosen might be summoned soon, and it would be a mistake to have so inexperienced a Swordsman?"

The old man snorted. "No," he said. "Or not entirely. Rather, it occurred to me that if the Wizard Lord knows of my suspicions, then once I am no longer the Swordsman he might well decide to dispose of me as a threat. Oh, I can't hope to kill him without the magic, but I can still speak, and because I served so long, people might listen."

"But . . ."

"Remember, if the Swordsman dies, the Wizard Lord loses one-eighth of his magical power. If an ordinary old man dies, it costs him nothing. He could say it was an execution, that I had slain someone unjustly, and who could argue with him?"

"Oh." Breaker looked up at the spider. "So you wanted to hold on to the magic to protect yourself."

"Yes. And *you,* of course, since you would no longer be involved."

"But the rabbit called out, and I won."

"Yes. And all day, I have been wondering *why* the rabbit called out. I think it's clear that the Wizard Lord wanted me to pass the role of the Swordsman on to you—but why?"

"Because I wasn't suspicious of him," Breaker said bitterly. "Because I'm young and naive."

"That would be my guess, yes."

"But now you've ruined that by telling me."

"And now we may discover whether he is as vengeful as I fear, or whether my worries are all imaginary. If he *is* turning to evil, I don't expect to live very long."

"But I . . . No, I won't allow that." Breaker turned to face the spider. "If you're listening, Wizard Lord, know this: If this old man dies under circumstances suspicious in even the slightest degree, then I will know my duty as one of the Chosen, and I will remove you!" He brandished the talisman at the web.

"If he's listening, it's probably not really through the spider."

"Oh, I know," Breaker said, "but where else should I direct my warning?"

"True enough. And thank you, lad, for giving that warning—I appreciate it more than I can say. Even if it looks and sounds like nothing more than the posturing of an overconfident child, the fact that it comes from the Chosen Swordsman gives it weight. But even so, if the Wizard Lord has gone mad, it may do no good."

"Well, then let us both hope that your worries are groundless. You don't want to die, and I . . ." Breaker swallowed, and grimaced. ". . . and I don't want to kill."

[9]

Neither swordsman said a word of any of this to anyone else in Mad Oak, of course. The Young Swordsman claimed to be tired from the duel and the magical rite that had bound him to the *ler* of muscle and steel and kept to himself, and after Breaker clambered back down the steps the Old Swordsman made sure he was too busy tending his wound and preparing to depart to talk to anyone else.

The wizards had all flown away by midafternoon; Breaker's younger sisters watched the four departures and came running in speckled with snow, gasping and giggling as they asked each other repeatedly, "Did you *see* that?" Fidget tried to pantomime the whole scene for her parents, spreading her arms, flapping, twirling, and leaping, while Spider wildly applauded her performance.

The familiar Greenwater Guide arrived at the pavilion that evening, as the lanterns were being lit, and word was sent to the swordsmen. Breaker was told first, and in fact, it was he who carried the news up to the loft.

"The road to Greenwater is supposed to be open, if you aren't in a hurry," he said from the open trap. "The guide made it here from Ashgrove in about half a day; he's staying with Elder Priestess tonight, and will meet you at the pavilion in the morning. But he says the roads beyond Greenwater may still be blocked; he has no reports from the *ler* there."

"I think I have outlasted my welcome in Mad Oak," the old man replied from his bed. "Greenwater can surely tolerate me for a few days." He shuddered. "Though I'm not looking forward to that walk through the snow, with this hole in my shoulder, and I don't know how the High Priestess will receive me, this time of year and in my condition. The lake must be frozen, and I have no idea what that does to their customs and rituals—and when I visited there before I was one of the Chosen, not a mere outcast."

"You aren't an outcast."

"Well, I . . . no, I suppose not." He shifted on the bed, whether to get more comfortable or disguise embarrassment Breaker could not be sure.

"And the guide wouldn't be willing to take you if he thought they would not tolerate your presence."

"True enough. But my wound and the snow are real enough, even if my other worries aren't."

"Yes, they are. You should have asked one of the wizards to carry you."

"Oh, they hate that. It would probably take more than one of them, for one thing. They'll *do* it, if they must, but they hate it."

"Surely the Council of Immortals owes you that much for forty-four years of service!"

"You'd be surprised how few of them see it that way."

Breaker nodded, and hesitated. He had delivered his news, but there were still so many things he wanted explained to him, so much to ask about how the Council of Immortals and the eight Chosen operated, so much more he would like to know about what the other Chosen were like, so many details of why the Old Swordsman was suspicious of the Wizard Lord, so much about what he could expect in the days and years ahead, that he scarcely knew where to begin.

"You know, lad, you're one of eight—don't take *too* much weight on your own shoulders," the old man said, obviously guessing the trend of Breaker's thoughts. "It's not just up to *you* to decide anything, or to kill the Wizard Lord single-handedly should it become necessary—there are seven others with just as much say and just as much responsibility in the matter. Perhaps more, given that one of them is the Leader of the Chosen, with the magic to make others heed his words."

"How does that work, then?" Breaker asked, taking another step upward. "You said something about that before. How strong is his hold on the Chosen? And does everyone else simply obey his commands, whether they want to or not? It seems to me that such a power could be as easily abused as the Wizard Lord's own!"

The old man snorted. "If that were how it worked, it could. No, his magic is only that others will *listen* to him, no matter how dire the circumstances or how distracted they may be, and take seriously what he tells them—he can always command the attention of everyone in earshot, should he choose to do so. He can't outright control them unless he knows their true names, any more than anyone else can, but they can't ignore him. The Chosen *can* ignore him, but he's very persuasive, even to us—to you, I mean. The *ler* guide him to choose wisely when presented with a clear choice of paths, and that's important to consider before refusing his instructions. He will listen to what others say, weigh the options, and then quickly reach a decision; the magic ensures that he will never hesitate in finding his course. It may not always be the best course—even the *ler* aren't infallible—but he will always be confident in his actions. He has an aura of certainty about him—you'll see, when you meet him."

"And how will I ever meet him? You said I was to travel, but surely the Chosen are scattered all across Barokan; what are the chances I'll stumble across the others?"

"Who said it would be left to chance? The wizards and the *ler* will see to it, when the time seems right—you may never meet them all, but at some point you'll meet Boss. Everyone always does, somehow. And you can seek the others out; most of the Chosen aren't hard to find. They have their homes and their preferred routes when they travel, like anyone else. And if you find the Seer, she always knows where the others are."

"I may go looking for them in the spring."

"You could do that."

"I might see what they think of the present Wizard Lord."

"You might well do that, yes."

"Do you know where you're going, from Greenwater?"

"Home to Dazet Saltmarsh; I still have land and family there."

"Is it far?"

"Yes." He did not go into detail, but the tone of that single word convinced Breaker that wherever Dazet Saltmarsh was, the old man would not be there any time soon.

But the Chosen were expected to travel, and Breaker was now one of the Chosen—the still-new sensations of his magical transformation constantly reminded him of that. He nodded. "Perhaps I'll see you there someday."

"Perhaps you will," the old man agreed.

And with that, Breaker decided he had had enough of his former teacher for the moment; he looked down, and began his descent. The old man said nothing as the youth sank out of sight, but Breaker thought he heard a sigh just before he closed the trap.

Breaker slept late the next morning, after a restless night of strange dreams about swords and rabbits, and by the time he awoke the old man had left the house and headed up the ridge to the pavilion.

For a moment Breaker considered going after him to ask more of the endless questions that troubled him, but then he thought better of it. The old man's answers were never satisfying, but only led to more questions, and breakfast was waiting.

By the time he did finally get to the pavilion the former Swordsman and the guide had departed, their footprints leading up the Greenwater route, past the boundary shrine and past the immense gnarled tree the town of Mad Oak was named for. Breaker stared at the broken snow for a long moment before turning back.

He had better things to do than run after the old man. For one thing, he needed to practice his swordsmanship. He needed an hour of practice, he knew—and he could feel the *ler,* and the talisman in his pocket, impatiently waiting for him to begin.

He quickly settled back into a daily routine much like the one he had followed before the duel—he would practice for an hour each morning, do the chores that needed doing, and then spend time with friends and family. He practiced alone now, of course, but the biggest difference was the loss of the evening talks with the old man. He could no longer ask questions about the wizards or the Chosen, or about points of swordsmanship, or about the world outside Mad Oak; instead he talked to his mother and sisters about the ordinary affairs of the village, or walked up to the pavilion and listened to the other young men boast about their amorous accomplishments, or discuss their plans for the future—plans that usually centered on growing barley, bedding women, swindling bargemen, and the like.

And the old dissatisfaction that had prompted him to speak up when the Swordsman and wizards first arrived, the dissatisfaction that had faded away during his training and been replaced with frustration with his inability to best the old man, gradually returned. Mad Oak seemed to close in around him; the ordinary concerns of the people around him seemed petty and meaningless. Even Little Weaver's chatter about her dreams or the fanciful things she hoped to create on the loom one day, which had always delighted him, seemed pointless and silly.

The frustrations of practice, though, had vanished. Anything that it was physically possible for a man to do with a sword, he could now do. He had nothing more to learn, nothing anyone human could teach him about using a blade—the *ler* had seen to that. He was, indeed, the world's greatest swordsman. The purpose of practice was no longer to learn, but merely to do each move more smoothly, more quickly, than before.

In a way that made it less interesting and less challenging, but on the other hand there was still a great deal of simple satisfaction in doing the incredibly difficult just a little bit better, a little bit faster, than he had ever done it before.

On warmer days he sometimes acquired an audience, but it usually didn't last long; as Harp told him when he discussed it with her, utter perfection quickly became boring.

"Besides," she said, "you're so fast sometimes now that we can't even see you move—one instant you're standing with the sword at ready, and the next you're in a different position and whatever it is you've sliced to ribbons is falling to the ground, and we haven't seen a thing in between!"

Breaker had not realized he was *that* fast. *He* could still see—or at least feel—every move he made. He grimaced, and dropped the subject.

One day in midwinter, when his father was ill again and the supply of firewood low, he came in from practice and flung coat, sword, and pouch on his bed, then emerged from his chamber to find his mother waiting for him.

"Swordsman," she said, "could you fetch a few sticks for the fire from the pavilion's woodpile?"

He looked down at her, really looked, and for a moment he hardly recognized her. His mother had always called him "Breaker," not "Swordsman," and was she really so small and old as this, her hair gray, her skin more red than the white that had won her her nickname? Was this the first time she had called him "Swordsman"? He could not recall with any certainty, and that made him uneasy and eager to escape.

"Of course," he said, stepping back in his room and grabbing his coat. He pulled it on quickly and hurried out the door.

He was halfway to the pavilion when he began to feel the wrongness. He might have sensed it sooner had he not already been confused by the meeting with his mother, and he tried to tell himself that that encounter was responsible, that he was merely upset because his mother was getting old and he was growing apart from her; he pressed on, but a few steps later his stomach clenched and his skin began to crawl, sweat breaking out on the back of his neck despite the cold, and he knew something more was at work.

He swallowed hard, and stopped in his tracks, trying to feel what was wrong.

He had done his daily practice, so it was not that. He could think of nothing he had done, or failed to do, that might have displeased the village *ler*—yet he could definitely sense something very wrong, and getting worse.

His gloved hands were shaking, and his knees felt weak, as if he were frightened or ill, but he knew he was not afraid, and he had been well enough to wield a sword just a few minutes before. He looked down at himself, at his heavy brown coat and sturdy gray boots.

He was not wearing his sword belt, he realized—but he didn't always carry a sword, not here in Mad Oak, so it wasn't that.

He swallowed again, struggling to stay upright and not to vomit or piss himself, and tried desperately to think what it might be. This was nothing he had experienced before, nor did he recall hearing anyone else describe such a thing, so he guessed it had something to do with being Chosen. Was this some warning? Did it have something to do with the Wizard Lord? Had some wizard put a curse on him? He reached for the pouch where he kept the silver talisman, to see whether it was glowing or otherwise acting strangely. . . .

The pouch wasn't there, and he realized he had left it at home, on his bed—and he further realized that this was the first time since becoming the Swordsman that he had ever been more than a few feet from the talisman, and comprehension burst upon him.

"Oh," he said, to no one in particular. He turned around, and the wrongness faded—though he still felt weak and sick.

With each step back toward his family home, his room, his bed, his talisman, he felt stronger. His vision cleared—he had not even consciously noticed that his sight had been blurred and dim. His stride lengthened, his throat relaxed.

At the door of the house he burst in without knocking, and almost collided with Harp; he hurried past without apology, and snatched the pouch from his bed.

Strength and joy surged through him now that the talisman was in his grasp, and he laughed aloud.

"Sword?"

His mother was standing behind him, in the door of the room.

"You're back quickly; did you get the wood?"

"No; I forgot something," Breaker replied, turning around and grinning broadly. The euphoria of restored health was already fading.

"Well, hurry up, then."

His smile vanished. He wanted to say something to her, to explain about what had happened, how strongly he was bound to the talisman, how careless he had been to leave it behind, but the words did not come; she wouldn't understand, he was sure of that, and might instead see this as a chance to berate him once again for agreeing to become one of the Chosen. He closed his hand more tightly on the pouch and nodded wordlessly.

When he returned with the wood he said nothing to anyone.

Being the Swordsman was not just a job, he knew now—it was a part of who he was, and a burden he could not walk away from. Even a simple bit of carelessness like leaving his talisman behind could sicken him; who knew what might happen if he did something *really* wrong? He was bound by rules he barely understood, and could not afford to test them, let alone break them, until he knew more of what it meant to be Chosen.

After that, he always checked to be sure the talisman was secure before he set foot outside the house—and he never spoke of it to anyone. He did not think anyone in Mad Oak would understand—or care.

The days came and went, and his vague dissatisfaction grew.

Spring was not long in coming; the snow melted quickly that year. For the most part life returned to normal as Breaker helped with the cleaning, the plowing, the planting—but he still spent an hour of every day practicing with the sword the old man had left him. There were times when taking an hour to himself was inconvenient, and angered friends or family, but he had no choice. Even when the spring plowing kept him in the fields from dawn to dusk, he lit a lantern after supper and carried it out behind the house to practice in the dark.

He still spent time with Joker, Brokenose, and the other young men, and danced and flirted with Curly and Little Weaver, but somehow he felt more detached than ever. Jokes about his role in the Chosen that had been common at first faded much more quickly than he had expected, leaving only an odd sense of disconnection. It was as if the *ler* of Mad Oak knew he was no longer truly part of the town—as, Breaker realized, they probably did. *They* would have observed his connection to his talisman, and understood that it replaced and weakened his link to his old home.

And then at last the planting was done, summer coming on, he was no longer urgently needed to tend the crops, and in the idleness of the lengthening days the feeling that he no longer belonged in Mad Oak became overwhelming. He bore it for a time, but finally one day Breaker informed his parents that he felt it was time he did some traveling—it was his duty as the Swordsman to see more of Barokan.

To his mild surprise no one argued; if anything, his father looked relieved by the announcement. As Breaker looked around at the faces of his family, he realized that the disconnection he felt had not been one-sided.

"Where will you go?" his mother asked.

He shrugged. "I'm not sure yet—I've never traveled before, I don't know what it's like. If I can, though, I think I should visit the Wizard Lord in the Galbek Hills, and see what I think of him." He smiled, as if uncertain he wasn't joking.

No one said a word in reply; no one smiled back.

And why should they? There was no reason that would be a joke. For an ordinary traveler it might be, but not for one of the Chosen. His smile vanished.

"I'll go where the *ler* guide me," he said. "It may be to the Wizard

Lord's tower, or it may just be to Greenwater—I'll see how it goes. Don't worry; I'll be fine, and I won't make any trouble."

"Be careful, then."

"I will."

And it was decided, far more easily than Breaker had expected.

[10]

He spent the next few days trying to decide what to bring, and how much he could comfortably carry. He had a barley sack that would serve as a carry-all, and he obviously needed to bring his sword, his talisman, and an assortment of clothing appropriate for all weathers, since he had no idea how long he would be gone or what the climate was like in the Galbek Hills, but beyond that he was at something of a loss.

On the fourth day, around midafternoon, the Greenwater Guide arrived, which decided his route—he had been considering bartering for passage with the bargemen, should a southbound barge come by, and there was always a chance the Birches Guide would make her annual visit early, or the long-promised new Willowbank Guide the now-retired one had supposedly been training would finally arrive, but Greenwater had seemed like the most promising destination.

As soon as Breaker heard the guide was in town he hurried up to the pavilion, where he found the traveler sitting on a bench surrounded by women. It was not immediately obvious just what had attracted them all; they were staring at something spread on the bench beside the guide, pointing and chattering happily.

"What's that?" Breaker asked.

Several of the women turned. "Jewelry," one of them said.

"Ah." Breaker knew that the guides sometimes brought trade goods of one sort or another; there weren't enough people along their routes who needed guiding or had messages to send to make constant traveling worthwhile, so they augmented their regular services with lace, cosmetics, jewelry, tools, spices, feathers, and the like—small, valuable items that wouldn't weigh them down and that the barges didn't bother with.

"Was there something I can help you with, Young Swordsman?" the guide asked.

Breaker took a deep breath, and said, "I need a guide. I'm going to the Galbek Hills."

"Oh? I've never been there. I can get you as far as Valleymouth, at the edge of the Midlands, but from there you'll need to find someone else."

"Good enough." Breaker tried not to notice that several of the women were staring at him now.

"Would tomorrow morning suit you? I'd like to stay here tonight, perhaps sell some of this jewelry."

"Of course. Tomorrow would be fine."

"Then shall we meet here, tomorrow at midmorning?"

"That sounds very good," Breaker said. "Thank you."

"Make sure you bring your pack—we'll leave directly from here."

"My what?"

"Your pack. Your luggage. The belongings you're bringing with you."

Someone giggled.

"Oh. Of course." Flustered, Breaker turned away, his face reddening.

He felt foolish—and he resented that. He was a man—a young one, still unmarried, but a man. Furthermore, he was one of the Chosen. He should not, he told himself, be so easily thrown off-stride. An unfamiliar term and a girl's laugh should not leave him blushing like a silly child.

And the next day he was waiting in the pavilion, his barley-sack pack at his side, his talisman secure beneath his tunic, and his sword on his belt, when the Greenwater Guide arrived.

The guide was a stocky, middle-aged man, the same man who had brought the former Swordsman to Mad Oak, and who had led him away three months earlier; he alone had worked the roads from Mad Oak to Ashgrove in the north and Greenwater in the southwest for as long as Breaker could remember. Despite the warmth of the late spring day he wore a long leather coat with *ara* feathers around the collar, across the shoulders, and down the sleeves and back, as well as the traditional guide's feathered hat. He glanced at the sack, but made no comment about it.

He did ask, however, "How do you plan to pay me?"

"Uh . . ."

That caught Breaker completely off-guard; he had not thought about payment.

"Do you have any money?"

"No—why would I have money? I'm going overland."

The guide sighed. "The bargemen aren't the only ones who use money, lad—you'll see that soon enough. In the Midlands *everyone* carries money, and everything is bought and sold; they'd laugh if they saw how you people up here manage."

"What's wrong with how we manage?"

"Oh, nothing, for a village of brewers and bean-farmers, but in the wider world things get too complex for your everyone works, everyone shares system. No matter, you'll see soon enough—and you'll want to get your hands on a few coins as soon as you can. For now, though—do you expect me to see you safely to Valleymouth out of the kindness of my heart?"

Breaker had, in fact, expected exactly that, but it was clear that saying so would not be wise. "Do the Chosen get no special privileges, then?"

"Not from me."

Breaker frowned. "Then my mother will cook you a dinner, when next you come to Mad Oak—will that be sufficient? Perhaps Harp might play a tune for you, as well."

The guide nodded, a sharp motion that set the long white plumes on his hat bobbing. "Good enough," he said. "And you think you have everything you need?"

"I hope so," Breaker replied. He hesitated, glancing at the guide's clothing, then said, "Except perhaps a few *ara* feathers, to guard me on the road."

"You're one of the Chosen, are you not?"

"Yes."

"Then surely the *ler* protect you, and you don't need feathers."

"You're sure?"

"The old man got here without any."

"So he did. Lead on, then."

The guide snorted, but without another word he did exactly that, picking up his own pack and slinging it on his shoulder as he led the way toward the uphill door.

Breaker heaved his own bulkier load onto his back and followed, bound for the wilderness—or at least, the lands beyond Mad Oak that he had always thought of as wilderness.

The two of them marched quickly along the ridgetop, out of the village, past the herbalist's gardens, and up to the boundary shrine. The guide marched past it without hesitation, but Breaker could not so easily overcome a lifetime of training; he paused at the little stone structure, unable to continue immediately.

This was it; this was the point at which he would leave Mad Oak behind—though he could see the tree itself looming ahead of them, this was where the village ended. Beyond this point the town's priests could no longer talk to the *ler,* could no longer bargain with them and coax them to be generous. This was where he left his old life behind and entered the larger world beyond.

The guide glanced back and slowed his pace, but obviously did not intend to stop, despite his charge's hesitation.

Annoyed, Breaker bobbed his head quickly and said, "I thank you, spirits of my homeland, and pray that I may return safely to your protection." The prayer seemed appropriate—he had heard it said by others as they left Mad Oak—and provided an excuse for his delay.

Then he hastened past the shrine to catch up with the guide on the path—the trail was too narrow and faint to really deserve the name "road," Breaker thought.

And the minute he crossed the boundary, the world around him felt different; the air was suddenly cooler and somehow harder, the ground rougher beneath his boot soles, and everything felt somehow less unified, less part of a harmonious whole. He had always heard that the difference between a place where the *ler* knew you and one where you were a stranger was noticeable, but he hadn't expected it to be quite so abrupt a transition—especially not after having spent the last several months feeling ever more disconnected from Mad Oak. He gasped.

The guide did not respond, and Breaker broke into a trot to catch up.

He stumbled on the hostile and unfamiliar ground, but hurried on, and a moment later he came alongside the guide. "I've never been outside town before," he explained. "It feels so different!"

The guide acknowledged this with a grunt.

"It's . . . it's a bit frightening, really."

That drew only a nod, and the guide's silence began to worry Breaker. "Have I done something to annoy you?" he asked.

The guide sighed, and turned. "Do you think I'd have become a traveler if I liked talking to people?"

"Oh," Breaker said. "But you . . . I mean, you talked back in town, and you don't always travel alone . . ."

"I have to earn my keep, don't I?"

"Oh."

"And as for doing that earning, do you see that tree ahead? The big oak?" He pointed.

The tree the guide indicated was gigantic, and very familiar; Breaker had seen it from Mad Oak every time he looked to the southeast, as it towered above its surroundings. "Yes, of course," he said. "That's the Mad Oak that the town is named for; there are all sorts of stories told about it to scare children, so they won't cross the border. I don't know why it's *really* called that, though."

"Oh, it really *is* the main reason the town's lands come no farther along the ridge, and why the priests have made no attempt to tame the *ler* beyond the shrine. Those scary stories you heard may well be true. It's called the Mad Oak because the tree's *ler* has gone mad, more than a century ago, and will not speak to the other *ler,* or to the village priests. If you speak in its hearing it will strike at you; if you sleep beneath it, it will devour your soul, and what's left of your body will go to feed its roots. If you touch it, it will poison you or cut you or club you. If you move swiftly and silently beneath it, without stopping and without speaking, it will not notice you. Now, be silent, and follow me."

With that the guide crouched and began hurrying forward in an odd, stooped posture. Breaker did his best to imitate this.

Together, the two men dashed across the broad clearing around the oak—a clearing that Breaker noticed was brown and dead, despite the lush green of the surrounding area and the blossoming leaves of the Mad Oak itself. Dead leaves rustled and crumbled beneath their boots as they hurried, brown powder scattering in all directions and staining Breaker's legs. There were no green shoots anywhere, no weeds, no moss, no mold, just dead leaves. It was plain that nothing lived in the clearing, nothing at all but the immense oak.

Stooped as he was, Breaker found himself looking down at the deep layer of dead leaves, surely the accumulation of many years, as he ran, and he realized that here and there low mounds rose above the even surface, and that here and there these mounds revealed curves and corners of white bone, gleaming amid the rotting brown leaves.

This was a *bad* place; he could *feel* that. The air around him felt wrong, far more than it had when he first passed the boundary, and that strange and horrible ground cover only confirmed the wrongness. The sensation reminded him somewhat of the wrongness he had felt that day when he went out without his talisman, though there was no weakness or illness this time—just a certainty that this place was *wrong*.

And he knew that just as he had felt the wrongness of the place, *it* had felt something of *him*. He could not have explained how he knew, but he did.

The oak knew he was there, he was sure of it—it must have sensed his magic.

He looked up, trying to see how much farther he had to go, and saw that he had somehow veered from the guide's path, toward the great oak—the oak he could now see was twisted and bent, despite its size. Its house-thick trunk was distorted by bulging growths, its limbs crooked and spiraling; these abnormalities that had been largely hidden by the canopy of healthy green leaves, but he was under the leaves now . . .

That wasn't right. Why was he under the leaves, so close to the tree? The guide had not ventured so near, and Breaker had certainly not *intended* to.

But something was urging him even closer, drawing him in. The oak's *ler* was pulling at him, closing its hold around his own spirit.

He slowed, and tried to turn his feet back toward the guide's track, clearly marked by the line of crushed and scattered leaves his boots had left.

His feet would not turn. The oak had hold of him. He struggled, trying to turn.

He could not. Against his will, he was still placing one foot directly in front of the other, walking toward the hideous tree.

He could not turn, but he could slow his pace. He could not *stop,* though—he tried, and his own legs refused to obey him. Dead leaves and distorted limbs filled his sight and his mind, and even as he struggled to stop his movement forward he could feel his own thoughts becoming twisted and somehow treelike.

At last, though he could not stop, he stumbled, and the dry snap of old bones breaking echoed in the unnatural stillness beneath the great tree. One hand dropped toward the ground to steady him if he fell, and the other hand closed instinctively on the hilt of his sword, as his sack shifted awkwardly and almost fell from his shoulder.

Touching the grip of the sword seemed to wake him, though he had had no awareness of being asleep; the cold ferocity of the weapon's *ler* was like a rush of wind in his face, and he was suddenly free again, able to turn his steps and break into a flat-out run directly away from that hideous tree. His booted feet sent clouds of crumbled leaf into the air, and scattered bits of bone across the clearing; he ducked his head to avoid touching the lowest branches.

And then the guide was beckoning him forward, out of the clearing and into the shade of a towering ash, and the malign influence of the oak faded from his mind like a warm breath vanishing in midwinter air, replaced by the calm presence of the ash tree's sane, if disdainful, spirit. Breaker turned to look back, and started to say, "I never . . ."

The guide pressed a finger to his lips and shook his other hand side to side, indicating that he should not speak. Breaker snapped his mouth shut and nodded, and the two men proceeded in silence, under the ash and on into the forest beyond.

Breaker could sense the *ler* of every tree they passed, and they were all *different;* in Mad Oak the trees were cooperative parts of a greater whole, but out here they were all individuals, pressing close to one another but caring for nothing but themselves. Breaker would have liked to slow down and take time to feel their spirits, to see how this strange wilderness worked, but the guide was hurrying him on.

At last, when they were safely clear of the oppressive atmosphere of the Mad Oak, the guide said, "I thought you were one of the Chosen."

"I am," Breaker said, glancing up at the sunlight in the leaves overhead.

"Shouldn't you have greater resistance to magic than that, then? That's the closest I've come to losing a customer in the past ten years. I didn't bother giving you any feathers or casting a spell because I assumed your magic would protect you. It *should* have protected you; it protected the Old Swordsman well enough when he came north. Going south with me he used feathers, of course, and a talisman, but he said he'd never needed them when he was one of the Chosen."

"I'm sorry," Breaker said, lowering his gaze. "I'm new at it. I didn't know how to use my magic to protect myself. The tree's spell broke when I touched my sword, though, so I think I . . . It did help. Being Chosen."

"It shouldn't have gotten a hold on you in the first place. Maybe you should wear a feather after all . . ." He reached for his pack.

"I'll be fine," Breaker said, holding up a hand. If the Chosen were supposed to be immune to the hostile *ler* on the road, then he would play that part, he would focus himself on his sword and talisman and not use the magic-blocking feathers the Uplanders sold. Maybe assuming it was true would make it so—and if not, he had the guide to save him.

"If you ever have to fight the Wizard Lord, I hope you do better," the guide said.

"So do I," Breaker said, looking back at the Mad Oak with a shudder. Then he squared his shoulders, straightened his sack, and marched onward at the guide's heel.

A few moments later he asked, "If the Mad Oak is so dangerous, why do you take this route? Isn't there any other path to Greenwater?"

"The others are worse."

Breaker opened his mouth, then closed it again.

"Oh," he said at last.

The Mad Oak was the worst of the hazards they encountered, but by no means the only one, and their route detoured around several areas the guide said made the oak seem like a mere game. Even as they made their way through the forest along the supposedly safe paths, vines twisted around Breaker's feet, hostile eyes watched him from the shadows, branches whipped at his face—he began to see, he thought, why the guide wore that leather coat.

But when he looked at the guide, somehow nothing seemed to be bothering him—even as branches slashed at Breaker's arms, they seemed to move aside for the guide. Breaker remarked on this.

"They know me," the guide said. "I've made my peace with them. And they know this coat will protect me, too. They might well do far worse to you if I weren't with you, or if you had no magical protection—as it is, you might have a slap or a scratch here and there, but nothing that will leave a permanent mark. If you weren't one of the Chosen and tried to make this trip alone, you might not make it to Greenwater alive."

"But they don't touch you at *all.*"

"They know me," the guide repeated.

"So you're a priest of this road, then? You speak to the *ler,* and treat with them?"

"I'm no priest. I don't know any secret tongues. I speak with some of the *ler* along my route, the ones that deign to understand human words, and I know which to avoid entirely, but there are no compacts or covenants, no cooperation between them. I don't know their true names, I can't tell them what to do, who to let pass—if you seriously anger them, I can't save you. These are *wild ler,* boy, every one for itself, not a peaceful little community like your town of Mad Oak."

A dry twig snapped beneath Breaker's foot, and the sharp broken end leapt up to slash at his shin; he winced, though the scratch did not break the skin or draw blood. "I see that," he said.

"This is what most of the world is like, you know—wild and uninhabited."

"I know."

"You mean you've been told that; you won't *know* it until you've seen more of the wild."

Breaker knew better to argue with such a statement.

"So without you, Mad Oak and Greenwater would be cut off from each other?"

"Oh, there would still be other routes, but it would be a long way around—maybe a *very* long way."

"Do you have an apprentice, then?"

"No. Your townsfolk might want to think about that."

That was another statement that Breaker did not care to reply to. Instead he asked, "What's Greenwater like? I mean, I've heard stories about it all my life, but I've never been there."

The guide shrugged. "It's a town. A hundred families or so. They mostly eat fish and berries, and do some fine woodwork, and they make wine rather than beer. They have priests who deal with the *ler* so the crops will grow and the fish will stay in the nets, same as any other town. And they have one priestess, who runs the place."

"I've heard that their priests live underwater." He had actually heard that they could turn into fish, but he decided to start with the more believable part of the tale.

The guide snorted. "No, they live *in* the water much of the time, but not *under* it—they can't breathe water any more than we can, and they'd freeze in the winter, and no, they aren't part fish, they're men like any other. But it's true that Greenwater's most powerful *ler* are in the lake, the soul of the village is the lake, and the priests spend hours standing in water up to their chests, coaxing favors from the water *ler*."

"I've never seen a lake."

"Then look over there." The guide pointed ahead and to the right.

Breaker looked.

When not dodging supernatural hazards their path had led them more or less along a ridgetop for a distance of several miles, but the surrounding trees had blocked most of the view; now, though, as Breaker looked where the guide pointed, the ground fell away steeply ahead of them, and through gaps in the trees he could glimpse the far side of the valley.

Except the valley was far wider than it should be, and its far side more distant than Breaker had thought possible—it seemed as distant as the Eastern Cliffs. He had been to the ridgetop in Mad Oak many times, and had looked out across the wilderness of Greenvale to the next ridge, and it had been much, much closer than this, closer than the northeastern side of Longvale. Here it was so distant it seemed hazy. The trees on that distant ridge were merely an uneven green blur.

"Down there," the guide said.

Breaker's gaze dropped to the valley floor ahead of them, and he saw the lake, a vast blue-green splotch gleaming in the afternoon sun—Greenwater's water was indeed greenish, though not the vivid verdigris color he had always imagined it. It was closer to the dull green of a spruce tree.

"Oh," he said. The sheer size of the lake was overwhelming. It was many times as broad as the Longvale River was anywhere in sight of Mad Oak. The bargemen said the river grew much wider to the north, toward its mouth in the icy seas, but Breaker had never been sure whether they were telling the truth or just spinning yarns to amuse the townsfolk—and even if the stories were true, Breaker had never seen that. He had never imagined that as much water as he saw down in the valley below could be in anything but the ocean.

"We should be there in an hour or so," the guide said.

"Oh," Breaker said again.

Then he began pointing, and asking confused fragments of questions, and the guide took pity on him and explained as they began picking their way cautiously down the surprisingly steep southern side of the ridge.

"Not all the valleys in this part of Barokan are nice and straight like Longvale or Shadowvale," he said. "Greenvale is almost triangular—it's wide here and narrows sharply to the northwest. If we'd gone the other way along the ridgetop, toward Ashgrove, you'd have seen it narrow down to nothing, and this ridge we're on merges with the next. North of that it wouldn't be Greenvale over there at all, it would be Deepvale."

"But Deepvale is on the other side of Greenvale!"

"Here it is, and at Mad Oak, but by the time you get to Ashgrove or Bell Hill, Greenvale is gone, and Deepvale is next to Longvale."

Breaker turned and peered through the trees on the other side, over the ridgetop, and was relieved to see the Eastern Cliffs were still where they ought to be, two valleys away.

"I thought all Barokan was . . . there's Shadowvale, and Longvale, and Greenvale, and Deepvale, and Ravenvale, and so on to the sea, lined up nice and neat."

The guide snorted. "No," he said. "The ridges are just in this area, where the land jams up against the northern wall of the Eastern Cliffs, and only the first two are nice and neat. The farther you go from the cliffs the more the ridges wiggle and split. That's why Longvale is *long*, you see—it's between the two long, straight ridges. Even so, it doesn't go on forever; I've never been to the northwest end, but I've been to the southeast, where it empties into the Midlands. If you think Greenvale over there is broad, you should see the Midlands! Flat as a table, almost, and fifty miles across, maybe more! Some of the towns there are so close they share their boundary shrines—you can step from one to the next with nothing between. And beyond the Midlands are the southern hills, and the western marshes—Barokan is *big,* my boy."

"Have you seen all of it, then?"

"No. Didn't I just say I'd never been to the far end of Longvale? And I've never been into the southern hills, or beyond the nearest edges of the marshes. I've never seen the sea, or the islands, or been up the path to the clifftops—I didn't catch these *ara* feathers myself, I bought them from a Winterhome trader. I know half a dozen safe routes around Longvale where I work, from Bell Hill to Valleymouth, and I've traveled a little in the Midlands with someone else leading the way, but that's all."

"Oh. But . . ."

"We turn here," the guide interrupted. "And the *ler* in this next stretch like it quiet, so if you have any more questions they'll just have to wait. Watch your footing; the stones like to slip out from under your feet and make you stumble."

Breaker fell silent, but found himself staring through the trees at the lake, and thus distracted he quickly discovered that the guide's warning had been apt. When the two of them passed the boundary shrine into Greenwater he was still wiping the dust from the seat of his pants.

[11]

Greenwater was arranged along the lakeshore, with every house and workshop facing the water. The village did have a central structure Breaker took for a pavilion, like the one in Mad Oak, but instead of being built into the ridge it stood on wooden pilings in the lake. There were docks and boats along the water, as well, and then a broad clear area, and then the houses in three parallel rows. Above that were the orchards and gardens and vineyards, stopping abruptly at the boundary. There were no broad fields in the river bottom—but then, there was no river bottom, but a lakeshore.

Breaker had expected to see many different places in the world, but he had not expected one so different to be so close, less than a day's journey from Mad Oak. He stared at the unfamiliar surroundings as he followed the guide down the slope and into the village.

People working in the vineyards and gardens glanced up from their labors as the pair approached; some then turned back to their duties, while others stared at the stranger the guide had brought.

Breaker found it uncomfortable to be the object of such scrutiny; for that matter, he found it unsettling simply to see so many unfamiliar faces. These people were still people, with the same sort of eyes and hair and skin he was accustomed to, but their clothing was slightly odd—the colors seemed darker than they should be, and the sleeves were neither the full wrist-length sleeves of winter nor the short, loose sleeves of summer, but tighter than they should be and reaching to just below the elbow.

And there were so many of them, without a single face he recognized!

The guide did not speak, but led Breaker down the slope; Breaker followed silently, for fear that so much as a single word might violate the demands of the local *ler* and bring misfortune down on him. He stayed close to the guide, for while the man was a foreigner, and neither kith nor kin, he at least was someone Breaker had *spoken* to before.

When they crossed the boundary Breaker felt the transition clearly—the air became softer and more welcoming. At the same time, though, it was not the air of home; this was not Mad Oak, and he did not belong here as he had there. This place was not his own, it was merely not hostile.

The guide seemed to straighten a bit when they were within the town's limits; despite his earlier claims to dislike people and be at home in the wild, he, too, clearly felt more comfortable here.

Together the two of them passed the vineyards, then the orchards, and the gardens, and one by one the three rows of houses, and Breaker began to wonder whether the guide intended to march directly into the lake—was some sort of ritual ablution required? But in the open space below the houses the guide turned aside and headed for the plank walk leading out to the pavilion.

Breaker followed, noticing that the earth beneath his feet had a slightly peculiar feel to it, packed hard, but with a faint sponginess. He looked down at the black soil, and when he looked up again there was a woman walking out from the pavilion to greet them.

She was stark naked.

He stumbled, and barely caught himself before falling. His mouth opened, but at the last instant he caught himself and did not speak. He glanced at the guide.

The guide seemed utterly undisturbed by this apparition, and somewhere in the back of Breaker's mind old stories and rumors bubbled up, and he remembered that he had heard, often accompanied by adolescent giggling, that in some places the *ler* required their priests perform various rites in the nude.

And yes, Greenwater was said to be such a place—it went with the story about the priests living underwater, since clothing would scarcely be practical in an aquatic environment, and would have fallen away when they transformed into fish.

Maybe they really did turn into fish, after all—he hadn't actually asked about that.

More likely, though, the nudity was just something the *ler* required. There were far more lurid and unsettling tales of priestcraft in more distant lands, of blood sacrifices and horrific rituals, but those were all just rumors from afar; Greenwater was merely said to keep their priesthood as naked and submerged as the fish in the lake—sometimes literally as the fish in the lake.

It appeared that however exaggerated the guide might say the stories were, they were based on truth.

With this, he finally noticed a few details of the woman's appearance other than her lack of clothing—for example, that her waist-length black hair was dripping wet, and that there were green marks on the skin of her face and arms, marks that probably had some priestly significance, like the embroidery on the priests' garments back in Mad Oak. And while she was still young and slim enough to be attractive, she was not a mere girl; she had filled out, and begun to show the effects of time. Breaker judged her to be at least a decade older than his own nineteen years, perhaps as much as twice his age.

The guide led Breaker on, until the two men stood at the end of the wooden walkway; there he stopped and knelt. Breaker hastily followed his example.

The naked woman walked up to the very last plank to be over water instead of soil, and stopped as well, about twelve feet from where the guide waited.

"Oh, glorious bridge between human and spirit, grant us entry to your realm," the guide called out.

"Say first who you are," the woman replied, in a startlingly deep voice.

"I am the traveler known to you as the Longvale Guide, who the spirits recognize by a name that begins Kopol," the guide answered.

Then for a moment no one spoke.

Then the guide cast an angry sideways glance at Breaker, and the nude priestess said, "And you?"

"Ah," Breaker said. "Oh. I am . . . I am the Chosen Swordsman."

It was clear from her expression that that was not sufficient, and he hastily added, "The *ler* call me by a name beginning with Erren." He grimaced slightly, wondering whether it had been wise to give even that tiny fragment of his true name; in Mad Oak true names were not used in ordinary conversation. Breaker had heard that other towns were less strict, that in some places people actually called each other by their true names as casually as the people of Mad Oak used nicknames, but back home no one but the priests or the visiting wizards would ever have dared ask for even a syllable of it, and even they would never ask it in so public a setting.

But then, this woman *was* a priestess!

It was hard to think of anyone but Priest, Elder Priestess, and Younger Priestess as priests, though. He had never met any others before.

In any case, his answer seemed to satisfy her. "Then let me ask the spirits if you are welcome here," she said. She turned to face the pavilion and the lake.

That view had its points of interest, Breaker thought, but overall he preferred the front.

Then he reprimanded himself for thinking such a thing about a *priestess,* and one from somewhere other than Mad Oak, at that.

The priestess called out something in a language that was nothing Breaker had ever heard before, and as she finished a bird cried out somewhere, and a series of splashes sounded from the lake; reflected sunlight sparkled across the priestess's gleaming black hair.

Then she turned around again. "Well," she said, "that takes care of the formalities. Come on, then, you two, and tell me why the Swordsman has come to Greenwater." She beckoned.

The guide got to his feet and stepped up onto the walkway; Breaker followed. The priestess waited until they were almost close enough to touch, then turned and strolled toward the pavilion.

It felt very odd, to be walking so close to a naked woman in front of all the world like this. Everyone in town, looking down from their homes or fields, could see Breaker, the guide, and the priestess walking out across the lake.

Then they stepped into the pavilion, where the priestess led the way through various rooms to a verandah overlooking the lake, on the far side from the village.

This pavilion was very different from the one in Mad Oak; in fact, Breaker was not entirely sure "pavilion" was the proper name for it after all. He saw no dance floor, no storerooms; there was no reassuringly solid stone, nor fireplaces. Everything was built of wood and oilcloth, and the seams in the floor were so wide that he could catch glimpses of moving water through them, and hear the faint splashing of the lake against the pylons. Rooms and corridors opened into one another in confusing fashion, and it was not at all clear what most of them were for.

And the whole thing smelled of fish, rather than woodsmoke and beer.

There were other people present in the building, Breaker glimpsed at least half a dozen, but they vanished at the approach of the priestess and the travelers, quickly slipping into other rooms and closing the doors behind themselves—clearly they did not want to be around the threesome, but he could not tell whether they were avoiding the strangers or their own priestess.

The *ler* were moving around him as well, he could sense them; they did not seem as bashful as the humans.

Once the little party had reached the verandah the priestess settled into a large wooden chair, and gestured for the others to find themselves seats. There were half a dozen similar chairs, and a wooden bench along one wall; Breaker settled gingerly into one of the chairs.

The priestess smiled at him, then turned to the guide. "I didn't expect you back so soon, Kopol."

The guide shrugged. "He wanted to come to Greenwater," he said, jerking a thumb at Breaker, "and I was in no hurry to reach Ashgrove or Bell Hill."

"So you're only here to guide him?"

"That's right. I'll be taking him as far as Valleymouth, unless his plans change."

She nodded, and turned her attention to Breaker. "And you're the new Swordsman? One of the Chosen Heroes?"

"Yes." He wanted to say more, and not sound like an idiot, but he couldn't think what to add.

"So why have you come to Greenwater? Why are you bound for Valleymouth?"

Breaker stared at her face helplessly for a few seconds, then swallowed.

"I'm not entirely sure," he said. "I wanted . . . you see, I . . . I take my responsibilities seriously. If I am to judge whether or not the Wizard Lord should be slain, then don't I need to see more of Barokan than my own hometown? Shouldn't I try to see him and judge his character for myself? What if he is truly an evil man, but has simply not had occasion to direct his evil at Mad Oak? The Old Swordsman said I must travel, to learn more of the world, and so I am traveling."

"But why Greenwater and Valleymouth? Are you planning to spend much time in the Midlands?"

"No—I'm going to Valleymouth because it's on the way to the Galbek Hills."

"You're going to visit the Wizard Lord?"

"Yes. I thought I should meet him."

She smiled again. "Well, that's simple enough, isn't it?"

"Yes," Breaker said, with a sigh of relief.

"So you're just out to see the world, and meet the Wizard Lord, to reassure you that he's protecting us all properly. And how can we help you in this task?"

"Well, I . . . I need a place to sleep, and something to eat . . ."

"Of course."

"And I'd be happy to hear anything you can tell me about the Wizard Lord."

"Of course. Though it won't be much beyond the usual songs and stories."

"Or about anything else, for that matter. Greenwater is different from Mad Oak, and I'm . . . I'm curious about why, and what all the differences are."

"Are you?" She straightened in her chair.

"Yes, I . . . yes."

"Good. You should be."

Breaker's mouth opened, then closed again.

"You know, young Swordsman, you're doing quite well for a first-time traveler. I think the spirits did well when they led the Old Swordsman to you. You haven't stared at my chest or my crotch, though I know my appearance must be a shock to you—women don't go abroad nude in Mad Oak, do they? Not even the priestesses?"

"No. No, they don't. They wear robes."

"But you haven't stared, or made any rude comments. That's very good. That's better than many male travelers can manage."

"Oh." That remark somehow made it *much* harder not to lower his gaze and stare, and Breaker forced himself to focus all his attention on the tip of her nose.

"I suppose you've guessed that I'm Shilil, the High Priestess of the Lake, and my pact with the spirits, the *ler,* forbids me to wear any clothing in the warm months. I'm quite sure your guide didn't bother to mention any of that; Kopol likes to watch his charges make fools of themselves. It's a particular foible of his; most guides prefer to show off their knowledge, rather than hoard it."

The guide grunted at that, but did not deny the accusation. Breaker threw him a resentful glance.

"I'm sure you're tired and hungry from the journey; I'll have someone find you food and drink, and when you've rested and eaten, I'd be pleased to talk with you further—you can tell me about Mad Oak and how you became the Swordsman, and I'll tell you about Greenwater and what little I know of the Wizard Lord. Would that suit you?"

"Very much indeed."

"You said your name is Erren?"

"I . . . We . . ." he stammered helplessly.

"They don't use true names in Mad Oak," the guide interjected. "Not at all. They just call him Swordsman."

"Oh? Oh! I'd forgotten that." She frowned. "But have they always called him that? Did they *know* he would be the Swordsman?"

"No," Breaker said. "I was called 'Breaker' until I took up the sword."

" 'Breaker'? I don't think I like the sound of that."

"Oh, it's just from childhood. When I was little I didn't know my own strength, and didn't always look where I was going; I broke a lot of dishes and toys and the like."

"Ah—nothing deliberate, then?"

"Well, no more than any other boy." He smiled at her.

She smiled back.

"Let us hope you break nothing you shouldn't here in Greenwater, then." With that she rose; taking his cue from the guide, Breaker remained seated as she headed for the door.

She did not actually go *through* the door, however; instead she merely opened it and called, "See that our guests are fed, and given beds!" Without waiting for a reply she closed it again, then turned back to the two men.

"Someone will be with you in a moment. I will be back before sunset."

And then, to Breaker's astonishment, she ran across the verandah, sprang over the railing, and plunged into the lake. He leapt from his chair and hurried to the rail.

She was swimming smoothly away, obviously not in any distress.

"They all swim like fish here," the guide said, coming up beside him. "She more than any of them; she spends more time in the lake than on land."

"But she just jumped!"

"Yes. I suppose she's going to confer with the *ler* and ask what they think of you." He turned and eyed Breaker. "Can you swim?"

"No—at least, I don't think so. Most of the river below Mad Oak is shallow and muddy, and the water's *ler* don't speak to our priests, and the bargemen don't like townspeople intruding in their water, so I never saw any point in swimming. Even if I fell off the dock, it'd be easier and cleaner to wade than to swim." He had never tumbled off the dock himself, but Digger had once when trying to show off how much he could lift, and had simply walked ashore, cursing the *ler* at length for allowing his fall. They had rewarded his blasphemy with a cold that lasted for weeks.

"That's a pity. It would be useful here."

"Can *you* swim?"

The guide smiled. "No. A girl here tried to teach me once, but we didn't get very far in the lessons before I left."

Breaker had no answer to that; he looked out at the lake again, and at the dwindling figure of the priestess, swimming easily through the greenish water.

And then the door opened and a woman entered with a tray of food—a properly clothed woman, though her dress did have the odd tight half-sleeves. The smell of fried fish pierced the more general fishy odor of their surroundings, and Breaker suddenly realized just how hungry he was.

Their hosts spoke very little, but the supply of food and drink was generous, and kept Breaker's mouth busy enough without words. He didn't always know what he was eating or drinking, but all of it seemed tasty enough.

By the time the priestess finally returned, and climbed dripping from the water onto the verandah, Breaker was well stuffed and well rested, and eager to talk.

[12]

Except for old songs about hunting down criminals and stories about saving lost livestock, the High Priestess knew no more about the Wizard Lord than Breaker did—perhaps less, as she had not known he could make a rabbit speak.

"I had heard that he could see through the eyes of birds and beasts, but to speak with their mouths—this is new to me," she said, when Breaker described the day of the duel.

"I hadn't heard of it, either, but the Old Swordsman knew it could happen." It was odd, Breaker thought, how quickly he had grown accustomed to the lake priestess's nudity; he only noticed it now when she moved in certain ways.

"Well, he *is* supposed to have greater magic than a dozen lesser wizards combined, far greater than any priest who ever lived. He can probably do a thousand things we never heard of."

"I suppose so," Breaker agreed. He grimaced. "If he *did* go mad, I don't know how I could ever hope to kill him."

"You have your own magic, surely."

"Yes," Breaker said, very aware of the talisman in his pocket and the sword on his hip—and the need to get his daily hour of practice before he slept that night; he had been too busy packing and worrying to do it that morning. "But nothing like his!"

"And you wouldn't be alone; you would have your seven companions."

"I've never met them," Breaker said. "I don't know how much help they would be."

The priestess stared at him for a moment. "You haven't met them?" she asked at last.

"No. Not yet, at any rate. I suppose I should try to find them."

"I should say so, yes. Ask them what *they* know of the Wizard Lord, and what they think of them—surely, they will have given the matter some thought, and they have all held their roles for years, have they not?"

"I suppose so. I don't really know."

"You know very little, it seems."

Breaker started to protest, then stopped. He paused, considering. "That's true," he admitted at last. "The Old Swordsman taught me a great deal about the use of the sword, but not as much about the Wizard Lord or the Chosen. He told me a few things, but somehow now it seems as if he missed the most important ones."

"Then you should find the other Chosen, and talk to them, and ask them about the Wizard Lord, as well as visiting the Wizard Lord himself. Ask anyone who knows the Wizard Lord—there must be men and women who work with him in his tower."

"Just a few women, I'm told—and in all likelihood, they would not dare to speak ill of him, would they?"

"Perhaps not. You could speak to his friends and family, though, to the people who knew him before he became the Wizard Lord, perhaps even people who knew him before he was any sort of wizard at all. He's not so very ancient, after all, is he? Not yet ten years in the role? He might have brothers yet alive who would tell you all his secrets, from the name of his first girl to when he stopped wetting his bed."

"Brothers?" That possibility had never occurred to Breaker, that the Wizard Lord might have family. Wizards were not tied to a single village like ordinary people, nor to a few known roads like a guide; they traveled freely, their magic protecting them from hostile *ler*. Breaker had never stopped to consider that they must nonetheless have come from somewhere, that they would have parents like anyone else, and homes, but of course they would. They could not, after all, spring full-grown from the forest, as if they were *ler*. Wizards might have strange powers, and might accomplish wonders, but they were still human. "Does he have brothers?"

"I don't know." The priestess shrugged, and her breasts bobbed distractingly; it took Breaker a moment to compose his thoughts.

"Where is he from? One of the valleys?"

The priestess glanced at the guide, who shrugged. "I have no idea," he said. "His tower is in the southern hills, so maybe that's his homeland, but I don't know."

"His tower is in the Galbek Hills," Breaker said. "Is that in the south?"

"Yes," the guide said. "I haven't been there, but I know that much."

"I think it would be very strange, to talk to the Wizard Lord's family," Breaker said.

"Perhaps," the priestess acknowledged.

"I think I would like to do that."

"As you please; you are one of the Chosen, and all in Barokan are obliged to lend you aid, within reason."

"I suppose that's true," Breaker said slowly. He thought for a moment, glanced at the guide, and then said, "I know the Old Swordsman came this way, months ago, and I had thought I might follow his route for a time, in hopes I would catch up to him, so that I could ask him more questions. I didn't know anyone else outside Mad Oak. But if he wanted to tell me more, he could have done so, couldn't he? No one compelled him to leave Mad Oak so hastily. If I found him, he might have no more to say than he did at home. But as you say, *everyone* is supposed to aid the Chosen in their duties, even complete strangers—I don't need to seek him out to find people who can help me learn what I want to know."

"I suppose not," the priestess agreed.

"I'll want to find the Wizard Lord's home village, if I can; surely, the people there can tell me whether he is a good and trustworthy man, or not."

"I'm sure he is," the priestess said. "Otherwise, why would the wizards and their *ler* have accepted him as the Wizard Lord?"

"They could have made a mistake; it *has* happened before," the guide pointed out.

"Not for a century," the priestess replied.

"Then perhaps we're due."

Breaker grimaced, his eyes meeting the priestess's, and the two of them shared a moment of silent derision at the guide's suggestion that Dark Lords happened on a schedule.

"How will you find his home?" the priestess asked.

"I'll ask, until I find someone who knows where it is. I'll start in the southern hills."

"That's a long walk, out of the valleys and across the Midlands."

"Then I should get started as soon as possible."

And with that, the conversation came to its close. Breaker excused himself and set about his required hour of practice, leaving the guide and the priestess to chat.

As he went through a familiar routine of thrust and counterthrust against an imaginary opponent, he mentally reviewed the day's events, and found himself pleased. He had left his home for the wider world, and so far the adventure was going well. The incident with the oak was unfortunate, but educational, and his stay in Greenwater was proving entertaining, as well. He was interested to notice that while he felt just as disconnected from this town as he had from his own, it bothered him less here, because he was not *expected* to feel at home in Greenwater. Mad Oak was still nominally his home, the place where he should fit in, but he no longer felt at home there, or in his proper place; here in Greenwater he was a stranger made welcome, and he *felt* like a stranger made welcome. It was oddly comforting to no longer have that disjunction between expectation and reality.

Late that night, as he lay drowsing but not yet asleep upon the bed they had given him, the door opened silently and a figure slipped in. He held his breath and tried to see who it was, but the darkness was too complete; his hand slid toward the hilt of his sword, lying close by the bed.

"The spirits command me to attend upon worthy visitors," a familiar alto voice said. "As their High Priestess I am forbidden a husband, but must instead be wife to the lake itself—but the lake cannot easily get a child on me, and my line must continue if Greenwater is to thrive."

Breaker withdrew his hand and began to breathe. As with her nudity, Breaker had heard tales of such things, but had never entirely believed them.

"Besides," she said, "the rumors say that the spirits give you superhuman skill with *both* your swords, not just the steel one, and your predecessor lived up to that legend, despite his age. Shall we see whether you do as well?"

Certain remarks he had heard among the women back home suddenly made sense; Breaker had never heard such rumors himself, but obviously they had reached female ears in Mad Oak, just as the tales of naked priestesses seducing strangers had come to his own. Magical speed, strength, coordination, endurance, the ability to anticipate another person's actions and respond appropriately—perhaps his newfound talents *did* have another use.

"I make no promises," he said, sitting up, "but I'll do my best."

And his best was apparently good enough; Breaker had never heard a woman squeal so, certainly not any of the few girls he had bedded back home. He worried that some listener might think her cries needed investigation, but no one interrupted them.

And as he fell into an exhausted slumber at last he found himself thinking that, quite contrary to what he had been told since infancy and his own initial expectations, he *liked* traveling.

In the morning, at first light, he awoke as Shilil left his bed, and he looked out his window just in time to see the priestess leap into the lake again. A few moments later Kopol appeared at the door of his room, eager to hustle Breaker through his preparations for departure—"It's farther to Hartridge than to Mad Oak," he explained. "We need to get an early start if we want to be sure of arriving before sundown."

And scarcely an hour after dawn the two passed a wooden fence carved with prayers, and were out of Greenwater and in the wild again, making their way south along the slopes above the Greenvale River.

The Longvale River flowed south to north, and Breaker found it mildly disorienting that the Greenvale did the opposite, but he adjusted to it readily enough.

The sun was indeed skimming the western ridgetop when they reached Hartridge, where the priests were all men who had seen eighty summers and the *ler* respected only age. Although the guide showed him to a guesthouse, no one there seemed interested in speaking with him, nor admitted to any knowledge of the present Wizard Lord or his origins.

They stayed the night before continuing on to Bent Peak, where the half-dozen priests and priestesses were as ordinary as those in Mad Oak but the brightly clad farmers had a custom of gathering in their odd, dirt-floored pavilion and telling tales in the evening. He heard a score of fine stories about the Wizard Lord, none of which he believed; somehow he doubted even a Wizard Lord could fly to the moon and challenge the sun to a game of riddles, or build a tower of nothing but *ara* feathers to hide his sea-sprite mistress from other wizards. Alas, as Breaker had no good tales to tell in exchange, his welcome wore thin quickly.

The next day they headed for Valleymouth, the walled city at the edge of the Midlands, where the numerous priestesses attending to the *ler* in the gigantic stone temple and the dozens of scattered shrines were all young girls—the *ler* there would treat only with female virgins—whom he was forbidden to approach or address, or even to look at for more than a heartbeat or two. Other townsfolk were friendly enough, but greeted almost every question with "I'd need to ask a priestess," and considered it bad luck to mention the Wizard Lord at all, lest he think them rude and punish them with bad weather.

The guide greeted people in each town as old friends, and always knew where they could find food and shelter—the lake pavilion in Greenwater, the guesthouse in Hartridge, the bachelor barracks in Bent Peak, an upstairs room at the trading post in Valleymouth—but did not provide a great deal of assistance beyond that. With each new town Breaker had to adjust to the local accent; by the time he reached Valleymouth he sometimes had to ask for words to be repeated, but with a little coaching from his guide he picked up the differences readily. He also had to learn new customs, and cope with new *ler*—while he never felt as unwelcome in any town as he did in the wild, each community had its own feel, its own rules, its own prayers and attitudes.

The guide—despite the habits of the people in the towns of Greenvale, Breaker could not bring himself to call the man Kopol—helped him out a little, but as the priestess Shilil had warned him back in Greenwater, Kopol liked to keep his secrets and took mild pleasure in watching his charge's discomfiture as he learned the differences for himself.

He discovered that visible *ler* of the sort that sometimes manifested in Mad Oak as lights or shadows were unusual, as was the constant coddling and coaxing Mad Oak's priestesses used to make the *ler* cooperate with humans. Styles of prayer, styles of clothing, and styles of speech all varied more than he had imagined, almost more than he had thought possible—and this was all just in Greenvale.

No one in any of these towns seemed to know much about the Wizard Lord beyond the same stories he had grown up with and the absurd fancies of the Bent Peak farmers, but in Valleymouth he began to hear new stories about one of the Chosen.

The Leader—"Boss," he called himself, as the Old Swordsman had said—had come through there once or twice; he was reported to be tall and handsome, as might be expected, with a thick black beard and dark eyes. Several of the priestesses seemed smitten with him, though of course none had succumbed to his charms, since anyone who *had* would no longer be a priestess. There were rumors that two young women had indeed given up the *ler* for the sake of the Boss at some point in the past, but no one was willing to give Breaker any details; he suspected they thought he might use them as his model in seducing a priestess or two himself. Most of the girls were too young to be much of a temptation, but there were a few he glimpsed fleetingly who might have been worth the effort.

Breaker was hesitant to leave Valleymouth, even though he could see other towns from atop the town's ramparts; the flat open plain of the Midlands made him nervous. He had lived his entire life between two forested ridges, with the Eastern Cliffs guarding one side of his world, but here the cliffs were so far distant they appeared little more than a gray line on the horizon, and there were no ridges at all, nor forests, just flat land for as far as the eye could see, land covered with fields and farms, villages and towns, boundary shrines or fences or walls scattered everywhere. Actual roads—like streets, but between towns instead of inside them—crossed the landscape in the distance; the towns here were not all on rivers or lakes, and the land was flat enough to make wheeled vehicles practical, so a great deal of trade was conducted overland, hauling goods not on barges, but in giant carts called "wagons" that were pulled by oxen.

Breaker had never seen oxen before reaching Valleymouth, and did not much like them—placid as the beasts were, their mere size and obvious strength was frightening.

And the towns in the Midlands were so close together that there were no guides; to reach the next he would have to venture through wild country unescorted. Even with the roads, that was a daunting prospect.

"I've done it," Kopol told him. "It's not hard."

"But you're a guide!" Breaker protested.

"Not here; I learned the routes up through Greenvale and part of Longvale from my mother, but in the Midlands I just set out at random, and I did fine."

"But still . . ."

Kopol shrugged. "Please yourself," he said. "But I'm heading north again tomorrow, and you're on your own from here. The Galbek Hills are somewhere to the south, across the Midlands—you'll have to find your own way."

Breaker still hesitated.

Good as his word, the Greenwater Guide left the next day, leaving Breaker alone in the upstairs room of the trading post.

Eventually, after four days in Valleymouth, he gathered his courage and set out to the south. He arrived in Barrel unscathed, after a completely unremarkable walk.

It was in Barrel that he first learned to use money. The people of Longvale bartered goods and services, and sometimes used a measure of barley as a standard, but they had no coinage other than the copper tokens they traded with the bargemen, and a great many things were held in common by the entire village, to be used as needed. The people of the Midlands, as Kopol had warned, considered this foolish and old-fashioned, and used stamped silver disks as their medium of exchange. It took Breaker three or four days to get the hang of using the silly things, and to earn a modest supply by displaying his prowess with a blade and then passing a mug around.

He had developed his act little by little as he traveled; in every village since Hartridge, as soon as his identity was known, he had been asked to demonstrate his supernatural skills in exchange for his meals.

The stunts the Old Swordsman had taught him served him well; people were entertained by even the simplest tricks—slicing a tossed pear into three pieces before it hit the ground, deflecting a ball flung at his head without warning, disarming a stick-wielding attacker, snuffing a candle with the tip of his blade. He had gradually developed a standard performance, and could use it as his daily hour of practice. In the towns of Greenvale the end of the hour had usually meant a flurry of admiring questions and perhaps a little flirting from the local women; in Barrel it became his cue to hold out a mug and gather coins.

He was not the only one providing entertainment in the taverns and public houses—Barrel had no village pavilion, but instead several separate businesses arranged around a central square served the same purpose, and several people seemed to make their living by amusing the patrons of these establishments. Singers and storytellers would pass a mug or hat before and after each performance, and anyone who made a point of dropping in a larger coin than the usual could request a particular tale or tune.

Breaker bought himself a few stories and songs about the Wizard Lord, but alas, none of them were about the *present* Wizard Lord; instead he got to hear several familiar pieces about how this lord or that had turned aside a flood, or driven murderers to their doom, or fetched runaway children and cattle safely home again.

And of course, he heard the old ballads about how the Chosen slew the Dark Lords of Goln Vleys and Spider Marsh, though in versions not quite the ones he had learned back in Mad Oak.

In truth, Breaker thought he learned more talking to the townsfolk than he did listening to the professional storytellers. Here in Barrel, as in

Valleymouth, Boss was a known and familiar figure, and several of the locals claimed to have met the Scholar, as well. Three men even mentioned encountering the Speaker once, when traveling.

"What are they like?" Breaker asked as he stood in a public house, a mug of ale in his hand.

The locals glanced at one another.

"What do you mean, what are they like?" a fellow not much older than Breaker himself asked.

"I mean, are they short, tall, thin, fat, jolly, sad, quiet, loud—what are they like?"

"Scholar's pleasant enough," one man said. "He's about my height but thinner, with gray in his beard. He's good company, will trade tale for tale, and takes his turn buying the beer."

The man in question was of average height and stoutly built, which would make the Scholar a man of ordinary dimensions.

"He collects gossip like an old woman," another man said. "Always wants to know the news since he last came through."

"That's true enough—he'll remember everything you told him last time, about your sister's boyfriend and your mother-in-law's bad knee, and he'll ask you what's become of them, whether your sister's married her man and how that knee's been doing." This third speaker shook his head. "Filling his head with gossip instead of studying the lore he should be!"

"Well, it's not as if the Chosen will ever be called upon," said the stout man. "He has the gift of learning, so why not use it to make himself pleasant?"

"Pleasant?" the young man said. "How is it pleasant?"

"Everyone likes a good listener."

"And it's not as if he spreads it about—he *listens* to all the news, but when it's his turn he'll tell a story about some wizard dead a hundred years."

Breaker nodded. "And the Speaker?"

The men suddenly fell silent, the eyes of the others turning toward the three who had traveled; after an awkward pause, the man who had spoken of a mother-in-law's knee said, "I think she's mad, if the truth be told."

"Aye. She'll sit in the corner with her head tilted to one side, staring at nothing, and then she'll startle at nothing, and when she speaks she interrupts herself with nonsense."

"She's a crazy old woman, and the magic should have been handed on long ago," the stout man agreed.

"Is she old?" Breaker asked. The Old Swordsman had implied otherwise.

The men exchanged glances.

"She still has her teeth."

"And her hair hadn't gone gray as yet, when we saw her."

"Not so very old, then."

"I'd be hard put to guess her years," the stout man acknowledged.

"I think the madness makes her seem older," said the man who had called her mad.

"I know that the Chosen guard us all against the Wizard Lord going bad and we owe them respect for that, but it's hard to think well of such as her."

"Scholar and Boss, though—they're both fine men, and I'd not like to be a Wizard Lord who'd done evil."

"And show us that sword of yours again! I saw some of the tricks you did, and I wouldn't care to have *you* after me, either!"

"Buy me something to eat, and I'll show you how fast steel can move," Breaker agreed. "I can't do my best on an empty stomach!"

"Fair enough." The stout man beckoned to the landlord.

"Do you know who *I* would like to meet?" one of the others began.

"The Beauty. We know. We all would."

Breaker smiled. "The most beautiful woman in the world—who *wouldn't* want to meet her, if just to see the standard by which all others might be judged?"

"And is that why you agreed to be the Swordsman, then—so you'd have a chance to get to know her?"

Breaker shook his head. "No—fool that I am, I didn't even think about that aspect of it until after I'd started my training. It certainly wouldn't have discouraged me, though!" His smile faded. "Would you have any idea where she might be found?"

"None at all."

"Nor I."

That was hardly a surprise. The Old Swordsman had said she lived in Winterhome, at the base of the Eastern Cliffs where the trail came down from the Uplands into Barokan, but Breaker was not sure how reliable the old man had been. He had been vaguely hoping these people might know more—if the Beauty were nearby, then visiting her, getting to know another of the Chosen, might have been a good idea.

But she apparently wasn't, and before he could say anything more the landlord was there, and the men fished out a few coins to cover the cost of a platter of ham and vegetables.

As they did, Breaker was thinking over what he had learned. The Leader, or Boss, or whatever he called himself, sounded like a good strong man and a useful ally, worthy of being one of the Chosen, but there was nothing to indicate that he would know much of anything about the Wizard Lord. And the Speaker, if she was truly mad, would be useless.

The Scholar, though—if he had been collecting gossip for years, he might well know more about the Wizard Lord than anyone else. So far, Breaker had not heard a single negative word about the current Wizard Lord from anyone but the Old Swordsman—but he was beginning to notice he hadn't heard anything *positive,* either. There were hundreds of stories about Wizard Lords righting wrongs and saving lives and so on, but they were all about *former* Wizard Lords, not the current holder of the title.

Someone must know something about the man, and the Scholar was more likely than anyone else to be that one.

"When was the Scholar last in Barrel?" Breaker asked.

The men looked at one another.

"Last summer, was it?"

"Spring. I'd just been planting the north field."

"That's right—remember, he left just before the priests started looking for the solstice sacrifice."

"Right. Last spring, then."

A year's head start was more than enough to be discouraging, but Breaker had little else to guide his travels; he knew he wanted to head generally southward, toward the Galbek Hills, but other than that his plans were vague. He refused to be distracted by the mention of a solstice sacrifice, and asked, "When he left, which way did he go?"

"Toward Blackwell."

The others nodded.

And the following morning Breaker passed by an exceptionally ugly boundary shrine and headed southeast toward Blackwell.

[13]

Crossing the Midlands took almost half the summer; midsummer found Breaker in the foothills on the southern edge of the plain, in a town called Dog Pole—a name no one could explain. The local dialect was sufficiently different from the language spoken in Longvale that Breaker was not entirely sure he would have understood the explanation, in any case.

He had noticed as he moved south that the names, for both towns and people, seemed to make less and less sense. Some of them seemed little more than random syllables, rather than descriptions. Most people used the beginnings of true names for each other, as the people of Greenwater had, but nicknames, often bizarre ones, were common; a complete avoidance of true names, as in Mad Oak, was rare.

He had always wondered what "Galbek" meant; he now suspected that it didn't mean anything, but was just a meaningless name given to a particular set of hills. That seemed to be how these Southerners operated.

Of course, he reminded himself, he wasn't really *in* the South yet, but only just approaching its boundaries.

Along his way he had heard descriptions of several of the other Chosen—the handsome Leader, the gossip-loving Scholar, the mad Speaker, the short-tempered Archer, the motherly Seer. The Beauty and the Thief remained completely unknown; no one would admit meeting either of them.

He had learned very little about the Wizard Lord. Several people had told stories about the *previous* Wizard Lord—Breaker had not visited Spilled Basket, where he had made his home, but he had passed within about twenty miles of it—or about others even farther back, but hardly anyone knew anything about the present incumbent. The most common response to questions was a shrug and a remark, "The weather's been fine."

He wondered whether the Old Swordsman's fears might have been completely baseless; certainly, he saw no sign that anyone else suspected the Wizard Lord of any sort of misbehavior. No one actually professed to *like* him, but neither did they fear him. As far as Breaker could tell his journey to visit the Wizard Lord at his home in the Galbek Hills was largely pointless, but he was not inclined to turn back yet; overall, he was enjoying the trip.

He had asked sometimes about other wizards, as well, and had been surprised at how few reports he heard about them. None seemed to make their homes in the Midlands, or at least not in the portion of the Midlands he crossed; a few vague tales and legends trickled in from the west and south, but Breaker was unsure how much credence to give them. He supposed wizards preferred the less-crowded parts of Barokan, but it still seemed somewhat odd.

He had encountered hundreds of strange customs and unfamiliar rites in his traveling, and had become largely inured to them. People did what they had to to live with the *ler,* and he was no longer surprised by any demands the spirits might make. Appalled, sometimes, but not surprised. He still had trouble believing that people would willingly live in a community whose guardian *ler* demanded a human sacrifice every spring, but he had encountered at least three such towns.

He had continued to follow reports of the Scholar's presence, which had led him almost directly south—he was unsure what to make of that, whether it was merely coincidence or something else at work. He had gained some ground; the Scholar had reportedly passed through Dog Pole in early spring, no more than three or four months ago.

The Seer had also come this way not so very long ago; he wondered about that.

All in all, he was enjoying his journey, but found it worrisome that he was not learning more about his own role in the world.

One morning he was sitting at a battered table in Dog Pole's one and only public house, wondering whether he should continue following reports of the Scholar's route or try to find his way directly to the Galbek Hills, when the door opened.

He didn't look up at first; he was trying to estimate how long it would take to get back to Mad Oak if he took as direct a route as possible and only stayed a night in each town along the way. If the snows didn't come early he might take another two months to find the Wizard Lord's tower and still be home . . .

"Swordsman?"

Startled, he looked up, his right hand falling to the hilt of his sword. That had become a completely involuntary habit, but one he could *not* break; he suspected it was part of the magic his role entailed.

The speaker was a somewhat elderly man, rather weathered-looking but still straight-backed and apparently vigorous, clad in well-worn deerhide. "Yes?" Breaker said, returning his hand to the tabletop.

"It's a pleasure to meet you," the white-haired man said, holding out a hand; he spoke the Midlands dialect, but with a thick southern accent. "I'm here to take you to Tumbled Sheep."

Breaker blinked at him. "What?"

"I'm a guide—I know every road in the hills from here to Crooked Valley. I'm here to take you to Tumbled Sheep—it's a village about fifteen miles southeast of here."

Breaker frowned. "Who told you I want to go to Tumbled Sheep?" He was tempted to remark on the bizarre stupidity of naming a village "Tumbled Sheep," but restrained himself; that would just prolong a conversation he wanted to end quickly. He wanted this person to go away and let him think; he was in no great hurry to go anywhere but home, and did not think Tumbled Sheep sounded like a promising destination. He guessed the old man had heard the Swordsman was traveling the area, and wanted to earn himself a guide's fee and the enhanced reputation that aiding any of the Chosen might bring.

"The Seer," the guide said.

Breaker abruptly sat up straight, suddenly attentive. "What?"

"The Seer sent me to fetch you; she and the Scholar are waiting for you in Tumbled Sheep."

"The . . . They are? But how would they know I was here?"

The guide snorted. "There's a reason they call her the Seer, you know."

Breaker had known, of course, that the Seer had magical abilities, and always knew where the other Chosen were, but somehow it had never occurred to him that she would be using that knowledge to find *him.*

But he supposed it made sense.

"Why do they want me there?"

The guide smiled crookedly. "Swordsman, she didn't tell me that, but she *did* say you might not remember right away that you were *looking* for the Scholar, and if so, I should remind you. Well, consider this your reminder—here's your chance to talk to him."

That was true—but if they wanted to talk to him, why hadn't they come to Dog Pole?

"But why Tumbled Sheep?"

"Because that's where they *are.* They didn't tell me anything; they just sent me to get you and bring you there."

"Oh." He supposed it was perfectly reasonable for the Seer and the Scholar to want to meet the new Swordsman—after all, as the guide had pointed out, *he* had wanted to meet *them.* Simple curiosity was more than adequate to explain their interest.

And thinking about other possible explanations, he very much hoped mere curiosity *was* the only motivation. He stared at the guide for a moment longer, then rose. "Let me get my bag."

Ten minutes later the two of them marched past a boundary shrine, out of Dog Pole, and into the southern hills.

The rolling country was not as strange as the flat plain of the Midlands, but in a way it was even more disorienting to someone from the northern valleys; none of the hills seemed to line up into ridges, but instead they thrust up here and there, apparently at random—and every hill had its own *ler,* of course, some of them visible as lights or mist or shadows, like the *ler* of Mad Oak. The guide led Breaker along a winding, circuitous route that dodged most of these, but he stopped in a few spots to placate the local spirits; in one case this required a libation from a wineskin he carried, at another he recited an elaborately worded prayer, and so on.

In short, save for the odd landscape, the journey was much like others Breaker had made in his travels, and like those others it went smoothly, and late in the afternoon, as the sun neared the western horizon, he and the guide made an uneventful arrival in the town of Tumbled Sheep, which nestled beside a river at the foot of an unusually steep hillside. Breaker supposed that the hillside was connected with the silly name somehow.

The guide paused at the boundary shrine only long enough to kneel briefly, then led Breaker to the largest building in town, a wooden structure with wide but sagging porches on every side. Breaker was unsure whether it was a public house, a community center like the pavilions in the northern valleys, or a temple to the local *ler,* but whatever it was, several people were sitting on the porches. They had been chatting quietly when Breaker had first glimpsed them from well beyond the boundary shrine, but someone had spotted the approaching travelers, and now every eye was focused on them, every tongue still.

A month or two before that would have made him unbearably nervous, but his travels had accustomed him to this sort of reception—it was not at all unusual. He ignored the stares as he followed the guide around to the north porch and up the two low steps.

A woman rose at his approach, a woman roughly his mother's age, but shorter and plumper, her hair gone prematurely silver-gray. She wore a white cotton tunic embroidered in red and gold, and a long green wool skirt, both worn soft with long use; her hair hung to her waist. The top of her head barely reached Breaker's chin, but she looked boldly into his eyes, clearly not intimidated by his size. Her own eyes were green and intense, her nose long and prominent; she was not smiling. She did not look as if she smiled often.

She held out a hand. "Hello, Swordsman," she said. "I'm the Seer."

Behind her a man got to his feet, a thin man of medium height with a graying beard and a cheerful grin, clad in a long vest of brown leather.

Breaker accepted the woman's hand and bowed to her. "I am honored," he said.

"Oh, nonsense. You're one of the Chosen, I'm one of the Chosen—we're equals, and there's no honor involved in meeting me."

Before Breaker could reply, the thin man held out his hand and said, "Call me Lore."

Breaker released the Seer's hand and turned to look at this other person.

He was midway between Breaker and the Seer in height, his dull brown hair pulled back in a tight braid, his face tanned but not heavily so; Breaker could not guess his age, though he was sure that it fell, like his height, somewhere between the Seer's and his own. His eyes were a soft brown, and reminded Breaker of the puppy one of the bargemen had brought along two summers back; unlike the Seer he was smiling, though his grin seemed a bit tentative.

He wore a long, many-pocketed vest over a tan blouse and brown denim pants—practical garb, appropriate for most circumstances. And his grip was surprisingly firm.

"You're the Scholar?" Breaker asked. The man's healthy color, cheerful expression, and sensible clothing hardly fit the stereotype of a man devoted to learning.

"I am. I understand you're from Mad Oak in Longvale?"

Startled, Breaker nodded.

"Is the Mad Oak still standing?"

"Yes, it is; it almost got me when I left."

"As bad as ever, then? A shame. And is Flute still in mourning?"

That was more than startling, that was astonishing. Breaker glanced at the Seer, then said, "No, he's done grieving. When I left he was courting Brewer's sister Sugar Cake."

"Lore, that can wait," the Seer interjected before the Scholar could ask any more questions. "We have more urgent concerns."

Up until then, everything they had said and done had been consistent with simple curiosity, a desire to meet their new compatriot—but "urgent concerns"? That did not sound so benign, and the Old Swordsman's words came back to him.

Breaker glanced around, and realized that at least a score of the residents of Tumbled Sheep were staring at the three Chosen. The guide who had brought him from Dog Pole was standing a few feet away, making a point of *not* staring.

That was hardly surprising; after all, seeing even one of the Chosen must be fairly unusual, and to have three of the eight gathered here, and to have one of those three speaking of "urgent concerns" . . .

Breaker swallowed. These people knew what the Chosen had been chosen for; they would undoubtedly be guessing what could gather three in one place, and probably guessing one thing.

Breaker hoped that obvious guess was wrong, but he remembered the Old Swordsman's suspicions. The old man might have been right—and if so, then Breaker would need to do something about it. He might have to become the killer his mother had feared he would be.

The old man had tricked him—but it didn't matter. He was here now, and he had accepted his role, regardless of whether he had been deceived about its nature.

"Should we be speaking out here in the open?" he asked.

"No," the Seer replied immediately. "Just a moment." She turned to the guide, pulled something from a pouch on her belt, and thrust it into the guide's hand. He opened his hand and counted the coins.

The Seer did not wait for the guide to total up his pay; she took both Breaker and Lore by the hand, one on either side, and led them across the porch and into the building.

It appeared to be a public house, or perhaps an inn; there were several tables, dozens of chairs, and a row of barrels along one wall in the main room, but the Seer led them quickly past that and down a corridor. She found the door she wanted and opened it, ushering the two men into a small room where a narrow bed stood against either wall, a nightstand at the head of each bed, a pitcher and basin on each nightstand. There were no other furnishings, but a large rucksack stood at the foot of one bed, and shutters were closed over the window, leaving the room only dimly lit.

"Sit down if you want," the Seer said, gesturing at the nearer bed. "You must be tired after the long walk."

Breaker didn't argue—he *was* tired, and hungry, as well. He sat and reached for the pitcher.

It held a modest amount of water; he poured it into the basin, then rinsed his hands and splashed a little on his face while the Scholar settled on the other bed and the Seer placed herself between them.

"Now," she said, "let's speak frankly."

"About what?" Breaker asked, wiping his face.

"About the Wizard Lord, of course. You're traveling around Barokan looking for information about him, aren't you? You're on your way to visit him, to see whether he might need to be removed?"

Breaker shook his hands dry, then turned to face her. "How is it," he asked, "that you two know so much about me and my home and my intentions, when I know nothing about *you*?"

The Seer and the Scholar exchanged glances.

"I'm the *Seer,*" the Seer said. "I *always* know who and where all the eight Chosen are, and where the Wizard Lord is, and whether he's watching us. Which, I am pleased to say, he is not, just now. He's eating his supper, and not worrying about us."

"I wish *I* were eating supper," Breaker muttered to himself.

"They'll be serving here in half an hour," the Seer replied. "We'll eat then."

That was heartening news. "I still don't understand how you know these things," Breaker said.

The Seer gave him a look, one he had gotten from his mother on occasion, a look that clearly meant he was being stupid.

"I'm the *Seer,*" the Seer repeated. "It's my magic—I know where all Chosen are just as you know how to use a sword."

"I had to *learn* to use a sword," Breaker protested. "How do you learn knowing things you can't see?"

The Seer scowled at him. "All right, fine—it's not the same, but it *is* my magic, as one of the Chosen. I always know where the nine of us are, and more or less what condition we're in, though I usually have only a vague idea what we're all doing. And sometimes I see other things, as well. So I know who you are, and where you've been. Is that clear enough?"

"I suppose it is," Breaker conceded. Then he turned to the Scholar. "But how do *you* know about the Mad Oak, or about Flute?"

"That's *my* magic," the Scholar explained. "I learn things—and I don't forget them. I never forget a true story, *any* true story. It's not just the old tales and legends I remember, it's *all* the stories I've ever heard, and it doesn't matter whether it's how the first three Chosen slew the first Dark Lord, or how a girl from Mad Oak almost ran away with a guide from Willowbank, but changed her mind at the last minute when she realized he was so scared she could smell it."

Breaker blinked. "Oh." He frowned as he thought this over. "Only true stories? Do they have to be entirely true? I mean, what if someone gets a few things wrong?"

"I remember the true *parts* of every story I hear, but I can forget the lies and exaggerations and embroidering. For some stories that doesn't leave much—with made-up stories sometimes I only remember what the tale told me about the author, and not a word of the story itself." He smiled. "It's not a very useful sort of magic as a general thing, but I enjoy it."

"But you said the first three Chosen slew the first Dark Lord—my mother said there were eight Chosen, just as there always are, and the Dark Lord killed six of them."

The Scholar shrugged. "Your mother was wrong. There were only three then—the Swordsman, the Seer, and the Leader. The Dark Lord killed the Leader, and the other two survived. The Council of Immortals chose a new Leader, and added the Beauty after that. Your mother probably only heard that two survived, and assumed that meant six had died."

"How do you know it was my mother who was wrong, and not *your* version of the story?"

"Because I'm the Scholar. It's my magic."

"But . . ."

"How do you know what your opponent is going to do before he does it?" the Seer interjected.

"Oh, because you can see his muscles tense, and his eyes adjust, and his weight shift," Breaker said.

"And how do you know how to see and interpret those signs, and do it so quickly that you can counter every move? Have you had years of training to learn this?"

Breaker was at a loss for a moment, then yielded. "All right, it's magic," he said. "But I still think my magic makes more sense than yours."

"It's more like ordinary human skills, certainly," the Scholar agreed. "My magic was created hundreds of years later than yours, when the wizards of the Council had learned greater subtlety and finesse."

Breaker resented the implications in that, but before he could think of a reply the Seer said, "Fine, that's all settled, then—you appreciate each other's magic. Now, could we get down to business?"

"I assume," Breaker said, "from your summoning me here, and saying we had urgent matters to discuss, that the Wizard Lord has done something unfortunate. I haven't heard anything about it; everyone I've spoken to seems satisfied with him. Still, he must have done *something*. What is it? When did it happen?"

The Seer and the Scholar exchanged glances.

"It's not that simple," the Scholar said.

"It started years ago," the Seer said. "About five years ago, in the third or fourth year of the Wizard Lord's reign. I saw him kill several people—not with my own eyes, but with my magic. I couldn't see any details, but I *knew* he had killed people—I didn't know exactly how many, or who they were, but he had killed. I could feel it. So I went to the Leader and told him—that's my job, after all. And I spoke to two wizards from the Council of Immortals, as well. And they all asked me to please not say anything about it yet—there was no point in starting a panic if the Wizard Lord was behaving himself, and no reason to warn him that he was discovered if in fact the Chosen would have to remove him. So I didn't say anything more, and then Boss came back and told me that it was all right, that the Wizard Lord had merely been doing his job, wiping out a group of rogue wizards who were organizing to overthrow him and destroy the Council. These wizards supposedly intended to set themselves up as overlords of Varagan . . ."

"Of what?" Breaker interrupted.

"Varagan—oh, Barokan. In my native tongue we call it Varagan. At any rate, the Wizard Lord said that he had killed a group of rogue wizards, and of course that's *his* job, and Boss and the Council had investigated and it was all in order. So that was fine, and I didn't worry about it anymore. The Wizard Lord had done his job, just like in the old songs. The next time I saw Lore, here, I told him about it—I thought he should know, as one more item for his collection of facts and stories. And then we went our separate ways, and I forgot about it for years."

Breaker glanced at the Scholar, who shifted on the bed and grimaced.

"And then last year old Blade went looking for a replacement—the Old Swordsman, I mean. I knew he was doing it, and I knew he found you and trained you, and I didn't think much of it; he wasn't a young man, in fact he was the oldest of us all by a few years, and if he wanted to pass on the talisman and retire, that was his business. I wanted to say farewell, though, and wish him well, so I met him on his way home to Dazet Saltmarsh this past spring, after he had lost the duel and you had become the new Swordsman. We chatted a bit, and then went our separate ways—but he mentioned that he had some doubts about the Wizard Lord. He knew he could speak freely to me, since I always know when the Wizard Lord is listening, so he told me that it wasn't anything specific, and that he'd told you about his worries, as well."

"Yes, he did," Breaker agreed.

"I thought he was worrying about nothing—after all, the Wizard Lord has been in power for eight or nine years now, and nothing dreadful had happened, so far as I knew. So I wished him well, and he went west, and I came south. And then just recently, I saw you were coming this way, and realized you were following Lore, so I found him and told him you wanted to meet him."

"That was just a few days ago," the Scholar added.

"And I thought it would be nice to meet you, too, so we settled in together to wait for you, and we talked, as people will . . ."

"I wanted more stories," the Scholar interrupted. "I always do."

The Seer's expression suddenly changed. "And you know, I think that's a lovely sword the Old Swordsman gave you, but wouldn't it be nice to have a new one, made to fit your own hand? Isn't it awkward, fighting with someone else's sword?"

"What?" Breaker said.

"The *Old* Swordsman had a sword made for him, you know—he went to the best swordsmiths, right under the cliffs in Winterhome, and had them make it just the way he wanted."

"Yes, he did," the Scholar agreed, nodding vigorously. "He told me the whole story."

Breaker was not sure what was going on, but he was bright enough to play along. "Wouldn't that be expensive, though? I'm just a barley farmer, after all—I don't have much to trade."

"Oh, but you're one of the Chosen," the Seer said. "I'm sure the armorers would be honored . . ."

She stopped in midsentence and let her breath out in a rush. Then she turned and deliberately stamped on a spider that stood on the floor by the corner of Breaker's bed.

"I hate it when he does that," she said. "Wouldn't you think someone who's ruling all Varagan would have better things to do with his time than spy on us?"

"The Wizard Lord was watching us?"

"And listening," the Seer confirmed. "Through that spider."

Breaker stared at the gooey smudge on the floor.

"As I was saying," the Seer continued, "the two of us were waiting here for you—we both wanted to meet the new Swordsman. And we talked, and we discussed the Old Swordsman's worries, and I mentioned that incident with the rogue wizards five years ago, when the Wizard Lord had killed people for the first and last time."

"And I didn't remember a word of it," the Scholar finished.

[14]

Breaker stared at the Scholar. "But I thought you said you remember *everything.*"

"Only if it's true."

Breaker looked at the Seer's face.

"It was lies," she said grimly. "The whole story about the rogue wizards must have been lies, from beginning to end."

"But you're a *seer*—couldn't you *tell*?"

She shook her head. "No. I'm a seer, yes, but not that sort of seer. Sometimes I can't tell truth from falsehood any better than any other woman my age—and I heard the story from Boss, from the Leader, and he can be very convincing. You'll see when you meet him. He and the Wizard Lord both draw on the *ler* of persuasion for some of their magic; after all, they're both expected to command people. As one of the Chosen the magic doesn't work as well on me as it does on most people, but there's still a little bit of an effect, or maybe Boss has just had so much practice being believed—whatever the reason, it's *hard* to see when he's lying, even when it would be obvious nonsense from an ordinary person."

"But . . . I don't understand. If there were no rogue wizards, then why did he say there were?"

"There were people who died, Swordsman; there's no doubt of that. I felt it, *knew* it—the Wizard Lord killed them himself, summoning *ler* of fire and plague and storm. And they weren't rogue wizards."

"But then—who *were* they? Why did he kill them? Why did he lie about it? Or why did the *Leader* lie about it?"

"It may have been a misunderstanding," the Scholar suggested. "You would be amazed how often stories are distorted, quite unintentionally, in the retelling. Especially stories about the Wizard Lord—there are several I remember very differently from how they're usually told."

"He's been trying to convince me that that's what it is," the Seer said. "That the Wizard Lord told Boss that these were people who had to die, and Boss assumed that meant they were rogue wizards, and they weren't. He might even be right—but who else would the Wizard Lord be called upon to slaughter? Common criminals are usually dealt with by local priests, you know that, unless they flee past the boundaries, and most aren't stupid enough to do that—they know the old stories, they know the Wizard Lord probably won't bother with any trials or mitigating circumstances, he'll just kill them, while the town priests and magistrates generally won't do anything more than a flogging unless their crimes are unspeakably vile. Oh, one or two fugitives, that could happen, certainly, but this was more than two killed, all at once. And you know Blade said he never trusted this Wizard Lord. I fear Blade was right, that innocents were slain five years ago and we did nothing."

"We didn't know. We still don't, not for certain."

"But it's our *duty* to know! It's what we were chosen to do!"

Breaker shifted uncomfortably, but before he could speak the Scholar said, "It is perhaps what *you* were chosen to do, but *my* role is to learn everything I can of the world, past and present, so as to advise you and the others how best to deal with the Wizard Lord."

"Well, isn't the murder of innocents a part of the world's history, and a fit subject for your study?" the Seer demanded.

Before the Scholar could reply, Breaker asked, "If this happened, if the Wizard Lord killed innocent people, why didn't we hear about it? Why wasn't the news in every public house in the Midlands and every pavilion in the valleys? The guides carry gossip everywhere—why hadn't the Scholar heard the *true* story somewhere?"

"That's a very good question," the Seer said.

"Indeed," the Scholar agreed. "We have been discussing this while we awaited your arrival, and the only conclusion that seems to make sense is that there were no witnesses to the killings, no survivors to spread the word."

"Except the Wizard Lord himself," the Seer added. "I know he was there."

"But wouldn't these people be missed? Wouldn't their families and townsfolk notice their absence? One person might disappear without anyone thinking it especially strange, but you said there were . . . You didn't say. How many were there, three or four?"

"More," the Seer said. "I don't know how many."

Breaker felt as if he had been punched in the gut. "*More* than four? The Wizard Lord murdered more than four people?"

"Killed them, yes," the Scholar said. "Seer seems sure of that. We don't know yet whether it was murder or execution, though." Before anyone else could respond, he added, "Or self-defense."

"It wasn't an accident," the Seer said. "You don't summon a plague by mistake."

"I concede that much."

"We have to *do* something," Breaker said, overwhelmed by the thought of half a dozen people dead at once.

"What we must do," the Scholar said, "is determine the facts of the matter."

"Talk to the Wizard Lord, you mean?"

"No. If he lied to Boss, he would lie to us," the Seer said.

"But the Scholar would know, when he didn't remember the lies."

"That could take months," the Scholar said. "And if the Wizard Lord has indeed given in to darkness, he could dispose of us all during those months."

"But how? We're the Chosen!"

"He might find a way, all the same."

The Seer interrupted. "We aren't going to talk to the Wizard Lord. We are going to go and see for ourselves what happened to those people."

"But . . . I don't understand."

"I know where they died—my magic, the *ler* of location, will guide us there. It's in the Galbek Hills—and yes, the Wizard Lord lives in the Galbek Hills, but the deaths were at the other end, about thirty miles east of his tower. We'll go there. Then we can talk to the people nearby, and see what's left, and perhaps my other magic will let us know more. I'm not omniscient, but I do sometimes see with more than just my eyes, even when neither the Chosen nor the Wizard Lord are involved."

"And the Wizard Lord *was* involved, in this case," the Scholar pointed out.

"When you say 'we,' " Breaker said, "are you including me?"

"Yes, of course!" the Seer said, startled. "It might be dangerous, and neither of us is a fighter. We may need you to protect us. After all, you *are* one of the Chosen."

"One of them. Will you be gathering the other five, then, before we set out?"

The Scholar snorted.

"No," the Seer said. "That would take too long, and I'm not sure all of them would cooperate. And wouldn't that be as good as shouting to the Wizard Lord, 'We think you've gone mad!'?"

"What about the Leader, then? Isn't it his decision? Shouldn't he be involved?"

The Seer and the Scholar exchanged glances. "Ordinarily, you might have a case," the Scholar said.

"But it was Boss who told me not to worry about these killings," the Seer said. "He'll be reluctant to admit he could have been fooled—and if he wasn't fooled, if there's really an innocent explanation, I'd rather not look like *I'm* a fool."

"Besides, he's nowhere near here," the Scholar said.

"That's true—he's traveling well north of here, in the eastern Midlands," the Seer said. "It might take months to catch up to him and bring him."

"And I would prefer not to gather too big a crowd," the Scholar said. "Even three of us traveling together might be viewed with some suspicion. Seer assures me that the Wizard Lord *does* keep track of us all—that incident with the spider shows as much."

The explanations all had a superficial logic, but Breaker was not entirely satisfied. He had already had one of the Chosen mislead him, and for all he knew these two were even less trustworthy than the Old Swordsman. He had lived with the old man for months and still been deceived, while he had only just met these two—why should he trust them? He had a sudden momentary suspicion that the incident with the spider might have been staged; after all, he had no proof other than the

Seer's word that the Wizard Lord had been watching them, through the spider or otherwise. The Seer and the Scholar might be fooling him as part of some elaborate scheme—or perhaps the Seer had fooled the Scholar, as well; maybe there had been no mysterious deaths, maybe she had never told the Scholar the story about rogue wizards being executed.

Maybe these two weren't really the Seer and the Scholar at all!

But that was absurd. Who would pretend to be the Chosen and make up such a tale? Why would anyone lie about such a thing? No, he had to trust these two—they were playing out their roles as he was playing his.

But they were not necessarily following the wisest possible course.

"Maybe we should split up, then," he said. "We don't want to arouse any suspicions. The Seer could go to investigate the killings by herself."

"I want to know what happened," the Scholar said.

"And I want witnesses along, to confirm my findings," the Seer said. "Boss might not take my word for it if I find something bad, but he can't ignore all of us. And the Scholar's knowledge may be useful."

"But do you really need me? You said you wanted protection, but wouldn't three of us traveling together attract so much attention it would be *more* dangerous than if I just went home?"

The Seer stared at Breaker for a long moment, then said, "I want you to see what there is to see, Swordsman. After all, if our ruler *has* become a Dark Lord, it will be *your* duty to kill him."

For a moment Breaker stared at her, unable to reply.

"It might be the Archer who kills him," he said at last. "Or any of us, really."

"In three of the five cases where a Dark Lord has been removed by the Chosen, the Swordsman was the one who actually killed the Wizard Lord," the Scholar said.

"Well, there, twice it was someone else!" Breaker said with a gesture.

"Once the Beauty put a knife in his ribs," the Scholar said. "That's unlikely to work again. And the other time the Leader carried the Wizard Lord over a parapet, and both fell to their deaths on the rocks below—the Leader's struggles, combined with previous injuries and the Thief's removal of various talismans, prevented the Wizard Lord in question from flying away safely."

"I heard that story," Breaker said. "My grandmother told me about that. That was the Dark Lord of the Tsamas, two hundred years ago."

"Two hundred and twenty-eight."

Breaker ignored the correction. "*He* wasn't killed by the Swordsman."

"Nor was the Dark Lord of Kamith t'Daru. But the Dark Lords of the Midlands, of Tallowcrane, and of Goln Vleys were slain by Swordsmen."

"Swordsman," the Seer said, "you surely knew when you agreed to take your role that it would be your responsibility to kill the Wizard Lord if he went mad or gave in to evil."

"Yes," Breaker admitted, "but I never thought it would really happen—and certainly not so *soon*!"

"It may not have happened—but it's our duty to find out. *Our* duty, all three of us."

"But won't the Wizard Lord notice the three of us traveling together?" He pointed at the Scholar. "*He* thought it would look suspicious!"

"Swordsman," the Seer said gently, "the Wizard Lord is going to know what's happening in any case. He's the *Wizard Lord.* He has magic that keeps him informed of everything of significance in all of Barokan. He has magic that allows him to locate every rogue wizard. He can see and hear through any pair of eyes he wants—well, any living eyes that aren't human. If he doesn't already know our true names, he can learn them in an instant, and surely you know that means he can always find us. We can't hide from him, and we can't keep what we do a secret. He'll know. The Chosen have *never* had the element of surprise in their favor; the Wizard Lord *always* knows when he's been marked for removal."

"The Chosen can use surprise in certain ways," the Scholar objected. "There are ways to limit the effectiveness of the Wizard Lord's divinations."

"But still, every Dark Lord knows the Chosen are coming well before they reach him, even if he doesn't know when or where or how."

"Well, that's true," the Scholar admitted. "It's inherent in the system, more or less."

"But then won't he try to stop us?" Breaker asked.

"Of *course* he will," the Seer said. "And we'll go on with the job all the same. That's what makes the Chosen heroes, Swordsman—we'll do what needs to be done, despite the danger."

"You must have known it might be dangerous," the Scholar remarked.

"Yes," Breaker said. "Yes, of course—but somehow it seems much more . . . more *real* now, more frightening. There's no way I can turn back, is there?"

"Not really, no," the Scholar told him. "If you were ill or injured or old, you might contrive to pass the title of Swordsman on, but as you're young and healthy I don't think the *ler* would accept that."

"You'll come with us into the Galbek Hills," the Seer said. "It's your duty. And with any luck at all this will all turn out to be nothing, some legitimate action the Wizard Lord took as protector of Varagan."

"I suppose," Breaker unhappily agreed.

He was not entirely convinced; he was unsure of everything now, unsure of whether these people were really the Seer and the Scholar, unsure what the Wizard Lord might be up to, unsure whether the Old Swordsman and the wizards might have tricked him somehow. Was he really the world's greatest swordsman, one of the Chosen, at all?

He didn't *know*. Since leaving Mad Oak he had often felt as if he didn't really know *anything* anymore, as if the entire world around him were shifting façades built upon mist and mud, liable to change or collapse or vanish at any moment. He had been *told* how everything was, told about the towns and roads, told about local customs and priesthoods and *ler,* told about the Chosen and the Wizard Lord, but how could he be sure that any of it was true? Back home he had seen the barley grow every year, seen the crops respond to the priests, seen the summers come and the winters go, and he had known how everything worked, but out here in the wider world he could only rely on what he saw and heard, and had no experience to guide him in telling truth from falsehood.

"We'll leave in the morning," the Seer said. "We'll go see what there is to see and settle this matter, one way or the other."

Breaker didn't answer.

"And Swordsman," she added, "I'm not any happier about this than you are. Do you think *I* want to confront the Wizard Lord? I'm an old woman, I should be safely at home in Sedgedown watching my grandchildren grow up, but instead I'm wandering around the southern hills and risking the wrath of the most powerful magician in the world. He's as likely to kill me as he is to kill you."

"I know," Breaker said quietly.

He wasn't sure what was going on, wasn't sure whether everything he had been told was the truth, but he really couldn't see any way out. If he went home to Mad Oak, or anywhere else other than accompanying these two, he would be failing in his duty, failing to live up to the role he had agreed to.

He couldn't do that, no matter how many doubts he had. He had agreed to this. His mother had warned him against it, he had had months to change his mind, and he had committed himself; he couldn't turn around and run home now.

"We'll leave in the morning," he agreed.

"I'll find the guide," the Seer said.

And in the morning, although the Swordsman was no more certain of anything than he had ever been, the four of them—the three Chosen and their guide—set out southward.

Breaker cast an occasional longing glance over his shoulder, toward his distant home in the north, but he trudged resolutely south.

[15]

Their progress was uneven; the Seer knew where their destination lay, but not how to get there, and the guides they hired along the way only knew routes between towns. The Seer would indicate a direction and distance, and the guide would do his best to deliver them to the town farthest along that line, but sometimes that town would prove a dead end, forcing them to double back or veer miles off their intended path.

As summer neared its end the weather began to turn cooler—but not as fast as Breaker felt it should have. When he remarked on this the Seer and the Scholar stared at him blankly for a moment; then the Seer said gently, "Swordsman, we're more than a hundred miles south of your homeland, perhaps more than two hundred. Winters are milder and arrive later here."

"Oh," Breaker said. He did vaguely recall hearing that the sun's path across the sky passed more closely over the southern lands, and that the

South was therefore warmer, but he had never expected to experience this firsthand; he had somehow assumed that those warmer lands lay thousands upon thousands of miles away, perhaps not in Barokan at all.

The journey itself was fairly uneventful; the guides knew their work, and in any case these hills seemed to harbor less danger, fewer hostile *ler,* than the northern lands—or perhaps the presence of three of the Chosen traveling together cowed the troublesome spirits with their partial immunity to magic.

The towns in which they stopped varied immensely in detail, but in time they all began to seem basically alike to Breaker. There would be a small priesthood that dealt with the local *ler,* a few tradespeople and shops clustered around the center, and dozens, or even a few hundred, of farm families working the land the priests had declared safe. The larger towns often had an inn, but the smaller ones made do with families willing to rent out extra beds.

And everywhere the three of them were quickly recognized as Chosen, regardless of whether any of them had ever before set foot within the borders. Breaker wondered just what made it so obvious—were travelers so very scarce that *any* group of strangers with no clear purpose was assumed to be the Chosen?

But then he recalled that he wore a sword on his belt and made no attempt to conceal it, and that the Scholar (whom Breaker was learning to call Lore) and Seer did not look as if they had any legitimate business that would send them traveling about. He wondered what would happen if they actually denied their identity, or hid the sword and pretended to be traders of some sort.

But there was no reason to do so; the one person they might have wished could not locate them, the Wizard Lord himself, would always be able to find them magically, no matter what they did to hide or disguise themselves. Trying to conceal their true nature would most likely simply arouse suspicion.

Furthermore, performing sword tricks was the most convenient way to raise a little extra money along the way, to pay for bed and board and guides, and he could hardly hope that his audience would not realize he was the Swordsman when he demonstrated his superhuman skill with a blade.

Of course, this meant that he found himself answering the same questions over and over, responding to the same requests. Had he ever killed a man with his sword? Had he met the Wizard Lord in person? Could he outfight two men at once? Three? Four? Where did he get the sword he carried—had he made it himself? And he would be asked for lessons in swordsmanship—both skill with a steel blade, and skill with what nature had provided.

Not all the questions came up every time, and some required some thought. Even some of the common ones could take a new slant, on occasion.

In a village called Cat's Whisker, in the town's one public house, a boy not much younger than Breaker himself asked, "How did you come to be chosen to be the Swordsman? Were you born with some mark on your skin, or under a particular sign in the heavens?"

"No," Breaker replied, as he had a hundred times before. "When the Old Swordsman asked who wanted the job, I said yes; that's all."

"But that can't be," the lad protested.

"Why not?" Breaker asked, amused.

"Well, because how would the *ler* know you were worthy, without some sign marking you? What if a cripple had spoken up, or an old man, or a woman in disguise?"

"The Old Swordsman did not ask any cripples or old men or women," Breaker said. "He asked the young men of the village as we drank to celebrate the harvest. He could see we were fit and strong by the barley we had brought in. He saw me drink and dance that night, and he taught me the basics of wielding a blade in the days that followed, and if he had found me wanting he would have said so and moved on to the next town. There were no signs or portents; he offered me the role, and I accepted."

"But that isn't *right,*" the youth insisted.

Up to that point the conversation had been similar to a dozen others, but the boy's persistence was new. "In what way isn't it right?" Breaker asked.

"The Swordsman is one of the Chosen," the youth said. "But you said you weren't chosen! You volunteered!"

"I chose myself, perhaps."

"You say he asked the young men of your village—what if one of the others had said yes, instead of you?"

"Then he would be the Swordsman now, talking to you here, and I would be at home—or dancing with Little Weaver in the pavilion, perhaps."

"But . . . but . . ."

"He would have been chosen, and I would not. And if none of us had spoken up—and that might well have happened, had I not been in the mood I was in—then the Old Swordsman would have gone on to the next town, and the next, until someone agreed."

"What if *two* of you had volunteered at once? Or three?"

"Then I suppose the Old Swordsman would have chosen between us, and picked the one he thought more promising. I don't think I take your point, lad."

"You're supposed to be the *Chosen,* the people fated to protect us from any Dark Lord! You're supposed to have a *destiny.*"

Breaker blinked silently at him before answering.

"We *are* the Chosen," he said, gesturing to take in himself and his two companions. "We were chosen by our predecessors, and chose to accept the roles they offered. The Chosen were created by wizards, boy, not by some mysterious destiny."

"But then how do you know you were chosen rightly? What if you're the wrong people for your roles?"

"Then you had better hope no Dark Lords arise," the Seer said before Breaker could respond.

"I took the job," Breaker said, "and I'll do it the best I can. I do have the wizards' magic to help me, and the *ler* they bound to me, and that's all the destiny any Swordsman has ever had."

"But you're the *Swordsman.* You're one of the *Chosen.* You're supposed to be someone special, something more than an ordinary man!"

"I am," Breaker said. "I am the world's greatest swordsman; the wizards of the Council of Immortals have bestowed that upon me with their magic."

"But you should have been special *before*!"

Breaker started to ask why, then stopped, thinking back to that evening in the pavilion when Elder Priestess had brought in the wizards and the Old Swordsman.

"I was," he said. "I was willing."

"That's not special!"

"No one else in my town was," Breaker said. "And I don't think it was the first town he'd asked in."

"But it's not enough!"

"But it is."

"Just because you were *willing*? Because you said *yes*? That can't be all . . ."

"Would *you* have said yes?" Breaker interrupted.

The youth stopped in midsentence and stared at him.

"If I were to have second thoughts—and believe me, I have—and decided that I did not care to be the world's greatest swordsman anymore, that someone else should take the honor from me, and if I came and asked you whether you would do it—would you? And do not answer hastily, because I may well be serious in this. Would you accept the role, knowing that it would mean you would be forever set apart from ordinary folk, and that you might be called upon at any time to fight your way into the Wizard Lord's stronghold and drive your blade through his living flesh and kill him?" Breaker had given that far too much thought of late, the image of the steel of his sword stabbing into a human body; he remembered what it had felt like to jab the Old Swordsman's shoulder, and he had exaggerated that memory and imagined what it would be like to kill the Wizard Lord.

It was not a pleasant thought.

"I . . ." The youth looked at him uncertainly.

"Would you?"

By this time the entire room had fallen silent, and all eyes were upon the two of them. For a moment no one spoke.

Then the youth's gaze fell.

"No," he admitted.

"Then do not chide me for being born without a caul, on a day of no astronomical distinction, to an ordinary mother and father."

"But you didn't do anything to earn it," the boy said.

"Oh, yes, I did. I practiced for months."

"But you didn't go on a quest or have any adventures . . ."

"I worked long and hard. That's more useful."

The boy shook his head, but said nothing more; while he was plainly not yet convinced, he had run out of arguments that he could put into words.

Breaker turned away as someone else asked, “Do you need to use a particular sword, or could you fight with another one?”

Breaker answered that, and a dozen other questions, but while he did a thought nagged at the back of his mind. The boy seemed dissatisfied because Breaker had not proven himself worthy by mystical means—but in fact, he *had* done exactly that by defeating the Old Swordsman in their staged duel. Why had he not mentioned that to the lad?

Because, he decided, it hadn’t seemed important. What was important was that he had spoken up, saying he would take on the role, and that he had worked hard to learn it. The actual ritual conflict that convinced the *ler* to transfer their magical aid had been a mere formality.

He thought perhaps he should explain this to the boy, but when he looked around during a lull in the questioning the youth had gone.

And the following morning the three of them, Seer, Scholar, and Swordsman, accompanied by a local guide, continued on their southward journey.

It was three towns, two guides, and four days later that they found themselves in a village so small it had no agreed-upon name, where the Seer’s inquiries about finding a guide to lead them just a little farther into the Galbek Hills encountered worried silence.

“That way,” she said, pointing. “Perhaps half a day’s walk.”

“Oh, we know where you mean,” the village’s one priest replied. “You mean Stoneslope. That’s the only town there. But you can’t get there anymore.”

“Why not?” the Seer asked.

“Because there aren’t any guides,” the priest explained. “The last one died five years ago.”

“Five years?” Breaker looked at the Seer. “How did he die?”

“She. She died in childbirth. Had the child lived . . . but it did not. Her family’s secrets are lost, and there are no more guides.”

“Then how do the people of Stoneslope trade with the rest of Barokan?” the Scholar asked.

“They don’t.”

“Is there another route around the other side, perhaps?” Breaker suggested.

"No. They no longer have any contact with the outside world. To the best of our knowledge no one has entered or left Stoneslope for five years now."

The three Chosen looked at one another.

"What do we do now?" Breaker asked.

"We go there without a guide," the Seer replied.

"But the *ler*! We don't know the path, don't know the dangers!"

"We'll just have to find our way. And our magic will protect us."

"Not from *everything*."

"From most ordinary dangers. And we know the path can be found," the Seer said, "because it *was,* once."

"After all," the Scholar said, "someone had to find the safe paths in the first place; no one is *born* knowing the route to another town."

"I suppose, but I'm no explorer . . ."

"We were chosen to be heroes," the Seer said, and the rebuke in her tone was unmistakable. "A hero does what he must."

Breaker sighed. "As you say," he agreed.

"Does this have something to do with the Wizard Lord?" the priest asked, looking from Breaker to the Seer.

"Not *everything* the Chosen do need be in connection with the Wizard Lord," the Seer said—which Breaker knew was true, but irrelevant.

"Well, yes, but Stoneslope—the Chosen wanting to go to Stoneslope . . ."

"And what does Stoneslope have to do with the Wizard Lord?" the Scholar asked.

The priest looked startled. "Why, I assumed you knew. He was born and raised there. Back then he was sometimes called Feather, because he was so thin and frail—his father had said he was as light as a feather, you see. He was called other names as well, less pleasant ones—he wasn't a popular child. He left home to learn wizardry when he was just a boy, younger than the Swordsman is now, and we never saw him again, but we would hear about him sometimes; when news came that he had been chosen as the Wizard Lord we were all quite excited, and wondered whether he might build a stronghold here." He sighed. "But he built it all the way over near Split Reed, at the other end of the Galbek Hills. He never even visited us here. I know there were some in

Stoneslope who wanted to apologize to him for not treating him better, but they never had the chance."

Breaker stood silent for a moment, absorbing this information.

Somehow he had always had trouble with the thought of the Wizard Lord growing up somewhere. Obviously wizards started out as human as anyone, they weren't born with talismans in hand and spells in their heads, but he never pictured them as children, growing up like anyone else. The Wizard Lord had had parents and neighbors, perhaps siblings, uncles, aunts, cousins, friends, and apparently enemies . . .

He found it difficult to picture.

And the Wizard Lord had killed people in or near Stoneslope, his old hometown—why? Who were they, and what had they done to deserve his wrath? Were they some of those people who had never had a chance to apologize? And was the guide's death merely a coincidence, or had the Wizard Lord arranged that, as well, so that the rest of Barokan would not hear what he had done?

No—surely, no Wizard Lord could be so petty as to kill a woman in childbirth just to keep a secret. Still, Breaker felt a certain foreboding; he hoped it was merely because he was among unfamiliar *ler*.

"Well, now we know why no word got out," the Seer said.

"We don't *know*," the Scholar said. "We merely *assume*."

"But his own townsfolk? Perhaps his own kin? Could it really be?" Breaker asked.

"We'll find out," the Seer said. "Tomorrow."

"Well, we will set out for Stoneslope tomorrow," the Scholar corrected. "We may not get there for some time, if the way is difficult, and we may not learn the truth of what happened there immediately upon arrival. The natives may be reluctant to speak to us—after five years of isolation they may view any stranger as an invader."

"Or a savior," the Seer suggested.

"Indeed," the Scholar agreed.

"Tomorrow, then," Breaker agreed.

[16]

As they set out across the grassy hilltop Breaker could not shake the feeling that he was being watched—and he suspected he probably was. The Wizard Lord could have eyes and ears anywhere, after all, and would certainly take an interest in three of the Chosen venturing out into the wilderness unguided, on their way to his own old home.

And then there were the *ler* around them, here as everywhere in Barokan—and once they passed the boundary stone halfway down the far slope those *ler* would be wild, untamed, and unknown. No priest had bargained with them, no pacts bound them, no powers restrained them except for the protections inherent in being Chosen, and the three travelers were deliberately walking into their territory uninvited and unguided; *ler* of land, tree, and sky would undoubtedly be watching them.

The people and priest of the nameless village had wished them well, but had declined to escort them to the border; the priest had admitted frankly, "We don't want to see anything terrible happen to you—and if we watch you cross the border we might not be able to *avoid* seeing it."

The boundary marker was old, a rough block of black stone with markings so worn by wind and rain that Breaker could make no sense of them. He hesitated beside it and looked at the others.

"Some *ler* prefer not to be bothered, and propitiatory rites only serve to wake and irritate them," the Scholar said as he came up behind Breaker, "but the majority appreciate indications that we are aware of them and respect their power." He knelt, bowed his head, and pressed his palms to the earth of the hillside below the black stone.

"To whatever powers may dwell beyond this point," the Scholar recited, "we give greetings, and offer peace. We wish you no ill, and intrude only because our duty compels us. Give us what guidance it may please you to give, ask of us what you will, and we will do what we may to speed our passage and fulfill your desires."

"I never heard *that* particular prayer before," Breaker remarked.

"I learned it from a Galbek guide years ago," the Scholar said as he rose. "It seemed appropriate."

"Let us hope it was," the Seer said. "That way." She pointed.

"That's where Stoneslope lies?" Breaker asked. "I thought it was more to the west."

"It is, but that's where the old trail was," she replied. "I can sense it."

Breaker peered at the ground, and at the brush ahead. "I see no sign of a trail."

"After five years of disuse that's hardly a surprise," the Scholar pointed out.

"Come on," the Seer said, marching past the boundary stone.

The three of them marched on into the wilderness, the Seer leading the way and Breaker bringing up the rear. Breaker could sense the change from tamed *ler* to wild immediately, and even more strongly than usual; the air seemed to almost buzz with hostility. The feeling of being watched grew more intense, and in fact every time he looked around Breaker seemed to glimpse eyes staring out at him from creatures perched on tree branches or crouching behind shrubs, eyes that would vanish the instant he saw them.

He could feel other *ler* moving invisibly about them as well, and not merely inhabiting the surrounding landscape—the air seemed to be full of them. Every so often his skin crawled, or turned cool, as a spirit brushed against him. The world around him was alive, not in the calm and ordered fashion of a priest-managed town, or even a trail accustomed to a guide's passage, but as chaotic and seething with life as a disturbed nest of hornets.

Any journey outside the safety of the towns and villages meant crossing the territory of untamed *ler,* but this area's intensity and alertness were unlike anything Breaker remembered. He wondered whether this was simply because no guide had come this way in years, or whether there was something more to it. Weeds and twigs tore at his legs, the ground was uneven beneath his feet, the breeze clammy on his skin even when no *ler* were making themselves obvious. And then he felt the eyes upon him again, and turned to look, and this time they did *not* vanish.

"Oh," he said, stopping where he stood. The others stopped, as well, staring up into the trees.

They were just squirrels, Breaker told himself. Squirrels, and birds, and chipmunks, and snakes, and lizards.

Nothing to be frightened of, surely; there were no monsters, no great beasts, just the ordinary inhabitants of the wood—but they were all motionless and staring, their gaze fixed on the three travelers . . . on *him,* Breaker thought. His hand fell to the hilt of his sword.

For a long silent moment everyone and everything simply stared; then a high, cracking voice broke the silence.

"You shouldn't be here," a squirrel said, speaking in the Galbek dialect.

Breaker let out a choking gasp of stifled laughter; the unexpected absurdity of a *squirrel* attempting to give them orders was too much to accept.

But then, he knew it wasn't really the squirrel speaking. He was fairly certain it wasn't even one of the local *ler.* The urge to laugh vanished completely, and he stared up at the squirrel unhappily.

He had not wanted this to happen. He had desperately hoped that they would go to Stoneslope and find a good, reasonable explanation of who the Wizard Lord had killed and why, and would share a laugh about their concerns and then go on about their separate business.

But if there were a good, reasonable explanation, this squirrel would not be telling them to go away.

"Lord," the Seer said, "it is our *duty* to be here."

The squirrel cocked its head and peered down at them from its branch. "Why do you call me 'lord'?" it asked.

The Seer grimaced, and turned away in disgust; it was the Scholar who replied.

"Lord, if the *ler* of this region made use of talking animals, not only would it have been reported in the local tales and legends, but this would not be wilderness. If *ler* will speak to us, then we can negotiate with them; if we can negotiate with them, then terms will be reached, sooner or later, and men and women will settle in the vicinity. This is how priesthoods begin."

"And what if the *ler*'s demands are too great?" the squirrel asked.

"Lord, you know the practices followed in Drumhead and Bone Garden; what demands could possibly be too great, if those were not?"

Breaker did not know what practices were followed in Drumhead and Bone Garden, but he had heard men and women calmly discussing the necessity of murdering an innocent child every year to please one set of *ler,* and visited two other towns that practiced human sacrifice as well, so he did not doubt that the Scholar knew of far worse—and he did not want to know the details.

"Lord," the Seer said, before the squirrel could respond, "I am the *Seer*. I know you, no matter what form you might take or what creature you might speak through. You know that."

The squirrel blinked, then turned and fled; it was a crow on a nearby branch that squawked, "Fine, then. Have it as you please. You still shouldn't be here."

"It is you who should not be here, Lord. We are doing our duty, weighing your deeds, and it is not your place to interfere."

The crow fluffed its wings and shook its head, and then a second crow spoke. "You're wandering in wild country. You might be killed—and if you die, then my own magic is lessened."

"If that is your concern, Lord, then you need merely see to it that we do not die. You are the Wizard Lord; surely, you have the power to see us safely to Stoneslope."

Another squirrel answered, "But I don't want you to go to Stoneslope. It's not safe there, either."

"Nonetheless, we must go."

"You won't like it," the second crow warned.

"That may be."

"The *ler* here don't like *you.*"

"We have done nothing to harm them. We have not seized control of their creatures as you have. We wish only to pass quickly through their realm."

The remaining leaves above their heads rustled at that; a murmur ran through the forest, and several birds and chipmunks stirred from their staring. The temperature seemed to drop several degrees.

Nothing spoke.

The sky began to darken; Breaker looked up through the trees at gathering clouds. "I think we had best move on," he said. His hand slid down to the pouch that held his talisman, reassuring him that it was securely in place.

The Seer glanced at him, then turned her attention back to the two crows.

"I think we should go *now,*" Breaker said, as the leaves stirred anew. "There's . . . the weather is strange. As if a storm were coming, even though it's daylight." As he spoke he noticed that the woodland's inhabitants, the birds and lizards and squirrels, were starting to slip away, taking cover wherever they could.

"He may . . ." the Scholar began.

Then there was a great fluttering of wings, a scampering of claws; Swordsman and Scholar both ducked as birds flew close overhead. The congregation of wildlife scattered in all directions, and wind whipped at the upper branches.

"He's gone," the Seer said, turning. Then she paused. "Mostly, at least . . ."

"We need to *go,*" Breaker bellowed at her over the rising gale. "We need to go *now*!"

"He won't harm us," the Seer said. "He wouldn't dare . . ."

"But the *ler* might!"

"He won't let . . ." Then she stopped in midsentence, looking around, as tree limbs began to creak.

Breaker grabbed her arm and tugged. "Come on!" he shouted. Shouting had suddenly become a necessity if one wished to be heard.

Slowly, as if confused, the Seer came, the Scholar close behind, and the three of them trudged on toward Stoneslope. They had taken no more than a dozen steps when the storm broke, and cold rain pelted at them from a sky that had been blue and white just a few moments before.

Breaker staggered in astonishment as the first drops struck his back. He had felt rain before, when he slipped out of the house late at night, but now it was *day*. It did not rain in the daytime in Barokan.

But that was because the Wizard Lord, who controlled the weather, did not allow it.

And obviously, right now the Wizard Lord was not playing by the established rules. After his initial shock, Breaker pressed on. Daylight rain or no, they had to reach Stoneslope.

The rain was heavy and soaking, but they ignored it as they half-walked, half-ran through the woods, in the direction of Stoneslope. The Seer was no longer pointing out the old guide's trail, but Breaker really didn't think it mattered anymore. The local *ler* knew they were there, certainly, and he could only hope that there was no local equivalent of the Mad Oak on the path they were taking—and such a menace could well have arisen in a formerly harmless spot in the five years since the path was abandoned, in any case, so the fact that they might have left the old path might not even matter.

Breaker prayed silently to the *ler,* telling them he was only doing what was required of him, that he was Chosen and doing his duty, and hoped that would be enough to protect him as he charged ahead through leaves and brush.

But then the Seer pulled at his arm, redirecting him. Breaker was unsure whether she was still following the old route or simply aiming them more directly toward Stoneslope, but he did his best to obey her and follow her lead.

The rain quickly became so heavy that they could see only a few feet, heavier than Breaker had ever seen even in the darkest spring night, heavier than he had known was possible, but that was not a real problem; the Seer was following something other than ordinary vision, and Breaker and the Scholar were following her.

They hurried on through the wilderness for hours, slipping on dead leaves or uneven stones, branches slapping at them, the rain beating down and the wind roaring, but there were no more talking animals, no more blatant manifestations of magic other than the unnatural weather. Breaker could not be sure, given the torrents soaking him, but he thought the hostile feel of their surroundings had lessened, despite the storm—perhaps the local *ler* had heard their conversation with the Wizard Lord and decided to tolerate them, as the less arrogant of the intruding factions.

And then at last they emerged from the forest into . . . not fields, as Breaker had expected, but younger forest. The great old trees were absent, but hundreds of saplings had sprung up on every side.

And the *ler* changed, from the vague inhuman hostility of the wilderness to screaming terror and agony. Breaker had never before experienced anything even remotely like it; he bent double at the initial shock as his shin brushed past an overgrown boundary stone, then fell to his knees, clapping his hands to his ears.

It did no good; the screams were not audible, but spiritual.

"Oh, my soul!" he gasped. "What *is* it? What *happened* here?"

"I don't know," the Seer said, and Breaker saw that she had remained on her feet, but was staggering. Lore had reacted in a more logical fashion—he had stepped back across the boundary, back out into the wilderness.

"We have to go on," the Seer said, her gaze fixed on something ahead that Breaker could not see.

"Yes," Breaker agreed. "In a moment." He tried to straighten up, and on his second try regained his feet. He closed his right hand on the hilt of his sword, and jammed his left into the pouch that held his silver talisman and closed his fingers around the sharp-edged shape.

That helped; the psychic battering of the town's *ler* weakened, as if a curtain had dropped around him.

Behind him the Scholar took a deep breath, and advanced again across the boundary. Together, the three of them pressed on, across what might once have been tilled fields but were now a tangle of shrubs and brambles.

And as if their persistence had broken the Wizard Lord's resolve the rain slackened at last, and ahead of them Breaker could see looming black shapes, the walls and roofs of the village of Stoneslope.

The structures did indeed look black; even when the rain subsided to a faint drizzle and the clouds thinned from black to gray, even as he stumbled nearer, Breaker still saw only vague black shapes.

And then at last he was close enough to see clearly in the dim light of the overcast afternoon, and he saw that the buildings really *were* black—or at least, what remained of them was blackened with soot and smoke. Shadows flitted among them—apparently the local *ler* had taken on some of the characteristics of smoke, and retained them.

Breaker staggered to a stop, and stared at the charred ruins. Not a single structure was intact, not a single roof whole; walls were broken, doorways shattered, and the greasy black smoke stains covered everything.

"What *happened*?" he asked again.

"That's what we're here to find out," the Seer said, slogging ahead through the flooded remains of what had once evidently been someone's garden.

"Is anyone here?" the Scholar shouted, in a passable imitation of the Galbek dialect.

"Hello!" Breaker boomed, cupping his hands to his mouth. "Can anyone hear me?"

"There's no one alive," the Seer said, pushing aside the bit of charcoal that still hung from one bent hinge in the doorway to the nearest house. "No one human, anyway. Not for miles. Just the three of us, and one of the Wizard Lord's creatures, watching us."

"But the village . . ." Breaker looked around, at the overgrown fields and the burned-out remains of the town. It appeared to have been almost as big as Mad Oak, covering the entire hillside for which it was named and a fair bit of the neighboring valley; that meant it had been home to dozens, or *hundreds,* of people, perhaps as many as half a thousand. "Where did they all go?"

"Nowhere," the Scholar said, stooping and pushing aside a charred beam. He held up half a skull. "They're all still here. That's what you feel suffering. Those screaming *ler* are the souls of the dead."

"*All* of them? They can't be!" He looked around, and was horrified to see lumps that looked very much like more half-rotted bones scattered and half-buried here and there.

"I wish you were right," the Seer said from inside the ruin. "This is what I saw, though. This is where I felt those deaths."

"But . . . you don't mean the Wizard Lord did this, do you? He can't have! It must have been rogue wizards—and then he killed them . . ."

"Swordsman," the Scholar said gently, "rogue wizards are the one thing we know he did *not* kill here."

Breaker stared at the Scholar, trying to absorb this. He knew it was true if what the Seer and Scholar had told him was true, but how could he really be sure? All he had was their word; the whole story of the Scholar only remembering the truth seemed so *convenient,* like something out of an old story . . .

But then, he was living in the realm of stories, of heroes and villains—he was the Swordsman, one of the Chosen. He was a hero—and someone here was unquestionably a villain.

But it didn't have to be the Wizard Lord; what if it was the Seer? The Scholar didn't even need to be in on the plot; perhaps he didn't remember the rogue wizard explanation because *she had never told it to him,* not because it was a lie.

Or wait—it could even be an honest mistake. Maybe she *thought* she had told him, but she never had; perhaps she had told someone else and confused that unknown listener with the Scholar. She wasn't a young woman, and Breaker knew that older people sometimes had trouble remembering things accurately. Maybe there *was* no villain.

But there was a destroyed village strewn with human skulls, *ler* that reeked of horrors they had experienced, and the Wizard Lord had tried to prevent them from coming here.

Or *something* had; did he really know it was the Wizard Lord who had spoken through the squirrels and crows? He glanced back at the rain-blackened forest.

"We need to be sure," he said. "You're telling me that the Wizard Lord slaughtered an entire village, and that would mean he's become a new Dark Lord. If he has, I have to kill him. I want to be absolutely certain of the truth before I kill *anyone*."

"Of course," the Scholar agreed. "And it may even be that he had a legitimate reason to do this—though it's hard to imagine what it might be—but you can't seriously doubt that something very wrong happened here, and that the Wizard Lord was involved."

"I can tell that much, yes," Breaker admitted. He could feel the souls of the dead—and now that he had been told, he could not deny that that was what he sensed—shrieking in lingering pain and fear, and he could feel it spike in intensity when the Wizard Lord was mentioned.

And beneath the fear and pain, he could feel hatred, and a desperate need for something—though he was not entirely sure yet what it might be. To tell him something? For him to understand something, or do something?

He could not be sure.

The Seer reappeared in the doorway, holding something in her hand. "It's *very* hard to imagine anything that would justify this," she said. She raised her hand, and Breaker saw that she held another skull—a tiny one.

A baby's.

"There's half a cradle in there," she said, gesturing. "This was in it." Then she looked up suddenly. "He's watching us."

Breaker turned to follow her gaze and saw a crow flying toward them; he had no way of telling whether it was one of the crows they had seen before, but it easily could have been.

The three of them stood in the muddy dooryard, waiting silently, as the bird came to them and landed atop a broken beam.

"Tell us what happened, Lord," the Seer said. "Did you do this? How did it happen, and why? Tell us what these people did to deserve this. And tell us the truth—Lore won't remember anything else, and we'll know if you've lied to us."

The Scholar started to open his mouth, then stopped; Breaker guessed he had been about to explain that he didn't *necessarily* forget lies, but thought better of undermining his companion's argument. Instead he said, "This was your home village, wasn't it?"

"I was born here," the crow croaked. It shook itself, then gestured awkwardly with one wing, trying to point. "In that house over there," it said, indicating a pile of blackened stones at the foot of the hill. "My mother died of me; my father died when I was eight."

"And you destroyed your childhood home? Slaughtered your friends and neighbors?" the Seer demanded. Breaker could feel the angry *ler* pressing toward her, urging her to speak.

"I *had* no friends!" the bird croaked. "They hated me, all of them. I was small and weak and ugly, and I had killed my mother—they hated me. They called me Stinker, and Pigface, and Killer—I didn't even have a real calling name once my father died, not for years, just insults. They threw mud at me, and chased me through the stubble until my ankles ran with blood, and beat me when they caught me, and I swore by all the *ler* that when the time came I would return their cruelty tenfold. I ran away to become a wizard when I was fifteen, and never came back—until five years ago, when I honored my childhood vow."

"This infant never taunted or tormented you," the Seer said, holding up the tiny skull.

"Her father did!" the crow exclaimed. "Or at any rate, her mother's husband; I would not be surprised to learn someone else had sired the whore's brat."

Breaker's blood ran cold at that. "Then you know who this was?" the Seer said. "You killed them deliberately?"

"Of course I knew who it was! I sent my spies and watched them for more than a year before I brought my vengeance upon them; I had to plan, to prepare. I knew that people like you, you Chosen, might not approve, might not understand that I *needed* to do this for the sake of justice, and so I wanted to ensure that the outside world would never know what I did here. I killed the guides, father and daughter and grandson, to cut Stoneslope's ties to the rest of Barokan, to the *decent* part of the world, so that I could do as I pleased to the filth that lived here, and I made sure I knew who every soul in the village was, so that I could be certain none escaped my wrath."

Breaker, already strained by the oppressive *ler,* went numb with horror as he listened to this speech; he wished he could convince himself that it was merely a nightmare, and certainly the talking crow seemed dreamlike, but his rain-drenched clothes and the mud beneath his feet were much too real to be so conveniently dismissed. He stared silently at the bird.

"And did everyone in Stoneslope deserve to die, then?" the Scholar asked. "Were there none who had taken your side, or even stayed aloof, when you were a child here?"

"None!" the crow squawked. "None, none!"

"You had no family here?" the Seer asked.

"I told you, my parents were dead!"

"But who took you in after your father's death? What of the town's priesthood, and the *ler*? Didn't they defend you, as one of their own?"

"Does it matter? They're all dead, five years dead. And I had *sworn,* by the *ler,* that I would take revenge. I had no choice."

"You hadn't sworn revenge on *everyone,* had you?"

"Yes! I had! Those who didn't torture me allowed it to continue!"

"How . . ." Breaker's voice came out almost as much a croak as the crow's; he swallowed, and tried again. "How did you do it?" he asked.

The crow cocked its head. "You don't want to know," it said. "I'm the Wizard Lord, master of wind and fire and steel—do you really want the details?"

"I think we would like to know whether you deliberately tormented any of them, or whether you made their deaths as quick and easy as you could," the Scholar said. "As a matter of record, you understand."

"I struck them down with a plague first," the crow replied. "So they could not flee. When all were in their beds and many dying I sent fires to cleanse, and storm winds to whip the flames, then rain to douse the flames and cool the ashes. Then I came myself, not in this crow or any other such puppet, but in my own flesh, with some of my creatures, to make sure the job was done. I chopped the heads off anyone who appeared intact enough that a spark of life might possibly have remained, and then I left them here to rot. I did not taunt or torture anyone; I would not stoop to that level. I was ridding Barokan of a blight, not taking pleasure in anyone's suffering."

Breaker thought he could hear a note of satisfaction in these words, even spoken in the crow's unnatural squawking voice.

For a moment no one replied; then the crow asked, "And will you call me mad or evil now, and seek to slay me?"

"I don't know," the Seer said, before the others could speak. "We will need time to consider the matter, and we should confer with the rest of the Chosen. We are three out of eight, less than half the total—it is not our place to make the decision."

Breaker turned to stare at her.

"I don't want to kill you," the crow said. "But I will if I must, even though it would destroy a portion of my own power."

"And it would certainly mean that the other Chosen would vote to kill you," the Scholar said. "Slaying any of the Chosen is one of the things absolutely forbidden to a Wizard Lord."

"And not just the other Chosen would seek to avenge you, but the Council of Immortals," the crow agreed. "Even if I slew all eight of you, every wizard in Barokan would be out for my blood, and I'd have almost no power left to oppose them."

"I don't think any of us want that," the Seer said. "But you know we'll need to tell the others about what you did here."

"And then the eight of you will decide whether my vengeance was justice or madness, and if you choose to deem me mad, then it will mean war between us, war to the death."

"It needn't be to the death. You could resign your title," the Scholar suggested, "as the Dark Lord of Spider Marsh did, two hundred years ago."

"Perhaps," the crow croaked. "Perhaps."

Then the bird twitched, flapped its wings, cawed, and flew away.

Breaker did not need to hear the Seer's words to know that the Wizard Lord was gone—for the moment.

And he knew now what the ghosts of Stoneslope's murdered inhabitants wanted.

They wanted justice—or no, that was not quite right.

They wanted *revenge.*

[17]

They were eager to get out of Stoneslope, away from those haunted, overgrown ruins and the restless souls of slaughtered innocents, souls who had had no surviving priests to guide them from this world to the next; there was no need to find more evidence when the Wizard Lord had admitted what he had done, almost boasted of it. They had left swiftly, eager to reach shelter elsewhere—anywhere but Stoneslope—before full dark.

The journey back to the nameless village was relatively uneventful. The mud underfoot seemed even slicker than it naturally should be, and one vine draped itself around the Scholar's throat with malicious intent, but careful walking and a swipe from Breaker's sword disposed of these hazards.

They saw no animals of any kind this time. Breaker wondered about that. What was the Wizard Lord doing? What was he thinking? He knew they had seen Stoneslope, and he must know how horrified they were, but he was not doing anything, so far as Breaker could see. The clouds had scattered, the trail was less hostile—apparently he was making no attempt to prevent them from reaching the outside world, even though he must know they would tell others what they had seen.

What *was* he doing? Fortifying his tower? Preparing magic to protect himself from their inevitable assault?

He considered asking the Seer, but a glance at her expression convinced him not to address her—and in truth, he was not sure he could speak calmly at the moment, as the emotions of the ghosts of Stoneslope still lingered in his head, ready to burst out.

Besides, what if the Wizard Lord was listening? Or what if ordinary *ler* were listening, that might pass the word to others? Breaker knew that news could sometimes spread through the land itself, without human intervention, and he was not at all sure that they wanted this news to be turned loose just yet.

So he said nothing, the whole way back to the nameless village.

The sun was low in the west and the priest was waiting for them just beyond the boundary shrine when they emerged from the forest; some *ler* must have informed him that they were coming. "You're alive!" he said, without preamble.

"I certainly hope so," the Seer muttered as she stumped past the black marker, ignoring the faces that peered at them from the distant cottages.

"Did you expect the wild *ler* to kill us, or the Wizard Lord's creatures, or what?" Breaker asked, genuinely curious, as he paused and leaned against the weathered boundary stone.

The priest shrugged. "Who knows? All I knew was that no one had come alive from Stoneslope in five years. Out *ler* had said something about a plague—but the *ler* can be vague and unreliable sometimes."

"Just like anyone else," the Seer said, stopping some twenty feet inside the village and turning.

"There was a plague," the Scholar said. "Stoneslope's people are all dead, and the secrets of their priests presumably lost."

"Horrible, horrible! What can I do to aid you, then?"

The three Chosen exchanged glances.

"A warm bath, a hot fire, a hot meal, and a warm bed would be welcome," Breaker said.

"Of course, of course! I'll have them prepared." The priest turned, and ran toward the village square in a thoroughly undignified fashion, as the weary Chosen followed at a more leisurely pace.

The baths were not as warm or as generous as Breaker would have liked, the fire was distressingly smoky because the unnatural rain had soaked much of the village's stock of firewood, the meal was just oatmeal, and the beds were straw ticks in the village's communal hay barn that crunched and rustled underneath them, but the villagers did their best to provide what the three had asked for. In exchange, once they had bathed and before heading to their beds they described what they had found in Stoneslope; for the most part they answered the villagers' questions as best they could, but by unspoken mutual consent they never mentioned that the Wizard Lord had been responsible for the plague or the subsequent fires. They were not yet ready to tell all the world that a ninth Dark Lord now reigned over Barokan. Breaker was not entirely sure of his own reasons, but he knew he did not want to be the first to reveal the truth; he knew that once released, that truth could never be recaptured, and that he did not know what the consequences might be.

"I suppose no one was well enough to fight the flames," Breaker said, when asked directly what started the conflagration.

"Why didn't their *ler* protect them?" a girl of ten or so asked.

"Perhaps their priest angered the *ler* somehow," the Seer suggested. "We don't really know. All we know is what we found."

"And you found your way there safely?"

"Easily," the Scholar said, setting down his half-eaten oatmeal. "The *ler* of the forest did try to hinder us, but their efforts were really quite trivial. If anyone should care to negotiate new terms with the *ler* of Stoneslope, a new settlement might be established there."

Breaker stared at him in astonishment. No one could live there until the ghosts were exorcised, the spirits of the dead calmed and sent on their way! What was Lore thinking?

The Seer saw Breaker's expression and gestured for silence.

The villagers stirred, muttering and shuddering. "And risk another plague? I don't think so!" a woman responded.

"And we have no idea how the priesthood there operated, in any case," the priest said. "We don't know whether they negotiated with the *ler,* or commanded them, or were enslaved by them. Anyone trying to create a new priesthood would be risking his life if he chose the wrong strategy."

No one could deny that—and Breaker supposed the Scholar had known this would be the response. Still, his suggestion had seemed bizarre.

When at last the crowd had dispersed, and the three travelers had retired to the barn to sleep, Breaker asked quietly, "Now what?"

"Now we gather the Chosen," the Seer said. "The Speaker lives just a few days' travel northwest of here, the Archer not much farther. The Thief lives in the eastern Midlands and the Leader is traveling not far from there, while the Beauty lives in Winterhome. We're fortunate that no one is in the northern valleys, or out on the islands, or in the far marshes."

"That's assuming they don't move around," the Scholar pointed out. "Just because most of them are home at the moment doesn't mean they'll stay there. They may well *be* on the islands by the time we catch up to them."

"We can send word somehow," the Seer said. "Especially once we find the Speaker."

"But we're in the Galbek Hills," Breaker protested. "The Wizard Lord's tower is just a few miles away, isn't it?"

"About thirty miles," the Seer agreed, pointing to the southwest.

A little of the remembered fury of the ghosts of Stoneslope scratched at Breaker. "But you want us to go wandering all over Barokan, while the Wizard Lord builds up defenses and prepares for us, instead of just going there *now* and killing him?"

The Seer sighed. "That's right," she said.

"You can go try to kill him yourself, if you want," the Scholar said, "but you would be acting alone, and the rest of us would feel no great need to do anything about it if the Wizard Lord were to kill you in self-defense. Once we have agreed that he must be removed, *then* any harm he does to you would bring our collective wrath down upon his head, but now? Seer and I saw Stoneslope, and felt the *ler* there—while I can't speak for her, I think killing the Wizard Lord is more than justified, it's essential. But we are only three; the other five were not with us."

Breaker frowned. "The three of us could go to his tower together," he said.

"Are you that eager to kill him?"

Breaker bit off his immediate reply of "yes," and before he could say anything else the Seer spoke.

"Are you that eager to die?" she asked. "He could kill us easily."

"But . . . very well, then, would eight be so much more formidable than three? He could kill *all* of us, just as he wiped out that village."

The Seer shook her head. "No," she said. "He would destroy his own magic in the process, and the other wizards would make quick work of him."

"And we are immune to his magic, his diseases and fires," the Scholar added. "He could undoubtedly kill us, but not in the same way he slaughtered his townsfolk."

"But . . . he could still kill us, surely."

"Three of us, yes," the Seer said patiently. "But if the eight of us act together, he cannot kill us without destroying his own power and leaving himself defenseless against the other wizards. If he knows he faces all the Chosen he may see sense and surrender his position without a fight; against three, that's far less likely."

Breaker wanted to argue further, but he knew his companions were right. He had wanted to go and get it over with, to confront the Wizard Lord while the horrors of Stoneslope were fresh in his mind, to avenge the dead swiftly, but he knew that would not work. The Chosen were chosen to act *together,* and not in haste.

The idea that the Wizard Lord might surrender peacefully, and not be punished for his butchery with death, did not suit Breaker just now, but he knew intellectually that it might be best.

"The Speaker," he said. "You want to find her first?"

"She's the closest."

Breaker hesitated, then said, "I heard she's mad."

The Seer and the Scholar exchanged glances.

"She wasn't when last we spoke," the Seer said, "but I can see how some might think she is. After all, she can hear things no one else hears, and aside from priests, most people who hear voices no one else can hear *are* mad."

"Is that what it is?" Breaker asked. "I thought she could speak any tongue, I didn't know she heard voices."

"She can hear, speak, and understand every tongue in Barokan," the Seer explained. "And not just the human ones. She hears the *ler,* the birds and beasts, spiders and flies, earth and flame, the messages that wizards send one another on the wind—everything. If she ever does go mad she'll have good reason, after living with such a constant din!"

Breaker tried to imagine what it would be like, hearing everything, and quickly gave up. That was not a role he would have accepted; being the Swordsman was far simpler and more straightforward.

"If she were to die," the Scholar said, "the Wizard Lord would no longer be able to command other creatures, nor speak through them. That's the portion of his magic bound to her."

This was interesting information, not something he had known before; Breaker nodded. Then a sudden thought occurred to him.

If he were to kill the Speaker, the Wizard Lord would be a less formidable foe. If he were to kill all the other Chosen, the Wizard Lord would be almost defenseless.

But that was insane; the Chosen were his equals, his helpers and partners. He had no reason to kill any of them, nor any intention of harming anyone but the Wizard Lord.

The Wizard Lord deserved to die for what he had done to Stoneslope, and it was Breaker's duty as the Swordsman to see that justice was done, but that hardly gave him the right to kill anyone else, let alone betray and murder his own companions! Where had such a horrible notion come from?

Was the Wizard Lord influencing his thoughts somehow? That was a terrifying idea.

No, he told himself, that was foolish. The idea of killing the others was just one of those strange passing thoughts that sometimes wandered through a tired mind—especially one that had just suffered something like seeing and feeling the horrors of Stoneslope!

"I need some rest," he said—but then another, more urgent thought struck him.

He had not yet practiced his swordsmanship for the day. The trip to and from Stoneslope, and the brief investigation there, had taken up the entire day and thrown his usual schedule into disarray. Perhaps that was where the morbid thoughts were coming from—the *ler* that gave him his skill, and who sometimes seemed to glory in the thought of bloodshed, were affecting him.

"Oh, blood and spirit," he said, rolling off his mattress and getting to his feet.

"What is it?" the Seer asked.

"Practice," he said, drawing his blade.

There was no need to go outside; the barn was spacious enough, and with the sun down the candlelight inside provided better visibility. He sighed, and began running through his usual exercises, thrusting the sword to either side of a pillar, lunging and feinting.

The Seer and the Scholar watched, but by the time he finally sheathed his sword and blew out the candles they had both been sound asleep for several minutes. Whatever requirements their magic might make of them—and Breaker knew that the Scholar, at least, did have some sort of daily requirement, something about learning new facts every day—had apparently been met earlier.

They set out without a guide the following morning; the Scholar was sure he could remember exactly the route by which they had arrived and the prayers their guide had spoken along the way, and surviving the previous day's ordeal had given them all confidence in their own abilities to cross hostile territory unscathed.

"I've done this before," the Scholar admitted, as they ambled along. "Not this particular route, but retracing a path I'd been guided on. It's one of the more useful manifestations of my magic."

"Are you sure it's really safe?" Breaker asked, as he dodged a low-hanging branch that seemed to be trying to poke out his left eye.

"No," the Scholar said. "But then, what is?"

Breaker had no reply to that.

They reached the town of Argand Wager an hour or two past noon; here they had a choice of routes, rather than the single link that joined the nameless village to the rest of civilization, but the Seer had no doubt of which they should take, and a guide was expected that very evening.

They made good progress. They spoke very little on the road; Breaker was not sure just why. It certainly wasn't that they had nothing to discuss; there were hundreds of questions he wanted answered. How could the Wizard Lord have done such a thing? When the Seer felt the deaths, why hadn't she realized how many there were, and that they could not possibly have just been the handful of rogue wizards Boss had said they were? Why had she taken the Leader's word and done no investigation of her own?

Was it really necessary to find the others before doing *anything* about the Wizard Lord's crimes?

Now that they were set out upon out their appointed task of removing a Dark Lord, why did he feel no different? Why was the sun still bright and warm, the countryside calm? Shouldn't there be some outward sign of the atrocities in Stoneslope, something that would show anywhere in Barokan?

If he was one of a brotherhood of heroes, on their way to avenge murdered innocents, why did he feel no particular kinship with the Seer or the Scholar? He was as detached as ever. The Scholar was pleasant enough company, but they were not close, and the Seer seemed like a combination of his mother and Elder Priestess rather than a companion and equal. Shouldn't they be bonding into the sort of team that the Chosen were in all the old stories, ready to die for one another, understanding each other so well that they could anticipate each other's actions without words?

And they weren't. They were just three people traveling together. Breaker had no feeling that they were on any sort of adventure; he could not imagine that anyone would ever tell epic tales of the three of them walking from town to town.

But then, *why* was there no adventure? Why wasn't the Wizard Lord trying to stop them? Why were there no monsters, no traps, no messages trying to deter them, no threats nor bribes?

It was all very strange, and didn't seem entirely real, somehow—until he closed his eyes and remembered the blackened ruins of Stoneslope, there beneath the overcast skies, with the scattered mounds that hid the bones of the dead. He remembered that tiny skull in the Seer's hand, and he shuddered.

That seemed far more real than the sunny skies, the light scattering through the leaves or shining off the farmers' fields, as they walked behind their hired guide, watching the *ara* feathers on his hat flutter in the gentle breeze.

The Speaker had been a good hundred miles away when they left Stoneslope, the Seer reported, but by the third day she had begun moving toward them. "Something probably told her we were coming," the Scholar said.

And on the fifth day they found the Speaker sitting in the central temple of a large and prosperous town called Blessed of Earth and Sky, waiting for them. Several priestesses were going about some ritual, so that the temple was full of women walking to and fro, and Breaker would never have noticed the Speaker if the Seer hadn't tugged at his sleeve and pointed her out.

She was a tiny little thing in a dark brown cloak, curled up on a bench, knees tucked in, leaning one shoulder against the wall. Breaker thought at first she was a child, from both her size and her posture, but then she turned her face so it caught the sunlight from the open door and he saw that she was perhaps twice his own age, though not as old as the Seer. Her hair was still dark and curly, her skin still mostly free of wrinkles and blemishes, but there was no question that she was past the full bloom of youth.

And her dark eyes seemed touched with madness. Even before she said a word, Breaker understood why so many people thought she was mad—her face was full of irrational intensity. Her fragile form hardly seemed suitable for a Chosen Hero, but those eyes were another matter entirely.

She looked at the three Chosen but did not say anything, nor make any move to leave the bench. For a moment the three of them stood staring silently at her, while she stared back. Then Breaker bowed.

"I am the new Swordsman," he said. "I am honored to meet you."

"Erren Zal Tuyo kam Darig seveth Tirinsir abek Du," she said, in a soft, unsteady, high-pitched voice, her eyes fixed on his face.

Breaker jerked upright at the sound of so much of his true name; he could feel its power close on his heart. "Yes," he said.

"And Shal Doro Sheth tava Doro kal Gardar."

The Seer grimaced.

"And Olbir Olgurun pul Sasimori ken ken Frovor."

The Scholar flinched.

"We are met, four of the eight, half the Chosen," she continued, in a sort of singsong. "You want to decide the fate of Laquar kellin Hario Vor Tesil sil Galbek."

"Yes," the Seer said.

"So much *ler* have told me," the Speaker said, straightening a little. "The winds and sky have told me this, because I could hear your soul, Shal Doro, calling out to mine, asking where I could be found, and so I asked the *ler* why you sought me. But all they could tell me were certain of the words you had spoken as you traveled, and thus I learned that you wanted to speak to me of the life of Laquar kellin Hario, but did not learn why. I have come here to meet you, in this quiet place, so that you can tell me why."

"Quiet?" Breaker looked around at the hurrying priestesses, listened to their footsteps on the stone floors echoing from the stone walls, heard a dozen voices chanting in another part of the temple and echoes answering them, as well.

"Remember," the Seer said, "she hears everything. In here she hears people and stone, but there are no birds nor beasts, the *ler* speak in concert . . . and I'm starting to talk like her." She sighed. "She always has this effect on me."

"It's because she uses true names," the Scholar said. "It creates a bond."

Breaker refused to be distracted. "Speaker, as I said, I am honored to meet you," he said. "I hope we will be friends, as it appears we are fated to be companions."

"I have no friends," the Speaker replied, a note of woe creeping into her singsong. "I have no time for friends, when so many voices call to me."

Breaker did not know what to say to that; he looked helplessly at the Scholar, who shrugged.

"There are things I would say that I would prefer the priestesses of this temple not hear," the Seer said. "Is there somewhere we can go where no other people will hear us?"

"We are heard everywhere, always," the Speaker murmured.

"No *people,*" the Seer repeated. "I know *ler* will hear us, and probably spiders and insects and the birds above, and quite possibly the Wizard Lord himself if he's listening, but I would prefer not to be heard by any other *people.*"

The Speaker sighed, lifted her head and shoulder from the wall, and uncurled her legs. "Come, then, Shal Doro, Erren Zal, and Olbir Olgurun." She rose from the bench and led the way down a corridor and out of the temple.

Now that she was upright Breaker could see that she was close to the

Seer's height, but probably only weighed half what the older woman did. Beneath the brown cloak she was dressed entirely in black, though golden embroidery shone at collar and cuffs.

As they walked, Breaker asked, "Why do you use our true names?"

She threw him a startled glance. "*Ler* know no others," she said. "Your souls speak your names to me endlessly." She hesitated. "Would you prefer I call you something else?"

"Among my people, using true names is considered . . . well . . ." Breaker groped for the right word to express the normal Mad Oak attitude, and finally found it. "Bullying. It's considered bullying. Because true names have power."

"Of course they do. I see." She almost stumbled as they reached a short flight of stairs leading down, but caught herself. "Then what would you have me call you?"

"I'm the Swordsman. Most people call me that."

"Ah." They reached the bottom of the stair, and she said, "But you do not truly think of that as your own name yet—it's a title, more than a name. Your predecessor was known as Blade to his friends; do you have a nickname like that? Or would you like to be called Blade?"

Breaker shook his head. "No, he can keep that name; I don't want it."

"You were known for more than half your life as . . . Shatterer? Divider? The *ler* do not speak our tongue . . ."

"Breaker."

"And you still think of yourself as the Breaker."

Breaker glanced back and saw the Scholar listening with obvious interest.

"I suppose I do," he admitted.

"I will call you Sword."

It was Breaker's turn to almost stumble; he had assumed she was about to settle on using his old nickname, and the sudden change of direction startled him—not to mention the coincidence that she had happened on the same nickname his neighbors had used, back in Mad Oak. He opened his mouth to say something, then stopped.

He did not really want his old name back; he did not want to break anything.

"Sword is good," he said.

The Seer and the Scholar glanced at one another.

Then the four of them stepped into a small room of bare stone, and the Speaker closed the door behind them, plunging them into utter darkness, before Breaker—or Sword—could take in much of their surroundings.

He could hear something crunching underfoot, though.

"A storeroom," the Speaker said. "It held grain for the winter, but winter is done and the new harvest not yet in. The room is strong, the walls thick stone without seam, to keep out mice. We won't be heard by human ears, and the *ler* of the grain are slumbering. Only the stones speak, and their words are slow and gentle."

"Good," the Seer said; the other two made no comment, but Breaker, for one, found the darkness uncomfortable.

"Tell me, then, why you believe Laquar kellin Hario must be removed."

"Have you ever heard of a town called Stoneslope?" the Seer asked.

"Not that I recall, not by that name," the Speaker replied. "The *ler* would have another name for it, of course."

"Of course. It's the town where the Wizard Lord was born and raised; he left when he was fifteen."

"Ah! Yes, I know of it. What of it?"

"It's gone," the Swordsman said—partly just to hear his own voice and remind everyone that he was there in the dark.

"The Wizard Lord destroyed it," the Seer said.

"But—a moment, then."

For what seemed several minutes, no one spoke—though Breaker was unsure exactly what they were waiting for. Then the Speaker said, "And he slew all who lived there?"

A new note had crept into her voice, the singsong become a dirge.

"So it appears, and so he believes," the Seer said. "The air was thick with the souls of the dead, all full of fear and anger."

"The aunt who took him in when his father died? His childhood betrothed? The cousin he deflowered instead?"

"If they were there, he killed them," the Scholar said.

The Speaker made a noise of strangled disgust. Then silence descended again, broken only by the grinding of spilled grain beneath Breaker's boots as he shifted nervously.

"We must find Farash inith Kerra das Bik abba Terrul sinna Oppor, and the others," the Speaker said.

"Farash . . ." Breaker did not recognize any part of the name.

"The Leader," the Speaker explained. "Boss."

"Yes," the Seer replied. "We agree. Boss and the others. The Archer is nearest; could you send him word to meet us halfway?"

[18]

The Speaker could speak to anything that lived or had any spiritual existence, but she could not easily command anything; the birds and *ler* she asked to convey the message did not cooperate. She could have forced them by using their true names, but did not want to, as it would bring protests only she could hear.

At last, though, she found a stray dog that agreed to carry a note tied round its neck, and to find the man with the scent the Speaker described.

"You can describe a person's scent well enough to identify him?" Breaker marveled, as the dog ran off.

"Only in the languages of dogs," the Speaker said. "Half their vocabulary—more than half—is about smells. They have no words for color or music, but a thousand shades of acrid, a thousand kinds of sour."

"And how do you know the Archer's smell well enough to describe him that way?"

"It's in his true name," she said. She hefted her pack. "Shall we go?"

They went.

Two days later the four of them were sitting in a tavern in a town called Seven Sides, talking to some of the locals. The townsfolk had recognized Breaker as the Swordsman immediately—not difficult, given the sword on his belt—and then guessed that the people with him might also be Chosen. They had quickly identified the Seer, and guessed the Speaker; now they were trying to determine which of the Chosen the fourth might be. The travelers had agreed to play along with this guessing game in exchange for bread, ham, gravy, and beer. They sat, eating silently, and listening while the natives argued.

"He doesn't have a bow or any arrows."

"I think the Leader would have to be taller."

"That leaves the Thief and the Scholar."

"And the Beauty, but I think we can rule *that* one out."

That evinced a round of laughter. "How do we know he even *is* one of the Chosen?" a boy asked as the laughter subsided. "Maybe he's just a friend of theirs."

"The lad has a point."

"But they agreed to our game! They wouldn't have done that if he wasn't one of them; it wouldn't be honest."

"Are the Chosen necessarily honest?"

"I certainly *hope* so!"

"Then he's the Thief or the Scholar."

"Or he left his bow and arrows somewhere else."

"Look at his arms—he's not one accustomed to drawing a bow. The Swordsman has the shoulders of a fighting man, but this other one . . ."

"The Scholar or the Thief."

"The Thief, I'd say."

"Uh . . . isn't the present Thief a woman?"

That brought a sudden startled silence, followed by a burst of argument.

"She is! She is, I tell you!"

"Who knows? Would a thief *admit* to being a thief?"

"Then who's the woman?"

"She's just trying to get attention!"

"The real Thief wouldn't *want* attention."

"I don't think she's trying for attention."

As they argued, Breaker finished the food on his plate, gulped the remainder of his beer, then wiped his mouth with the back of his hand and looked around at the crowd.

There were at least a score playing the game, and a score more watching; the tavern's dining room was packed full. They seemed friendly enough, and so far the game's arguments had remained calm and not turned into quarrels. They all wore the town's standard garb of white blouse and leather vest—apparently the local *ler* demanded this attire.

All, that is, except the man in the doorway, who was watching and listening with amused interest; he wore a dusty deerskin tunic, instead. And he carried a bow on his back.

He was a tall, broad-shouldered, slim-waisted fellow with a narrow face and pointed jaw; he wore his light brown hair long and loose, but his beard was trimmed short and to a point that exaggerated the sharpness of his chin. His clothes were worn and not particularly clean, from square leather cap to muddy brown boots. He smiled crookedly at Breaker.

No one else seemed to have noticed him yet.

Breaker cocked his head, and the man with the bow nodded an acknowledgment.

"Excuse me for a moment," Breaker said, getting to his feet.

People moved aside to let him rise from his chair and slip out of the crowd; oddly, none of them looked where he was looking, and no one else seemed to notice the man at the door.

The man stepped to one side as Breaker approached, as well, but then turned his back to the tavern wall and said, "So you're the new Swordsman?"

Breaker looked him in the eye—the two men were very close in height. "And you're the Archer."

"I got Babble's note—the Speaker's, I mean. So we're finally going to do what we swore we would when we accepted these roles, then? We're going to kill him?"

Breaker hesitated. "So it would seem," he admitted.

"Do you want to do it, or should I?"

"I . . . I don't know," Breaker replied. "I assumed that whichever of us had the better opportunity would do it. I mean, if it needs to be done."

"That's fine, then. You don't mind if I do it? You won't feel I've cheated you out of the glory?"

Breaker blinked. This was not at all the conversation he had expected. "No, I don't mind," he said. "If you have the chance, go ahead."

"That's fine, then!" The Archer reached out and clapped Breaker on the shoulder. "I think we'll get along just fine, lad—you've got more sense than your predecessor, that's plain!"

"I don't . . . I wouldn't say that."

"Oh, no question about it. He kept insisting he didn't want to kill anyone, which is all very well, but then he said *I* shouldn't, either, and really, what's the point of being one of the Chosen, then? Our whole *purpose* is to kill the Wizard Lord!"

"Well, if he deserves it," Breaker said. "If he's turned wicked." He hesitated, unsure what to say next, because after all, as he well knew, the Wizard Lord *had* turned wicked and needed to be removed. The *ler* of a hundred dead innocents had said so, and the Wizard Lord himself had admitted murdering them.

"And if he hasn't, we don't do anything at all? That's just so pointless. I knew when I agreed to become the Archer that we'd have a Dark Lord soon—I could just *feel* it, as if *ler* were whispering to me. And sure enough, we do—though old Blade never wanted to admit it, and I don't think the others even realized it." He smiled, and leaned against the wall. "So how did you convince them?"

"I didn't," Breaker said. "*They* convinced *me*. Something the Scholar said made the Seer suspicious, and they dragged me along, and we all went to the Wizard Lord's home village, a place called Stoneslope, and we saw what he'd done to it. And that's when the three of us knew."

"Something *Lore* said? The Seer always did take his stories seriously, but they all just sounded like a lot of dusty, useless nonsense to me."

"It's complicated," Breaker said—he did not feel like trying to explain anything to this strange man, who seemed downright *enthusiastic* about killing the Wizard Lord.

"So the Wizard Lord did something bad to his old neighbors?"

"He killed them," Breaker said.

The Archer seemed suddenly wary. "Were they wizards? We aren't supposed to interfere if he kills wizards—we're to assume they'd gone rogue and started raping girls and eating babies."

"They weren't wizards. Not all of them, anyway—there might have been a wizard in there somewhere."

"Not all . . . ? And somewhere . . . ?" For the first time the Archer's confidence looked slightly shaken. "Ah, how many people did he kill?"

"All of them."

For a moment the Archer stared at him, confused. "What do you mean?"

"I mean he killed them all. The entire town. He sent a plague, and then killed the survivors and burned the town."

The Archer stared for a moment, then shook his head. "No, he didn't."

"Yes, he did. Five years ago. We only just found out."

"No, that's insane. Why would he slaughter a whole *town*? What about his friends and family there?"

"He claims he had no friends—and yes, it's insane. That's why we need to kill him."

"By the ghosts of my ancestors," the Archer said quietly. "He's gone completely *mad*?"

"Yes, of course—why else would we be planning to kill him?"

"Well, I . . . well, yes, I see. You're right, of course." He stared thoughtfully at Breaker.

Breaker stared back, then glanced at the open tavern door.

"The Scholar!" someone was shouting. "He's the Scholar! Must be!"

"Why didn't they notice you?" Breaker asked.

"Because I didn't want them to," the Archer said. "That's part of my magic—not being noticed."

"They can't see you?"

"They *don't* see me. It's not the same thing. If they were actually *looking* for me, or if they happened to glance right at me without any distractions, then they *would* see me, but I can just . . . fail to attract attention. Not stand out. It's all part of the magic."

"I thought your magic was just archery—hitting what you aim at."

"Oh, that's the other half—but the ability to wait, to lurk, to go unnoticed until I can make my shot, that's all part of it, too. After all, don't you have superhuman speed and agility even when you don't have a sword in your hand? Aren't there things you can do without a blade?"

"I suppose," Breaker agreed, remembering the women he had bedded over the past few months, and how they had reacted. How did *that* fit in with the skills needed to slay a Dark Lord?

"And Lore doesn't just remember stories about the Wizard Lords, and Seer can do more than tell us where the Wizard Lord is, and Babble can understand every language there is as well as speak it, and knows all the true names—we all have more than one skill, more than one *ler* bound to us."

"I suppose."

For a moment the two of them were silent, contemplating one another; then the Archer said, "So then, we're agreed that the Wizard Lord must die, and you don't mind if I take care of it?"

Breaker hesitated. "The Seer says we need to find the others, first." It occurred to him to wonder just why he was so willing to yield to her in this, when they were nominally equals, but he knew why—she was his senior in every way, and knew things he did not. She had decades of experience, while he was not yet twenty. And she reminded him of the women he had obeyed back in Mad Oak; he deferred to her without thinking about it.

The Archer frowned. "Oh, I suppose she's right. How very tedious—but we want to do things properly." The frown vanished. "And this means we'll meet the Beauty, doesn't it? That should be pleasant—I've always wondered what she really looks like."

Breaker started. "You don't know? Haven't you met her?"

"No, I haven't. Have you?"

"No—but I've only been the Swordsman for a few months."

"And I've only been the Archer for . . . oh, I suppose it's seven years, now. Not so very long, at any rate, and the Beauty keeps to herself. I've met Lore and Seer and Babble and Boss, but until today I hadn't met *you,* and I haven't met the Thief or the Beauty."

"You'd met the Old Swordsman, though."

"Blade? Oh, once or twice. Not often."

"But not the Thief or the Beauty?"

"No. They don't . . . well, I don't know what the story is, really. Maybe they're supposed to remain hidden, so the Wizard Lord won't know who they are and they can take him by surprise."

"But he can find all of us, just as the Seer can, I thought. I mean, he's the *Wizard Lord*—he knows where *everybody* is. It goes with the job."

"Probably. I don't know."

"He knows where we are right now. Everyone knowing who we are—I wonder about that," Breaker said. "I mean, wouldn't it be better if we could take the Wizard Lord by surprise?"

"Oh, I . . ."

The Archer's reply was interrupted by a man emerging from the tavern, calling, "Swordsman? Are you . . . hey! The Archer! You're the Archer, aren't you?"

The Archer sighed and acknowledged his identity, and the two men allowed themselves to be herded inside, questioned, studied, toasted, and admired. Later in the evening the Archer demonstrated his skill by putting a dozen arrows, one after the other, through an iron ring swinging on the end of a string; when the performance was over he explained quietly to Breaker that quite aside from satisfying the locals' demands for a display of magical skill, this fulfilled the daily ritual the *ler* demanded of him—he didn't need to spend an hour in practice, but was required to hit twelve difficult targets with missiles of one sort or another.

"Sometimes I just toss pebbles, or other things," he said, "but in that case the targets need to be *very* difficult."

Breaker nodded, and wondered what demands were made on the other Chosen, but then the townsfolk came roaring up to him demanding a display of *his* prowess.

Well after midnight the five of them were at last permitted to retreat to the special compound where the town's visitors could spend the night without being possessed by the local *ler* as they slept, and where they could speak more privately. No ordinary inn or guesthouse was available in Seven Sides because the town's spirits, rather than merely sending dreams into sleeping minds, had a habit of animating sleeping bodies and using them to act out their favorite tales of olden times. The presence of strangers meant the possibility of new and dangerous stories—the *ler* sometimes got carried away, and people often awoke to find they had sustained bruises and scars reenacting ancient battles. The presence of a swordsman and an archer—well, no one wanted the Chosen sleeping in the village itself.

Breaker shuddered as they made their way across the compound yard to the guesthouses, not at the habits of the local *ler,* nor at the memory of Stoneslope or the prospect of confronting the Wizard Lord in a battle to the death, but merely at the feel of his environment; the air in this place was cool and dead. The village's *ler* not only did not trouble sleeping visitors here, they did not enter at all, and sealed the area off from any other spirits that might seep in. As a result the entire compound was lifeless and inert; the dirt underfoot was bare and packed hard, unbroken by any trace of green. The air was still; the half-dozen little cottages were dull and dim, with no bright colors nor the slightest glint of light.

Breaker had never before experienced lifeless surroundings, and he did not like the sensation—or rather, the eerie *lack* of sensation—at all.

"I wonder whether the Wizard Lord can hear us *here,*" the Archer said.

"Probably," Breaker said, trying to distract himself. "Isn't a wizard's magic independent of place?"

"But still, he works his will by commanding *ler,* like any priest or wizard, and there are no *ler* here."

"There are *ler* here," the Scholar corrected. "There are the *ler* we brought in with us, the *ler* bound to us by the talismans of the Chosen. And the Wizard Lord can send *his ler* here, as well."

"We might notice them a little more easily," the Seer said. "There are no others to confuse the matter."

"I see no sign of them," the Archer said.

"I hear almost nothing," the Speaker said, looking about with the calmest expression that Breaker had ever seen on her face, plainly visible even in the faint moonlight. "This place is so *quiet.* No plants speak, the earth is silent . . ."

"It's a dead place," the Seer said.

"Yes. I love it," the Speaker said. "I have a small place at home that is sealed away and lifeless, but it's smaller, and the voices from outside can still be heard faintly. Here it's so quiet! I have been here before, but not for some time, and I had forgotten how pleasant it is."

"Pleasant? It's . . . it's *dreadful,*" the Seer said, as she reached the door of the first guesthouse and stopped.

"It's strange, certainly," Breaker said, stepping up to the second doorway.

"And it's irrelevant, isn't it?" the Archer asked, as he neared the third. "Can we get down to business now?"

"Business?" the Scholar asked, pausing between Breaker and the Archer. "Do we have business to attend to?"

"Don't we?" the Archer asked. "I thought you four wanted to discuss whether or not to kill the Wizard Lord—and how to go about it."

"He has to die," the Seer said. "He destroyed an entire town. But we can't act without all eight of us, so there's no need to discuss anything until we find Boss, and the Thief, and the Beauty."

"Why do we need all eight?" the Archer asked. "There are five of us here; if we all agree then that's a majority, and we can get on with it."

"We need the Leader, at the very least," the Scholar said. "After all, he's meant to *lead* us."

"We must all agree," the Seer said.

"Why?" the Archer insisted.

"The Old Swordsman didn't tell me we needed to be unanimous," Breaker agreed.

"If there are only five, the Wizard Lord can kill us all and still have enough magic to rule," the Seer said.

"Can he?" the Archer asked.

"I wouldn't say it's certain," the Scholar said. "We don't have much precedent, since every previous Dark Lord who slew any of the Chosen was removed from power soon afterward. If he killed us, the remaining Chosen and the Council of Immortals would certainly want to remove him, and powerful as the Wizard Lord is, I don't know that he could defeat the entire Council with a mere three-eighths of his magic available."

"Are we all agreed that he must die, though?"

"I take it that young Sword told you about Stoneslope?" the Seer said.

"He did—not that it really matters; I've been willing to kill this Wizard Lord for years, just on general principles. I became the world's greatest archer to slay Dark Lords, not just to win wagers."

"We'll see what Boss says," the Seer replied. "If he thinks six of us are enough then we'll go without the Thief or the Beauty, but I want the Leader to guide us, to devise our approach. I don't want to just walk into the Wizard Lord's stronghold and say, 'Hello, we've come to kill you.' I want a plan."

"When he sticks his face out of his tower I could put an arrow through his eye from a nice safe distance," the Archer said. "How's that for a plan?"

"A little rudimentary," the Scholar said. "What constitutes a safe distance with a wizard whose power extends over all of Barokan?"

"We'll talk to the Leader," the Seer said.

"You know, *you* aren't Boss," the Archer said. "You're the eldest here, but all the same, you're not in charge. What if the rest of us don't want to take the time to find him?"

"He's in the Midlands," the Seer said. "It's not that far."

"But why should we bother? Why not go straight to the Wizard Lord *now,* before he has time to prepare?"

"He's had five years to prepare. He must have known when he destroyed Stoneslope that we would find out and come after him eventually. We need to prepare as much as *we* can."

"You're scared," the Archer said, pointing a finger at the Seer.

For a moment no one spoke; then the Seer said, "Of *course* I'm scared—I felt the terror his victims felt in Stoneslope, and some of it stayed with me. And even without that, I'd be scared. If you weren't a fool you would be, too. We're planning to kill the *Wizard Lord,* Bow. To kill a man—that's a grave responsibility to begin with, and *this* particular man is dangerous and powerful. We saw what he did to Stoneslope, and it was horrific—you have no idea how bad it was. Yes, if he kills us he'll be terrifically weakened, and he'll be slain anyway, but *he may not care*—he may kill us anyway. He's mad, he must be, to do what he did to his own hometown, and that means he may not have the sense to not kill us. If he has *any* sense he'll abdicate, give up the talismans and tell the Council to choose a new Wizard Lord, and retire, and if he did that we would have to let him live—and I pray to all the *ler* that he does that, and soon, so that we don't have to fight him."

"You're giving him time to realize it's hopeless," Breaker said.

"Yes, I am—that, and I do want Boss to help us. He's the Chosen Leader—he has magic, just like the rest of us, but *his* magic is in planning and scheming and improvising, persuading people to help us and directing our attack. I want that magic on our side, to give us every advantage we can get. I don't want to die. I don't want to kill anyone if I don't need to, either."

"The third, fourth, and seventh Dark Lords all retired peacefully when confronted with their sins and failures," the Scholar said. "Our current lord hasn't chosen that path yet, but it really would be better for all concerned if he did."

"It would be even better if you people just went home and dropped this whole mission," a high-pitched, inhuman voice said; Breaker started, and looked down to see an immense rat sitting up on its haunches by the corner of the nearest guesthouse. "I'm not going to hurt anyone else who doesn't deserve it; all my old enemies are already dead."

"So you say now," the Seer said. "Get away, and let us talk!" She swung her walking stick at the rat, which dodged and vanished into the shadows between houses.

"How much did he hear?" Breaker asked, worried.

"Not much," the Seer said. "He manifested in that rat just as you said I was giving him time to see it's hopeless."

"Is he gone now?"

"Yes. For the moment."

"He's not going to surrender peacefully," the Archer said. "I vote we go kill him as quickly as we can, and get it over with."

"And I say we need the Leader's magic," the Seer replied. "I vote we go to the Midlands and find Boss."

"Lore?" the Archer said, turning to the Scholar.

"I think he may yet see reason," the Scholar said. "I vote with the Seer."

"There is no reason to see," the Speaker said, startling Breaker. "Kill him now."

"The deciding vote is yours, Sword," the Seer said, turning to Breaker.

"I . . ." Breaker hesitated, looking at the Archer and the Speaker. This was his chance to get on with it, to get it over with sooner—but it didn't *feel* right. Perhaps the Leader's presence would remedy that. He turned back to the Seer. "I think we should find the Leader. What you say about his magic—that's true and important. We should talk to him before we rush in."

"Three to two," the Scholar said.

"I hope you won't do anything foolish, like going in alone," the Seer said to the Archer.

The Archer sighed. "No," he said. "I'll behave. But no dawdling—tomorrow we head for the Midlands by the fastest route, agreed?"

"Agreed."

"And so to bed," the Scholar said. "Let us get as much sleep as we can before we go!"

"I'll miss this place," the Speaker said. Then she stepped back and vanished into one of the guesthouses.

A moment later all five had gone to their separate beds, and the only sign of life in the *ler*less compound was a lone rat, sniffing at the foundations of the Seer's chosen shelter.

Breaker's dreams that night were vague and jumbled, unguided by *ler,* but he awoke with a fading memory of the bone-strewn hillside in Stoneslope and was unusually quiet for much of the morning.

[19]

They made good time on their northward journey, but to little initial avail; to their extreme annoyance the Seer reported one morning, as they marched across a broad and peaceful meadow behind a taciturn guide, that the Leader had packed up and headed east, moving farther away.

"What does that idiot think he's doing?" the Archer complained.

"He probably has no idea we're looking for him," the Seer said. "After all, how could he know? And better to the east than into the western marshes, or out to the islands."

"He can't go *too* far," Breaker said. "Not to the east—he'll reach the cliffs."

"Is there any way we can *tell* him we need to talk to him?" the Archer asked. "The way the Speaker sent me that message, perhaps?"

"I don't know of anything I can—no, be still—I don't know of any spirit I might convince to go so far," the Speaker said. "Even if I spoke a bird's true name, the compulsion would not last long enough to cover such a distance." She was walking ahead of the other four Chosen, close behind their hired guide, with her head down; every so often she started as some part of the surrounding landscape spoke to her, unheard by the others.

"Perhaps we could find a wizard who could fly a message to him?" the Scholar suggested.

"There are no wizards any closer to us than Boss is," the Seer reported.

"But isn't there some way we can contact them magically?" Breaker asked.

"I tried, days ago," the Seer said. "I had a talisman that was supposed to summon a wizard I know. No response."

"We have to go as far as Winterhome to find the Beauty anyway, don't we?" Breaker asked. "He won't go any farther than that, will he?"

"You mean up on the plateau, above the cliffs?" The Seer shrugged. "I can't imagine why he would. If he does, though, we can't follow him—our magic won't work outside Varagan."

"We *could* follow him," the Scholar said. "We'd just need to use more mundane methods."

"*I* don't know anything about tracking," the Seer said. "Do you?"

"Well, a little," the Scholar said. "It does come up in certain stories, of course."

"Why would he go somewhere *his* magic doesn't work?" the Archer asked. "He won't go up the cliffs."

"We'll probably catch up with him in Winterhome," Breaker said. "And the Beauty, too."

"You're really looking forward to getting a look at her, aren't you?" the Archer asked, grinning. He jabbed Breaker with an elbow as the two of them drew slightly ahead of the Scholar and the Seer. "Well, maybe we will, and maybe it'll be worth it. We'll see."

"I'd like to see what she looks like, of course," Breaker agreed, as he trudged onward, "but mostly I want to get on with business. We need to remove the Wizard Lord, and the Seer says we can't do that without the Leader."

The Archer glanced back over his shoulder, then leaned closer and said quietly, "You know, we don't need to do what the Seer says. We could turn around right now, just the two of us, and go kill the bastard. We don't need to go all the way to Winterhome just so Boss can tell us what we already know."

Breaker glanced at their guide, wondering if the bent little man had heard the Archer's words. "He'd see us coming, and probably kill us both," the Swordsman said. "The Seer is right about that."

"We aren't that easy to kill."

"We aren't wizards, either. I agree he needs to be removed, but I'd like to survive the process."

"But we're the Chosen! He won't kill us—it would destroy his magic."

Breaker sighed, and picked up his pace—he thought he would prefer the guide's company to the Archer's, and in any case the group was becoming uncomfortably spread out. "He's a human being—or at least he used to be, I suppose it's not quite so certain anymore, but he still acts like one. If he's got a choice between being killed *right now,* or giving up his magic and living a while longer and maybe talking his way out of it altogether—well, I don't expect him to stand there playing target."

"But you think it'll work any better with eight of us, instead of two or three?" the Archer demanded, hurrying after him.

"I don't know," Breaker admitted. "I'm beginning to wonder how our predecessors killed those five Dark Lords—how did it ever get that far? Why didn't they all resign, rather than fight to the death?"

"Three *did* resign," the Scholar reminded him, from behind the two. "I think it's safe to conclude that the five who died were either completely irrational in their madness, or convinced they could win the battle somehow."

"Or they were caught by surprise, and dead before they could react," the Archer suggested.

"That might be," the Scholar conceded. "Certainly, the Dark Lord of Kamith t'Daru was caught off-guard."

"That's the approach I'd prefer," the Archer said. "An arrow through the eye before he even knows we're near!"

"We noticed," Breaker said dryly, as he approached the guide. "But the way it's supposed to operate is that the eight of us work as a team—a band of heroes, not a handful of assassins." As he spoke, Breaker wished that the five of them felt more like a team; he hoped that the Leader's presence would bring them together. That was perhaps his strongest reason for voting to find Boss before turning back toward the Galbek Hills.

"I don't see much of a difference," the Archer said.

"In many languages there *is* no difference," the Speaker murmured.

Breaker glanced at her, startled. He found that very strange—how could a language not distinguish between defenders and predators?

"Really," the Archer said, "if the idea is simply to remove a wizard who threatens all of Barokan, does it matter how it's done? Do we really need all this rigmarole gathering the Chosen?"

"That's how it works," Breaker said. "That's the system that protects us all. The *ler* guard the world. The priests and wizards control the *ler* and guard us from any that turn hostile, the priests in our homelands, the wizards in the wider world. The Wizard Lord protects us against bad weather and bad men and any wizards who go bad, and the Chosen protect us when a Wizard Lord goes bad. That's how the Council of Immortals set it up, and it's why we're all here instead of safe at home with our families."

The guide, who had apparently been listening to at least this speech, asked quietly, "And what happens if the Chosen go bad?"

"That's why there are eight of us," the Scholar said. "If there's just one of us who goes mad, then the Wizard Lord or the other Chosen can deal with him."

"And what if all eight of you go mad?"

"How likely is it that *eight* of us would go mad?" the Seer responded, catching up.

"If you travel together often, and go astray on certain routes, it's not that unlikely," the guide said.

"We *don't* usually travel together," Breaker said—but he glanced around uneasily at the surrounding forest, aware that the spirits of the trees were watching him, and that some of them might well be just as mad and just as predatory as the Mad Oak back home.

"The five of you are here," the guide said.

"And this is the first time in the twenty years I've been the Scholar that we've had so many together," the Scholar said.

The guide glanced at him, startled.

"Then—you really *are* going to kill the Wizard Lord? This isn't just . . . But why? What did he do?"

"He wiped out an entire town," Breaker said. "He killed every man, woman, and child in it, deliberately."

The guide looked from face to face; the Speaker was listening to something off to the side that the others couldn't hear and didn't meet his eyes, but the Scholar and the Archer nodded.

"I didn't see it myself," the Archer admitted, "but they swear to it."

"I did see it," the Scholar said. "So did Seer and Sword. We saw the bones and the burnt-out ruins, and felt the lingering spirits of the dead crying out for justice."

"Why did he do it?" the guide asked, obviously frightened. His voice dropped to a whisper. "Is he *mad*?"

"Revenge," Breaker said. "He wanted revenge."

"What?" The guide's expression was so astonished Breaker almost laughed. "Who could have harmed the *Wizard Lord* so badly that he needed vengeance?"

"He killed the people who had teased him as a child," the Scholar said.

"And everyone else in town, while he was at it," Breaker said.

"That's insane!"

"That's why we're going to kill him," the Archer agreed.

"And . . ." The guide paused and looked around, then leaned forward and whispered, "Does he know you know?"

"He knows," the Seer said.

"Then—then isn't it dangerous? Isn't he likely to try to kill *you* before you kill *him*?"

"Quite possibly," the Scholar said. "Though so far he hasn't tried."

"Am *I* in danger, for guiding you?"

The Chosen glanced at one another. None of them had considered that possibility.

"I don't know," Breaker said. "I hope not."

"But I could be?"

"He knows that if he harms any more innocents he'll only make it worse," the Archer said.

"But you're already planning to kill him! How could it be worse?"

"Oh, so far we'd settle for his resignation," the Scholar said. "If he kills any more people, we may not give him that option."

"And . . . why are you going north? Isn't his tower to the south, in the Galbek Hills? You just *came* from there!"

"We need to find the other three Chosen," the Seer said.

"Or at least the Leader," Breaker said.

"You know where he is?"

"I do, yes," said the Seer. "And right now he's moving east, while we're just standing here talking. Can we move on?"

"Oh!" The guide started. "Oh, of course." He looked around. "We need to bear to the right up ahead to avoid the *ler* of the ancient ants . . ." He started walking.

The five Chosen followed.

Six days later they were in a town called Dust Market, going through the cleansing ritual that the local *ler* required before permitting them to stay the night, when the Seer said, "He's gone past her—Stealth is now closer than Boss."

"Stealth?" Breaker asked, as one of the naked priestesses poured a pitcher of scented water over his head.

"The Thief," the Scholar explained. "Seer calls her Stealth."

"Ah." Breaker would have nodded, but he was afraid he would get water in his eyes. "Lore, Boss, Blade, Babble, Bow, Stealth—but she's just Seer."

The Scholar shrugged. "Why not? And Blade is gone—you're Sword now."

"What do you call the Beauty?"

"I've never met her," the Seer said. "I call her the Beauty."

That startled Breaker. "You've never met her?"

"Not the present one. I knew the last one; we called her . . . well, we had a name for her. It wasn't a nice one, and I regret it now."

"How long has this one been Chosen?"

The Seer glanced at the Scholar, but had to wait until most of the just-poured water had run off before he could reply.

"Twenty-three years," Lore said.

"That long? And you've never met her?"

"*I've* met her," the Scholar said. "She's been Chosen a little longer than I have. Not long after I became the Scholar she found me to ask a few questions about Barokan's history, and about the Uplanders. But I haven't seen her since."

"I haven't met her," the Seer said.

"I have spoken with her memories, but never seen her face," the Speaker said.

Breaker wasn't sure how literally to take that; he glanced at the Archer, but then remembered that he had already admitted never meeting the Beauty.

"I'm surprised you haven't," he said.

"Don't be," the Seer said. "It's deliberate. I don't *want* to meet her—but we'll probably have to, now."

"I don't understand."

"You don't need to. But you do need to help us decide—now that the Thief is closer than the Leader, do we go on chasing him, or do we talk to her first?"

"You said you just wanted to get Boss and his magic," the Archer said, as the priestesses began distributing towels.

"Historically, the Thief has sometimes been essential," the Scholar pointed out. "The Thief's magical talents with locks and stealth have been very useful in two of the five killings our predecessors carried out, and in the case of the Dark Lord of Goln Vleys, it's possible that the Swordsman might not have ever managed to gut him at all had the Thief not safely opened the seals on the fortress gate."

Breaker swallowed. Although he had become accustomed to talking about killing the Wizard Lord, every so often a particular turn of phrase would bring it home to him once again that in a few months at most he was almost certainly going to be trying to kill a *person,* that he was planning to stick his sword right through someone. Yes, the Wizard Lord was a special case, being a wizard and a mass murderer, but he was still a human being.

"I have never heard the Thief's voice," the Speaker said. "I cannot judge her worth."

"I haven't talked to Stealth in, oh, fourteen or fifteen years," the Seer said. "That would have been just before you were Chosen, Babble. She doesn't travel much."

"Is she along our route?" Breaker asked.

"We don't know where Boss is going," the Seer said. "How can we tell?"

"Well, if we head directly for Winterhome, how far out of our way would the Thief's home be?"

"Not far," the Seer said. "Not far at all."

"Then why not? We'll probably want her to join us eventually."

"Sword has a point," the Archer said.

"Then we'll go there next," the Seer agreed. She accepted a towel and began drying her hair as she got to her feet.

"Agreed."

[20]

The farmhouse stood well off the road, surrounded by bright yellow flowers of a variety Breaker did not recognize; the five Chosen approached cautiously.

"I would have thought a thief would live in town," Breaker said, as the others slipped through the gate he held open. "In the largest town she could find, in fact."

"She's here," the Seer said, as she stepped through. Her tone did not allow further argument, and Breaker shrugged as he latched the gate behind her. He turned to see the Archer trotting unhesitatingly up to the door, and hurried to follow.

The others were still hastening along the graveled walk when the Archer rapped loudly on the blue-painted door.

No one answered at first, and the five of them had time to cluster around the threshold before the Archer grew impatient and knocked again.

This time Breaker heard a faint voice from within, and the Speaker announced, "She's coming. Her feet are heavy on the floorboards, and the spirits of home and hearth . . ."

She was interrupted by the rattle of the latch, and the door swung open to reveal a rather tired-looking woman in apron and cap. She was of moderate height, taller than the Speaker or the Seer, and thin; the thick curls that escaped her white cap were straw-colored, her skin pale. Her ears appeared oversized to Breaker, but he knew that was exaggerated by the way her tucked-back hair pushed them forward, and by the narrowness of her face. Her dress was a faded blue that did not quite match her eyes, the apron stained a dozen shades of off-white and gray.

She blinked at the five visitors—or perhaps at the bright sunlight—and said, "Yes?"

The Archer started to speak, but Breaker cut him off. "Please pardon us for disturbing you, ma'am, but we're looking for someone . . ."

"It's her," the Seer interrupted. "She's the Thief."

The woman blinked again. "The what?"

"You're the Thief," the Seer said.

The woman stared at her five visitors—the two strong young men and the ordinary older man, the sturdy white-haired woman, and the tiny dark-haired woman who seemed to be whispering silently to herself. "I haven't stolen anything!" she protested. "If you've been listening to that silly redheaded boy and his gossip, I'll have you know that he tells so many lies the *ler* themselves despair of him! Ask his mother, she'll tell you!"

"We haven't spoken to any redheaded boy," the Seer said, "and we didn't say you'd stolen anything. I said you're the Thief—the world's greatest thief, one of the eight Chosen, one of the heroes who are charged with protecting Varagan from the Wizard Lords."

"I am no such thing," she said. "Now, go away." She tried to close the door.

The Archer thrust his foot in the way. "If the Seer says you are the Thief, then I believe you are the Thief," he said. "How you might not *know* that baffles me, though."

She glared at him, then turned that withering stare on the rest of them. "I am not a thief," she said. "I may have made certain foolish decisions when I was young, and agreed to things I shouldn't have, but that was a long time ago and I know better now, and I am *not* a thief. I have not kept anything that belongs to another, and I have nothing here that isn't mine by right."

"No one said you had," Breaker said mildly. "If you'd prefer a more diplomatic phrasing, we believe you are the one chosen to be the best in the world at those skills associated with housebreaking and thievery, just as I am the one chosen to be the best in the world at wielding a sword. That does not mean that you have stolen anything, any more than my own title means I have killed anyone."

"You know who you are," the Seer said wearily. "Arguing semantics won't change that."

"I am Merrilin tarak Dolin, wife of Sezen piri Oldrav, mother of

Kilila tesh Barag and Garant asa Dorhals," she said defiantly. "I have a name and a place here, and they have nothing to do with any legends about Chosen Heroes."

"But you are *also* the bearer of the talisman of thievery," the Seer said.

The Thief snorted. "'Bearer'? I have it somewhere, put away in a drawer—I don't carry it around the house with me."

"But you *have* it," the Archer said. "That makes you one of the Chosen."

"It makes me someone who did something foolish when I was seventeen, and was too embarrassed to admit it and pass the silly thing on," Merrilin retorted. "I should have gotten rid of it years ago."

Breaker remembered his own unpleasant experience back in Mad Oak when he had left his talisman behind, and wondered whether the Thief *could* get rid of it—had she ever tried? Was the illness he had felt something shared by all the Chosen, or unique to the Swordsman?

"Your pardon, ma'am," the Scholar said, "but might we take a moment of your time to discuss this, please? It's a matter of some concern to us all. Might we come in?"

"No. Garant's taking his nap."

"Then I'm afraid we'll have to wait out here until you speak with us."

She glared at him, then looked down at the Archer's foot. "When my husband gets home . . ." she began.

"Your husband is not going to interfere," the Seer said. "Not only are there five of us to the two of you, but we include the world's greatest swordsman, and the world's greatest archer! We are equipped to slay the Wizard Lord himself; do you really think your husband frightens us?"

She stared at the Seer for a moment, then glanced back over her shoulder, then looked out at her unwelcome visitors again. "Why can't you just leave me alone?" she asked.

"If you speak with us, that may well be explained," the Scholar said.

"Your children will be safe," the Speaker said, startling everyone with her high-pitched singsong. "*Ler* will watch over them. Garant will sleep an hour and a moment more, and Kilila's game with her dolls will occupy her even longer. The *ler* will see to it."

The aproned woman stared at her. "Who are *you*?" she demanded.

"I am Gliris Tala Danria shul Keredi bav Sedenir, who hears all tongues and answers when I must." The Speaker jerked her head suddenly in the middle of this reply, but completed the sentence without interruption.

"The Speaker," the Seer said. "And I am the Seer, and he is the Scholar, and he is the Archer, and he is the Swordsman."

"You're *all* Chosen?"

"Yes."

She frowned, glanced back into the house again, then at the Speaker. Then she reached a decision and stepped out onto the path, pushing Breaker and the Archer aside and closing the door behind her.

"We can speak here," she said.

"Good. We've come because we have learned something terrible . . ."

Merrilin ignored her and asked the Speaker, "How do you know that, about my children and the *ler*? Are you a priestess?"

"I am the Chosen Speaker of All Tongues," the Speaker replied. "I can hear the *ler,* and speak to them—but I have no power over them save the power words give us all over each other. In this case the spirits of your home and hearth were troubled by our presence, and wish our business here resolved quickly, one way or another, and agreed to soothe and guard your children so that we might accomplish that."

"So you can't make the *ler* watch over them indefinitely?"

"No."

"Then how can you expect me to leave? Who would care for my children?"

"I am . . . no, no, no. Let me . . . no. I am not the one, Merrilin tarak Dolin kal Toria bal Siris, who expects you to leave."

The Seer and Archer snapped their heads around to stare at the Speaker, but neither Breaker nor the Scholar was surprised to hear this.

"Good," Merrilin said. Then she turned to the Seer. "So why have you come?"

The Seer quickly regained her composure, and said, "The Wizard Lord has done something terrible—the Scholar and I realized this a few weeks ago, and we and the Swordsman investigated and saw the proof. While we were there we heard the Wizard Lord confess his guilt through the voice of a crow, so there is no possible doubt. We're gathering all the

Chosen, so that we can confront the Wizard Lord and demand his abdication—and if he refuses, we will slay him, as we are bound to do by our oaths."

"I am bound by oath to stay by my husband and raise our children," Merrilin said. "I think that takes precedence over any oath I swore when I was just a silly girl."

"But you did swear!"

"Because I didn't think it meant anything. I thought it would be . . . I don't know, exciting, I suppose, to be one of the Chosen. One of eight in all the world, out of all the millions of people in Barokan—I thought I would be *special*!"

"You *are* special," the Seer insisted.

"Oh, indeed I am," Merrilin agreed. "If I do not take something that does not belong to me undetected, or open a lock without a key, or enter someone else's home uninvited and unseen, or perform any of a dozen other sordid acts three times each and every day, then I am struck down by headaches and chills and cramps. How *very* special! Thank all the *ler* that slipping my children's toys from their places is sufficient thievery, and nothing prevents me from then returning those toys to their rightful owners!"

"You must practice your skills," the Archer said. "So do we all. I must shoot at a dozen targets a day without a miss, Sword here must put in an hour of practice—your burden is not so great as all that!"

"And what do I get for my practice? Skills I cannot use! I am no thief; why should I take what isn't mine? You, Archer, you can boast of your skill, and show everyone what you can do—but what can I do? If I admit to being the Chosen Thief, everyone begins to check pockets and purses and locks, and no one will come near me. It doesn't matter if I promise not to steal, no matter how I swear it—I am the world's greatest thief, a master of subterfuge and deception! I cannot be trusted for a moment. And of course, by the time I realized this, my childhood friends all knew who and what I had become, and then all of Turnip Corner knew, and I was an outcast in my own home!"

"That's unfortunate . . ." the Scholar began.

"So I left," she said. "I told them I was going to travel, as the Chosen are said to do, and I left, and I came to Quince Market and told them I was an orphan and made a new life for myself, and I met Sezen, and he wooed me and wed me, and I'm *happy* here!"

"Deceiving your husband?" the Seer asked.

"No!" Merrilin turned to face her. "I told him, before we were married. He knows all about it—and he doesn't care. He loves me, no matter what silly oaths I may have taken, and that's why I'm staying right here, with him and with our children. You can go kill the Wizard Lord if you want, but you'll have to do it without my help."

"Why haven't you passed on the role, if you find it unsuitable?" the Scholar asked.

"And inflict it on someone else? Anyone who can be trusted with it wouldn't want it, and anyone who wants it shouldn't have it. And there are times—do you have any children?"

"Not that I know of," the Scholar replied.

"Well, there are times when it *is* useful for a mother to know how to open things, how to take things from their owners, and so on. But when the children are grown, then I *will* find a wizard and choose someone else, and free myself of this curse."

"The Wizard Lord slaughtered an entire town," the Seer said angrily. "Men, women, and children, down to the babes in their cradles. Your so-called curse can help us avenge them, and prevent him from ever doing it again."

Merrilin hesitated.

"He did?"

"Yes."

"Where?"

"Stoneslope, in the Galbek Hills."

"I never heard of it."

No one had an immediate response to that, and after a moment Merrilin added, "It isn't any of my business. I never heard of this place. It's all a long way off."

"But you're one of the Chosen," the Archer said. "We're supposed to protect *everyone* from the Wizard Lord."

"You said he *already* destroyed this town."

The Archer looked to Breaker for support.

"He did," Breaker said. "And we need to avenge them and make sure he never does it again somewhere else. Next time it might be my home, or yours."

"There's no reason for him to hurt anyone here," Merrilin said. "We never bothered him. I've never even *seen* him. Why would he bother us?"

"Because he's mad," the Archer said. "There's no telling *what* he'll do!"

"Who says so?"

"*We* do!"

"And why should I believe you?"

"Because we're the Chosen! And so are you!"

"I don't want to be, anymore."

"Then you should pass the talisman on," the Seer said. "Find a wizard and arrange it."

" 'Find a wizard'? Where? I haven't seen a wizard since I first accepted that thing! And I can't go looking for one; I have a family to care for."

That caught Breaker's attention—she hadn't seen a wizard in all those years? While it was true that wizards seemed to be very scarce in the Midlands, hadn't the Old Swordsman said that wizards checked on the Chosen every so often?

If so, they presumably must have missed one.

And Breaker hadn't seen a wizard since the day after he became the Chosen Swordsman; was that significant? Wizards seemed less common than he had expected.

But that had nothing to do with the Thief's reluctance to join them.

For a moment the five of them stared at her; then the Scholar said, "The next time we meet a wizard, we'll tell him you'd like to hand on the responsibility. I'm sure the Council will send someone to attend to it."

"I . . ." Merrilin hesitated, looking from one to the next, then shrugged. "Good. Do that, then. But I'm not coming with you."

"Fair enough," the Scholar said.

"No, it isn't!" the Archer protested. "She has an obligation! A role to fill!"

"I think we can manage without her," the Scholar replied. "The Chosen have before, after all."

The Archer had opened his mouth to argue, but then stopped. "They have?" he said.

"Three times," the Scholar said. "The first two Dark Lords were deposed before the first Thief was chosen, and in the three hundred and fifth year of the Wizard Lords, the Dark Lord of Kamith t'Daru killed the Thief before the Chosen had gathered to oppose him."

"He did?"

"You see? I can't risk it!" Merrilin said. "Now, go away, all of you!" She turned to go inside.

"You knew this might happen when you first agreed," the Seer called angrily.

"No, I did not," Merrilin retorted over her shoulder. "We had a wise and honorable Wizard Lord, and there hadn't been a bad one in a hundred years! I didn't think there would ever be another Dark Lord. If I had, I'd never have let myself be talked into anything—and I am not letting myself be talked into anything now. Now, go away, all of you!" She stamped into her house and slammed the door.

The five of them stood for a moment; then the Archer asked, "Should I go in after her?"

The Scholar, rather than replying, asked the Seer, "Where is Boss?"

The Seer blinked, then looked at him, and pointed to the east. "That way," she said. "Near Winterhome."

"Is he with the Beauty, then?"

The Seer shook her head. "No. But they're not far apart."

"Then perhaps we should just go find Boss, and if he thinks we need the Thief, we can stop here on the way to the Galbek Hills. It *is* almost on the way, isn't it?"

The Seer glanced to the southwest—toward the Wizard Lord, Breaker was sure—and then to the east. She nodded.

"Almost," she agreed. "I think you're right. Let Boss decide."

"Then I shouldn't go in?" the Archer asked, audibly disappointed.

"No, of course not," Breaker said. "It's her home. She has children in there—you'd scare them half to death. And we can't *force* her to help—how would *that* work? She'd probably just get some of us killed." He nodded at the others. "Seer's right. Let the Leader decide what to do about her."

"I don't like it," the Archer said.

"I thought you were the one who said the two of us should go kill the Wizard Lord by ourselves!"

"I . . . well, you . . . Um." The Archer considered that for a moment. He grimaced. "Fine, then. Let's go to Winterhome. Where do we find a guide for the next leg?"

[21]

By the time they first glimpsed the pennants of Winterhome the Eastern Cliffs towered far above them and seemed to block out half the sky ahead. The sun had not become visible until well after dawn that morning, and they had begun the day's walk in the shadow of the cliffs.

The experience was a strange one—predawn gloom on the ground, but a bright blue sky above. Breaker had seen similar conditions down by the river below Mad Oak sometimes, when he wandered through the ridge's shadow at just the right time, but there it had been just a matter of minutes before the sun broke over the ridgetop and full day arrived. Here, the sun did not appear until well after the sky had turned blue and the western world come alight.

And when at last the sun did clear the clifftops it was as if the travelers had suddenly been flung from dawn to midday—the temperature seemed to soar, and the whole world around them to blaze up in color and light, while the still-shaded terrain ahead was plunged into darkness as their eyes adjusted.

Their guide on this route was a tall, thin man who wore an entire crest of white *ara* feathers rather than a mere decorated hat, the feathers' curling tips fluttering above his head as he marched up the gentle but increasingly rocky slope that seemed to extend endlessly eastward. When Breaker glimpsed the flutter of a pennant deep in the shadows ahead he thought at first that it was one of the guide's feathers, but then he realized that what he saw moving was red and gold, not white.

"Is that a bird?" he asked, pointing.

"It's a flag," the Archer said. "There are more of them farther on, see?"

"Pennants," the Scholar said, peering into the gloom. "The Uplanders use them to mark each clan's holdings."

"Are the Uplanders here, then?" Breaker glanced around; the weather was pleasantly cool, but definitely not yet winter. The world around them was still more green than brown, and a few late wildflowers bloomed here and there.

"No—they would still be atop the cliffs, though perhaps the earliest are making their way toward us. The pennants are so they can find the right place when they come down for the winter."

"Don't they get tattered and faded, if they fly constantly from spring to autumn?"

"The Host People take care of them somehow, I suppose."

"Who are the Host People?" the Archer asked, turning. "I know the Uplanders are the people who live atop the cliffs and come down to shelter for the winter, but I've never heard of the Host People."

Breaker wondered where the Archer was from, that he had never heard of the Host People—in Mad Oak everyone knew how even the Uplanders could not survive winters on the plateau, and that the Host People readied Winterhome for them each year.

"Well, look at the place—those buildings the flags are on? Someone has to take care of those the rest of the year," the Scholar explained. "And someone has to set up the markets where the Uplanders buy their supplies, and make everything ready for them, and stock the warehouses and granaries to see them through the winter. That's the Host People. They live in Winterhome year-round."

"Wait a minute." The Archer stopped walking. "You mean this place we're going, Winterhome—it's where the *Uplanders* spend the winter?"

"Yes, of course."

"But I thought they weren't subject to the Wizard Lord! What would Boss and the Beauty be doing there?"

"No, no," the Scholar said. "The *Uplands* aren't subject to the Wizard Lord—his authority stops at the cliffs, just as Barokan does. You're quite right about that. But the Uplanders are subject to the same laws as anyone else in Barokan when they come down here for the winter. Winterhome doesn't get any special treatment—well, no more so than anywhere else; naturally, it has its own *ler* and its own priesthood and so on."

"But . . ." The Archer fell in step beside the Scholar, while Breaker walked on the other side. For a moment he fumbled for words, while the other two men waited.

"The stories I heard as a child," the Archer said finally, "said that the Uplanders had climbed the cliffs to get away from the whole system of priests and priesthoods—that the land of the great plateau doesn't have *ler* the way Barokan does, it's dead and barren, without soul or spirit, and the Uplanders *like* it like that. That's supposed to be why there are no trees up there, just grassland and *ara,* and why *ara* feathers are protection against hostile *ler*—because *ara* are the only living creatures with no *ler* of their own, and the feathers shield them from any *ler* that might want to invade and possess them."

"Yes, I've heard that story, among others," the Scholar agreed. "But I discover that I can't recall the details of any of the accounts that say there are no spirits in the Uplands. I therefore believe there may well be *ler* atop the cliffs, and the Uplanders may well have priests—but they don't speak of these things to outsiders, so I can't say for certain."

"Wouldn't it be easy to tell, though?" Breaker asked. "You've been in a *ler*less place, when we stayed in the guesthouses in Seven Sides; you know what it's like. Couldn't you climb the cliffs and see whether the plateau has that same dead feeling?"

The Scholar looked at him, then looked to the east. He pointed.

"Climb *that*?" he said.

Breaker saw his point—the cliffs loomed over them like a dark wall across the world, impossibly high and forbidding, blotting out the eastern sky. Still, everyone knew there was a way up on the far side of Winterhome, where a portion of the cliff had crumbled and a path had been made. "The Uplanders do it every year," he pointed out.

"The Uplanders have far better reasons than I!"

Breaker was not entirely convinced—after all, the Scholar was supposed to learn everything he could about the entire world. Before he could argue, however, the Scholar turned to the Archer and said, "At any rate, whatever may hold true in the Uplands, the Host People have priests and *ler* just like anyone else, and the Uplanders live by their rules during the winter."

"But if they fled to the Uplands to escape the priests . . ."

"Apparently, if they did, then they found Upland winters to be even worse than priests."

Breaker grimaced. He thought that would depend *which* priests. Presumably the priesthood of the Host People was not particularly dreadful.

"And be glad they are," the Scholar added. "Else we would have no *ara* feathers, nor beaks nor eggs nor meat, nor the hollow bones. The Uplanders bring those down to trade, but I doubt they would bother if they were not coming down to shelter here."

By this time the party was past the customary boundary shrine and approaching the first of several immense buildings. It was constructed with massive stone walls rising for two stories, and a third story of wood and plaster atop that, all beneath a steep overhanging roof; the windows were all shuttered and barred, save for a few on the top floor. A long red pennant bearing an elaborate golden design flew from a pole at the eastern gable; Breaker could see that the heart of the design was a running bird, presumably an *ara*.

And beyond this first structure stood another, similar in outline but different in detail, flying a red banner that showed three golden hawks.

And beyond that was a third, whose pennant bore a crown and spear, and across the road from it a fourth with a dragon banner, and so on, deep into the cliffs' shadows.

And with each of these great buildings, the road in front showed more wear. When at last the sun broke over the clifftops Breaker could see that the road ahead grew ever wider as it climbed the slope to the east, and that it was churned into mud for as far as he could see.

"I would guess preparations are being made for the Uplanders' arrival," the Scholar remarked.

"Boss is still down here, though," the Seer said. "That way." She pointed ahead and to the right.

"What about the Beauty?" the Archer asked.

"That way," the Seer replied, pointing ahead and to the left.

"So they're both staying with the Host People?"

"So it would seem."

"I wonder why?" Breaker said.

"Well, the Beauty has lived here for years," the Seer said. "I have no idea why Boss is here."

"Which one do we find first?" the Archer asked.

"Boss," the Seer replied. "He's the Leader."

The Speaker interrupted her perpetual mumbling to say, "Farash inith Kerra das Bik abba Terrul sinna Oppor carries the talisman of the Leader of the Chosen, but the *ler* say he has never truly led anyone."

"Well, he's never had a *reason* to," the Seer retorted.

"Until now," the Archer said.

"He has used his magic, and called upon the *ler* bound to him," the Speaker said. "He has cajoled and wheedled and deceived, planned and devised, seduced and appeased, ordered and commanded, but never truly led."

"That doesn't sound good," Breaker said uneasily.

"Oh, ignore her," the Seer said. "I've known Boss for ten years, since he wasn't much older than you are, and he's a decent enough man."

Breaker glanced at the Speaker, but having said her piece she was now bent over, hands over her ears, reacting to some other unheard voice by muttering "No, no, never that, no, no, never," endlessly.

He could have interrupted her mumbling and asked her to say more, but as usual, her behavior put him off.

They had been traveling together for some time now, and Breaker knew that she was not insane, despite appearances, but at times it was difficult to remember that. It was hard to believe that she had lived fourteen years under this constant barrage of inhuman chatter without genuinely going mad. Unlike the Archer or himself, the Speaker had no daily task she had to perform to satisfy her *ler;* instead the requirement was that she could never stop hearing them, could not simply learn to ignore them. How she slept was a mystery, how she retained her sanity a much greater one. Breaker knew that he should listen to her when she spoke, but he was never comfortable doing so.

The Seer, with her motherly impatience, seemed much easier to believe—and besides, whether he had ever actually led anyone or not, Boss was the Leader of the Chosen and they were supposed to follow him.

"This way," the Seer said, and Breaker shrugged off the Speaker's words and followed.

Winterhome, he discovered, was huge—but largely empty with the Uplanders gone. There were three streets of the great shelters, each miles long, radiating to the west, southwest, and northwest from a central plaza; to the east of the plaza a gigantic steep slope of broken stone led up toward the only break in the Eastern Cliffs, a trail zigzagging across it. Where most of the world was green and inviting now that the sun was above the cliffs, this slope was mostly reddish brown, though here and there a few patches of moss and lichen showed that the rocks were not utterly lifeless.

To the north and south of the square lay the homes and businesses of the Host People—or at least those who were not employed as live-in caretakers of the clan houses. When the travelers reached the plaza the Seer dismissed their guide, and led the way into the tangle of streets and alleys to the south.

Here, at last, the streets were inhabited, and Breaker got his first real look at the Host People.

He was not particularly impressed; they all wore black from head to toe, with tight black hoods hiding their hair and ears. The few visible women added a black scarf pulled up over their mouths and usually their noses, as well; the men wore bristling beards instead.

The men's garments were tunics and breeches, cut generously, but bound at wrists, elbows, knees, and ankles with black garters to keep their clothing from getting in the way. The women's floor-length robes, on the other hand, were great baggy swirling things, almost tentlike, that were worn loose, without any sort of belt or binding; combined with the hoods and scarves it was impossible to tell what any of the women actually looked like. Wrinkles around the eyes gave some clue as to age, but beyond that all the females were simply interchangeable black shapes of varying size.

In all his travels so far, from Mad Oak to Stoneslope and Seven Sides to Winterhome, Breaker did not think he had ever seen less attractive feminine attire. There had been towns where he was not permitted to see the women at all, and others where women walked the streets stark naked, but never before had he encountered garb so utterly unappealing. He wondered whether this was ordained by the local *ler,* or was a purely human aberration.

"Do you know why the women dress like that?" he asked the Scholar quietly.

"For protection," the Scholar replied. "When the Uplanders come down from the plateau—well, you've got a lot of eager, active young men who are accustomed to roaming freely across wide areas who are suddenly thrust into close quarters with nothing much to occupy their time. They get bored and need outlets for their energy. Add in young women who are outside the protection of their clan system, and you've got a recipe for trouble—everything from rude remarks to outright rape and even murder. Hasty marriages, fatherless children . . ." He shrugged. "Not that those don't happen anyway, of course, but at least they're not common."

"But the women are still there," Breaker protested.

"But the Uplanders can't tell the pretty girls from the grandmothers. Easier to talk to their own women, who *don't* dress like that—or to the Host People's whores, who also don't."

Breaker glanced around, and saw no exceptions to the smothering black garb. "They don't?"

"Indeed they don't, not when they're making themselves available—which they aren't right now, with the Uplanders not here, so you can stop looking."

"I wasn't . . ." Breaker began, then stopped. He grimaced. "All right, but I was merely curious about what they *do* wear."

"Furs, usually. The Uplanders find fur exotic, since *ara* and other birds dominate on the plateau and there are no fur-bearing beasts up there. And after all, it's in the winter that the Host People play host."

"If you two are done ogling the women," the Seer said, "Boss is in here." She pointed at an open door.

There was no signboard, no hanging tankard, no shop window, no bell, nothing to indicate that this place was open to the public; Breaker hesitated.

The Archer did not; he stepped forward and marched into the building. The Seer followed. Warily, Breaker and the Scholar stepped in; then Breaker paused on the threshold to make sure the Speaker was accompanying them.

Once she was past him, Breaker turned and found himself in what was plainly an ordinary inn or tavern; half a score of black-clad customers were scattered about several tables and benches, most of them holding pewter mugs. They had apparently been gathered around the one person not wearing black, a handsome man in his thirties who wore a tooled-leather vest over a fine white blouse, but all had now turned to stare at the newcomers.

The man in the leather vest had turned, as well. He was tall and muscular, though not quite a match for Bow or Breaker, with black curly hair and a magnificent black beard. Brown eyes and white teeth shone as he smiled at the newcomers, and Breaker felt an irrational urge to smile back—the man's charm was undeniable.

"Seer!" he said. "And Lore! What brings *you* here? And who—oh, wait, I recognize Babble, and that fellow looks like Bow. Is this other our new Swordsman, then?"

"I am," Breaker acknowledged—and he felt an odd warmth as he spoke those words.

"Then have you all journeyed here to introduce us? It hardly seems as if you *all* needed to come!"

"That's not why we're here," the Seer began.

The Leader held up a hand, and she fell silent. "Then perhaps this is not the best place to speak," he said.

"Perhaps . . ."

"Then come." He gestured.

A moment later Breaker was following the Leader up a set of stairs he had not even consciously noticed, not quite certain how he had come to be there. The man called Boss had taken control of the situation from the first, giving no one an opportunity to argue; he had instructed, and they had obeyed. The six Chosen had suddenly become the cooperating team Breaker had always thought they should be.

But now Breaker was not sure whether he was entirely pleased about that. Yes, it was good to have a leader who could actually lead, good to have everything falling into place, but this assumption of authority seemed a bit sudden. Being part of a team was good; being a subordinate on a team was not quite so clearly beneficial. Breaker liked to think he could make his own decisions.

Although he knew that far too often of late, he hadn't. He had just gone along with what was expected of him, playing out his role as the Swordsman, doing what the Seer and the Scholar wanted him to do. He had followed them halfway across Barokan without serious argument, but now that he was being guided by the Leader, the man he was *supposed* to obey, he balked?

He grimaced at his own foolishness.

And then the six of them were in an upstairs room, one that held them all well enough, but was somewhat crowded with half a dozen people in it. All of the new arrivals found places for themselves—the Speaker and the Scholar sat on the bed, the Seer took the room's only chair, the Archer settled on the windowseat, and Breaker perched himself on a trunk. The Leader closed the door, then turned and leaned against it.

"Now," the Leader said, "since there's really only one reason I can think of that three-fourths of the Chosen would be gathered together, I assume someone's heard something terrible about the Wizard Lord, and you want a decision on whether or not we need to remove him. I don't think that's something we want to discuss in front of the Host People, or anyone else but ourselves, so I've brought us up here—but you know they'll figure it out quickly enough, word will be all over Winterhome in an hour, and the Wizard Lord himself will know by morning."

"He already knows," the Seer said.

"You're sure of that?"

"Absolutely. We've spoken to him. And we told at least one of our guides, come to that, so there's no secret to keep."

The Leader nodded. "Then there's no element of surprise to consider, and it may not matter if rumors are all over Barokan. *That* would seem to mean there's no need to rush. So I'll be happy to hear all about whatever atrocity has been alleged, but first let's take a minute to get to know our own situation." He pointed at Breaker. "Stand up, Swordsman, and tell us about yourself."

Breaker rose. "What would you like to know?" he asked.

"To begin with, what's your name?"

Breaker glanced at the Speaker, then said, "I'm called Sword now; for most of my life I was known as Breaker."

"Those aren't your *name*."

"No, of course not. My people don't use true names."

The Leader nodded. "And where are those people? Somewhere in the northern valleys?"

"A town called Mad Oak, in Longvale," Breaker acknowledged.

"And old Blade showed up there, asking for someone to replace him?"

"Yes."

"Why did you volunteer?"

"Someone had to do it."

The Leader looked at him for a long moment; Breaker looked calmly back. Then Boss nodded again. "I see," he said. "Someone had to—but why you?"

"Because no one else was speaking up."

"And the glory of being the world's greatest swordsman, one of the eight Chosen . . . ?"

Breaker smiled. "That didn't hurt."

"And you had no ties holding you to Mad Oak?"

Breaker shrugged. "I had friends, and my family, and I had never seen anywhere else, but nothing that prevented me from taking on the role."

"Family? You're married? Children?"

Breaker was genuinely shocked. "Oh, no, of course not! But there are my parents and my sisters."

"Ah. Of course. So you trained with old Blade, and fought him and won—how did that go?"

Breaker frowned. "That was . . . odd. I cut him worse than I had intended—he was distracted and dropped his guard. The Wizard Lord spoke up during the fight, you see. Through a rabbit."

"Did he? How do you know it was the Wizard Lord, and not some other magician? Perhaps one of your local priests wanted to ensure your victory, as a matter of local pride."

Breaker blinked.

"Our priest couldn't do that," he said.

"Another wizard, perhaps?"

"I suppose it's possible," Breaker admitted. "No one else mentioned that possibility, though—not Blade nor the wizards present."

"Perhaps they were fooled as well—or perhaps some of them were part of the scheme."

"Or perhaps it really was the Wizard Lord," the Seer interjected. "Boss, can we get down to business?"

"In a moment. I like to know who I'll be working with." He looked around at the others. "I've met the rest of you, of course, though I don't know as much about some of you as I would like. I notice that the Thief isn't here, nor the Beauty—why is that, Sword?"

"The Thief wouldn't come," Breaker explained. "She says she regrets ever taking the role, and she won't leave her husband and children. As for the Beauty, we found you first."

"Fair enough. Where is the Beauty, Seer? Up north? Out on the coast?"

"That way," the Seer said, pointing. "About half a mile."

The Leader blinked in apparent surprise. "Is she?"

"Yes."

"I had no idea! Interesting." He smiled. "Well, then, we're all accounted for, and I'm sure I'll get to know all of you as well as I could ask if we do indeed join forces to destroy the Wizard Lord, so let me get to the point. Lore, tell me what this is about."

"The short version, or with all the details?" the Scholar asked.

"The short version, for now—we can fill in the rest later."

Lore nodded. "When the Seer and I compared notes recently, we realized that the Wizard Lord had lied to us about killings he performed in Stoneslope, about five years ago. You'll remember that the Seer discussed those with you at the time—well, we discovered that the explanation he gave could not be true. We felt we had to investigate further. The new Swordsman was nearby, and we thought it might be useful to have a good fighter along, since there might be dangers, so we met with him, and asked him to accompany us to Stoneslope to explore the situation."

"The *short* version, Lore."

"Yes, I'm sorry, Boss. The short version is that Stoneslope isn't there anymore; five years ago the Wizard Lord slaughtered every man, woman, and child there in revenge for what he saw as childhood abuse."

"He did."

"Yes."

"How do you know?"

The Scholar looked confused, and glanced at the Seer for support. "We saw their bones," he said. "We saw the burnt-out remains of the village. We felt the ghosts that linger there. We talked to the people of the neighboring village. And we talked to the Wizard Lord, who admitted what he had done."

"So you know the village was destroyed, and the people killed—but how do you know it was the Wizard Lord who did it?"

"He *said* so," Lore replied, baffled. "Through a crow."

"And how do you know this crow . . ."

"Save your breath, Boss," the Seer said. "I was there, and it was the Wizard Lord speaking to us—and don't ask how *I* know, because you *know* how I know."

"Ah. Your magic."

"Yes."

"And do you know that he spoke the truth, through this crow?"

"Why would he lie?" Breaker asked, puzzled.

"I remember every word," the Scholar said. "Every word, just as he spoke them. You know what that means."

The Leader nodded. "All right, then, he did it—he killed everyone in his home village. And for that you believe we should remove him, am I correct?"

"You know you are," the Seer said.

"Then let me ask—why?"

[22]

The others stared at the Leader in astonishment.

"What do you mean, why?" the Seer demanded. "Because he's a murderer, a butcher, who killed dozens of innocent people, and he needs to be removed before he does it again!"

"But what makes you think he would ever do it again?" the Leader asked. "After all, he has no other enemies, does he? And by your own account it's been five years since the killings; has he killed anyone else in those five years?"

"No," the Seer said.

The Archer glanced at her, startled. "No rogue wizards or other wandering criminals?"

"No one," the Seer said. "I'm certain of it."

"But shouldn't he have?" the Archer persisted. "Weren't there any fleeing murderers? In all the old stories . . ."

"The stories sometimes exaggerate," the Scholar said. "Most of them are about events that happened centuries ago, even if the tellers may say otherwise."

"The Wizard Lord hasn't killed anyone since the slaughter in Stoneslope," the Seer insisted. "Perhaps he *should* have killed someone, I can't tell that, but he hasn't."

"Then why not recognize this one instance as a special case?" the Leader asked, spreading his hands. "He's been a good Wizard Lord otherwise—the weather has been pleasant, the crops good, there are no reports of bandits or disorder. Why is this so unforgivable?"

"He killed *babies,* Boss. He killed his own aunt, and his betrothed, and his first girl. He's a monster."

"Seer, it is his *duty* as Wizard Lord to kill those who deserve to die. We have all of us *made* him a monster, if that's what he is, because that's what we need to protect us from ourselves . . ."

"That's ridiculous," the Archer said, interrupting. "*We* didn't make him anything. The Council of Immortals made him, and made us to keep him in check."

"And he *is* held in check—he has killed no one for five years!"

"Boss," the Seer said, "I held a baby's skull in my hand. It takes more than five years of mercy to atone for what he did—it takes a life."

"Agreed," the Archer said. "He has to die."

"The devastation in Stoneslope was quite impressive," the Scholar said. "And while he made no attempt to deny it, which is good, he made no apology for it, either. He still felt that he was justified in slaughtering his entire village, and furthermore he said that if we attempted to remove him from power he would kill us. I do not believe we can trust him to behave himself in the future, five years of good behavior notwithstanding."

"He deliberately killed innocents," Breaker said. "We are supposed to punish him for that. The ghosts in Stoneslope are . . . they want . . ."

"The souls of the dead cry out for vengeance," the Speaker interrupted, her singsong startling everyone. "The *ler* of the lost yet linger, seeking justice for their slayer."

"Yes," Breaker said. "They do. I felt them."

"As did I," the Seer said.

"And I," the Scholar confirmed.

"All of you agree, then," the Leader said. "Then why did you come here?"

"Because you're our *leader,*" the Seer said. "It's your duty to lead us against him."

"But if I don't believe it wise . . ."

"He killed an entire village!"

"And if he had done that last month or last year, I would indeed be packing my belongings and preparing for the march to the Galbek Hills—but it was *five years ago,* and he has done no more harm! A man can change, and repent his deeds, and if he is no danger . . ."

"There is a story," the Scholar said, "that I remember well, so I presume it to be true—though perhaps it merely struck my fancy, and I recall it for that. In any case, it tells of a man who built a home in Shadowvale, close beneath the cliffs, in a spot where the *ler* were gentle and generous, so that the land was rich and the crops munificent, despite the great barrier blocking out the eastern sky. This man built his house atop the scree, up against the cliff itself, and when he was building it his neighbors, who had come to assist him after the northern fashion, looked up, and noticed that far above them, at the very top of the cliff, was a section that had cracked and leaned out from the surrounding stone. This great block of stone, fifteen or twenty feet wide, was hanging by a corner.

" 'You can't build here!' one of them said to the homeowner. 'Look, that stone is ready to fall and crush you!'

"But the builder laughed. 'That stone has hung from the cliff for as long as I have lived in this vicinity,' he said, 'and it has never fallen yet. Perhaps the *ler* hold it, or perhaps that corner is stronger than it appears, but I will be as safe here as any of you.' And he completed his house, with his neighbors' aid, and moved in, and lived there in peace—perhaps more peace than he had intended, as the hanging rock made many reluctant to visit him.

"And one day, a dozen years after the house was finished, with no warning, the stone fell, and crushed the house to splinters, killing the man and his young daughter. His wife had been down at the river, and she lived, but lost her home and family.

"Boss, *you* may choose to live beneath the hanging rock, but the rest of us do not. We have seen what the Wizard Lord can do, and we do not want to risk seeing it happen again."

"Lore, we will *always* have a Wizard Lord—the question is not whether we will always have the threat of a Wizard Lord going mad hanging over us, but whether this particular Wizard Lord deserves to be removed, perhaps killed. You all seem to believe that this particular stone is leaning out too far and must be removed for those beneath to be safe, but it seems to me that it has been secure enough for five years. Yes, it slipped once, but now it seems to me to be as solid as ever."

"And the man who built the house thought that because the rock above him had never fallen after the initial crack, it never would."

"Boss," the Seer said, "if the Wizard Lord is truly as sane and harmless as you think, then wouldn't he simply acknowledge that our concerns are reasonable, and resign? After all, ending his reign as Wizard Lord simply means retiring to the long and peaceful life of a member of the Council of Immortals, whereas resisting us means his death. How sane can he be, to refuse to resign?"

"Has he refused? Have you *asked* him?"

"We suggested it," Lore replied.

"And he said . . . ?"

" 'Perhaps,' " Lore said. "He said, 'Perhaps.' "

"Then any talk of killing him is premature, isn't it? Perhaps he'll resign and we can end all this worry calmly and sensibly."

"That would do," the Seer said. "Mind you, I still think he deserves worse for what he did to the children of Stoneslope, but if he resigns, then we, as the Chosen, will have done our duty and fulfilled our role."

"Well, then!"

"He hasn't resigned," the Seer said. "We have not spoken with him in . . . some time."

"Almost a month," the Scholar said. "And even that silence is indicative. He knew our intentions, and could have told us he was resigning, if that was his intention. He could have bargained with us. He has not done so."

"Perhaps he thought you would come to your senses, and realize we aren't a bunch of heroes out of some ancient legend."

"But, Boss," the Seer said, "we *are* heroes out of legend."

"We are sensible modern people."

"We are the Chosen, and more than mortal," the Speaker sang.

"Listen," the Archer said. "If he wants to resign rather than face us, he's welcome to do that, but so far he hasn't. Until he does, it's our job to go to the Galbek Hills and try to kill him, and that's what we're going to do. If he wants us to stop coming after him, he can resign at any time, and we'll stop—but for now, I say we get on with our business. If we just sit here in Winterhome arguing, he won't think we're serious. If we march to Galbek either his nerve will crack, and save everyone a lot of trouble, or we'll get there and kill him; either way, our mission will be accomplished and we can split up and go home and get on with our lives. So we march. That's sensible—*and* heroic."

"Yes," the Seer said. "We must go after him as if we mean to kill him."

"We really *do* mean to kill him," Breaker said. "But he can stave us off by resigning."

"Fair enough," Boss replied. "That's fair enough all around. We'll head to the Galbek Hills, then. Now, you say the Thief won't come with us?"

"We couldn't convince her," the Seer said. "You might do better."

"What about the Beauty?"

"We haven't spoken to her," the Scholar said. "We found you first."

"Then I'd say it's time we found her, wouldn't you?"

"I suppose it is," the Seer said.

"Then let's do that, shall we? You said she was half a mile from here?"

"That way." The Seer pointed.

"Should we all go?" the Scholar asked. "I wonder whether a small delegation might not be a better idea; it seems she's been living among the Host People for some time, and a group of half a dozen descending upon one of their women might not make the right impression."

The others glanced at one another.

"A fine suggestion," the Leader said. "Seer, I'll need you to find her, and of course I'll go, but that should do, and the rest of you . . ."

"A third," the Speaker interrupted. "The *ler* counsel a third."

"I agree," the Seer said. "I'd like to have someone else."

The Leader shrugged. "If you want." He looked over the candidates.

"I'll wait here," the Scholar said.

"The streets do not welcome me, the Beauty's words need no interpretation," the Speaker said.

That left the Archer and the Swordsman; the Leader glanced at the two of them, then said, "Come on, Sword—it'll give us a chance to get to know one another a little better." He clapped the young man on the back.

"All right," Breaker agreed.

The Archer grimaced. "Enjoy the view, Sword," he said. "I suppose I'll get a look at her soon enough."

That reminded Breaker that most of his companions had never met the Beauty; Lore had, but none of the others he had traveled with. As the threesome descended the stairs he asked the Leader, "Have you ever met her before?"

The Leader glanced at him. "No," he said. "I understand she was already something of a recluse by the time I was Chosen."

"She was," the Seer agreed.

"How long has she been Chosen?" Breaker asked. "I mean—she's supposed to be the most beautiful woman in the world, so . . . I mean, she . . ."

"You mean, doesn't she have to be young?" the Seer said, as they walked across the common room to the door. "Well, let's just say she can't hold the title forever. The present Beauty took on the role when she was only fifteen or sixteen, and has held it more than twenty years—she doesn't need to find a successor quite yet, but she probably will before she reaches *my* age."

Breaker did not know just what the Seer's actual age was, but he was not fool enough to ask. At a glance she appeared to be in her fifties.

Breaker had no trouble imagining a woman in her fifties who was still handsome, and perhaps even beautiful, but the most beautiful woman in the world? That didn't seem possible.

Of course, the Beauty's appearance was magical, so anything might be possible, but so far nothing Breaker had seen of magic had been so . . . so unnatural. Magic came from *ler,* and *ler* were a part of nature—to an extent they *were* nature. Magic shaped nature, exaggerated it, redirected it, but it was still nature; a rabbit or a crow might speak, but with the voice of a rabbit or crow, not in a human voice. The

Wizard Lord might summon wind and storm, but those winds and storms were no different from natural ones—the clouds were not red or blue, the rain still fell down and didn't fly sideways or spiral about.

And it was natural for a woman's beauty to fade with time, like a man's strength.

But the Beauty was not yet forty, if the Seer had the numbers right; she might have several years left before she would have any reason to seek out her successor.

"This way," the Seer said, as they emerged into the street, and the three of them marched northward, up the street.

A few moments later, sooner than Breaker had expected and scarcely out of sight of the inn where they had found the Leader, the Seer pointed.

"There," she said.

The stone-and-wood structure the Seer indicated was no inn; the blackened oak door was closed tight, the windows small and shuttered. The Leader said as much.

"She's in there," the Seer said.

The Leader nodded. "Very well, then," he said. He stepped up and rapped on the door.

For a moment nothing happened, and the Leader looked questioningly at the Seer.

"She heard you," the Seer said. "And the Wizard Lord is watching us." She pointed at a bird perched on an adjoining rooftop.

The Leader looked where she indicated. "He's using the bird's eyes? Has he been watching you often? With five of you traveling together, I assume he's noticed."

"He's looked and listened from time to time," the Seer agreed.

"Then he knows what you have in mind."

"Of course."

"Is she coming?" Breaker asked. Now that the possibility of seeing the Beauty was so close, he found himself growing impatient, trying to imagine what the most beautiful woman in the world would look like.

The Seer turned her attention back to the closed door. "No, she isn't," she said.

"No?" The Leader knocked again, more loudly.

"She's moving now, but she isn't coming straight to the door," the

Seer said. "I'm not sure why. If the Speaker were here she could ask the *ler,* but I'm not . . . my magic doesn't . . ." She glanced up at the bird again.

"Is he interfering somehow?" Breaker asked, following her gaze.

The Seer shook her head. "No, that's not it," she said. "At least, I don't think so. He's still watching *us,* not her. But he's watching *me,* trying to see what I'm seeing."

"Can he *do* that?"

"I don't think so—but he can try."

The Leader gave the bird one last look, then knocked again.

"She's coming now," the Seer said.

Breaker turned back to the door expectantly. The latch rattled, and the door swung inward; a face appeared in the opening.

Or part of one, in any case; the woman in the door wore the black hood and scarf of the Host People, so that all Breaker could see of her face was her eyes.

Those eyes were startlingly lovely—a deep, rich green, surrounded by smooth, perfect skin—but still, Breaker had expected more. He had expected an entire face.

Though now that he thought about it, he should have known better; he had been told that the Beauty lived in Winterhome, so naturally she would take on the customs of the Host People. The delay in opening the door might well have been to fetch her scarf and pull up her hood.

And all he could see of her was those lovely, lovely eyes, and a vague outline in black. He could see she was tall, and the outline of her hood suggested the shape of her head, but beyond that she was invisible.

"Beauty," the Leader said. "We meet at last. I am the Leader of the Chosen. We need to speak with you."

The veiled woman glanced quickly at the other two. "There must be some mistake," she said, in a soft voice that sent a thrill through Breaker—though he was not pleased by the words; had she, like the Thief, come to regret her role? Would she, too, refuse to help?

"There is no mistake," said the Seer. "I am the Chosen Seer, and I know you for what you are."

"And what is that?" the woman asked, an edge of annoyance in her voice.

"The most beautiful woman in the world, made so by magic, chosen by the Council of Immortals as one of the eight heroes who will depose the Wizard Lord should he stray into madness or evil."

"I don't suppose you would believe me if I denied it; the mere fact that you found me would seem to indicate that you're what you say you are. Which is intriguing, to say the least." She looked at Breaker. "And who's this? Is this another of the Chosen, or a witness to some atrocity? I can see by his attire he's neither Host nor Uplander."

"I'm called Sword," Breaker said.

"And you're the world's greatest swordsman?"

"So they tell me."

She stared at him for a moment, then stepped back and swung the door wide. "Come in, then," she said. "And try not to track mud on the carpets."

[23]

The interior of the Beauty's home—and it was instantly obvious that this was indeed someone's home, and not a business or shop of any kind—was warm and cozy. Two rocking chairs stood on either side of a broad hearth, where a moderate fire burned; a rag rug covered much of the plank floor. Two of the walls were dressed stone, and two were dark wood hung with simple tapestries; a rough table held a bowl of nuts, a basket of sewing supplies, and scraps of black fabric that Breaker only belatedly recognized as the pieces of an unfinished garment. A vase on a shelf by the hearth held a dozen curling white *ara* feathers.

A ginger cat had been curled on the corner of the hearth, but it leapt up and bolted at the appearance of strangers, vanishing through an open door at the rear of the room.

"I'm sorry I haven't enough chairs for everyone," the Beauty said as she led them inside. Her voluminous black robe swirled about her as she moved, and Breaker tried not to notice when it happened to shape itself briefly here or there to the curves of her body. "I live alone, and have few guests."

"Why?" Breaker blurted, before he could catch himself.

She turned to stare at him, then said, "Because it suits me. Now, why have you come?"

The Leader replied, "I think the Seer can best explain."

The Seer frowned at him, then turned her attention to the Beauty.

"Five years ago," she said, "the Wizard Lord slaughtered the entire population of his home village of Stoneslope, men, women, and children, to avenge childhood slights. We cannot . . ."

She stopped abruptly and turned toward the open door; Breaker, startled, directed his own gaze there.

The ginger cat had reappeared.

"Slights, you call them?" it said.

The Beauty screamed, a short, wordless shriek, and clapped a hand to her heart.

"Yes, slights," the Seer replied.

"Say rather 'torments.' Say 'heartless abuse.' Say 'vicious cruelty' and 'unrelenting evil.' "

The Beauty stared in horror at her cat.

"Are you all right?" Breaker asked, stepping forward to offer support; the Beauty looked none too steady on her feet.

"He talks!" she said. "He never spoke before!"

"It's not your cat," Breaker said. "It's magic."

"It's the Wizard Lord," the Seer agreed. "He's speaking to us through your cat."

The Beauty's head whipped around so fast her scarf slipped, and Breaker glimpsed the most perfectly shaped nose he had ever seen or imagined; he felt a stirring in his loins that he would never have guessed a mere nose could inspire. Then she tugged the scarf back into place and said, "He can do that?"

"Obviously," the Seer said.

"It must be a shock," the Leader said. "Here, sit down." He took her elbow and guided her to one of the rockers. She settled warily into the seat.

The cat strolled across the room and leapt up on the hearth, where it turned to face the four Chosen; the Beauty watched it as a trapped mouse might.

"She says I killed my tormentors," the cat said. "I admit it; I did. I sent fire and plague and killed them all—and I say that they deserved it. They had made my life constant unremitting pain for fifteen years, from my birth until I fled. I tried to forget, to put it all behind me, and to ignore them, and for all the years when I was an ordinary wizard I did them no harm, despite the lingering nightmares and the countless opportunities; when I first became the Wizard Lord I still had no intention of avenging the countless wrongs they had done me. As the time passed, though, and I carried out my duties and sent the freshening rain and warming sun across the southern hills, and warded away the great storms, and listened for reports of fugitives, and watched everywhere for the depredations of rogue wizards, the temptation grew. I began to watch my old foes through the eyes of birds and beasts, to see whether they had repented of their crimes, and I saw that they had not, and finally I could bear no more. I could not stand the thought that I was repaying their offenses with the blessings of fine weather and safety, and in a fit of cold rage I destroyed them.

"It would have been wiser to have resisted, I suppose—but in all honesty, these past five years I have lived content for the first time in my life, happy in the knowledge that all those who wronged me when I was an innocent child have paid for their crimes, and that their feet no longer soil the earth, their breath no longer fouls the air.

"Now the Seer and her comrades seek to slay me for my actions, but why? I wish no one else any harm. I am content. I am satisfied. I have done what needed to be done, and no more remains. Let us live in peace."

"You killed innocent children," the Seer said. "Babies. Old women. Your own aunt. Their *ler* are screaming for justice."

"I removed a blight from the face of Barokan, as is my duty as Wizard Lord. No more than that."

"Teasing children do not deserve slaughter."

"If by 'teasing children' you mean my torturers, I disagree. I have done nothing unjustified—and if you use this as an excuse to attack me, then I will be justified in defending myself by any means necessary. I truly hope it won't come to that."

"You killed people who hadn't been *born* yet when you left Stoneslope."

"But their families were my tormentors, and if I had left the children alive, what would have become of them? They would have spread lies about me through all Barokan."

"So you killed them just to not leave any witnesses?" Breaker asked.

The cat glowered at him, then turned to the Beauty. "I hope you will be reasonable, and not let these misguided people sway you. Think of the risks and dangers in opposing me, and consider what I have said. I mean you no ill—but I will defend myself. Now, let me go before I wear out your poor cat's jaw with all this talking—the beast is not designed for such speeches!"

And with that something seemed to change in the cat's eyes; it meowed loudly, once, then jumped from the hearth and ran for the door again.

The four of them watched it go; then the Beauty turned to the Seer. "Can he still hear us?" she asked.

"Not at the moment," the Seer said, "but he could begin listening again at any time—if not through your cat, then through a spider or a beetle, a mouse in the wall or a bird in the chimney."

"We have to kill him," the Beauty said. "We have to kill him *now,* as soon as possible. He's a monster."

"Yes," the Seer said, startled. "Yes, we do."

"There's no need for haste," the Leader said. "We want to do this right."

"But *soon,*" the Beauty said. "Before he remembers some other youthful horror he needs to avenge." She shuddered, but Breaker thought he saw an odd light in her eyes.

"We're gathering at Karregh's Inn," the Leader said. "We'll be making plans there tonight."

"I'll be there," the Beauty said, rising from her chair. "I need to pack, and find someone to watch my cat, but I'll be there."

"Good," the Leader said. "Good! I'll see you there this evening, then." He held out a hand.

The Beauty looked at it in confusion for a moment, then shook it. "The Host People don't shake hands," she said. "You might want to remember that while you're here."

"Ah, thank you," the Leader said. "I hadn't noticed that."

There were dozens, perhaps hundreds, of questions that Breaker wanted to ask the Beauty, about why she lived in Winterhome as she did and how she had made her decision so swiftly, and of course he wanted a look at her face more than ever after that tantalizing glimpse of nose, but he did not say anything; instead he followed Boss and the Seer to the door, only glancing back once at the Beauty as she stood in the center of the room, watching her visitors depart.

After all, he told himself, they would be traveling together all the way to the Galbek Hills; he would have plenty of time to ask his questions, and he would undoubtedly see plenty of her face along the way.

And then the three of them were in the street, and marching back down the street toward the inn where they had left the others—Karregh's Inn, Breaker supposed it was.

They found the Scholar trading stories with half a dozen Hostmen while the Speaker listened to the walls; the Archer was nowhere to be seen. At the sight of the returning trio the Scholar stood and politely took his leave of his listeners, and the Speaker wandered away from the wall.

"Well, then," the Leader said, turning to the others, "we'll want to take a few days to prepare . . ."

"Why?" Breaker asked, startled.

"I would think the sooner we left, the better," the Scholar agreed.

"We need to get this done," the Seer agreed. "The longer we put it off, the more chance the Wizard Lord has to find a way to stop us."

"But no Wizard Lord has ever stopped the Chosen," the Leader pointed out. "We are *destined* to succeed—that's the whole point of being the Chosen. We want to do this as carefully as we can, so that none of us die in the process, but the eventual outcome is assured!"

"No Wizard Lord has stopped the Chosen *yet,*" the Seer corrected him. "This system of ours was not divinely ordained, Boss; it was created by the Council of Immortals, and they're not infallible. It's been a long time since the Chosen were called upon to serve, and we can't be sure this won't turn out to be the Wizard Lord who finds a way to defeat the system."

"Oh, nonsense."

"The Wizard Lord doesn't think so—if he was certain we'll defeat him, wouldn't he retire right now, rather than waiting for us to act?" Breaker asked.

"You're assuming he's rational," the Leader replied. "I think his actions in Stoneslope and his words just now demonstrate otherwise."

Breaker started to open his mouth to protest, to say that less than an hour before Boss had been arguing the opposite, saying that a single massacre did not indicate the Wizard Lord had gone mad, but then he stopped, unsure just why he would want to argue when the Leader's new position matched his own.

It was still unsettling that his position had changed so quickly. Breaker remembered that part of the Leader's magic was the ability to make swift and firm decisions; was this an example?

"He thinks he's going to win," the Seer said. "After all, none of us were even alive the last time a Dark Lord had to be removed—how will we know what to do? It's never been so long between Dark Lords before!"

The Scholar cleared his throat. "Actually," he said, "this isn't even close to the longest hiatus. The Dark Lord of the Tsamas was not removed until the four hundred and seventy-fourth year of the Council of Immortals, some one hundred and sixty-nine years after the Dark Lord of Kamith t'Daru."

The Seer glared at him.

"But this is the *second*-longest gap," the Scholar added hastily. "It's been a hundred and three years since the Swordsman of Crab Leg Key killed the Dark Lord of Goln Vleys, and the other gaps have never approached a century."

"If we just rush to the Galbek Hills without a plan or strategy, maybe the Wizard Lord *will* be able to stop us," the Leader said. "We need to decide how we want to approach him."

"We need to see just what the situation is before we can make plans," the Seer said. "What his tower is like now, how it's defended—we need to go look. Maybe we don't want to just march in the front door when we get there, but there's no reason to sit around *here*—we can make our plans along the way, and adjust them once we've seen what his stronghold is like."

"I agree," Breaker said.

"As do I," said the Scholar.

"The *ler* don't understand why we even need to discuss it," the Speaker said. "They think we're already—yes, I know—on our way."

Before anyone could reply the door opened, and the Archer stepped in, bow in one hand and an arrow in the other.

"Just practicing," he said. "So, you found the Beauty?"

"Yes," Breaker said.

"Then we leave in the morning?"

"We were just discussing that," the Leader began.

"Yes," the Seer said.

"Yes, we do," Breaker said. "As soon as I've had my morning practice." He glanced at the Leader. "*Some* of us are going, anyway—Boss, here, isn't entirely sure he'll be coming."

It was very odd, but even while the Leader's mere presence seemed to have transformed the Chosen into a unified team, Breaker did not necessarily want Boss to *lead* that team—his switching positions so quickly and carrying on as if he had always agreed with the others made Breaker nervous.

But that was foolish, surely.

The Archer eyed the Leader with interest. "Really?"

"He's joking," the Leader said. "I had suggested we might want to rest and prepare a little, that's all." He shrugged. "I realize now that the sooner we leave, the better."

"Will we be stopping to talk to the Thief again, or heading directly for the Wizard Lord's tower?"

The Leader looked at the Seer. "I believe the Thief's home is on the way?"

"Almost," the Seer agreed. "We might find a route a day or so shorter if we skipped it, but no more than that."

"Then we'll stop and have a word. Her talents may well be wanted."

"What about the Beauty?" the Archer asked.

"She'll be here this evening," the Leader said.

"She's coming with us," Breaker agreed.

"Is she . . . I mean . . ."

"We didn't see her face," Breaker said. "She kept her scarf and hood up."

"Seems to defeat the whole purpose," the Archer said.

A realization finally flickered into Breaker's mind.

"I think that's why she does it," he said. "In fact, I think that's why she lives here in Winterhome—so she can keep her face hidden."

"Several of the Beauties have lived here," the Scholar said.

"Have they?" Breaker nodded. "That would make sense. I never heard it mentioned, though."

"I don't understand," the Archer said.

"She probably wants to be able to lead a normal life," Breaker said. "She has a house and a cat, she sews—if she showed her face she would spend all her time fending off suitors." He remembered those eyes, the glimpsed curves, and the sultry voice—if the rest of her was equally alluring, then he knew that men would flock to her like crows to corn.

And the prospect of traveling in her company, which had seemed so appealing before, suddenly lost its charm—he would be around her constantly, hearing that voice, seeing those eyes, perhaps seeing more, and he almost certainly wouldn't be permitted to touch her. They would have urgent business, and he would be one of four men . . . He suspected he would be living through weeks or months of frustration.

"That didn't bother Slut," the Seer said bitterly. "She enjoyed it."

"That was the previous Beauty?" Breaker asked, startled.

The Seer nodded.

"You called her *Slut*?"

"I regret to say we did."

Breaker had more questions he wanted to ask, but hardly knew where to begin—and then he was interrupted before he could choose.

"Don't call this one that," the Leader said. "Nor Whore or Trollop or any of the other names of that sort. You understand me?"

"I wasn't going to," the Seer said. "I understand very well how wrong I was, all those years ago."

"Good."

"But . . ." Breaker began, then cut off even before the Leader glared at him.

"If we're leaving in the morning," the Leader said, "then we should be gathering supplies, hiring a guide, and making sure we've had a good supper. There's a widow down the street who sets a fine table, though I don't know whether she could feed all of us on short notice."

"What about this place?" the Archer asked, gesturing at the room around them.

"Oh, they'll have something they call food, but I wouldn't necessarily agree. The Host People pride themselves on their hospitality, of course, but the truth is that this time of year they haven't much to offer—the Uplanders stripped their larders bare over the last winter, and they haven't yet restocked everything. Much of it will be arriving in the next few weeks, just before the snow. Nor would we, as mere travelers, receive their best, in any case—that's reserved for the Uplander clan leaders."

"Some of us should stay here, though, in case the Beauty comes sooner than we expect," Breaker said.

"A good point," the Leader agreed. "Then let it be you two, Sword and Bow—make her welcome when she comes, and the rest of us will see whether the widow can find room for us at her table. Come, then." He beckoned.

Breaker stood flat-footed and watched as the Leader led the Seer, the Scholar, and the Speaker out the door. Then he looked at the Archer.

The Archer looked back. "Now what?"

"Now," Breaker said, "we find out who's in charge around here, and what there is to eat!"

[24]

The Beauty did arrive before the others returned, securely wrapped in her hood and scarf, and once they were secure in the upstairs room Breaker introduced her to the Archer, who bowed elaborately.

"The pleasure is mine," the Archer said.

"You may not mean that, but it's largely true," the Beauty said. "I take no great delight in meeting you, since it is dozens of deaths that brought us here, and the need for one more that drives us forth. We are thrown together by the roles we live, not by choice."

"Yet I would have chosen to meet you, had I but known where you were."

"Of course you would," the Beauty said, and Breaker could hear the disgust in her voice. "You're a man, and I'm the most beautiful woman in the world."

The Archer opened his mouth to respond, but apparently could find no words.

"My mother used to say that true beauty comes from within, in actions and words," Breaker said, hoping to avert what he feared might become an ugly confrontation.

The Beauty turned her attention to him. "Your mother spoke platitudes. You don't know what beauty is, and neither did she."

"You could show us," the Archer challenged.

The Beauty sighed. "I could," she said. "But the sight of my face or body would arouse your lust, and I don't care to deal with that just now."

The Archer clapped a hand to his bosom. "Do you think so little of me, that you think I could not control my passion?" he asked.

"Yes," the Beauty said, before he could continue. Breaker smiled.

"It's magic," he said. "Remember, Bow? Her beauty is just as supernatural as your skill with an arrow, or mine with a sword, and would pierce our hearts figuratively just as surely as arrow or sword would do literally."

"Yes," the Beauty said, slightly startled.

"It must be a curse, really," Breaker continued. "Far worse than our need to practice our arts daily, perhaps even worse than the constant chatter the Speaker hears—you can never know what any man would think of you were the magic not there."

"That's right," the Beauty said, gazing at him with interest. "I'm surprised you understand so well—did the Seer or the Scholar explain it to you?"

"No," Breaker said. "It seems plain enough—how could it be otherwise? You live here so you can keep your beauty concealed without abandoning the company of others, yes?"

"Yes."

"And you only lower hood and scarf when no men can see, I suppose? Among women?"

"Not even then," the Beauty said. "Women—well, it's never so simple as the lust of men. There's envy in it, and lust of another kind, and often enough outright hatred."

Breaker blinked. "Ah," he said. "I hadn't thought of that. But of course, women aren't blind to beauty."

"Indeed."

"The Seer said she actively avoided meeting you. Now I think I see why. She would not like her reactions."

"You see much, for so young a man!"

"She knew your predecessor; they were not friends. I hadn't appreciated the reasons."

"I can guess."

"But I still cannot," the Archer said. "You speak of your beauty as a curse, but the mere sound of your voice has my heart pounding in my chest!"

"And other parts pressing at your breeches, I'm sure," the Beauty said dryly. "But what makes you think I *want* that?"

"But I . . . uh . . ."

"I can't make it stop," she said. "I can't turn it off. *Ara* feathers can help—they drive away the *ler* that provide the extra glamour. And in theory, the men of the Chosen are less susceptible to the magic than anyone else. But the feathers and the immunity don't change the sound of my voice, or the shape of my face, or the color of my eyes. They don't make my breasts sag or my belly bulge. I know from when I met the Scholar, long ago, that the Chosen are still men, and I cannot talk to a man without arousing him. I cannot walk down a street uncovered without drawing every eye. Men would follow me wherever I go—if I work in the fields, they trample the crops the better to gaze at me; if I fetch water from a stream, they muddy the water with their boots. Work goes undone, wives and lovers are abandoned—do you think I *enjoy* that?"

"I don't . . . uh . . ." The Archer muttered in confusion.

"For twenty-three years, since I was but fifteen, I have lived with this curse," the Beauty continued. "As did others before me, and for a hundred years it's been for nothing. We have had our lives ruined by it, our chances for happy families destroyed—but at least now I will be able to use it for its intended purpose, and *accomplish* something! I almost feel as if I should be thanking the Wizard Lord for his atrocity."

"I would hardly go that far," Breaker said.

"But at least now I can make my misery *mean* something!"

"Vengeance," the Archer said. "We can avenge the dead of Stoneslope."

"Justice," Breaker said.

"Call it what you will," the Beauty said, "so long as I have a purpose!" And with that she turned away.

An hour later the others returned, and the seven Chosen gathered in a council of war. The Beauty promised to hire the best guide in Winterhome to see them safely back west as far as Riversedge in the Midlands, and all of them reviewed their abilities and talents—and the accompanying burdens—for the group. Breaker was interested to hear that the Scholar was required every day to learn at least one true thing that he had not previously known, that the Leader's daily task was to convince someone (or something, if he was alone) to do something he or she would otherwise not have done, and that the Seer was required to wake for an hour each night and spend it in meditation, receptive to any visions the *ler* might see fit to send her.

"Not that they ever do," she added.

The Speaker and the Beauty had no burdens save their inability to cease their magic, and the Beauty's inability to conceive a child, but Breaker thought those quite enough. His own daily practice, or the Archer's, seemed trivial by comparison.

It was a pleasant surprise that the Beauty had some talent as a healer, but other than that the magical abilities described were no more than Breaker had expected. He wondered whether the others neglected to mention anything when listing their talents; he knew that he was not being completely truthful himself, since he said nothing about his skill with women, and he suspected the others of similarly keeping their own counsel about irrelevant matters.

When these introductions and explanations were complete the discussion moved on to the Wizard Lord—where he lived, how best to get there, what they might do to penetrate his defenses.

The Wizard Lord watched the proceedings through the eyes of a mouse; the Seer pointed it out, but no one saw any point in chasing the creature away, or killing it. The Wizard Lord would undoubtedly know their plans soon enough no matter what methods they tried; real secrecy was simply not possible. Details might be concealed, but at present they had no details to hide; the plan so far consisted simply of, "Go to the Wizard Lord's tower in the Galbek Hills and kill him."

That was hardly a secret worth worrying about.

The Leader assured them that he would devise a better plan in time, but as yet he did not have enough to work with. They knew little about what they might find in the Galbek Hills. The Wizard Lord was said to dwell in a lonely tower he had built atop a hill, attended only by a handful of young women from the neighboring town of Split Reed—and that was all they knew.

That did not lend itself to detailed schemes.

At last, later than Breaker liked, they all took to their beds. The Beauty invited the Seer and the Speaker to stay the night in her home, while the Leader had bedding brought for the Archer, the Scholar, and the Swordsman to sleep in his room at Karregh's Inn.

Breaker slept only fitfully; the excitement of finally having the Chosen gathered and agreed, the knowledge that they would soon be on their way to the Galbek Hills, kept him from resting soundly.

At one point as he lay half-awake he thought he heard voices outside the door of the room, but when he bestirred himself to listen, they stopped. He waited for a moment, but they did not resume, and in the end he decided he had imagined them—or perhaps, in his state midway between the waking and sleeping worlds, he had momentarily been able to hear the *ler* around him, talking among themselves.

At last he fell asleep again, though in his dreams he could sometimes still hear strange voices, murmuring just out of earshot.

In the morning the seven Chosen gathered at the inn, met the old woman Beauty had hired to guide them to Riversedge, and set out.

They began walking west while still in the shadow of the Eastern Cliffs, of course; all of Winterhome lay in that shadow for much of every morning, and they could hardly justify waiting until the sun cleared the cliffs before starting their journey. That meant that for the first hour or so the sky directly above was bright and blue, while the world around them remained dim. Clouds huddled on the western horizon, but the air in Winterhome was dry and pleasantly warm.

Before they cleared the shadow of the cliffs they passed the great guesthouses bearing the banners of the Uplander clans; the Beauty identified each banner along the route and provided a few details about the clan that flew it, facts she had learned in her years in Winterhome.

Breaker was only mildly interested in the stories, but the sound of the

Beauty's voice was a never-ending pleasure, so he listened avidly—as, he noticed, did the other three males in the party, while the other three women took the lead and paid no attention to her recitations.

The Scholar seemed genuinely fascinated by her account, and asked pertinent questions; he was undoubtedly adding to his store of historical and cultural knowledge, and had presumably filled his daily quota of new learning from this discussion. The Leader appeared to be listening out of habit. And the Archer was clearly only interested in the Beauty, and not what she was telling them; on the few occasions when he spoke, his remarks were always general and unrelated to whatever the Beauty had been saying.

When they passed the last of the clan houses Breaker asked, "Were you born among the Host People? You seem to know Winterhome well."

"No, I was born in a town called Hen's Corner, in Shadowvale, but I have lived here more than twenty years, since I was a girl of seventeen."

"Because of the attire?"

"Yes."

"We're out of Winterhome, though," the Archer said. "You can take off that hood and scarf now—the day is warm enough."

"I would prefer to keep them on," the Beauty replied. "These clothes are comfortable at this temperature, and I'm accustomed to them."

"We'll all see your face eventually, you know," the Archer said.

"Yes, I suppose you will," she agreed, "but could it please wait a while longer?"

The Archer glanced at the Leader, then shrugged. "As you please," he said. He looked up. "You might be glad of the warmer clothing soon, in any case."

Breaker looked up as well, and saw what the Archer meant—clouds were blowing in from the west and thickening rapidly, the blue of the sky fading. A cool breeze brushed his face, ruffling his hair.

"You think a storm is coming?" he said. "In the daytime?"

"And fast," the Archer replied.

"The Wizard Lord controls the weather," the Scholar said, in a surprisingly unsteady voice, "and I do not believe the storm he sent on our way to Stoneslope was even close to the worst he can do. That was just an attempt to discourage us; this time he may mean us real harm."

Breaker threw the Scholar a glance, then looked back at the sky.

The clouds were indeed thickening with unnatural speed—or at least, Breaker thought it was unnatural; since he had always lived in Barokan, where the Wizard Lord's magic moderated the weather, he could not be sure just what natural weather was like.

How bad could a storm be, though? There were tales of the great gales that swept across the Uplands, driving the flocks of *ara* before them and blowing down the Uplanders' tents, but what could the Wizard Lord send down here beneath the cliffs? Could he really do more than he had in the forests of the southern hills?

"He waited until we were west of Winterhome," the Leader said. "Away from shelter."

"The guesthouses are right there," Breaker said, gesturing.

"But we'd have to turn back . . ." the Leader began.

"And they're locked for the summer," the Beauty interrupted. "We can probably break in if we need to, but . . ."

"We aren't going back," the Seer said. She had heard the conversation and dropped back to join it. "We can't let him slow us down. After all, how bad can it be? We've all seen storms before, I'm sure."

"I don't know," the Beauty said. "The Uplanders say that we don't get true storms in Barokan, even at night, that the Wizard Lord keeps them back—they get *real* storms up on the plateau that make our worst seem like a summer breeze."

"Do you believe them?" the Archer asked. "They were probably just boasting to impress you."

"I hope you're right," the Beauty said, as the first clouds reached the sun and the light suddenly dimmed.

"It doesn't matter," the Leader said. "If the Uplanders can survive the worst storms, then so can we."

"He sent a storm when we went to Stoneslope," the Seer said. "We came through it well enough."

That memory cheered Breaker; the Seer was right. That storm had been impressive, and by the time they had reached Stoneslope he had been tired and soaked through, but no worse than that. The Scholar was surely worrying about nothing, suggesting the Wizard Lord could do much worse.

He glanced at the Scholar and noticed that Lore was huddling in his woolen coat.

"I think he can send much more severe storms than that one," the Scholar said. "But there's nothing we can do about it now. If we're ever to reach the Galbek Hills, we'll have to face his storms sooner or later."

Breaker had not thought about it in those terms, but the Scholar was obviously correct—any attempt to wait it out would be pointless, as the Wizard Lord could wait *them* out, and send a storm when they finally moved on.

The sun had vanished, and the sky was gray from end to end; the wind was starting to whip at their hair and clothes and stir the trees—not just the leaves, but the limbs. When Breaker glanced back he saw dust swirl from the rooftops behind them. The wind made his eyes sting, but squinting and blinking kept them clear enough.

"He must know this won't stop us," he said.

"He's just trying to discourage us," the Leader said. "To let us know he won't make it easy for us."

Breaker nodded; that made good sense.

They marched on—and the clouds continued to darken; by noon the sky was darker than when they had set out. The wind continued to rise, as well, until it not merely whistled in the trees, but screamed; dying leaves fluttered like bees' wings, and branches snapped like whips. Deadwood crackled and splintered, and broken twigs and shreds of bark flew in the travelers' faces as they walked.

And then the storm broke, and the rain poured down in blinding torrents.

This was far worse than the path to Stoneslope—but then, the Wizard Lord had taken longer to build it. Lore had been right, and Breaker wrong. Breaker had never imagined such a rain was possible; within seconds his cloak was soaked through, his boots filled by the water streaming down his legs. Even when he had cleared the water from his eyes and sheltered them as best he could, he could barely see the Scholar to his left, the Beauty to his right; the Leader's laden back, ahead of him, was just a vague gray shape, and the others were invisible in the downpour. He tried to keep staggering forward, but every step was a struggle, as the wind pressed him back, his saturated clothing weighed down his limbs, and his waterlogged boots seemed to weigh a hundred pounds apiece. The pack on his back seemed heavier than ever, and had presumably taken on water, but his back beneath it was the one part of him that remained dry.

The roar of wind and rain drowned out all other sound, and his attention was focused entirely on placing one foot ahead of another; it was not until he felt the Beauty's hand on his sleeve that he realized anyone was speaking.

"*What?*" he bellowed.

He could not make out all of her words, but he could see her gesture, and one phrase penetrated—". . . turn back?"

"*No!*" he shouted. "*No! We can't let him see . . .*" He realized she couldn't hear him, and just shook his head and roared, "*NO!*" He pointed at the road ahead.

She screamed something in reply, and he thought he heard her say, ". . . shelter!"

He nodded, and pointed ahead again. "*First chance we get!*" he agreed. "*Shelter, first chance!*" He turned to the Scholar.

"*I heard!*" the Scholar said, before Breaker could speak. Breaker was unsure whether it had something to do with the direction of the wind, or whether the Scholar simply had a far more powerful voice than he had realized, but the words were clear.

Breaker looked ahead, where he could see the Leader's back; he knew the guide, the Seer, and the Speaker were somewhere beyond, but he despaired of communicating with them. Then he looked to his right, past the Beauty, where he could see the Archer clinging to the Beauty's right arm.

He had obviously heard, just as the Scholar had.

Breaker considered taking the Beauty's left arm, to make sure they were not separated in the howling madness of the storm, but he dismissed the idea; he knew he was just looking for an excuse to touch her. If he had genuinely been concerned for the party's collective welfare he would have reached for the Scholar, who did not already have the Archer's aid.

He turned his gaze ahead again, and saw the Leader turning.

"*We're looking for shelter!*" the Leader shouted. "*We'll wait it out—he can't keep this up for long!*"

Breaker nodded, and waved an acknowledgment.

They pressed on, and after a few more minutes Breaker began to wonder how they would ever *see* any shelter if they reached one. The rain showed no sign of slacking; if anything, it was heavier than ever. The wind continued to blow directly in their faces, forcing them to keep their heads down.

After several more minutes Breaker was no longer worrying about such details; he was focusing all his attention on his feet, on simply continuing to walk. Lifting each foot meant pulling it out of inch-deep water and a thick layer of sticky mud beneath, heaving it forward against the wind's pressure, then dropping it back through the icy water and trying to find firm footing under the mud.

Breaker took some very, very small comfort in the realization that the road here was slightly elevated; if it had been sunken below the surrounding terrain it would undoubtedly be flooded up to his knees by now. The sheer volume of water spilling from the sky was incomprehensible, like nothing he had ever imagined; any crops that had been standing in this area must surely have been washed away. Fields would be flooded, drainage ditches becoming overflowing rivers. The soil would be too wet to work for weeks. Fruit would have been ripped from the orchards, as well—if the wind hadn't snapped the branches right off!

What could the Wizard Lord be thinking, unleashing such a disaster? He already had the Chosen after him, and a thing like this storm must unquestionably anger the Council of Immortals, as well.

The Wizard Lord, scourge of rogue wizards, had himself become a rogue wizard, misusing his magic and carelessly harming innocents.

If, of course, this storm was really the Wizard Lord's doing. Perhaps some other wizard . . .

But no. The Wizard Lord controlled the weather, for the good of all Barokan. A storm like this could not be natural, and surely no other wizard had the power to create such a thing. The Wizard Lord was doing this to delay them, to deter them . . .

There was a touch on his sleeve, and Breaker looked up to see the Leader's face just inches from his own.

"Barn!" the Leader bellowed, pointing. *"Barn, over there! Shelter!"*

Breaker had no extra breath to shout back; he nodded, and began turning his steps.

Their route took them across a hundred yards of pasture, and as Breaker had feared, it was flooded at least six inches deep with freezing-cold, fast-running water. He slogged on, his ankles and feet numb from the cold, water spilling from his boot tops with every step, only to be immediately replaced by new, colder rain.

The rain *was* getting colder, he realized. It had been chilly to start with; now it was icy. He risked an upward glance as he passed under a fair-sized oak, and saw that yes, the rain was freezing onto the branches, sheathing them in glittering ice.

That should not be possible this early in the year, Breaker knew; he shuddered with cold and dismay.

And then his shin collided with something hard, and he felt hands closing on his arms, pulling him upward. He stumbled across a platform, then through an opening into utter darkness.

And he was out of the rain.

It was as if he had thrown off a great weight; he straightened up, his back aching, and water spilled from his hat brim as if poured from a bowl. He flung open his drenched and freezing cloak and took a deep breath of the damp air—he had been unable to fill his lungs properly in the downpour.

Then he turned and saw the others, silhouetted against the door—the Seer and the Speaker helping the Beauty and the Scholar into the barn, the Leader guiding the Archer across the platform.

A light sprang up, and Breaker saw the guide kneeling on the barn floor, lighting a lantern.

"We're all here," he said, shouting to be heard over the roar of the rain on the barn's roof.

"Astonishingly, yes," the guide said, as the lantern flared up. "I'm amazed we didn't lose anyone in the storm."

"Yes," Breaker agreed. "It's very fortunate."

The Leader and the Archer staggered through the door, supporting each other; the Archer promptly slumped to the floor and sat, leaning against the wall beside the opening while the Leader panted, "Is everyone all right?"

"I'm *cold,*" the Beauty said.

The Archer looked up. "Perhaps I . . ."

"It's the wet clothes," the Leader said, cutting him off. "We'll all feel better if we get them off—at least, if we have anything dry to wear instead."

The Beauty looked at him, then at the Archer.

"I'll be over there," she said, pointing to the darkest corner of the barn. "Don't follow me."

"I wouldn't think of it!" the Archer protested.

The Scholar stopped peeling off his drenched cloak to look at the Archer. "You know, I don't think I'll remember you said that," he said, "and it's really rather a shame, to forget such audacity!"

The exhausted Archer needed a moment to puzzle this out, and before he managed a reply the Speaker said, "It's stopped."

[25]

All eyes except the Beauty's turned to the door of the barn, and all of them immediately saw and heard that the Speaker was right—the rain had stopped, almost as suddenly as it had begun. The wind was dropping, as well—but the clouds were still thick and dark. Ice still gleamed in the trees, and water still dripped from every tree branch and from the eaves of the barn, but no more rain was falling. The pounding on the roof had ceased.

"It's not doing him any good while we're in here," the Seer said. "Why should he waste his magic and ruin the crops if we aren't out in it?"

"No," the Archer said. "That can't be true."

"Do you really think that's it?" Breaker asked, as he pulled clothing from his pack. None of it was actually *dry,* but the garments that had been near the center of the pack were only slightly damp, and infinitely preferable to what he had on.

"Of course," the Seer said. "He didn't bother us when we were heading away from him—he probably hoped that the others would talk us out of going back. Now that we're actually marching toward the Galbek Hills, he's trying to stop us."

"Spirits of sky and sea, summoned by our foe, brought the storm," the Speaker said. "Sheltered as we are, they have no target, and the storm is no more." She looked up. "But the clouds linger, ready to renew their ravages, should we emerge. The *ler* of the land shriek with rage and woe, bent and buffeted, mad with fear and confusion—never has the sky abused them so."

This was perhaps the longest coherent, uninterrupted speech Breaker had ever heard from her; he turned to stare.

She met his eyes. "This is what I am *for,*" she said. "The *ler* bound to me are of one accord, for the first time in my life—they guide me as one, they direct me against the Wizard Lord as one, that he may be prevented from further disruption of the natural order."

"I hadn't realized," Breaker said, as he pulled at his soaked shirt. "I hope . . . I hope it's not unpleasant."

"On the contrary," she said. "I am at peace for the first time in fourteen years."

"I'm glad," Breaker said, feeling foolish at the banality of his words. He began to peel off his drenched clothing.

As his head came out of his shirt his gaze fell on the corner where the Beauty was changing, and although he could see almost nothing in the gloom he felt a sudden flash of modesty. After his months on the road and his encounters with some of the more exotic communities of Barokan he had almost forgotten the prohibitions on nudity he had grown up with, but now the Beauty's presence brought them all rushing back. He hastened to pull his drier shirt on, while carefully not looking in the Beauty's direction.

"This can't be right," the Archer said loudly. "It can't be." He stepped out the door onto the platform.

The wind, which had died to a stiff breeze, suddenly roared back to life, slamming against the western end of the barn so hard that the boards groaned and the entire barn shook.

"It's not because we took shelter," the Archer called from the platform, shouting to be heard over the wind. "He just needed to rest. You'll see. He can't be watching us *that* closely."

And suddenly it was raining again, the rain drumming heavily on the barn roof. Breaker shivered.

"You see? You're still inside!" the Archer bellowed.

"But you aren't!" the Seer shouted back.

"Wait, wait!" The Archer stumbled back through the door, water streaming from his hat.

And the rain stopped, as if some mighty being had turned a tap.

The Archer froze where he was; no one dared speak as the wind sank away again.

Then the Archer turned and looked out the door.

"I don't believe it," he said, "I *won't* believe it."

"Believe it," the Seer said. "He knows where we are as well as I do—and he doesn't need to watch every second; he can give the bound *ler* who serve him enough of our true names to identify us, and tell them what to do."

"I don't *like* it!"

"None of us do."

"Is it going to rain like that *all the way to the Galbek Hills*?"

"I don't know," the Seer said. "I profoundly hope not."

"He needs to get the moisture from somewhere," the Scholar said. "He can't just conjure it from nothing. So he may well run out, in time."

"Can't he get it from the ocean?" Breaker asked, as he tugged his fresh breeches into place. "I've never seen it, but I've heard it goes on forever, all around the world, covering everything but Barokan and the Uplands. I'd think that was enough water to rain on us forever."

"If he could get it all airborne, of course it would be," the Scholar said, "but I don't think his magic is *that* powerful. I think he has to wait for clouds to form naturally before he can direct them against us."

"Are you sure of that, Lore?" the Seer asked.

"No," the Scholar said. "It's just a theory, it's nothing I've been told. Oh, and Sword, there are other lands besides those you mention—there are unknown realms south and east of the Uplands, and there may be more beyond the sea, as well. There's much more to the world than just Barokan and the plateau."

"Barokan is more than enough for me," Breaker said. "I've been traveling all summer and most of the autumn and still only visited a small part of it. I've never even seen the sea!"

"Nonetheless, there are other lands."

Breaker shook his head. "Amazing," he said.

"Indeed," the Scholar said.

"So do you mean the Wizard Lord can rain the entire ocean down on us, whenever we set foot outside?" the Archer demanded.

"No," the Scholar replied mildly. "I don't believe he can. But he can certainly cause downpours and gales—and you saw the ice forming on the trees, and surely you feel the cold; he can do that, too. Let us hope he can't do anything too drastically unnatural—I do not care to experience earthquakes or lightning."

"You mean those are *real*?" Breaker said, astonished. "I always thought they were just scary stories, like the soul-eater, or the dead lands."

The Scholar grimaced. "I regret to say, Sword, that there are indeed dead lands, and yes, there has been a soul-eater—though I can't say for certain one still exists. And earthquakes and lightning are both real natural phenomena that the Wizard Lords have suppressed for these last five or six centuries."

"But . . . oh," Breaker said. He opened his mouth to say more, then simply repeated, "Oh."

"Fire from the sky?" the Leader said. "That's natural?"

The guide spoke up unexpectedly.

"The Uplanders say it happens frequently above the cliffs," she said. "Sometimes I've seen a flickering up there myself that the Uplanders say is lightning. And there's no true magic up there, is there?"

"I don't know," the Scholar said. "My magic is tied to Barokan, and does not tell me what's true in the Uplands."

"Well, that's what they say," the guide said.

"It's probably true."

"So in theory, the Wizard Lord could strike us down with fiery bolts from the heavens?" Breaker asked.

"Lightning isn't exactly fire," the Scholar said. "It's something else. But in any case, no, the Wizard Lord *cannot* strike us down. Our own magic protects us—lightning will not harm us, any more than the plagues he used in Stoneslope did."

"The lightning cannot touch us, yet must we guard against it," the Speaker said. "If a bolt should strike a tree as we walk beneath, the oaths of the *ler* are uncompromised, yet we are quite possibly crushed beneath falling limbs."

"Oh, *that's* a cheerful thought," the Archer said.

"The spirits that guard us would have us aware of the hazards," the Speaker replied. "I but relay their words."

"As I relay the words of the Wizard Lord," said a squeaky, high-pitched voice. The entire party looked up to see a rat atop one of the tie-beams above them, peering down over the side at them.

"What do you want, madman?" the Seer demanded.

"To bring a little sanity," the rat replied. "Won't you abandon this foolish mission of yours? Nothing good can come of it."

"On the contrary, your death would be a benefit to Varagan," the Seer retorted. "That's all the good *I* ask."

"And if the next Wizard Lord is even worse, what then? Will you hunt him down and kill him, as well?"

"Of course we will!" the Leader responded instantly. "Our duty is to remove *all* unfit Wizard Lords. We bear you no special grudge."

The Seer grimaced at that, and Breaker swallowed a protest—Boss had not been with them in Stoneslope, had not felt those poor ghosts. *He* had no special grudge against the present Wizard Lord, but there were those who did.

"So you say," the rat said, "but then why has it taken you five years—five exemplary years, in which I have carried out my duties faithfully and never hurt a soul—to decide that the filth of Stoneslope must be avenged?"

"Because we didn't *know,*" the Seer shouted. "We didn't know what you had done!"

"And now suddenly, you do. Who is responsible for that, I wonder? Could it be that my enemies on the Council of Immortals have decided the time has come for me to be removed, so that one of their own faction can replace me?"

"I stumbled upon the truth!" the Seer shouted. "No one schemed against you, and the Council had nothing to do with it!"

"*You* may believe that," the rat replied. "*I* don't. They got word to you somehow—perhaps a dream, or a whispered message you didn't even remember hearing."

"Lore and I compared notes, nothing more!"

"I don't believe it," the rat repeated. "One of you is working for the Council—perhaps one of you is *on* the Council! I wouldn't put it past them to have a spy among the Chosen, a wizard pretending to be one of you."

"A wizard can't be one of the Chosen," the Scholar said. "The *ler* won't permit it."

"Then perhaps one of you is not actually one of the Chosen at all."

"That's ridiculous," the Seer said. "I know who and where the Chosen are—it's my magic, my role as Seer."

"So you're working with the impostor."

"You're being absurd," the Leader said. "We've all known each other for years."

"If you say so—though I don't think Sword would agree, to cite only the most obvious. But ask yourselves—why are you so determined to depose me? Isn't it worth one town's destruction to protect the rest of Barokan? Will you risk far worse? Floods, famines, lost crops and lost lives—I don't need to attack you directly to cost you heavily. I can unleash plagues all across Barokan, wash away bridges and burn down towns. I don't want to hurt you, but some of you have friends and family you care for, and I can hurt them—will you risk *their* lives? And in the end, if you persist, I *will* kill you if I must. Don't think I value my magic more than my life, my power more than my position—I must and will remain Wizard Lord!"

"Why?" Breaker asked. "Why not just yield peacefully? If you resign, we are not to harm you—you know that."

"And be just another member of the Council of Immortals, an ordinary wizard surrounded by my enemies? They all hate me, and I despise them—death would be preferable to once again suffering the taunts and torments of those who would claim to be my peers!"

"Then how did you ever *become* the Wizard Lord?" the Archer asked. "Weren't you chosen by the Council?"

"Of course I was! They wanted to get rid of me. And none of them wanted the job—none of them could be bothered to hunt down traitors or regulate the weather."

Breaker and the Archer exchanged glances. Getting rid of someone by granting him vast power and authority did not sound like something anyone sane would attempt.

But the Wizard Lord was clearly not entirely sane.

"If you turn back," the rat said, "or scatter, then the rains will stop. If you continue toward the Galbek Hills as a group, then you will face storms every step of the way, and worse. Floods and wind and lightning are just the beginning. Turn back. Go back to Winterhome. Please." The rat's squeaky little voice cracked badly as it repeated, *"Please!"*

"His grip on the rat is weakening," the Seer remarked. "He put a lot into that storm, and is weary."

"So are you!" the rat squealed, and then it scampered away.

"He's gone," the Seer said.

"Good," the Leader said. "In that case, I can ask you—are you *sure* the Council hasn't deceived you somehow?"

"How?" the Seer asked angrily. "I realized the Wizard Lord had committed murder when I spoke to Lore, and then he and Sword and I went to see the remains of Stoneslope and heard the ghosts—how could the Council have intervened?"

"A hint, perhaps, as the rat suggested?"

The Seer shook her head. "There was no hint. I wish there had been. To know that those poor dead souls were trapped in Stoneslope for five years, waiting for someone to find them and avenge them, and I had never bothered to investigate—that weighs on my *own* soul." She turned to the Leader. "I believed you when you said he had only killed rogues! I never checked!"

"And I believed *him,*" Boss retorted. "I shouldn't have, obviously, but I didn't know that."

"But you do now," the Archer said. "How did that happen, exactly? Seer, might Sword have said something?"

Boss glanced at Breaker, then back at the Seer. "Do we truly know him to be the Chosen Swordsman? I said we've all known each other for years, but in truth, I never met Sword or Beauty until yesterday."

"Either they're who they claim to be, or my magic has failed me," the Seer said angrily.

"Or you are indeed lying, and conspiring with a Council spy."

"Boss!"

"Is it really so impossible?"

"You've known me for ten years! Do you really think I could deceive you like that?"

"We've met a few times, but really, Seer, how well do I know you? I've chatted with you a dozen times, perhaps."

"That's nonsense. If anyone has betrayed us, Boss, it was *you,* when you told me that the killings in Stoneslope were nothing to worry about. I am doing what I swore to do—I gathered the others to remove a Dark Lord as soon as I knew we had one."

"And do you really think that's our responsibility?"

The Seer gaped at him. "We . . . we are the *Chosen,* Boss! We are chosen to defend Barokan. We are *heroes.* It's our sworn duty to remove any Wizard Lord gone bad. Ask Lore and Sword what we need to do—they saw Stoneslope, just as I did. The Wizard Lord doesn't even bother to deny slaughtering them all. Even if the Council had somehow directed me there, what does it matter? The Council has the right to guide us, should they choose to do so."

"Good points indeed! Good. And of course, you're right—it doesn't matter whether or not the Council is involved. If you and Lore and Sword saw what you say you saw, and not some clever illusion, then indeed the Wizard Lord has gone mad."

"Exactly!" The Seer sat back on her heels. "Exactly. He's gone mad, and must be stopped. Just look outside at what that storm did—tree limbs are down all along the road, every ditch and depression flooded knee-deep, leaves frozen on the trees, all just to inconvenience us."

"To preserve his own life."

"To preserve his *power,*" the Seer corrected. "He could end this at any time by abdicating his post."

"He seems to feel death would be preferable," the Archer said—though his words were a trifle indistinct. Breaker noticed that he was staring at the corner where the Beauty was straightening her attire. The sky outside had grown brighter, and their eyes had adjusted to the barn's dim interior; Breaker realized that he could see a lock of the Beauty's long, dark, curling hair hanging free, and the approximate shape of her perfect jaw.

"You realize," the Scholar said, noticing the Archer's gaze, "that her glamour won't work on any of us, any more than the Wizard Lord can harm us with lightning or plague, or Boss use his magical persuasiveness to compel us? You will never see her as other men do, never see her as utterly irresistible."

"But she's still the most beautiful woman in the world, is she not?" the Archer asked, turning back.

"Indeed she is," the Scholar agreed. "But only to a natural extreme."

"Well, forgive me, Lore, but that's still enough to interest me."

"You might show a little more tact," the Seer said.

Then they all fell silent as the Beauty straightened up and moved to rejoin the group.

"She heard every word," the Speaker said.

The Archer threw her a quick glance, then essayed a bow to the Beauty, who was once again securely wrapped in black. "My apologies if I said anything that troubled you," he said.

"Oh, just shut up," she said. Then she turned to the Leader. "So we are continuing to the Galbek Hills, and the Wizard Lord intends to use storms to harry us every step of the way. What can we do about it?"

"We can dress for the weather," Boss replied. "If we *know* it will storm, we can wrap ourselves in oilcloth—at Riversedge we'll resupply accordingly. And perhaps some sort of cover—Seer, what are the paths like? Could we ride a covered wagon? Would the *ler* permit it?" He glanced at the guide, but that exhausted individual had dozed off, sitting slumped against the barn wall, and was snoring gently.

"Even if we can't take it all the way, a wagon would help . . ." Breaker began.

Outside the barn the wind howled anew.

[26]

They had traveled less than half a mile from the barn, fighting their way through pounding wind and torrential rain that had been building steadily since they stepped out onto the platform, when the first lightning flashed across the sky.

The Beauty screamed; Breaker started, throwing his head back in surprise and catching a faceful of rain. Several of the others stumbled or cried out, though Breaker could make out no words over the storm.

"What was . . ." the Archer began.

Then the crack of thunder stunned them momentarily; Breaker flinched, the Beauty gasped, and this time the Speaker screamed, though only softly. Echoes of the thunderclap rolled over them.

"Thunder," the Scholar explained, shouting. "The sound is called thunder. The flash is lightning."

The sky turned white, blinding Breaker momentarily, as another closer, brighter flash of lightning blazed out; this time the earsplitting roar of thunder followed almost immediately.

"What should we do?" the Beauty asked.

"It can't hurt us," the Scholar shouted back. "Our magic protects us."

"*What* can't hurt us?" the Archer demanded. "It's just light and sound!"

The Scholar shook his head. "No, it's more than that. It's . . . the flash is from a *thing,* an effect, a force. The actual lightning bolt. It can knock down trees, start fires, kill a man by touching him. I don't really understand how . . ."

And then the third bolt flashed, and the thunder boomed, and all of them were blinded and deafened momentarily.

Even before Breaker could see again the smell reached him, a strange, sharp odor he had never smelled before, and then the scent of cooking meat.

And then the Seer was screaming, and the Speaker was babbling, and the Leader barking orders, and the three of them were kneeling in the mud and rain, huddled around something, something lying on the ground, something that smoked . . .

"The guide," the Scholar said. "Lightning hit the guide!" He turned and ran to help, Breaker and the Archer and the Beauty close behind.

It was obvious at a glance that nothing could be done; Breaker took one look and turned away, sickened by the sweet smell of cooked meat.

He had thought he had seen horror in the scattered bones in Stoneslope, the tiny skull the Seer had displayed, the pitiful remnants of ordinary life, but now he had learned a new and greater horror. A woman he had known and liked, however briefly, had just died before his eyes, roasted like a pig by magical fire from the sky—and for what? Surely the Wizard Lord must realize this would only increase their determination!

Rain spilled from his hat as he straightened up, and rain ran down his face; Breaker did not know whether he was crying, whether the moisture on his cheeks included his own tears.

"She must have died instantly," the Leader said.

"Lightning can stop a person's heart as if a hand grabbed it and squeezed," the Scholar said. "It can blast one's brain to pudding. She probably never felt a thing; she was most likely dead before she hit the ground."

The Seer gagged.

"You aren't helping, Lore," the Archer said.

Breaker was unsure whether the Scholar's words were any comfort or not; so far his reactions were too visceral for mere words to matter. The odd smell of the lightning and the ghastly smell of cooked meat, the memory of the guide's blackened and smoking face, were far more immediate.

"No more guides," the Beauty said. "We'll have to travel unaided."

"Indeed," the Leader agreed.

Breaker swallowed, and forced himself to speak. "Did the Wizard Lord do this intentionally?" he asked. "Can he steer these lightning bolts so precisely?"

"Yes," the Scholar replied instantly.

"Then you've all seen, now," Breaker said. "He killed an innocent woman. We can no longer doubt the need to remove him."

"I think we've all seen enough," the Leader said, getting to his feet. "Come on—we still need to reach shelter before nightfall."

"Are we going to just *leave* her here?" the Archer asked, shocked.

"We can't spare the time to do anything else, not in this storm," the Leader said. "We'll tell the townspeople in Riversedge."

Lightning flashed anew, and the crack of thunder blended with the crack of breaking wood.

"Stay away from any trees," the Leader said. "Lore says lightning can knock them down—that means it can knock them down on *us*. We need to stay in the open."

"Where the storm is worst," the Archer said.

"Of course."

"You know, I wanted to kill him anyway, but now I am really beginning to *hate* the Wizard Lord."

"I don't blame you," Breaker said.

"Come on," the Beauty said. "All of you. We can talk in Riversedge." She matched her actions to her words, rising and trudging onward.

One by one, the others followed.

They reached Riversedge around sunset—they had not seen the sun in hours, of course, but the skies were growing even darker, and there could be little doubt that the faint daylight was dying.

The boundary shrine had tilted slightly in the mud, but was still easily seen; Breaker stopped to say, "We come in peace, O *ler,* and beg you receive us kindly." The Speaker paused as well and said something that sounded like no imaginable human language; the others marched past without stopping.

They passed the farmers' fields, now flooded and lost beneath black water; before them the village was a darker gray outline in the deepening gray gloom. Breaker saw no lights, and for a moment felt an uncontrollable surge of terror—had the Wizard Lord destroyed the town, as he had Stoneslope, so that its residents could not aid the Chosen? Would they find roofless ruins and staring corpses, rather than welcoming fires and cheerful hosts?

But then he glimpsed a yellow flicker, and another—the lights were there, but doors and shutters were tightly closed, shutting out the storm and the encroaching night.

"Hey!" the Archer shouted, as they entered the main street. "Hello in there!"

"Shut up," Breaker told him. "We'll knock at the inn—there's no need to wake the whole town."

"And where is this inn?" the Leader asked. "I was the high priest's guest when I came through before, and needed no inn."

"There," the Seer replied, pointing.

A moment later the Seer and the Archer were pounding on the door of the inn, calling for succor, while the other five stood back.

And a moment after that—a long and frightening moment, in which Breaker feared that his fantasy was true after all, despite the lights—the door swung open, and the seven tumbled in, one after another, spilling rain from cloaks and hats and packs.

The landlord stared at them.

"What's happening?" he demanded. "Who are you people? What were you doing out in this storm?"

The Leader spoke, of course, as the others shook off the worst of the rain.

"We are traveling from Winterhome, on our way to the Galbek Hills," he said.

"In *this* storm?"

The Leader grimaced. "We didn't have much choice."

"And where is your guide?"

At that, the seven Chosen fell silent. They stopped wringing out sleeves to stare at one another.

"Dead," the Leader said at last. "She's dead. On the road, a mile or two east."

"Dead? The *ler*?"

"The lightning."

The innkeeper flinched. "The flashes—that was lightning? And it really can kill?"

"Yes."

"What's happened? Why is this happening? Are the *ler* angry? Is a rogue wizard responsible? Why doesn't the Wizard Lord *do* something?"

"The Wizard Lord has gone mad," the Seer said, before the Leader could reply.

"Indeed," the Leader agreed, not bothering to hide his annoyance at the Seer's interruption. "The Wizard Lord *has* gone mad, and sent that storm to stop us."

"To stop *you*?"

"See for yourself," the Leader said, gesturing at the still-open door. "Now that we're safely inside—well, look!"

The Scholar opened the door wide so that the innkeeper could see that the wind had dropped, and the rain and lightning had stopped.

"But—are you wizards, then?"

The Leader gave an exasperated sigh. "We are the *Chosen,*" he said. "Not wizards."

"The Chosen—going to the Galbek Hills?" The innkeeper gaped at them. "The Wizard Lord has gone mad? What, have I fallen into one of the old stories? That's absurd! It's been a hundred years!"

"Do you think we don't know that?" the Archer snapped, as he tugged at his wet garments.

"That doesn't make it any easier for us," the Beauty said, as she struggled to squeeze enough water from her scarf that it would stop falling from her face.

"Did you think it could never happen again?" the Seer demanded, as she found the poker and began stirring the fire. Breaker thought that was unfair; the innkeeper almost certainly *had* thought it would never happen again. Breaker had thought so, or he would not have taken the role of Swordsman in the first place. Thinking it would never happen again seemed very common.

"Regardless of who or what else we may be, my good man, right now we are customers—cold, damp, hungry, tired customers," the Leader said. "We'll have all night to tell you our tales, if you wish."

"We need to sleep," the Seer said. "We'll need all the rest we can get. We'll face more of the same tomorrow."

"Eat first," the Archer protested.

"And find a guide to our next destination . . ." the Scholar began.

"*No,*" Breaker interrupted. "No guide. No more guides, ever."

"Oh," the Scholar said, as several of the others glared at him. "Of course. No guides."

"I can guide us," the Speaker said. "Now that my guardians are agreed on our goal, I can bespeak the *ler* of the road and find our path."

"Good," the Leader said. "I'm pleased to hear that. Landlord, you're still here? Food! Drink! Seats! Beds!"

With that, the innkeeper finally remembered his duties, and hurried toward the kitchens, calling, "Wife! We have customers!"

Breaker looked around, then, and realized that the seven of them *were* the only customers—save for themselves and the innkeeper, the common room was deserted. The fire was banked, chairs and benches pushed against the walls, tables bare and empty.

But that made sense; after all, who would venture out on such a day, in such a storm? The people of Riversedge were undoubtedly safe in their homes, huddled around their hearths, waiting out the weather.

Though now that the rain had stopped, some might well feel like discussing the storm with their neighbors over a good mug of beer; Breaker suspected that the tavern would not remain empty for long.

And that would undoubtedly mean explaining the situation several times.

Breaker was not looking forward to that—especially not when it came to their poor guide. He really did not want to think about that.

How could the Wizard Lord have done such a thing? Burning down an innocent old woman like that!

But then, the Wizard Lord had slaughtered an entire village. It was hard to think about that, too.

At least in Stoneslope Breaker hadn't *seen* anyone die—or worse, smelled it; he had seen the bones and the ruins, and felt the fear and anger of the dead, but that had been less immediate. Those were quite bad enough, horrifying and infuriating and frustrating, but not nauseating. He doubted he would ever forget the smell of the guide's death, that strange mix of that sharp, magical odor and the stench of charred flesh.

He pulled a chair over to the nearest table and sat down; a moment later the Scholar was seated at his left, the Beauty at his right. She had somehow managed to get her scarf secured in place, despite its utter saturation, but it was clinging, outlining her jaw; Breaker found himself staring without meaning to. He had never seen so lovely a chin. And he could see her fingers, though she had tucked her hands back into her sleeves, and they were beautiful, long and tapered . . .

Then he realized what he was doing and tore his gaze away.

The Archer had sat down on the far side of the table; he was staring openly at the Beauty. Breaker frowned.

"We can't go on like this," the Beauty said. "We need that wagon."

"Getting it ready may mean staying a few days here," Breaker said.

"It would be worth it," the Beauty said.

"I believe she's right," the Scholar said.

Breaker nodded. "I won't argue." He looked at the Scholar—partly just to avoid looking at the Beauty again—and asked, "In all the stories about the other Dark Lords, is there any mention of storms or lightning?"

"Oh, yes, of course," the Scholar said. "The Dark Lord of the Midlands was before the Wizard Lords had full control of the weather, but he did manage to gather clouds around his fortress—I'm not sure why. The Dark Lord of Tallowcrane brought landslides down on the Chosen, and killed the Seer that way. The next two retired, rather than be slain, but the Dark Lord of Kamith t'Daru used rainstorms to create floods to slow the Chosen when they neared his keep. The Dark Lord of the

Tsamas used a lightning bolt to burn a siege engine the Leader was constructing, and rain to make footing treacherous." He frowned. "The Dark Lord of Spider Marsh and the Dark Lord of Goln Vleys did not use weather—I don't know why not. And I don't recall any tales of using storms as the Dark Lord of the Galbek Hills does."

"The Dark Lord of the Galbek Hills." Breaker had never heard that phrase spoken before, had never thought it himself, but it was now obvious that was indeed who and what they were up against.

"The Dark Lord of the Galbek Hills." He, as the Swordsman, was on his way to kill the Dark Lord of the Galbek Hills. It still didn't seem entirely real, somehow. Dark Lords were monsters of the ancient past, not part of the peaceful modern world.

But the present Wizard Lord had slaughtered a village—and killed their guide.

The Seer, satisfied with the fire, pulled another chair up, between the Scholar and the Archer. The Leader and the Speaker remained apart, seated on a bench by the far wall, talking quietly.

"How many people has the Wizard Lord killed?" Breaker asked the Seer, without preamble, as she settled onto her chair.

"What?"

"All told, in his eight years, or nine, how many people has the current Wizard Lord killed?"

"I . . . I don't know, exactly. I don't know how many were in Stoneslope—enough that I sensed them as a mass, rather than individuals."

"Well, other than that, then—how many besides the people of Stoneslope?"

"Well, you *saw,*" she said, startled. "He killed our guide!"

"No, besides that. How many rogue wizards, real or alleged?"

"Oh! None."

It was Breaker's turn to be startled. "None?"

"No, of course not."

"But isn't it his duty to kill rogue wizards?"

"Yes, of course, but he hasn't found any to kill."

"Have you asked him?"

"No, I . . . No."

"Do you think he's *recruited* them?" the Archer asked. "That they're working for him?"

"Maybe," Breaker said—though in fact he had not thought anything of the sort; he hadn't yet worked that far through his ideas.

"I don't think there were any," the Seer said.

"Seer, how long have you been the Seer?"

"Thirty-two long, tiresome years. Since a little after my twentieth birthday. Why?"

"How many Wizard Lords have you known?"

"Three. I don't see why this matters."

"The other two—how many people did *they* kill?"

"None. They weren't Dark Lords."

"But rogue wizards . . . ?"

"There aren't . . . oh, I don't know."

"There aren't any more rogue wizards?" Breaker asked. "Is that what you mean?"

"Maybe. I don't know. There haven't been any for thirty-two years."

"Longer," the Scholar said. "The last confirmed instance of a Wizard Lord killing a rogue wizard was during the reign of the Wizard Lord of Greensand, about three hundred years ago. In fact, when the Dark Lord of Spider Marsh resigned he cited the dearth of rogue wizards as one reason he had attempted to alter the system."

Breaker and the Archer exchanged glances.

"It seems to me he had a point," Breaker said.

"The Council of Immortals felt otherwise," the Scholar said. "They said that it was proof the system was working just as it was—the presence of the Wizard Lord prevented wizards from going rogue in the first place."

"The presence of the Chosen is supposed to prevent Wizard Lords from going dark, but how many have there been since then?" Breaker asked.

"Since the Dark Lord of Spider Marsh? Just the Dark Lord of Goln Vleys, and now the Dark Lord of the Galbek Hills."

"So we've had three Dark Lords, and no rogue wizards, in that time?" the Archer asked. "That sounds to me as if the cure is worse than the disease."

The Scholar shrugged. "Perhaps. But remember, the Wizard Lord also regulates the weather, to ensure good crops and safe passage, and his presence deters bandits and other criminals as well as rogue wizards."

"Don't the priests bargain with the *ler* for good crops?" Breaker asked. "Ours certainly did in Mad Oak."

"Well, with earth *ler,* certainly," the Scholar answered, disconcerted. "But the wind and rain . . ." He hesitated. "You know, I don't know whether that can be controlled locally. I would think it could be—but then why *do* we have the Wizard Lord do it?"

"My parents told me the Wizard Lord spent his time hunting down rogue wizards," Breaker said.

"But if there *aren't* any . . ."

"I thought there were," the Seer interrupted. "I swear by all the *ler,* I thought there were still rogues, and they had simply gotten better at hiding themselves. When the Wizard Lord told us he had wiped out a nest of them at Stoneslope I believed him, because I *wanted* to believe him—it meant the system was working. But I should have checked, I shouldn't have just *accepted* it without question for five years!" Her face crumpled as if she were struggling to hold back tears; Breaker had never before seen a woman her age look like that.

"But there's no real harm done," Breaker said soothingly. "He didn't kill anyone else—well, not until today. And now we know, and we'll stop him."

"But the guide—if I had checked years ago, she might . . ."

"She might have been just as horribly dead five years sooner," Breaker said. "And when you saw your mistake, you set out to correct it, didn't you? And here we are."

"But *five years*!"

"Are you worried about the ghosts of the dead that cannot rest until they're avenged?" the Archer asked. "I've heard that they aren't really aware of the passage of time."

"I don't . . ." Breaker began, but then he was interrupted by a shove at his elbow. He turned to see a plump woman heaving a large, heavily loaded tray onto the table.

"Your supper," she said.

"At last!" the Archer said, and for the next twenty minutes no one mentioned Dark Lords or rogue wizards; for the most part the conversation was limited to requests to have one food or another handed over or replenished.

The Beauty took her dinner to a room upstairs, to eat in private; the Archer watched her go, but then, resigned to not yet seeing her face, returned his attention to the meal.

[27]

Few townspeople appeared at the inn that evening; although the rain had stopped the wind still howled through the muddy streets, and few cared to venture out in such conditions. Those who did appear did not intrude on the party of strangers. Thus the six of them—seven, when the Beauty emerged again from her room—were able to discuss and plan.

"We can expect storms every inch of the way," the Leader said, "and I, for one, don't want to slog through them the way we did today. We need a wagon. A covered one that will keep the rain off."

"Solidly enclosed, I would say," the Archer said. "A cloth covering will be blown away or flogged to pieces."

"Good point—yes, a good solid wagon, all wood."

"What will lightning do to a wooden wagon?" Breaker asked.

The Leader frowned, then looked at the Scholar.

"Lightning can shatter trees, or set them afire," the Scholar said. "I'd suppose it can do the same to a wooden wagon."

"What can we do about it?"

The Scholar hesitated. "I'm not sure," he said. "There are a few very old stories—I suppose they must be true, since I remember them, but I don't know what they *mean.* One speaks of a thing called a 'lightning rod,' made of copper or iron, but I don't know what one would look like, or how it would work, or how we could make it."

"Metal?" the Speaker asked.

Startled, the Scholar turned. "Yes, metal."

"But metal *draws* lightning, it doesn't keep it away."

"Does it? How?" the Leader asked.

The Speaker looked confused, then turned to the empty air and murmured gibberish for a moment, then cocked her head as if listening. The others waited.

At last, she spoke.

"Lightning is . . . not a fluid, but something that behaves somewhat like a fluid. It seeks the ground, as water seeks to flow downward. To lightning, the air is like sand is to water—it seeps through it by the easiest route, though a thousand thousand times faster than water through sand. And metal—to lightning, metal is a hole in the sand, a hole in the air. The *ler* of lightning will seek out metal as a path through the air, a shortcut to the ground."

"Oh, but then a lightning rod is easy to understand!" the Scholar said enthusiastically. "A metal rod reaching from above the wagon down to the ground will draw the lightning through it, and it will all pass through so quickly it won't have time to harm the wood!"

"The sand around a hole still gets wet when you pour water in the hole," the Leader said doubtfully.

"But only the water close to the hole! If we set our lightning rods out on iron brackets, along either side of the wagon, then we should be safe."

"I suppose it won't hurt to try it," the Leader said. "Of course, it will take some time to construct such a thing." He considered, then asked, "Does anyone see a better alternative?"

No one did.

Their manner of transport settled, they then discussed routes, and whether or not to hire guides.

"The Speaker can speak to *ler,*" Breaker pointed out. "And we are all supposed to be immune to much of the magic we meet. We don't need guides anymore."

"But guides do more than speak," the Seer protested. "They know the safe routes, and ways to appease the dangers."

"We will not be crossing wilderness," Breaker said. "We *came* here from the Galbek Hills, and the paths were mostly well-worn and clearly visible, with no grave dangers to dissuade. We made do without a guide to and from Stoneslope. I think we can manage to find our way without endangering any more guides."

"Would we be endangering them?" the Leader asked. "This lightning cage the Scholar proposes should make our wagon safe for anyone, not just us."

"How well can they guide us from inside a wagon?" the Archer asked. "Besides, as Sword says, we don't need them."

"We got *here* without one," Breaker said. "At least, for half the distance."

"And we don't know how well the cage will work," the Scholar said. "Devices do not always behave as expected."

"Let us try the next leg of our journey without a guide," the Beauty said. "At least until we know whether this magical cage works. If we encounter unexpected difficulties on the road, we will know better next time."

"Agreed," the Leader said. "We will try it unguided, and see how we fare. After all, we are the Chosen!"

Although he had been arguing for exactly that, Breaker was not particularly happy at the Leader's words—he was all too aware that merely being the Chosen did not mean they would win out, or that they would all survive. He worried that they would become overconfident.

But then he remembered the long, weary slog through the rain, lightning flickering around them, thunder echoing dully, mud sucking at their boots. They could hardly be overconfident in such conditions; it was only here in the inn, safe and dry, that they were regaining their self-assurance.

He thought the Wizard Lord could be counted on to provide them with reminders of their own fallibility.

The planning and plotting continued well into the night; at one point the Seer warned them that the Wizard Lord was listening in through the innkeeper's cat, and they shifted the focus of their discussion for a time.

And finally, not long before midnight, they found their way to their two rooms.

In the morning they set about implementing their schemes—a wagon and oxen were bought, a smith hired to construct a protective cage. Wind howled through the streets constantly, but rain only fell when one or another of the Chosen was out in the open.

The wagon was stocked, supplies laid in, while the cage was built; the project used almost the smith's entire supply of iron and took three days to complete, but at last the wagon stood ready.

Breaker looked at it with mixed feelings.

The wagon itself was nothing very special—a large unpainted wooden box on four sturdy wheels, a bench at the front, drawn by four oxen. The metal lightning cage, however, gave it a strange and mechanical appearance. Four long metal rods stood a foot out from either side, mounted on iron brackets, and extending from two feet above the top of the wagon to a few inches from the ground; two more were mounted at the front, another pair at the back, making a dozen in all. Because the Scholar had been uncertain what would be most effective, half the rods were iron, and half were copper, alternating. Iron scrollwork formed a protective web above the top of the wagon, connecting all twelve, and chains dangled from the bottom of each rod, dragging on the ground.

"How much does that *weigh*?" he asked.

"A great deal," the Leader said. "We may need more oxen, especially in the mud—but let us try it as it is and see how we fare."

Breaker nodded.

At dawn the next day they boarded the wagon; the Archer claimed to know how to drive a team of oxen, so he took his place on the bench while the other six climbed into the cramped interior and settled onto the boxes of supplies that served as seats. The Leader lit a small and distressingly smoky lantern and hung it from a hook in the ceiling—the wagon had no windows, as no one had thought them necessary, and the light that leaked in around the Archer's back was gray and unsatisfying. Rain drummed heavily on the roof.

Then the Archer shook the reins and called "Hyaah!," and with a jerk, the heavy contraption started forward.

They had scarcely left Riversedge when the first rumble of thunder sounded—at first Breaker had taken it for the cart's wheels rolling over something, or something shifting in the wagon, but then it sounded again and he knew. He glanced out at the Archer's back, hunched against the rain.

"How close is it?" he called.

"Flickers on the horizon," the Archer replied. "And we need to put an overhang on this thing—I'm getting soaked!"

"We'll do it at our next stop, then," Breaker said. "You'll survive one day, won't you?"

"Do I have a choice?"

Breaker felt a moment's guilt that the Archer was working in the rain, while he was safe and dry—albeit crowded and likely to get bruised from banging against wooden boxes as the wagon bumped along. "I'll take a turn later, if you show me how," he said.

"I'll . . ." the Archer began, but then a sudden flash blinded them both for a moment, and half a second later a crash of thunder broke over them.

"Closer," Breaker said.

"Just ahead," the Archer told him. "I saw it."

It occurred to Breaker for the first time that the Wizard Lord didn't need to hit *them,* or their wagon, to slow them down—if he were to knock down trees and block the road, that would certainly *delay* them, though it might not *stop* them.

He didn't say anything, however, for fear the Wizard Lord might be listening. The Seer hadn't mentioned the Wizard Lord's presence, but Breaker was not at all certain she always noticed it.

And then another flash came, and a blast of thunder simultaneously shook the wagon, which jolted and slowed, but did not stop; the Beauty shrieked, and the Leader cursed, and Breaker heard a strange crackling. He had been looking out at the rain when the flash came, and now he found himself blinking at pink afterimages of the Archer's silhouette; his ears were ringing. He did not resist when the Leader pushed him aside and barked, "What happened?"

The Archer's voice was little more than a croak as he replied, "The cage works."

"Are you all right?"

"I think so."

"Good. Keep going!"

"Yes, sir." Breaker heard the Archer calling to the oxen, but the wagon did not seem to pick up any speed.

And then another bolt of lightning crashed, deafeningly close, and the Archer screamed. The wagon jerked to a halt.

"What?" the Leader demanded. "What happened?"

Breaker thrust himself forward, close beside the Leader, as they both heard the Archer cursing elaborately.

"What is it?" Breaker called.

"The cage doesn't cover the oxen," the Archer called back, as he clambered from the bench. "One of them is down."

"Oh, by the black *ler* . . ." The Leader and Breaker both climbed out, and a moment later Breaker found himself slogging through mud in the torrential rain, helping the Archer cut the smoking carcass of a dead ox from the yoke and traces, while the Leader calmed the three surviving animals and held them back.

"It barely hit his nose," the Archer said as they worked. "I don't think he could get the lightning any closer."

"If we mount a metal bar above the yoke, leading back to the cage, then?"

"That should work, so far as I can see. We'll ask the Scholar and the Speaker."

"Can three oxen pull the wagon?"

The Archer glanced at the terrified beasts. "I don't know," he said.

Breaker glanced back along the path; even in the downpour he could still see Riversedge. They had come only a few hundred yards. "We could go on . . ."

"And if we try," the Leader said, leaning forward and shouting to be heard over the driving rain, "and he kills another ox, it'll be that much harder to get to shelter. No, we go back and mount a bar, as the Archer said, and get another ox. Then we press on."

"I hate to . . ." Breaker began.

"We don't really have a choice," the Leader said. "We can't risk another ox. We go back."

"Agreed," the Archer shouted.

Reluctantly, Breaker admitted that they had a point. When the last leather strap snapped free he began tugging the remaining lead ox's head around, getting the wagon headed back whence it had come.

The innkeeper was not happy to see them.

"Get out!" he bellowed, shaking with rage or fear. "Get out, and take this unnatural weather with you!"

"We would like nothing better," the Leader answered, "but the Wizard Lord has seen to it that we can't depart until certain matters have been attended to."

It took most of the day to install a long horizontal bar extending out from the wagon, but the Speaker assured them that it would indeed protect their draft animals—all six, as the Chosen took this opportunity to enlarge their team. They stayed one more night in Riversedge, and set out anew in the morning.

Once again, the rain was constant and drenching; the path beneath their wheels was usually inches deep in either mud or water, and lightning cracked and flashed around them.

The protective cage served its intended purpose, though; any lightning bolt that came close was drawn harmlessly through the metal into the ground. Sparks showered, and Breaker felt his hair stand on end, but no real harm was done. The wood around the supporting bolts did get slightly charred over time, and that strange magical smell—"ozone," the Scholar called it—followed them like a woman's perfume.

They had gone several miles before the Wizard Lord finally thought to attempt what Breaker had been expecting all along, and bring a tree down across their route. Breaker, the Archer, and the Leader managed to lever it out of the way eventually, but the delay cost them the better part of an hour—and of course the Wizard Lord repeated it half a mile later.

As a result they didn't reach the next town until well after dark, and the entire party was filthy, soaking wet, exhausted, half-deafened, and very, very angry.

"If he really wants us to turn back," Breaker said, as they unhitched the oxen for the night, "he's not going about it effectively. Irritating us with these stupid delays is just annoying, not discouraging."

"At least he's abandoned the 'Oh, I'm really harmless,' nonsense," the Archer said.

"These delays may be to give him time to prepare for us," the Leader suggested. "He may be setting traps of some sort."

"Oh, *there's* a cheerful thought!" said the Archer.

The Leader shrugged. "It's a possibility."

Breaker didn't argue, but he wondered whether the Wizard Lord's blockades would really make any difference. Yes, they had to waste time clearing them away, but they had still reached the next town in a single day—just much *later* in the day. And the time the Wizard Lord might have saved was probably devoted to casting weather spells and steering lightning bolts and so on, rather than setting traps. If this was to be the pattern for the rest of the journey, they would reach the Wizard Lord's tower on the same day as they would have anyway.

They would be far less well-rested and far more annoyed, though. That might make a difference in itself.

Still, if this was all the Wizard Lord had to throw at them, they would indeed reach the tower and kill its master.

He, the Swordsman, would presumably kill the Dark Lord of the Galbek Hills.

Breaker remembered his mother's words and the expression on her face when she asked, "You want to be a killer?"

He shuddered at the memory—and he hoped the Archer would put an arrow or two in the Wizard Lord's chest before anyone got close enough to draw a blade.

Nonetheless, after their late, cold, and tasteless supper, Breaker still attended to his required hour of practice.

[28]

The night sky was cloudy, but no rain fell—why would the Wizard Lord waste water when the Chosen were all safely indoors? Wind rattled the shutters, though, and whistled around the eaves. Tired as he was, Breaker lay awake listening to it for what seemed like hours before finally dropping off to sleep.

As a result he awoke stiff and foul-tempered in the morning. He did his share of the preparations for departure, but contributed little beyond grunts to the accompanying conversation.

It did not help his mood at all when the renewed storm broke and rain pelted down before they even had the oxen out of their rented stalls.

At last, though, they got out of the village, rolling west and south across open country—which meant no downed trees serving as roadblocks. That brightened Breaker's morning, and as his mood improved his weariness caught up with him. He dozed off in a corner of the wagon.

He was awakened by a sudden jarring and a crash; startled, he rolled from his niche and scrambled to the front of the still-moving wagon.

The air outside smelled of ozone, and Breaker saw that they had found their way into a patch of woods—and of course, the Wizard Lord had taken the opportunity to drop a tree across their path, a few yards ahead.

The Archer was reining in the oxen, preparing to stop; the Leader crouched in the wagon's doorway, ready to jump out and lend a hand in heaving the fallen timber aside.

Breaker sighed. "Again?" he said.

"I'm afraid so," the Leader said. "Nothing to do but get on with it, though—are you ready?"

"Ready enough," Breaker said.

The wagon slowed to a stop, and the Leader heaved himself through the opening; Breaker followed close behind. A moment later, when the wagon was secured, the Archer joined them.

The air was thick with confused *ler,* as well as rain—but they did not seem hostile; in fact, Breaker realized, as he splashed toward the fallen tree, that he had not felt any real hostility from any *ler* in any of the wilderness they had crossed since leaving Winterhome. Branches did not slap at his face, nor the ground make him stumble. Instead the *ler* seemed to be hanging back, watching them, making room for them. It appeared that nature itself preferred to let the Chosen pass unmolested, despite the Wizard Lord's efforts. That was heartening, and Breaker smiled as he followed Boss through the torrents.

They were heaving at a broken limb, trying to clear an opening the wagon could squeeze through, when the dog leapt at the Archer.

Breaker hadn't seen or heard the animal's approach; the steady downpour had hidden it effectively. It wasn't until the fast, close movement caught his eye, and he heard the thud of its forepaws hitting the Archer's bent back, that Breaker saw it.

It was a large black dog, a shepherd of some sort—between the rain and the combatants' thrashing Breaker could make out little detail beyond size, color, and general shape. The people of Mad Oak did not keep herd animals, and therefore did not keep herd dogs, so even after a year's travels Breaker was not very familiar with the specific breeds, but this one was big and fierce, and it was biting and clawing at the Archer with unnatural ferocity and in unnatural silence.

The Archer fell—not to the ground, but into the tangle of downed tree in front of him—as he tried to twist around to face his attacker, and as the dog's jaws closed on his neck.

The Leader called "Attack! We're under attack!" and turned, arms raised, to see whether any more animals were approaching. He made no move to aid the Archer.

Breaker, on the other hand, ran forward immediately. His hand fell instinctively to where the hilt of his sword should have been—but he had left the weapon in the wagon, to keep it dry and stave off rust. "Black *ler*!" he growled, as he hesitated.

If he ran for the wagon to fetch his blade, the Archer might well be maimed or dead before he returned, and he might collide with the others coming to help. If he dove in bare-handed, he might be taking his life in his hands—was the dog rabid, possessed, or mad?

But the Archer needed help, and there were weapons at hand—he snapped a branch from the fallen tree.

He had intended to wield it like a broom or a whip, to try to drive the dog away, but the minute his hand closed around one end of the stick his grip shifted, and he found himself falling into a fencing stance.

His first thrust caught the thrashing dog squarely in the back ribs, despite its twisting as the Archer struggled in its grip; the animal turned slightly, trying to face this new assailant, and that gave Breaker the opening he needed. He plunged the stick into the dog's eye.

It yelped, releasing its hold on the Archer, and Breaker automatically followed up with a jab at the dog's throat, and then a stab at its other eye.

"It's the Wizard Lord!" the Seer's voice shouted from the wagon.

"I guessed as much," Breaker called back, preparing for another thrust—but the dog had had enough; it leapt from the Archer's back over the fallen tree and bounded away, yelping and howling and stumbling.

Breaker dropped his improvised weapon and jumped to help the Archer; as he took one of the injured man's shoulders he found the Leader at the other, and together they got the Archer to his feet.

"Are you all right?" Breaker asked, although he could see that the

Archer was not—blood was streaming down his back, and his hands were red as well.

"I don't know," the Archer said. "What was that?"

"Just a dog," the Leader said, as he turned his wounded companion toward the wagon.

"A big one, with the Wizard Lord possessing it," Breaker added. They did not bother with further conversation as they hurried the Archer to the wagon and hoisted him in.

Breaker had expected confusion once they got inside, but instead he found three women waiting and ready, the Beauty in the middle, the Seer on her right, and the Speaker on her left; they stretched the Archer out and bent over him as the Scholar pulled Breaker and the Leader away.

"What . . ." Breaker began.

"It's part of their magic," the Scholar said. "Babble can talk to the *ler* to see the nature of the injury, Seer can see the strength of his spirit and judge what needs to be done, and the Beauty can heal with her touch—not completely, not any more than a strong priestess, but enough to help. Let them work."

Breaker nodded, but then shoved past the Speaker to fetch his sword; once armed, he climbed quickly back out of the wagon.

"What do you think you're doing?" the Leader demanded, as Breaker pushed past him.

"There could be more," Breaker said. "Why would the Wizard Lord stop with one? He hasn't stopped the lightning or the rain when his first attempt failed." He grimaced. "And we still need to move that tree."

"Good," the Leader said. "Come on, then." He turned, and the two of them climbed down side by side.

They had scarcely cleared the wagon when the buck charged at them, head down.

It was a large deer, its antlers tall and many-pronged. Without thinking, Breaker shoved the Leader aside and snatched his sword from its scabbard; he barely dodged the animal's antlers.

But then the sword slashed through the rain and pierced the big deer's neck. The speed of the charge almost yanked the weapon from Breaker's hand, but he withdrew it as the buck thundered past.

The animal turned, blood gushing from its throat, and dove for the

Leader; Breaker ran a pace after it and plunged his blade between its ribs as the Leader rolled in the mud, trying to get clear of the buck's hooves.

The deer thrashed, and tried to pivot, to get at Breaker, but he leapt nimbly away and thrust his sword into the beast's flank yet again.

He could see that its eyes were already clouded over, its movements unsteady, its left foreleg stiff and unresponsive, but still it came at him; he did not need the Seer to tell him that the Wizard Lord's magic was driving the dying creature far beyond its nature. Any ordinary deer would have fled or fallen long since.

He dodged again, and once again thrust his sword into the doomed animal, this time aiming a fierce slash just behind the shoulder, to cripple it—by rights it should already be dead, he knew, and the Wizard Lord's magic was keeping it alive, but could even the Wizard Lord force it to move severed muscles?

The deer's leg collapsed beneath it, and it fell on its side, panting, its flank heaving, blood pouring from every wound, but its head still turned, its gaze still fixed on Breaker.

He had had quite enough; he jammed his right foot onto one of the antlers to hold the poor thing down, and used his sword to chop off its head.

It took three blows, and when it was done Breaker was spattered from toe to waist with blood, mud, and gore, and dark blood drenched his rain-soaked sleeves to the elbow. He was shaking, whether from the cold rain or the aftereffects of the fight he wasn't sure, and the deer's body twitched for several seconds, as well.

"Are you all right?" the Leader asked.

Breaker didn't answer; he did not think he could speak yet without his voice shaking even more than his hands. He swallowed, and blinked rain from his eyes.

He had just killed a deer, he realized. He wasn't a hunter, hadn't been blessed by the priests, hadn't said the necessary prayers. He fell to his knees in the mud, bloody sword raised.

"Oh, *ler* of this land, spirit of this deer, spirits of all the creatures I have offended, I beg your forgiveness!" he called, and his voice did not shake at all. "I acted in haste, I acted to defend myself, and if I have wronged the *ler*, I ask that you instruct me in how I can atone!"

"We don't have time for this," the Leader said. "We still need to clear the path, and there may be more animals."

"Hear me, Erren Zal Tuyo!" the Speaker's voice called.

Startled, Breaker turned; the Speaker was leaning out the wagon's door.

"The *ler* of the deer and the land say you have done no wrong, that your acts freed the deer's spirit from enslavement, that it is the Wizard Lord who wrongs the land with his storms and distortions. Go about your business!"

Breaker blinked rain from his eyes and lowered his sword, simultaneously confused and reassured. How could the Wizard Lord wrong the land? Was he not *lord* of the land, of all Barokan? Had he gone *that* far from the right path?

But the Speaker could not be lying about such a thing; she would have had to listen to the *ler*'s protests.

"Come on," the Leader said. "Let's move that tree."

Automatically, Breaker drew a rag from his pocket and began wiping his blade clean, even though he knew he would not be able to dry it properly until he was back in the wagon, and therefore could not sheathe it safely.

He had killed a deer, and it had been the right and necessary thing to do, but he still did not like it. Killing animals was for hunters and herdsmen, not barley-farmers—or swordsmen. It wasn't his place to kill deer, and they should be killed with spear or arrow, not a sword.

And why hadn't the deer fled when wounded, as the dog had? Why had the Wizard Lord's hold been so much stronger?

Perhaps the Wizard Lord had been better prepared, or was improving with practice.

Breaker shuddered.

And then he was at the tree, and he and the Leader were too busy heaving at the unyielding wood to worry about anything else for the next few moments.

They had maneuvered the main bulk to one side, and had an opening that the wagon could probably squeeze through, when Breaker glanced uneasily toward the wagon. Something was bothering him, but he could not say what it was. He peered through the rain at the wagon, its outline weirdly distorted by the iron and bronze cage that protected it, as if someone had tried to cross it out of the world.

Something was moving across the top.

At first he thought it was a trick of the light, or rainwater splashing from the metal, or even perhaps a momentarily visible *ler* of some sort, but as he stared he realized it was not his imagination, nor any sort of illusion or spirit.

It was a squirrel.

He almost relaxed at that, then caught himself. What was a squirrel doing out in a downpour like this?

The Wizard Lord had just demonstrated that he was possessing animals to use against them, and while a squirrel might not be able to attack as directly as a dog or buck, that didn't mean it was completely harmless. And it might not just be the one squirrel—Breaker remembered the forest between Stoneslope and the nameless neighboring village, where it had seemed as if the Wizard Lord had turned every bird and small beast in the area to watch them, though he had not yet dared attack openly.

"Excuse me, Boss," he said, as he turned and began slogging through the mud, back toward the wagon.

"Sword, what are you . . . ?" Then the Leader saw the squirrels—two of them now—as well. "Squirrels?"

Breaker didn't bother to reply.

"Sword, what do you think squirrels are going to do?"

"They have teeth. They have claws. And there may be more of them."

In fact, a third was on the bench at the front of the wagon. One of the pair atop the wagon was now staring fixedly at Breaker and the Leader.

"Sword!"

Breaker did not turn around; he had his sword in his hand and was watching the squirrels closely.

There were more leaping up on the bench, he saw—climbing up the wheels or the dragging chains and making their way to the bench. This was *definitely* not natural. He began to run as best he could, splashing up to the wagon.

The squirrels did not flee at his approach; instead several of them gathered on the bench and turned to meet him.

He did not worry about killing them; he merely swept them aside with his blade, knocking them to the ground—or in some cases, only to the tongue beneath the bench. A small part of his mind worried about those, that they might bother the oxen, who were still standing placidly despite the various disturbances, but for the most part he focused on boarding the wagon and seeing what the situation was within. He clambered hastily over the bench and through the door.

The lanternlit interior was a scene so bizarre that Breaker had trouble comprehending it at first.

The Archer lay on his belly, head turned to one side, breathing in harsh, hissing gulps—despite the healing he was obviously still in pain. The others were still crouched over him, but most of their attention was on a small horde of squirrels that had climbed in.

The Beauty, at one side, was fending the squirrels away from the Archer; the squirrels were snapping and clawing, trying to bite the wounded man's legs. In the gloom of the rear the Scholar was rummaging through the packed supplies, looking for something—presumably a weapon of some sort. The Speaker, wedged into a corner out of the way, was shouting in a language Breaker had never heard before, a language that did not sound even remotely human—that sounded, in fact, like a squirrel's chittering.

And the Seer stood to one side by the Archer's feet, bent almost double, grabbing the squirrels one by one and wringing their necks; half a dozen broken little bodies already lay in the bed of the wagon.

Breaker watched her method for a second or two in astonishment; her hands moved with a speed he had never seen in anyone as old as she, and unerringly closed on the animals' necks. She did not seem to be aiming at where the squirrels *were* at all, but rather, on where they were *going* to be, after they had attempted to dodge. She would twist each head and snap the neck without even looking, her attention already focused on her next victim.

Without a word, Breaker joined in the slaughter, quickly spearing the remaining animals with his sword, and in a few seconds the chaos and noise had suddenly ceased. The only sounds were the drumming of the rain and the Archer's labored breath.

Breaker crouched in the wagon, unable to stand straight, and looked at the dead squirrels. He prodded a few with the point of his sword, and counted.

There were thirty-four dead squirrels scattered across the bed of the wagon.

"There were more outside," he said. "There were two atop the wagon, watching, and I chased more away when I came in."

"Fifty-four," the Speaker said. "That's the most he can control."

Breaker looked up at her. "How do you know?"

Just then the Leader arrived in the door, and the Speaker glanced at him before replying, "The *ler* told me, of course. The *ler* of the dead squirrels were furious, and eager to help—the Wizard Lord had summoned and bound them, but had made no death-bargain. He could not possess them outright, as he did the deer—he can control only a single body at a time—but he had spoken their true names and called them to his service, and they could not resist his commands while they lived. Once they were dead, though, their true names were altered and the spell no longer bound them, and they could tell me what they knew."

"And what was that?" the Leader asked.

The Speaker shrugged. "Very little. They knew very little. They were only squirrels, after all—their thoughts were of nests and climbing and nuts, and getting out of the rain, not of magic or human schemes. But they knew the names the Wizard Lord spoke, their own and the others, and they told me all of them, all fifty-four, and I called them aloud to free them from his power, but not soon enough and not loud enough, not clearly enough." She looked around at the dead animals, her face sagging with dismay.

"The two on the roof scampered away, looking very much like ordinary squirrels," the Leader said. "I believe you freed them, in any case, and perhaps some of the others."

"Fifty-four," the Seer said. "You're certain?"

"Fifty-four names were spoken," the Speaker confirmed.

"I couldn't count them," the Seer said. "They moved too fast, and there were too many. But when I focused on any one, I could see where it would be."

"Why fifty-four?" the Leader asked. "Was that all the squirrels in the area?"

The Speaker shrugged again. "I don't know," she said. "They told me he had summoned all he could, but whether because there were no more nearby, or because he did not have enough power to hold more, or because he only knew the fifty-four names, they did not say."

"There are certainly limits to how many creatures he can control at a time," the Scholar said, wiping his hands on his breeches as he emerged from the gloom at the rear. "That's been known for centuries. And the larger the beast in question, the stronger its will, the less complete his control, and the fewer he can command. The more aware a creature is, the more complex its relationship to its environment, and therefore the longer and more complicated its true name is, the harder to say correctly and the more subject to change in the latter portions." He glanced down at the dead squirrels. "These poor things can scarcely need more than a few syllables each, while as I'm sure you know, a human's true name is almost endless."

"True names can change?" Breaker asked.

"Only the later parts," the Scholar said. "Usually, the details are so far in the sequence that we don't consciously know them ourselves. If the opening syllables changed, why, then we wouldn't be *us* anymore, would we? We'd be someone else who happened to bear some similarity to who we were. But the later terms, a hundred or thousand syllables in—well, are you precisely the same person you were ten years ago, when you were a child? No? Then how could you have the same true name? A true name *is* what it describes, after all, and if the thing changes, so must the name."

"And that's why the Wizard Lord can't keep a strong hold on a human being," the Seer said. "By the time he's spoken enough of someone's true name to gain real control, the very act of doing things opposed to the victim's own will begins to alter the later syllables."

"So he uses animals."

"Because they're simpler, and naturally more prone to following their instincts or obeying commands. Yes." The Scholar nodded.

"How does he know their names?" Breaker asked. "Does he have some great list he's memorized?"

"The Talisman of Names," the Seer said. "It's one of the eight Great Talismans of power that make him the Wizard Lord, rather than just another wizard."

"It's bound to me," the Speaker said. "To my talisman, the Talisman of Tongues. It's why he dares not slay me."

"That's right," the Scholar said. "If she dies, the Talisman of Tongues dies with her, and the Talisman of Names dies with it, and the Wizard Lord could learn no more true names." He sighed. "Alas, he would still remember every one he has learned so far, as he has the Talisman of Memory, which is bound to my own Talisman of Truth."

"This is all very interesting," the Leader said, "but I don't think we need a lesson in the history of magic right now. I think we would do better to get moving—I believe Sword and I have opened enough of a path."

"But the Archer . . ." the Beauty began.

"I'll drive the oxen," the Scholar said. "I'm not as good at it as he is, but I'll manage."

"Good," the Leader said. "Now, this attack—have we learned anything from it? Are there precautions we should take? Do we know what to expect next?" He stepped aside to let the Scholar past.

A moment later, as the Seer and the Speaker explained to the Leader what had happened before his return, and as Breaker cleaned the blade of his sword, the wagon jerked, shuddered, and began rolling again.

[29]

Although the discussion of possible threats and methods of magical attack stretched on through much of the afternoon, at first Breaker did not dare voice his own greatest concern. This was a possibility that had occurred to him as he watched the squirrels he chased from the driver's bench scurry along the wagon's tongue.

He hoped that the Wizard Lord had not thought of it, and for that reason he did not mention it; while the Seer apparently always knew when the Wizard Lord was watching or listening, Breaker was not convinced the Wizard Lord might not have other ways to spy on them beyond direct observation. He did not intend to say anything about his worries lest the Wizard Lord overhear and decide to try out Breaker's idea.

If he could think of an effective way to *counter* it, then mentioning it to the others would make sense, but until he did he preferred to keep quiet.

Of course, he could ask questions that might lead to devising a defense. He mulled that over for a time, and when he had watched the largely recovered Archer return to the driver's seat and the drenched and shivering Scholar clamber back into the wagon, he finally spoke up.

"The Wizard Lord can possess any animal, can he not?" he asked.

"So long as he has the eight talismans, yes," the Seer replied, as she wrapped a dry cloak around the Scholar.

"And is there any way to reverse this possession, to free the beast from his control?"

The others exchanged glances.

"If you speak the beast's true name and order it to be free, you can counter the Wizard Lord's influence," the Speaker said. "I attempted to do as much with the squirrels. But you must speak the name clearly and fully, and be heard by the creature's *ler.* And it may be necessary to repeat this several times; it depends on how much of his own power the Wizard Lord has put into the enchantment."

Breaker hesitated, but decided this was the counter he had wanted. He said, "I think it might be wise, then, if all of us knew and could say the true names of our oxen. We can't afford to kill them, should they turn on us or lead us astray."

"The oxen?" The Leader glanced at the wagon's door. "A very good point, Sword. Very clever. Babble, could you help us out with this?"

"Of course." She muttered something incomprehensible, then went to the opening. "I'll be right back."

Breaker watched as she clambered out onto the bench beside the Archer, her hood pulled forward to protect her from the rain; then he turned his attention back to the Leader.

"I don't understand why he's giving us this chance to rest and recover," Breaker said. "Look at the Archer—he was down, but after the squirrels the Wizard Lord made no attempt to finish him off, and now he's back in the driver's seat. Why hasn't the Wizard Lord sent more animals after us, or used his lightning to knock down more trees?"

"He's only human," the Scholar said, shivering. "Surely he needs to rest, too."

"But he has his magic," the Seer replied. "He has superhuman strength and endurance—Sword's paired talisman provides that. And using magic isn't as taxing as lifting and hauling. No, I think he's giving us time to think; he still wants us to turn back, he doesn't want to kill us."

"Perhaps the *ler* are displeased with him, and it's *they* who are demanding a rest," the Leader suggested. "The Speaker said that the spirits of the animals resented what he did."

"But that's in the nature of his wizardry," the Scholar said. "His talismans let him *command ler,* not merely negotiate with them, or make requests, as priests and lesser wizards might. His talismanic *ler* are *bound* to him, as ours are bound to us."

"Give someone too many commands and he may rebel," the Leader said, "no matter what oaths he might have given. And isn't it so that the *ler* of the individual animals are not bound by talismans, but by their true names? He uses the talismans to learn those names, but it's the *names* that give him power over the beasts, and perhaps they're resisting that power."

"Or perhaps he can only learn and use so many true names at a time," Breaker suggested. "Magic does have limits, doesn't it? *Mine* certainly does."

"And the lightning?" the Seer asked. "That's not done with names."

"Perhaps those *ler* have reached *their* limit," the Leader said. "After all, while I don't know what lightning really is, it's natural, it comes from the sky—perhaps whatever reservoir it draws upon has run dry for the present, and needs to be . . ."

"He's listening," the Seer interrupted. She turned. "A spider, I think, somewhere in that corner."

"If it's a spider, then he's just spying on us," the Leader said, addressing the indicated corner. "I had wondered whether he might want to talk—whether perhaps he's come to his senses and is ready to resign."

"Somehow, I doubt it," Breaker said.

"You were just asking why he's paused in his assault," the Leader retorted. "Perhaps that's why."

"He released the spider, if that's what it was," the Seer said. "But I think he's . . . he's not entirely *gone,* somehow."

Her final word was partially obscured by the Speaker's scream.

Breaker and the Leader dove for the door simultaneously, and almost collided there; at the last instant Breaker caught himself, and the Leader plunged through first, out into the pounding rain—which abruptly stopped.

The wagon, too, abruptly stopped, just as Breaker thrust his head through the door, and he almost toppled forward onto the Leader's back.

The Speaker was standing in the mud beside the left lead ox, clutching the reins and looking the beast in the eye; the other oxen appeared confused, and were moving uneasily in their harnesses.

And the ox spoke, its voice a distorted bellow that was clearly audible, now that the rain's drumming had faded to the faint patter of water dripping from the trees and metal cage. The inhuman tone made the words hard to understand at first, but never quite unintelligible.

"*I* am not about to surrender!" it said. "I was allowing *you* time to come to your senses. Can't you see how much damage your attempts to destroy me will cause? You can still go home peacefully. We can all go on as before. I've shown you I can hurt you, despite your protections—and rest assured, I will kill you if I must."

"And for each of us you kill your power will be lessened, and the rest will be more determined to slay you," the Leader said.

"But we are a long way from that, as yet," the ox replied. "I have only begun to demonstrate how much I can make you suffer without killing you. You mourned that guide I slew, and you barely knew her—what, then, when I destroy your homes with lightning and fire? What will you feel when I kill the Thief and her children, or the Beauty's adopted clan sisters, or the Swordsman's family, off in the northern valleys?"

Breaker felt a sudden chill.

"You wouldn't dare," the Leader said.

"Wouldn't I? What about your useless brother, Boss? Do you want to see his daughter orphaned? His true name is Faral imz Dorra shadas Bik . . ."

"We know you can find names," the Leader interrupted. "And yes, I'm sure you found Faral and Wirra, and you could kill them—and do you think that would make me *stop*? Then I'd have a personal vengeance to pursue, as well as my duty!"

"And you'd have Wirra's death on your conscience—your own niece."

"You don't seem to be troubled by the slaughter of all *your* friends and family," the Leader retorted. "I think I could live with it, if I avenged them with your death. Why not resign now, and save us all the grief?"

"Arima first, in your family," the ox said, twisting its head in Breaker's direction.

"Arima?" Breaker said, blinking.

"Your older sister, the musician—her true name begins Arima sama Tisna."

"It does? You mean Harp?"

"You Northerners—you don't know your own family's names!" The ox shook its head. "Strange, strange people."

"You killed your own people, and you call *me* strange?" Breaker marveled.

"And after her, your other sisters, one by one, and then your father, and your mother, and your friends, those loutish barley-farmers—I can kill them all, one by one, until you give up this mad idea of defeating me."

Breaker stared at the ox, unable to frame a reply.

Did the Wizard Lord really mean what he said? Would he kill Harp and Fidget and Spider, and their mother and father, if Breaker kept going?

But it was his *duty* to go on, to destroy the Wizard Lord, precisely so that the mad Dark Lord would not kill more innocents. It was the role he had accepted when he became the Swordsman.

He had been warned that it would change his entire life, set him apart from everything he had known, but he had never thought it would mean his family, maybe all of Mad Oak, would be held hostage, perhaps killed.

The memory of the blasted wasteland that had been Stoneslope rose up before him, and superimposed itself upon his memories of Mad Oak, and he found himself imagining the desolation—the pavilion burned down to stone and ash, the houses roofless and empty, the square strewn with his friends' bones, Harp's harp broken apart in the wreckage, the strings snapped and curled.

That could happen—it wasn't an empty threat or some story from centuries ago, it could actually *happen*.

The old stories spoke of how some of the Dark Lords had laid waste to their enemies, in particular the Dark Lord of Kamith t'Daru, but

Breaker had never really thought about what that meant, what the survivors would have seen and felt. He felt physically ill, his stomach cramping—but he was not going to give in.

Because if he once yielded, where would it stop? The Wizard Lord could kill anyone who displeased him, and then threaten to kill more if Breaker and the others retaliated, and where would it stop? It could only end in the Wizard Lord's death, and the only question was how soon that end would come.

Breaker had agreed to be a hero, and now the time had come to mean it, to *be* a hero, despite what it would cost him. He couldn't surrender, couldn't give in to the Wizard Lord's threats, even if it meant his own family would die.

He thought he was going to throw up.

He had thought of heroism in the form of flashing swords and braving magical assaults, not of letting his unsuspecting sisters be murdered.

"Give it up," the ox said. "Go home."

"I can't," Breaker whispered. "You know I can't."

"You're only making it worse," the Leader said. "*You* surrender, resign, go home—no one more needs to die."

"Go *home*?" the ox lowed. "To where? To what?"

Breaker's memory of Stoneslope reemerged, and he shuddered.

"I am the Wizard Lord," the ox said. "I will always be the Wizard Lord; I will never return to anything less."

"Then you'll die," the Leader said. "Is that really better?"

"We all die, sooner or later," the ox replied. "Even the name of the Council of Immortals, like everything else they say, is a lie. We all die—but the question is when, and rest assured, if you continue your quest *you* will die before I do, and your families and friends with you."

"Do you have anything more to say, or are you just going to keep repeating this?" the Leader demanded.

"I have told you what must happen," the ox replied. "It is on *your* heads if you continue to deny my rightful authority as the Wizard Lord to slay those who defy me."

"Speaker, free that poor beast," the Leader said.

The Speaker nodded, then cleared her throat and made a low, sweet sound.

The ox trembled, stamped, shook its head—then lowed wordlessly.

"It's done," the Speaker said.

"Good," Breaker said, with a shudder. He did not like talking to the Wizard Lord; it never seemed to lead anywhere, and the constant threats and warnings made him uneasy—but most of all, such conversations reminded him that he was trying to kill someone, that he was expected to thrust a steel blade through that man's heart.

"The Wizard Lord" was an abstraction; killing the Wizard Lord didn't seem so very dreadful in the abstract. But when the Wizard Lord acquired a voice, even a borrowed one, and spoke to Breaker, that made it all more tangible, and uncomfortably so. That voice belonged to a person, one with a heart and mind of his own—albeit a sick, dark heart and a twisted mind. Breaker knew the Wizard Lord had killed dozens of innocent people, but except for the one guide he had known only briefly, none of those people seemed entirely real. They were dead, though not entirely gone, and Breaker had never met them, never spoken with them, while they lived. The pale suffering ghosts they had left behind were not *people,* but merely echoes and shadows.

But Harp, and Fidget, and Spider . . .

"Drive on," the Leader told the Archer, and with a command and a snap of the reins the Archer set the oxen in motion and the wagon rolling.

Breaker, the Leader, and the Speaker scrambled back inside as the rain began anew, and for the next half-hour or so, after the Beauty, the Scholar, and the Seer had been informed what the ox had said, the party concentrated on learning from the Speaker the true names of the oxen. Their pronunciation did not come naturally to human throats.

Only after conversation had ceased, bringing what might have been called a companionable silence had it not been for the creaking of wheels and the constant roar of the rain, did the Beauty stir and ask, "Is anyone considering it?"

Breaker glanced at her scarf-wrapped face and those deep, lovely eyes, gleaming warmly in the golden lanternlight.

"No, of course not," the Leader replied.

"Considering what?" the Scholar asked.

"Turning back," the Beauty said. "Letting the Wizard Lord be."

"Oh."

There was a moment of embarrassed quasi-silence; then the Scholar coughed, breaking the tension.

"This dampness is getting to me," he muttered.

"When will we reach the Thief's house, Seer?" the Leader asked, and the conversation turned to distances and routes and speeds—but Breaker found himself watching the Beauty, and saw that her eyes, all he could see of her, were troubled.

[30]

The Thief's home stood in a broad brownish green lake; the constant rain had flooded the low-lying surrounding yard three or four inches deep, so that the gardens and grasses brushed the water's surface from below, and a few yellow flowers still thrust up defiant blossoms. Rather than force the oxen down into the water the party settled the wagon into a secure and level position on the road above, the wheels firmly in ruts so that it could not slip sideways from its place, before debarking.

From there, a delegation emerged, wrapped in their cloaks—the Seer to locate her, the Leader to persuade her, the Speaker to consult the local *ler,* and the Swordsman to defend them from any physical threats. The Archer, the Beauty, and the Scholar remained with the wagon as the chosen four splashed down the path toward the door.

The low step at the threshold was awash; Breaker looked down at it and judged that the entire house must be on the verge of flooding; water would already be seeping in under the door. "Are you sure she's still here?" he asked the Seer.

"She's here," the Seer replied grimly.

Breaker shrugged, then knocked on the door—loudly, so as to be heard over the rain. Beside him the Leader straightened his cloak and lifted each foot in turn to drain some of the water from his boots, then stood ready.

"Your magic won't really work on her, you know," the Seer said, glancing at him.

"Oh, I know that," the Leader said, "but I was a persuasive fellow even before I got my talisman."

Breaker looked from the door to the Leader, and was turning back to the door, preparing to knock again, when a movement caught his eye. He looked up.

A raccoon was perched on the thatched roof, leaning over the edge and peering down at him.

"Yes, it's him," the Seer said, before Breaker could speak. "He possessed the raccoon a few minutes ago. I knew he would want to be here."

"You might have mentioned it sooner," the Leader said.

"I thought it was obvious," she replied.

Before the Leader could respond the latch rattled, and the door opened. The Thief stood there, staring at them, her cap askew and tangled blond hair spilling out; she wore the same apron, though it had been washed at least once, and the dress beneath it this time was brown. Behind her Breaker could hear a child crying.

"*What?*" Merrilin demanded. "What is it? What do you want?"

"I am the Leader of the Chosen," the Leader said, bowing, "and you, I presume, are Merrilin tarak Dolin, the world's greatest thief?"

"I'm not a thief!"

"We have come to attempt once again to persuade you to join us in our assigned task, and aid us in ridding the world of this madman, this Dark Lord, who slaughters innocents and drowns our lands in this unnatural rain."

"The Wizard Lord is doing this? He *is*?"

"Yes, of course. To try to stop us from doing what we must. Will you help? Will you help us stop him from drowning the fields and washing away the crops?"

"If you want to stop the rain," a high-pitched, nasal voice interjected, "just go home and leave me alone."

"What?" Merrilin twisted her neck, trying to see where the voice was coming from, and barely caught her cap before it slid from her head.

"Don't listen to him," the Leader said. "He's possessed an innocent raccoon so that he can spy on us . . ."

"If I just wanted to *spy*, I'd have used a mouse or a roach," the raccoon protested. "I'm trying to talk some *sense* into you!"

"What?" The expression of utter confusion and despair on Merrilin's face almost broke Breaker's heart, and he wished he could comfort her, but the Leader was speaking—and besides, Breaker was keeping an eye on the raccoon and his hand on his sword.

"These people are on their way to kill me," the raccoon said, "and I am using the rain and lightning and beasts to try to stop them, to convince them to just give it up and *go home.* I don't want any trouble, but I'm not going to just sit here and wait for them to walk in my front door and cut me down."

"Then resign!" the Leader barked. "That's all it would take to send us home."

"I am *not* going to resign!" the raccoon barked back. "I am the Wizard Lord, I was chosen to be the Wizard Lord, and I will be the Wizard Lord until I die! It's my role in this world, and I am not going to forsake it to appease a bunch of bloodthirsty, overeager idiots!"

"You slaughtered an entire town, you killed our guide, you set beasts upon us, and you call *us* bloodthirsty? We are doing our duty, fulfilling our roles by removing a power that menaces all of Barokan!"

"I don't understand," Merrilin said, leaning out to look up at the raccoon's face and shifting her feet as she tried to find a dry spot. "A talking raccoon that says it's the Wizard Lord? Is he a shapeshifter?"

"No, he's possessed it," the Leader said. "It's just a raccoon, but the Wizard Lord is speaking through it. He's possessed dogs and deer and squirrels and birds and so on to talk to us, or attack us."

"I don't want to hurt you," the raccoon said. "I just want you to turn back."

"Well, your threats aren't going to convince us!"

"They've convinced *me,*" Merrilin said. "Go away, all of you! I'm not going anywhere—not unless this rain floods us out."

"But don't you see how much damage he's doing?" Breaker said. "We can't leave him in power, knocking down trees and flooding farms!"

"It's *not my problem.* Go *away*!" she shrieked, stepping back and starting to close the door.

"Wait!" the Leader said, thrusting out a hand to catch the door. "Hear us out!"

"No! Go away!" She leaned on the door, but the Leader was solidly braced.

"Merri? What's going on?" a new voice asked from somewhere in the house—a deep voice, a human voice, a man's voice.

"It's . . . it's crazy people," the Thief said, still pushing the door.

"Maybe they can help." Breaker heard footsteps—the last few splashing, as the rain was over the threshold now. Then the door swung open, and a man stepped up beside Merrilin.

He was fairly tall but narrow-shouldered; he wore his black hair long and his beard trimmed short, with just a few gray hairs starting to show. A dark woolen tunic with rolled-up sleeves covered his chest, and Breaker could see that those sleeves were soaked—as were his hair, and his well-worn boots.

"Sezen piri Oldrav, I take it?" the Leader said, holding out an open hand. "I am Farash inith Kerra, known as Boss, the Leader of the Chosen."

"What?" The man blinked in astonishment.

"I am the Leader of the Chosen. These are the Speaker of All Tongues, the world's greatest swordsman, and the Seer of the Chosen."

"You . . . are you serious?"

"Go away, *please*!" Merrilin wailed hopelessly.

"Don't listen to them!" the raccoon squealed, in its unnatural voice. "Send them away, as she says!"

"*What?!*" Sezen said. "What was *that*?"

"It's the Wizard Lord," the Seer said. "Speaking through a raccoon on your roof."

"*What?*" Sezen leaned out into the rain, blinking, trying to see the animal.

"Please, Sezen, come inside and close the door," Merrilin pleaded. "Don't get involved. It's none of our business."

"But—but you're the Thief?" He pulled his head back and turned to look at her. "You really are?"

Merrilin stopped pulling at his arm and stared at her husband.

"I told you what happened," she said.

"Yes, you did, and I . . . well, I wasn't sure."

"Weren't sure of *what*?"

"Whether it was true. Whether it really happened, or whether maybe someone played a trick on you . . ."

"It wasn't a trick."

"She is the world's greatest thief, and one of the Chosen," the Seer said.

Sezen turned to the Seer. "My wife is really one of the Chosen? The heroes who guard Barokan? My *wife*?"

"She is."

"And that raccoon is the Wizard Lord?"

"No, it's a raccoon—but the Wizard Lord is controlling its actions and speaking through it."

"The raccoon's true name is . . ." The Speaker completed her statement with an untranscribable chittering. "It is not Laquar kellin Harrio, known as the Wizard Lord, now the Dark Lord of the Galbek Hills, though he guides its thoughts at the moment."

The raccoon suddenly turned and scrabbled up the wet thatch, then stopped, shivered for a moment, then came inching back, claws extended. Breaker only realized that he had drawn his sword when he saw it in his hand, ready to thrust upward.

"Don't say the names," the raccoon said. "You broke my hold, and I am not done speaking."

"This is insane," Sezen said, staring at the raccoon.

"No, it's . . . yes, it's insane," Merrilin replied. "It's not our business. Send them on their way; we have work to do."

"If you're the Wizard Lord," Sezen said, ignoring his wife, "then do you know why it's raining?"

"Does the rain trouble you? Then I'll stop it."

A roll of thunder sounded, and the rain began to let up.

"You see?" said the raccoon. "I am who I claim to be."

"Why was it raining like that in the first place?" Merrilin demanded. "We don't want anything to do with this, Sezen; they're dangerous, all of them."

"I can hardly deny *that,*" the Leader said. "And really, who *isn't* dangerous, under the right circumstances?" He smiled at Sezen.

Sezen paid no attention; he was staring up at the sky.

"You did it," he said. "You made it stop."

Breaker looked up as well, past the possessed raccoon; the skies were still gray, but the rain had indeed ceased, though water still ran from the eaves and dripped from the trees.

"And I can make it start again," the raccoon said. "I can summon the lightning and the storm, the wind and the rain; I can shake the earth and drive beasts mad, haunt your dreams and break your sleep. I am the Wizard Lord, protector of all Barokan, master of all that lies between the Eastern Cliffs and the Western Sea. Do not defy me."

"He is all that," the Leader said, in a conversational tone that seemed eerily loud in the rainless semi-silence, "but he's also as mad as a ferret, drunk with power, and a murderer many times over, and as the Chosen, we are sworn to remove him for his crimes."

Sezen's gaze fell abruptly from the sky to the Leader's face.

"Can you do that?" he said.

"I certainly hope so," the Leader said cheerfully. "And after all, the Chosen have removed Dark Lords before, half a dozen of them."

"You four?"

"No—we weren't even *born* the last time a Dark Lord was loose. Our predecessors. But we have the same magic they did. And there are eight of us, counting your wife—not four."

"And she alone, of the eight of you, has the sense not to defy me!" the raccoon squeaked. "Do you all *want* to die?"

"But . . ." Sezen glanced at his wife, then up at the raccoon, then at Merrilin again. "You're the Thief." It wasn't a question.

"You've always known that."

"But . . . I knew you had said so, but I . . . it didn't *mean* anything. Now it does. You have a *duty,* Merrilin, a role to fill."

"I have children and a home to care for," she replied, glaring at him.

"I can take care of the children. You're one of the *Chosen*!"

"You knew that."

"I . . . well, but it didn't matter; we didn't know the Wizard Lord had turned dark."

"You mean you never really believed me."

"I *did* believe you! But it didn't *matter*!"

"And now it does, and you think I should go off with these strangers to try to murder the Wizard Lord, and maybe get killed in the process, because of some foolish promise I made as a girl?"

"It's . . . you're one of the Chosen!"

"You keep saying that! What if I don't *want* to be?"

"But you *are*!"

"So you'd send her to her death?" the raccoon said. "I don't want to kill *her*—I would lose a part of my magic if I did that. But if she comes against me, perhaps I'll kill *you,* foolish man!"

Sezen's mouth fell open, and he stared up at the animal; then his jaw snapped shut and he said, "Well, then, if that's my part in it, then I'll die. We all must die someday."

"Sezen, you're being ridiculous," Merrilin said. "None of us need to die!"

"You've no fear for your own life, then?" the raccoon demanded. "What about your son and your daughter? Will you sacrifice *them* to this madness of sending your wife to slay me?"

"I . . ." Sezen hesitated. "You wouldn't do that. They're innocents, they have no part in this."

"If you harm her children, don't you think Merrilin would want revenge?" the Leader asked.

"No one needs to die!" Merrilin insisted. "No one needs to be hurt!"

"I regret to say, dear lady, that unless the Wizard Lord resigns, someone does indeed need to die," the Leader said.

"But it won't be me!" the raccoon said. Thunder rumbled in the distance. "I warn you, Thief, and you, husband, do not defy me. Do not aid these fools. If you do not go inside right now, and lock the door, I will give you a foretaste of what I can do to those who defy me."

"He can't really hurt you," the Leader said. "Not directly. It's a part of the magic of the Chosen—we are immune to the Wizard Lord's magic. He can strike at us in various ways, but he cannot simply turn his magic against us. He cannot use our true names, or send *ler* against us. And if he does manage to kill one of us, he loses a portion of his own power. He won't do that."

"But he . . . Sezen . . ."

"Oh, he can hurt your husband, yes—but do you really think he would risk angering you so? His threats are empty . . ."

"*Empty?*" The raccoon's voice broke in an unnatural squeal.

"Yes, empty!" the Leader shouted back.

"I will show you how empty my words are!" the raccoon said—and then it shivered, and something changed indefinably, and no one needed the Seer to tell them that the Wizard Lord had released his hold over the animal.

The raccoon shook itself, backed two careful steps away from the roof's edge, then turned and scampered up toward the ridgepole.

Thunder rumbled anew, and the sky darkened.

"I think he's going to make it rain again," the Leader said, squinting at the clouds. "That hardly seems like a really convincing demonstration of anything, at this point."

"Is that all?" Sezen looked over his four visitors, then his wife, "Merrilin . . ."

"I'm going," she said with a sigh. "I think you're all mad, but I don't want to argue about it any more, and really, Sezen, if you never even *believed* me when I told you I was the Thief . . ."

"I *did* believe you, truly I did, but I . . ."

The first fat raindrops began to patter on the flooded garden and soaked thatch, and Sezen and Merrilin ducked back inside; there they both paused, looking out at the travelers.

"You'll want to pack," the Leader said. "We can wait in the wagon . . ."

And then the flash blinded them all and the world seemed to vanish for an instant in blue-white light and an ear-shattering roar.

Breaker blinked, and for a moment seemed to see two or three doorways instead of one, in eerie afterimage; his ears rang, but then he seemed to hear crackling.

And then he heard screaming, and after a second or two it resolved into words, shrieked in a little girl's voice.

"Mama! Mama, help! Help, the roof's on fire! Mama!"

"Oh, my soul," Breaker said, as he charged forward, past the Seer and the Speaker, who stood frozen in astonishment.

Parental instinct had ensured that Sezen and Merrilin had not frozen; they had whirled and run in at the first scream. The Leader, too, had reacted quickly, and he and Breaker collided in the doorway before bouncing side by side into the interior of the Thief's home.

The stone-paved floor was awash, Breaker saw, but there were no rugs and little furniture—but then he saw where the rugs and smaller furnishings had been put, to escape the rising water. They lined the narrow staircase leading up to a loft.

And the children's screams—both children were screaming now, the girl calling for her mother, the baby wailing wordlessly—were coming from that loft. Sezen and Merrilin were squeezing their way up the stairs, past rolled rugs and precariously balanced tables.

And above them Breaker could see an orange glow, and rolling smoke, and dancing sparks. The thatch, despite the long rain, was ablaze—the outer layer might be saturated, but the straw beneath was still tinder-dry.

He hesitated, unsure what to do—crowding a third adult up the stairs would merely make it that much harder to get everyone safely down again. A pole of some sort, to knock away burning thatch, might be helpful, or a ladder so that someone could reach the flames directly . . .

Then the girl screamed again. "Mama! My hair's on fire! *Mama!*" And she came running out of the loft to the stair, arms flailing, and ran directly into her father on the top step.

Sezen staggered, swung his arms wildly, and managed to grab the back of a chair; he fell sideways rather than down, and caught himself just one step below his previous position.

The girl, though, rebounded from her father's belly and folded at the waist as she fell backward; her head struck the narrow stair rail, but then tucked down to her chest, and she tumbled under the rail and off the side of the step.

The snap when she hit the stone floor was clearly audible to everyone in the house, and Breaker knew where to go—he ran to the little girl.

Merrilin was screaming and hurrying back down the stairs; Sezen, seeing how matters stood, had pressed on into the loft to find the baby. The Leader was standing aside, taking in the extent of the fire, the fall of the sparks and burning straw, the rising wind and thickening rain outside the open door, the Seer and Speaker standing helplessly outside.

Then Breaker was at the little girl's side, where the first thing he did was to quickly stroke her long hair out on the wet stone and splash floodwater on it—her hair *had* been burning, and extinguishing that seemed the most urgent priority, as whatever other injuries she might have sustained had already happened and would get no worse.

Then he looked her over.

She had landed on her side, and her eyes and mouth were open, but she was no longer saying anything—the ongoing screaming came from her mother and baby brother. She was breathing heavily—that was good, that meant she was unquestionably still alive.

"Seer, get the Beauty!" the Leader shouted. "Speaker, get in here!"

"Where does it hurt?" Breaker asked. "Do you know what happened?"

"My arm," she said. Then her eyes focused. "Who are *you*?"

"My name is . . . is Erren," Breaker said. "I'm here to help."

Then Merrilin was there, and started to scoop up her daughter, but Breaker held her back.

"I think her arm is broken," he said. "Move her very carefully—we don't want to shift the pieces." He had known a man with a twisted arm once, back in Mad Oak, an old man who had broken his arm falling out of a tree as a boy; the break had healed, but healed crooked, and Elder Priestess had said it was because he had moved his arm wrong, trying to stop the pain, and moved the broken ends out of line. Breaker did not want this girl—Kilila, was it?—to grow up similarly crippled.

Merrilin sobbed, and nodded, and together the two of them carefully lifted Kilila to a sitting position.

"It's all wet," she said, with surprise. "My skirt is wet."

"We know," Merrilin said. "That's why we were moving everything upstairs, remember? The Wizard Lord is flooding everything—he's gone mad."

"The Wizard Lord?" The girl began crying. "My arm hurts so much!"

Then with a splash Sezen was standing there beside them with a baby in his arms, asking, "Is she all right?" The baby had stopped screaming, and was whimpering quietly as he clutched at his father's shirt.

"We think her arm is broken," Breaker replied.

Breaker thought the expression of helplessness on Sezen's face was somehow more dismaying than Kilila's obvious agony.

Then there was more splashing, and the Beauty was beside them, her face and figure still hidden in cloak and scarf as she knelt by the girl. Breaker heard her sharp intake of breath as she felt the broken bone.

"The break is high on her arm, but it feels clean, and young bones heal well," the Beauty said; Sezen started at the sound of her voice, its purity and musicality, and little Garant stopped sniffling, his eyes widening.

"Sword, if you're done there, I could use a hand," the Leader called.

"What?" Breaker looked up.

The Leader was at the top of the stair, leaning over. Now he pointed up.

"I think you might be able to cut away the burning thatch with that blade of yours, and we can keep this place from burning down."

"Oh!" Breaker started to rise, then realized he was still holding Kilila's shoulder. Carefully, he moved aside and let the Beauty take his place.

Then he stood and hurried up the stairs.

[31]

It took perhaps twenty minutes' work to extinguish the last traces of the fire, and by then Merrilin and the Beauty had set Kilila's broken arm and put her to bed—fortunately, her bed was in a corner of the loft well clear of the fire. Garant was now sleeping in his mother's arms as she sat, rocking and cooing, by the loft rail near her daughter's bed.

Sezen had joined Breaker and Boss in cutting burning thatch from overhead and stamping it to ash or kicking it into the flooded room below; the three men's eyes were watering from the smoke, and all were coughing sporadically, but the fire was out.

Amazingly, no rain had yet penetrated the burned area.

"It's not really so surprising," the Leader said, when Breaker commented on it. "After all, if water could get in, then the thatch wouldn't have been dry enough to burn."

"It's a good, thick roof," Sezen said. "I wanted it to last."

"Well, it's not as thick as it was," Breaker pointed out. "And I doubt it'll smell very pleasant. You'll want to repair that when the weather improves."

"Is the weather ever *going* to improve?" Sezen asked. "If the Wizard

Lord has truly gone mad, then how do we know he won't keep it raining until all Barokan is underwater?"

"I don't think he can do that," Breaker said mildly.

"For one thing, we'll kill him soon," the Leader said. "The eight of us."

Merrilin looked up from her children at that. "Seven," she said.

The three men turned.

"I'm not going," she said. "After *this*? I can't leave my children after this! Kilila needs me—I can't go anywhere until her arm heals."

"But . . ." Sezen began.

"I want him dead," she said. "Oh, believe me, after this I *really* want him dead! And if you seven can't do it, then maybe I will. But my children come first."

"But . . ."

"Sezen, if I go with them, the Wizard Lord will send more lightning. He might kill you all, and burn down the house—but if I'm here he won't dare. He knows that I'd come after him, and . . . well, he doesn't know what I can do, but *I* know. I did some experimenting, back when I was young, and the magic is still there. Maybe I don't have a magic weapon like the Swordsman, or a seductive voice like the Beauty, but I have my own ways. If the Wizard Lord defeats the others, he still won't be safe; he'll pay for this, for breaking my daughter's arm, one way or another. But *right now,* my family comes first, and I'm staying right here."

"And we have a reserve," the Leader said. "The seven of us will remove this monster from power—but if the *ler* betray us and we somehow fail, we have a second team." He bowed. "Thank you, Merrilin tarak Dolin."

And that settled it.

The party stayed the night at the house; the women slept in the loft with the family, while the Leader, the Archer, the Swordsman, and the Scholar slept in the wagon. Room was found in an outbuilding for the oxen.

Breaker noticed that the Beauty carefully slept as far away from Sezen as possible, in an unlit corner. And as had happened at the inn in Winterhome, Breaker heard voices in the night while half-awake, but they stopped when he tried to listen. He wondered, in his sleep-muddled state, whether Sezen or the Archer was troubling the Beauty, or whether one of the children had been talking while asleep, but he dozed off again before he could think of anything to do about it.

The rain had ended even before the fire was out, and there was no more lightning, but during the night the water in the house rose to a depth of three or four inches, and in the surrounding gardens to half a foot, before finally draining away. In the morning, as final preparations for departure were made, mere puddles remained, and the flowers, much the worse for wear, had emerged again.

The seven Chosen took their leave at midmorning, after the Swordsman, Archer, and Thief had practiced their skills, and they set out west and south—at least, once the wagon had been pried out of the mud.

The rain held off until surprisingly late; it was not until they were crossing the first low ridge and almost out of sight of the lightning-struck house that the first drops fell.

"I think he slept late," the Seer said. "He tired himself out yesterday."

"Or it may be that the rain *ler* themselves are getting weary of this," the Scholar suggested.

"Is that possible?" Breaker asked.

"Why not?"

"Well, I . . . I never really thought of *ler* as wearying of *anything* they do. I mean, year after year, the barley grows just as it always has, and the river flows over the same stones . . ."

"But it changes from one day to the next as the grain ripens—and not all *ler* are the same, as you certainly should have noticed! What are our souls, but the *ler* of ourselves, and surely *we* grow weary of things?"

"I . . ." Breaker stopped. Obviously, *some ler* could grow tired or bored—why not the ones the Wizard Lord used to bring the rain? After all, it never rained as much naturally as it had during these last few days.

Indeed, that day's downpour seemed a halfhearted effort compared with what they had seen before. The countryside did not lend itself to using lightning-blasted trees as roadblocks, though they did see some distant flashes and hear a rumble or two, and as a result they made decent time to Quince Market.

And in Quince Market, rather than the quiet village and dismal rain they had anticipated, they found smoldering ruins and excited natives.

They saw the smoke from an hour away, even through the haze of rain, and knew something was wrong, but it was not until they passed the boundary shrine and found themselves surrounded by townspeople that they had any clear idea just what had happened.

"You are the Chosen, aren't you?" a man demanded before the wagon's rear wheels cleared the shrine.

"Yes, we are," replied the Leader from the driver's bench. "What's happened here?"

"It's the Wizard Lord!" someone called from farther back. "He threatened to kill us all if we helped you!"

"He's gone mad," a woman added. "You have to kill him."

"He called fire from the sky!"

"He spoke through Doublethumb's dog!"

"How severe is the damage?" the Leader asked. "Has anyone been seriously hurt?"

"Four houses are burned!"

"And a stable!"

"Little Emerald has broken ribs!"

"My cat's missing!"

"Calm, people, calm!" the Leader called, rising to his feet and spreading his hands. "I know a Dark Lord is a terrible thing, and one we thought we'd never live to see, but it's nothing we can't handle. We are on our way to the Galbek Hills to deal with him, and this is just a desperate attempt to discourage us. I'm very sorry for Emerald, and about this woman's cat, and of course for the four families who lost their homes, but if that's the worst of it you've been fortunate—your *ler* are looking out for you."

"What are you going to *do* about it?"

"We are going to the Galbek Hills to remove the Wizard Lord, by whatever means may be necessary. What else *can* we do?"

"What about my *home*?"

"You'll rebuild, of course, and I'm sure your neighbors and priests will help you. But right now, we have a long journey ahead of us, and we need lodging . . ."

The crowd suddenly fell silent.

"You can't stay *here,*" a big man said.

"He'd kill us all."

A murmur of agreement ran through the gathered townsfolk.

Breaker peered out between the Leader and the Archer, and saw that the crowd, which up until then had been merely angry and upset, had now turned hostile.

"Ah," the Leader said. He glanced back into the wagon, as if asking if anyone had any useful suggestions, then turned his attention back to the crowd. "I see, and you have a good point. Then we will reprovision and move on . . ."

"We can't feed you," someone said. "He'd kill us."

"Ah," the Leader said again. He sighed. "Very well, then—we will be on our way, and rest assured, we will do our best to remove this nightmare from Barokan and restore peace and order. Bow, steer us around the village, please."

"But, Boss, you could persuade them . . ."

"I could, but I won't."

"But . . ."

"Do it."

The Archer shrugged. "You're the Leader," he said. He turned the wagon aside.

A halfhearted cheer went up. "Hail the Chosen!"

"Save us from the Dark Lord!"

"Go away!"

"Go quickly!"

"May the *ler* protect you!"

They bypassed Quince Market, and the next town, and the next, sleeping in the wagon by the roadside—a sleep troubled by unpleasant dreams. Breaker could remember no details of what he had dreamed when he woke, but he often awoke sweating, his hands clenched so tight they ached, and he always knew that whatever he had dreamed had been bad. When they met a guide upon the road, some four days past Quince Market, Breaker spent all his remaining funds buying *ara* feathers from him, in hopes the magic-blocking feathers would shield him from the nightmares.

They helped, but not as much as Breaker had hoped.

Obtaining water for drinking and bathing along the way was no problem, even without entering any inns or villages—the rain-swollen streams and overflowing wells and cisterns everywhere provided them with all the water they could want. Food was not so plentiful, however; their supplies ran out on the fifth day. They resorted to looting farms along the way, stealing grain and produce from outlying barns, and the Archer took to carrying his bow strung and ready, to bring down game for the cookpot. Rabbits, birds, squirrels, and a deer provided variety in their diet; they did not take down any livestock, preferring to keep their thievery to a minimum.

The Scholar turned out to be a reasonably competent butcher. "I had it all explained to me once," he said. "I couldn't forget it if I tried. But I've had very little practical experience until now."

The rain continued, but with ever less enthusiasm. Lightning seemed to be reserved for threatening any town they approached, and there were no more roadblocks. Animals attacked them occasionally, but now that the Seer and the Speaker knew to watch for those, they were easily dealt with—either the Speaker would use the beast's true name to release it from the spell, or the Archer or the Swordsman would dispose of it more permanently, often providing dinner in the process. The Wizard Lord could not mass enough animals in a single assault to overwhelm them all.

And these attacks, too, trailed off after a time. Even the nightmares, already weakened by the *ara* feathers, faded away to nothing.

"I think he's wearing himself out," the Seer said, when Breaker commented on the ineffectuality of the Wizard Lord's continuing efforts. "He *feels* tired, somehow. I could sense it in my meditation."

"I thought you just knew where he was, and whether he's killed anyone," Breaker said.

"That's all I can be sure of," the Seer agreed, "but sometimes I get these feelings about him, a little extra."

Breaker nodded.

They forged onward, passing town after town, entering none. A few showed evidence that their citizens had defied the Wizard Lord—burned houses and shops, thatch torn from roofs by storm winds, and so on—but most were unscathed, and the Seer reported mercifully few deaths.

Few.

Not none.

In all, the Wizard Lord killed five more people along the route to assert his insistence that no one aid the Chosen.

And no one did. The Chosen did not ask them to risk themselves. After all, it was the role of the Chosen, and only the Chosen, to defeat the Wizard Lord.

All the same, Breaker thought this hardly seemed like the heroic adventure the Chosen Swordsman ought to be having on his way to slay a Dark Lord. As the Swordsman he was supposed to fight other men, not struggle through rain and snow and mud, help push an overweight, metal-caged wagon out of ruts and mudholes and ice, or butcher possessed animals that attacked them—and not dragons or hippogriffs or even animals as exotic as *ara,* but just dogs and deer and the like, and once an immense bull.

He would have much preferred to be back in Mad Oak, growing barley and beans.

Still, he reassured himself that he *was* carrying out his role, he *was* performing his duties, he *was* doing the right thing. The dead of Stoneslope had to be avenged, and all Barokan defended from this mad wizard, no matter how tedious and unpleasant the job might be.

One meager comfort was that the Dark Lord of the Galbek Hills never made good on his threat to kill their friends and family—the Seer was able to reassure them on that count. It was theoretically possible that the Wizard Lord had sent others to commit such murders, but he never claimed to have done so, and such an action would have made no sense, so Breaker slept each night in reasonable assurance that his sisters and parents were unharmed.

Winter had come, and the constant rain turned to snow and ice, before they finally came in sight of the Wizard Lord's keep, perched on the highest peak in the Galbek Hills. They still had a good two or three miles to go when the stone tower's outline became unmistakable through lingering fog mixed with snow, and they paused for a moment to look at it—and for the Archer to take a look around for the evening meal.

It had been a tradition for centuries that each Wizard Lord used his magic to erect his home and headquarters, to demonstrate that he had indeed mastered enough *ler* to justify his title as Wizard Lord, and usually much of his power was tied to this place, as if he were a priest—that was one reason that the Chosen generally fought Dark Lords in their strongholds, rather than chasing them across the countryside. In his journey to meet the Seer and Scholar in Tumbled Sheep, Breaker had glimpsed from afar the remains of one such Wizard Lord's abandoned keep in the southern hills, and he knew the remnants of others had been incorporated into the surrounding communities—the onetime stronghold of the Dark Lord of the Midlands was now the central temple of the town of Drumhead, for example.

This tower, however, was clearly destined to be a ruin, not a temple—there *was* no surrounding community, the town of Split Reed was more than half a mile away and out of sight to the south, and Breaker doubted anyone would want the thing. It was crude and ugly, just a column of raw stone pierced by a few scattered windows; there was no ornamentation, no attempt at grace or elegant design. Even the snow could not soften its appearance into any semblance of beauty.

Breaker, the Beauty, and the Seer climbed a low, snow-covered hill for a better view while the Archer went in search of game and the Scholar, the Leader, and the Speaker stayed in the wagon. At the top they stared silently for a moment before anyone spoke.

"He lives in *that*?" the Beauty finally said. "By *choice*?"

"If I had any doubt that he was mad, the sight of that thing would dispel it," Breaker replied.

"I can't do it," the Seer said.

Breaker blinked. He turned to look at her. "Do what?" he asked.

"I can't go in there," she said. "I can't help you kill him."

"Why *not*?"

"I just . . . I just can't."

"Why?"

"I'm *scared,* all right? I can't do it!"

"But it was your idea! You were the one who knew he'd killed everyone in Stoneslope!"

"I know. He has to die, and it's my fault he didn't die five years ago, when the Swordsman was a wily old man instead of an untested youth, but I was afraid then, afraid to believe he had really become a Dark Lord, and I'm afraid now, and I can't go in there! The rest of you will have to do it without me."

"But how will we find him?"

"It's not very big. And he's always in there—he almost never leaves it at all, does everything with his magic. He has a room at the top, and then his workshop and sleeping quarters underground, and the rest is almost empty, he never spends much time there. You can find him without me. I'm not going in there."

Breaker stared helplessly at her, then turned back toward the wagon and called, "Boss! Could you come here, please?"

The Leader turned and waved an acknowledgment.

"You came this far," the Beauty said. "Why are you only losing your nerve *now*?"

"Look at that thing!" the Seer said. "I can't go in there."

"You've been in dead guesthouses, and temple cells, and the ruins of Stoneslope—why is that any worse?" Breaker demanded.

"Just *look* at it! It's a Dark Lord's keep, by all the *ler*! It even looks like one—I can't believe no one ever realized before, just from looking at it, that there's something wrong with this man."

"Who would notice?" the Leader asked, as he trudged up the hill to join them. "People mind their own business, they have their own jobs to do and roles to fill, and making sure the Wizard Lord hasn't gone mad is *our* job, nobody else's."

"The Seer is saying it's not her job after all," Breaker replied.

"She's frightened," the Beauty agreed. "She doesn't want to go any farther."

"Well, she doesn't need to," the Leader said. "She got us here, and that's her job—from now on it's up to the rest of us to do ours. What's a middle-aged woman going to do in our fight against a wizard? It's up to you, me, and Bow, Sword. The rest are just here to help us out—no one expects Lore or Beauty to do any fighting, and Babble's job is going to be countering spells, not attacking anyone. If the Seer's too frightened to continue, why force her? She'd be more hindrance than help."

"You're sure?" Breaker asked. "We already lost the Thief . . ."

"I'm sure," the Leader said. "She can stay with the wagon while the rest of us go inside—would that suit you, Seer?"

"That would be . . . yes. That would do," she said.

"Or you could take shelter in Split Reed . . ."

"No. The wagon is fine."

"Then that's how it'll be. You don't have to go inside."

"Thank you, Boss," the Seer said. "Thank you."

Breaker stared at them for a moment, but could not think of anything useful to say. The Leader surely knew what he was doing—after all, he was the *Leader,* with a magical gift for planning and persuading. If he said the Seer would be no more use, then surely she wouldn't be.

But somehow something felt wrong, all the same, and Breaker was troubled as he marched back down to the wagon. The Chosen were supposed to be a team, working together, each in his assigned role, but the Thief who would get them past locks and guards was not here, and now the Seer who was to tell them where their enemy could be found was refusing *her* role, as well. And the Leader who was supposed to ensure that everyone did his part was doing nothing to prevent this new defection.

It wasn't right—but he was the Swordsman, not the Leader, and could only play out his own role and hope that it would be enough.

[32]

They met no resistance as they rode up to the tower's base, which puzzled Breaker; he had thought the Wizard Lord would be making one last desperate attempt to get them to turn back, or perhaps even seriously trying to kill them. Instead the snow and rain, already thinned to little more than a heavy mist, stopped completely.

The wagon rolled up toward the crest of the hill, then stopped; the terrain was too steep and rocky for the last hundred yards. They would need to go the rest of the way on foot.

It was astonishing, really, that the wagon had made it this far. Only the fact that so many people had come and gone here over the past few years, clearing a path on their way to see the Wizard Lord, had made that possible.

"I'm staying in the wagon," the Seer said.

"And what about the rest of us?" the Archer asked, looking at the Leader. "What's the plan?"

The Leader climbed down from the wagon and stood on the gravel, looking up at the looming black tower.

"Who's still ready to go in and finish this?" he asked.

Breaker exchanged glances with the Scholar as they climbed out of the wagon. "All of us," he said. "Except the Seer."

"Then come on."

"Boss, shouldn't we have a plan?" the Scholar asked, as he hit the ground. "We want to use our magic effectively, don't we? If we just walk in, the Wizard Lord . . ."

"The Wizard Lord knows he's beaten simply by our presence," the Leader replied. "Once he sees us he'll surrender, I'm sure."

That was not what Breaker wanted to hear.

The group had discussed how they might deal with the Wizard Lord once they reached his keep, but they had made no definite plans; the Leader had always insisted that they would need to see just what the keep was like, what the situation was, before making any plans.

Well, here they were, there was the keep, and the Leader still had no plan—he appeared quite certain, despite months of the Wizard Lord insisting otherwise, that their foe would simply surrender.

"*I'm* not sure," Breaker said. "I expect I'll have to kill him."

"If I don't get him first," the Archer retorted.

"You don't need to sound so bloodthirsty about it," the Beauty said, as she clambered down from the bench. Her scarf had slipped, exposing most of her face, but that had happened several times over the course of the long journey, and Breaker no longer stared at her every time. The first few glimpses had been staggering, but apparently the old adage was true—one could become accustomed to *anything* eventually. Oh, she was still incredibly beautiful, not merely in appearance but in sound and smell, and living in close proximity to her for so long had meant many, many hours of frustration for Breaker and the other males, but right now there were more urgent matters at hand.

The Speaker paused on the bench, listening, before she climbed down.

"The *ler* are not happy here," she said. "This is a sick place, a *wrong* place, as bad as any I've ever heard."

"That's hardly news," the Archer said. Breaker did not bother to say so, but he agreed with Bow; *anyone* could feel the wrongness here, it didn't take the Speaker or a priest.

"I can't look at it," the Seer said from the wagon. "You go on. He's inside. He's on the stairs right now."

"You won't change your mind?" Breaker asked.

"I can't go in there. I *can't,*" the Seer said. "I've done my part—if I went in with you I'd just get someone hurt."

"Don't worry about her," the Leader called. "Come on, let's get this over with!"

Reluctantly, Breaker turned away and followed the Leader, as did the other four. Together, the six of them began the climb up the steep, rocky hillside. The ground was utterly barren, bare stone and mud, without any trace of greenery, and felt almost as dead as the guest compound in Seven Sides.

"The *ler* here are prisoners," the Speaker said. "They're bound, all of them—he's held them in bondage for years now, never letting them act upon their nature. He feared the Council of Immortals would turn them against him."

The Archer had his bow strung and ready, a full quiver on his back; Breaker's own hand fell to the hilt of his sword, but he did not draw it.

Then he heard the snap of a bowstring; he started to turn, to ask the Archer what he was doing, but then he realized that the sound had been much farther away, and that even with his supernatural speed and accuracy the Archer had not had time to nock and loose an arrow since last Breaker had looked in his direction.

Then he heard the whir of feathers passing, and the Speaker screamed. Breaker whirled.

An arrow protruded from the Speaker's right thigh, a few inches above the knee, and she was crumpling to the ground.

"There!" the Leader shouted. Breaker heard the Archer curse, and then draw, nock, and loose a shaft of his own, but he was too busy trying to catch the Speaker and ease her to the ground to turn and look.

Then the Speaker was laid out on the stones, the Scholar and the Beauty leaning over her, the Beauty with a hand to her forehead, the Scholar probing the area around the arrow, and the Archer said, "Missed! I don't believe it!"

"Look at the range, man!" the Leader replied. "Of course you missed! Even the world's greatest archer couldn't hit him at this distance."

"I *am* the world's greatest archer," the Archer replied angrily, "and *he* hit *her*."

"He had surprise on his side, he was shooting down, and she was out in the open—and for all we know, he was aiming at someone else," the Leader retorted. "You were shooting up at a man ducking behind a parapet—there's no way anyone could have hit him."

"Still think he'll just surrender?" Breaker asked bitterly, as the Scholar began to cut around the Speaker's wound with his pocketknife to free the barbs.

"It didn't cut the artery," the Scholar said. "We're lucky—she should live."

"Take her back to the wagon, you and Beauty," the Leader ordered. "Bow, Sword, and I will take care of Laquar kellin Hario." He gestured. "Come on, you two!"

"What, just the three of us?" Breaker said.

"Yes! Now, come on!" With that, the Leader broke into a trot, up the slope.

"Come on," the Archer said, following.

Unhappily, Breaker followed, as well.

This wasn't how it was supposed to go; they were supposed to be a team of eight, slipping into the Dark Lord's fortress unseen, protected by magic, following a carefully worked-out plan—not three men charging across open ground in broad daylight with ordinary weapons. This was nothing like the old stories; this wasn't heroism, this was madness.

But what choice did they have? The Thief had not come, the Seer had lost her nerve, the Speaker was wounded, the Beauty and the Scholar were tending to her—that left the three of them.

At least none of them had died yet—but he didn't want to think about that, lest the thought become fact. So far they had relied on the Wizard Lord's unwillingness to give up any of his magic, but surely, that only went so far—and that arrow might well have killed someone! If it had pierced the Speaker's femoral artery she would be bleeding to death even now, and Breaker doubted anyone could have saved her.

And why wasn't the Wizard Lord's archer, whoever it was, shooting more arrows? He peered up at the top of the tower, at the jagged parapet; he hadn't seen the archer, but the Leader had said he was behind that barrier.

And what if there were *several* archers?

Of course, all the reports said that this Wizard Lord kept less staff than any other in history—where the Dark Lord of the Midlands had kept a hundred guards at his keep, and the Dark Lord of Goln Vleys had dozens of spies and assassins, the Dark Lord of the Galbek Hills wasn't known to employ anyone but a handful of maids from Split Reed who did his cooking and cleaning, and presumably provided other services as well.

Was one of them a trained archer?

Looking up at the tower, and glancing back at the Speaker being helped back to the wagon, Breaker realized just how phenomenal that bowshot had been. It had been either fantastically bad luck that that arrow had hit anyone—or magic.

Breaker would have bet *his* money on magic.

Which might mean that the arrow had hit exactly who and where it was intended to hit, and that it had been intended to do exactly what it had done—to split the party of invaders without killing any of them.

He *really* didn't like that idea. He picked up the pace.

A moment later the three men were at the keep door—which was closed, of course. It wasn't the massive barrier Breaker had been expecting, though; it was simply a rough wooden panel set in an ordinary doorframe in the rough black wall.

"This is where the Thief would have earned her way," the Archer muttered, as the Leader tugged at the latch—and then, to everyone's surprise, something clicked and the door swung open.

"I don't understand," Breaker said.

"It's a trap," the Archer replied.

"Do you think so?"

"It must be!"

"Then what should we do?"

"We go in anyway," the Leader said. "Really, what choice do we have? We've come this far, we can hardly stop now because the door opened! Perhaps one of the maids unbarred it to help us—surely, they must know their master is mad, and isn't everyone in Barokan supposed to help the Chosen in their mission?"

"Or it might be a trap," the Archer said.

"Or it might be a trap," the Leader admitted. "But we'll just have to risk that possibility." With that he pushed the door wide and stepped in.

Whatever else Breaker might think of the Leader, he had to admit the man had courage, to simply walk through that door like that. Breaker drew his sword and followed, with the Archer bringing up the rear, and the three found themselves in a short, narrow, unlit corridor.

There was no choice of route; they moved cautiously forward, then paused as the gloom thickened.

"Wait a moment," the Archer said; then he took an arrow from the quiver on his shoulder and wedged it under the door to hold it open—not so much to preserve their escape route as to allow some daylight into the shadowed interior.

That done, the trio proceeded down the passage into a larger chamber, equally unlit, though enough daylight seeped in here and there for Breaker to see a central spiral stair and several doors. The stair went in both directions.

"Which way?" Breaker whispered.

"Well, he'll expect us to go up," the Leader said, "since we saw him up on the roof—and I'll wager that he's actually run down into the dungeons while we were climbing the hill, and is lurking downstairs, ready to cut us off once we ascend."

"Then we go down?" the Archer asked.

"We go down," the Leader agreed.

"Or we get the Seer," Breaker suggested. "She doesn't need to come inside—we could work out a few signals easily enough."

"We can't take the time," the Leader replied. "Besides, remember how badly she lost her nerve—she refused to come in here even before the Speaker was shot, and I doubt she'll be willing to come any closer than she is now. No, we'll have to rely on instinct, and my instinct says that he's down in the cellars, waiting to trap us above him when we climb the tower."

Breaker was not entirely satisfied with this, but they did need to go *somewhere,* and the Archer was already at the stair, starting down the spiral.

"I see a light!" he said. "Off that way." He pointed down at an angle.

"A light?"

"A lamp, I think, or a candle."

"That must be him, then! Hurry!" the Leader said. "You, too, Sword! A bow isn't the best weapon in a confined space like this."

Before Breaker could respond the Archer was galloping down the stairs, pulling an arrow from his quiver; after a moment's hesitation, Breaker followed, blade ready.

At the bottom of the stair he paused. He was in a large room, some fifteen feet below entry level, with half a dozen passages opening off it in various directions; the light was too dim to make out any details. The Archer was nowhere to be seen—but his footsteps were plainly audible, and Breaker glimpsed a faint flicker of light down one passage. Reluctantly, he moved toward it, sword raised.

This wasn't right, he thought. Rushing headlong down here—this could easily be the trap they had been worried about. This was *not* right. The Leader shouldn't have allowed this. He shouldn't be here.

But he couldn't let the Archer run off by himself.

"Bow?" he called.

"Over here, Sword!" came the reply. "It's someone with a candle, someone in a robe—this way!"

Cautiously, Breaker advanced into the corridor, past the first pair of doors—and then a woman's voice shouted from somewhere behind him, "Now!"

Breaker whirled instantly, his every instinct screaming "Trap!" A pair of heavy doors was swinging shut behind him; reacting without conscious thought, he thrust the blade of his sword between them, preventing them from closing completely. The doors had been shaped to overlap, and the sword prevented that; a tiny crack remained, his blade trapped in it.

That same female voice, muffled by the doors, squealed in surprise.

Behind him, farther down the corridor, Breaker heard other doors slam shut, and the rattle of locks and bars dropping into place. The distant candlelight vanished, plunging him into near-total darkness; the only thing still visible was the thin line of light above and below his sword.

Suddenly furious, Breaker raised one booted foot and kicked hard; the doors burst open, and he found himself staring at two young women. They stood in the corridor, staring back at him—and at the long, sharp sword in his hand, its tip mere inches from the nearer woman's throat. One of them held a lit lamp, but otherwise their raised hands were empty; a wooden bar thumped to the floor, obviously just dropped.

Two of the Wizard Lord's maids, obviously. They were thin, dark-haired, attractive enough, wearing knee-length white dresses—and clearly terrified.

"What's going on?" Breaker demanded, stepping forward and kicking the bar away.

One woman—little more than a girl, really—whimpered. The other, the one with the lamp, said, "Don't kill us!"

"I'm not planning to," Breaker replied angrily. "What's happening?"

"We were . . . we were supposed to close and bar the door, that's all," the whimperer said.

"To trap you," the other added. "We weren't going to hurt you."

"That's right. The Wizard Lord said that if we killed you, he'd beat us to death with his own hands."

And with that, understanding burst upon Breaker. It all made sense now. The Wizard Lord had made no serious attempt to kill them, had not fled from his keep, had not done any of a dozen things that might have delayed them longer, and *of course* had not agreed to resign, because this was what he had wanted all along, ever since he realized they could not be dissuaded. The Wizard Lord didn't want the Chosen dead, because that would destroy his own magic, but taking them prisoner—*that* would suit him very well indeed. They would be unable to harm him, unable to pass their magic along to anyone else.

The Thief might have been a problem to hold, with her magical skill with doors and locks, but she had not come—had the Wizard Lord arranged that somehow? Perhaps he had. And splitting the party with that arrow in Babble's thigh had almost certainly been carefully planned; it would obviously be easier to trap three people, rather than six or seven.

Everything suddenly made far more sense, and the Wizard Lord seemed far more sensible, than Breaker had thought just moments before.

But even so, the Wizard Lord had misjudged, had put too much faith in his maids and his own cunning, and Breaker was still free. What about the others?

"Bow!" Breaker bellowed, without taking his eyes off the women. "Are you there? Are you all right?"

No one replied.

"He probably can't hear you," one of the maids said. "The doors are very thick. And I'm pretty sure *he* didn't stop anyone from barring them."

"Damn," Breaker said. He hesitated.

He could go down the corridor to see whether he could free the Archer, but if he did these women would almost certainly lock him in, as they had originally intended—and even if he took them with him, there might well be more lurking out of sight, in whatever hiding place this pair had used. The stories said the Wizard Lord had half a dozen maids, which left four or so unaccounted for.

He could ask these two to help him get the Archer out, but he couldn't really trust them . . .

And where was the Leader? He suddenly realized he hadn't heard or seen anything of him since descending. He looked past the maids, back to the central chamber and the spiral stair, and saw no one else.

"Boss?" he called.

The maids glanced at each other, but said nothing.

"Boss?"

No one answered.

"Where is he?" Breaker demanded, lifting his sword to one woman's chin.

"I don't know!" the maid said, terrified. "I swear by all the *ler*, I don't know!"

"Damn," Breaker said again. Then he gestured behind himself. "Get in there," he said.

"What?"

"Get back in there!" He stepped to one side to let the two women pass. "And leave the lamp."

Reluctantly, watching him every step of the way, the first woman set the lamp on the floor, and then both sidled past him, into the dark, empty corridor.

Never taking his eyes off them, never lowering his sword, he closed the two doors. Heavy iron brackets were mounted on both of them, at exactly the height his sword had originally been caught between them; he found the dropped bar and set it in those brackets.

"It's so *dark*!" a muffled voice called.

Breaker ignored that; he scooped up the lamp and looked around.

There was a niche in the wall on either side, designed so that a person could stand in it with the door in front of him, and the door would fit in as if the niche was an ordinary doorframe leading into a room, so that someone walking down the passage would not realize the corridor could be closed off. This whole arrangement had clearly been *designed* as a trap, not improvised—how long had the Wizard Lord been planning this? Had he intended this when he first *built* the tower, eight or nine years ago?

Breaker began to wonder just what was really happening. Had the Chosen been gathered together and lured here deliberately? Had Seer and Lore been sent to Stoneslope on *purpose*?

But no, that was ridiculous. The Wizard Lord had done everything he could to keep the massacre secret. This was just his backup plan, his way of dealing with the Chosen if it could not be avoided.

But how elaborate was it? The Archer was undoubtedly trapped somewhere deep in the corridors, safe for the moment—but where was the Leader?

Breaker struggled to remember everything he had seen and heard since entering the tower, and concluded that he had never heard the Leader's footsteps on the stairs, had never seen the Leader's shadow blocking the light from above.

He had never come down here at all.

That was baffling; why hadn't he been right on Breaker's heels? Had the Wizard Lord somehow trapped him before he even got that far?

By the time he had thought this through he was on the stairs, climbing.

On the entry level he paused, and glanced around.

There were four doors and one open passage opening off the central chamber; all four doors were closed, and as far as he could see by lamplight did not appear to have been disturbed in some time—two were adorned with cobwebs that would have been broken had the doors been opened. The Wizard Lord and his maids clearly did not use those doors often.

The passage led back to the entrance, still held open by the Archer's wedged arrow.

The Leader might have gone back out to gather reinforcements, but would he have left the arrow? And . . . Breaker could hear voices. Faint, too faint to make out words, but definitely voices, and they were coming from above.

They were strangely familiar. They were very much like the voices he had heard now and then when he awoke in the middle of the night on the journey from Winterhome to this tower, the voices he had dismissed as dreams or audible *ler*—those same voices were speaking, somewhere higher up in the tower.

And one of them might have been the Leader's.

And every time he had heard those voices in the night, he now realized, one of them could have been the Leader's.

Sword in one hand, lamp in the other, Breaker headed up the spiral.

[33]

Once he was above the entry level's ceiling Breaker discovered that most of the tower was an empty shell; there were no intermediate levels, no floor across the beams that supported that ceiling, but simply a bare stone cylinder, some fifty feet in height, with a stone spiral up the center leading to the floor above.

And there were two voices coming from that upper level, one of them *definitely* the Leader's; he hastened his pace.

And then he stopped dead, just as his head reached the level of the floor, when he heard the Leader say, "I suppose they've realized they're trapped by now. You're sure there's no way they can escape?"

"I certainly *hope* not," the other voice said—a thin tenor Breaker did not recognize, but that he supposed must be the Wizard Lord's real voice. Up until now he had only heard the Wizard Lord speaking through animals, but this voice sounded human. "I suppose that eventually the Swordsman might manage to hack his way through the doors, but it should take hours, at the very least, and I'd expect my maids to warn me."

Breaker's hand trembled, and he felt ill.

"You can't just *tell* where they are?" the Leader asked.

"Not with those confounded *ara* feathers the Swordsman has—I'm not the Seer." At that, Breaker's hand fell to the feathers in his belt, the feathers he had bought from a passing guide to ward off bad dreams. They had apparently done more good than he realized.

"No, you're the Wizard Lord," the Leader said. "You're supposed to have *all* our magic."

"I have my *own* magic, not yours. Eight times as much, yes, but not the same."

"How long do you think I should wait before luring in the others?"

"You know them better than I do. My maids are undoubtedly setting up the next corridor by now, if you want to get on with it."

"Oh, there's no hurry. After all this time I want to enjoy this."

"You *enjoy* it? Betraying your comrades?"

"Of course! The seven people in all Barokan my magic can't affect, and who don't have the sense to see that our magic should make us rulers, and who dragged me halfway across Barokan in the rain—of *course* I enjoy knowing where their folly has brought them."

"It's not all seven. The Thief is still back on her farm outside Quince Market, with her husband and brats."

"It's six of them; that's good enough for now."

"We've only trapped two so far."

"The dangerous two."

"True enough."

Breaker heard the gurgle of wine being poured. He swallowed bile.

"Was it hard, keeping up the pretense for so long?" the Wizard Lord asked.

"Sometimes. But they were all so very sure of themselves—the idea that one of the Chosen might want to join you in ruling Barokan doesn't seem to have ever even occurred to them. Even when I kept telling them not to make any plans, not to make *any* sort of serious preparations, they never got suspicious—you probably didn't need to set that stag on me at all."

"I was trying for the Swordsman," the other said. "But then I couldn't just ignore you. If I had, they might have realized something was wrong."

"I know, and I'm sure it removed any doubts they might have had. Later I was a bit worried that the Thief's refusal to accompany us might get them thinking in unfortunate directions, but apparently it never did.

I was very relieved when she didn't come along, you know—she thought differently from the others, more sensibly, not all caught up in our preordained roles, so she might have been harder to fool, and of course her magic would make her hard to capture and hold. And I almost couldn't believe our luck when the Seer said she wasn't going to set foot in the tower—if she'd been here I couldn't have sent them down into the cellars, she'd have *known* where you were."

"I was planning to shoot *her,* rather than the Speaker, for exactly that reason," the Wizard Lord replied. "But having them both out of the way was even better. Though you know, she must know where we are, that the two of us are up here and the others are downstairs—I wonder what she thinks of that?"

"She probably thinks it's all part of some grand scheme of mine, some ploy to convince you to surrender."

The Wizard Lord snorted derisively. "As if I would *ever* give up any of my magic! It's all that makes life worth living."

"As you say. I always wanted to be a wizard, or at the very least a priest, but I couldn't find any wizards to train me, and the *ler* back home in Deepwell wouldn't have me. Becoming one of the Chosen was the only magic I could get."

"You could do worse. After all, here we are!"

It might just be a trick, Breaker told himself. This might all be some scheme to get the Wizard Lord to lower his guard. After all, the Leader knew what the Wizard Lord had done, knew about the deaths and disasters he had caused.

"Here we are," the Leader agreed. "And you know, when they're all captured, and the Council has been dealt with, I think I might just go back to Deepwell and gut all the priests. If the *ler* there won't have me, why should they have anyone?"

"Indeed, indeed! A toast, then, to the priesthood of Deepwell—may their deaths come soon!"

Glasses clinked.

If that was a trick, it had succeeded too well—Breaker was convinced. There was no need to say anything like that as part of a ruse.

The Leader was as mad, as evil, as the Wizard Lord.

That explained so much. It explained the disorganization, the lack of planning the Chosen had suffered—it hadn't been simple inexperience, but that the man charged with organizing and planning had been working against them. It explained why the Seer had accepted the Wizard Lord's lies about Stoneslope for five years—it had been the Leader who told her, the Leader she trusted, the Leader whose opinion she respected, the Leader who had been scheming with the Wizard Lord all along. Those voices in the night—that must have been Boss and the Wizard Lord conspiring together, making their plans, discussing the next move.

"Now, I think it's time to bring in the others," the Leader said, after a moment's silence. "What do we have planned for them? I don't want to foul anything up at *this* point."

"Can you separate them, so they'll be easier to deal with? Individually they shouldn't be any problem—the Beauty can't seduce my maids, the Scholar's knowledge won't help him here . . ."

"Is that why all your servants are female? The Beauty?"

"Of course! I thought that was obvious, and I still don't know why Goln Vleys didn't do it."

"I don't either—Goln Vleys must have been a fool."

"All of them must have been. I'm not."

"Goln Vleys didn't need to fight a Speaker. The Council hadn't invented that role yet. The Speaker can break most of your spells."

"The Speaker has an arrow in her leg—she's the least danger of any of them, now!"

"True. So we have a cripple, an old woman, a pretty little nothing, and a harmless tale-spinner. Suppose I tell them that you're going to surrender after all, and resign, and that you have healing magic you've agreed to use, and the Beauty can help Babble in, while Seer and Lore wait with the wagon? Then later I can ask them to come in and lend a hand with the cleanup."

"That should work. I'll have my maids ready another corridor."

And Breaker heard a wineglass set down, and footsteps approaching, and he knew that the time had come at last. He charged up the last few steps.

His training and countless hours of practice kicked in immediately, and as he had been taught he took in his surroundings as swiftly as he could, looking for foes and traps and anything he might want to use as a weapon, all while keeping much of his attention on his intended target. The room at the top of the tower was round, of course, lit by five windows spaced around its circumference; cluttered shelves covered much of the walls between the windows. Several chairs were scattered about. A small table with three chairs stood to one side, a bottle, corkscrew, and two glasses upon it, and the Leader seated comfortably in one of the chairs. And halfway between that table and the stair was his enemy, his target, the Wizard Lord.

The Wizard Lord was a little below average in height, a little thinner than most, wearing a loose gray robe that might once have been black; he had unruly brown hair, and a surprised look on his face—though Breaker supposed anyone would look surprised to have a swordsman come bounding up the stairs at him like that. He jerked aside at Breaker's sudden emergence, and dove for a staff that leaned against a nearby chair, and even as he did one hand was scrabbling at his robe, clearly groping for a hidden talisman.

For an instant, as he saw the Wizard Lord as an ordinary man rather than a mysterious magical presence, Breaker thought he should offer the man one last chance to surrender—after all, up until now he had always had his secret final defense in the form of the Leader's treachery. Now that that was exposed, he might see reason. . . .

But the ghosts of Stoneslope, the memory of little Kilila's screams, the months of dismal rain, burned homes, drowned fields, and bloody butchered animals, all swept over him in a wave of weary anger, and Breaker did not bother saying a word before knocking the staff away with the sword and then thrusting the blade through the Wizard Lord's unprotected heart.

It was easy, astonishingly easy. This was the moment that all his practice, all his training back in Mad Oak, had been meant for, and now that preparation paid off; he had no trouble at all in slipping his blade past the Wizard Lord's arm, past the man's last desperate attempt to ward off his doom, and punching the point through cloth and skin and flesh, putting his shoulder and muscle and weight behind the blow.

For a few strange seconds, as he struck, everything seemed to slow down; Breaker was horribly aware of the feel of the sword in his hand, the resistance the blade met as it scraped across a rib, pushed through muscle much tougher than he would have expected in so small a man, and pierced the Wizard Lord's beating heart. He heard the tearing of the robe's fabric, the rattle as the dropped staff hit the floor, the sound of the Leader's chair being pushed back. He saw the Wizard Lord's mouth and eyes go wide, saw the man's eyes glaze over, and dark blood bubble up in his mouth. A choked gasp came from the Wizard Lord's throat, cut off almost instantly by the surge of blood.

From the corner of his eye Breaker saw the Leader fall backward, across the chair he had been sitting in a moment before, and sprawl awkwardly to the floor. He was no threat, not yet; Breaker could take the time to be sure that the Wizard Lord was dead.

But that did not take long at all. He could see the light going out of the man's eyes as they rolled back, could hear his breath catch and cease, could feel his heart spasm into stillness around the sword's blade.

The Wizard Lord was dead.

A weird feeling of anticlimax struck him; he had just killed a man for the first time, and no ordinary man, but the Wizard Lord himself—and it had taken a single thrust, catching the man by surprise, and really, physically it hadn't felt very different than killing a dog or a deer.

But at the same time he knew it *was* different. The expression on the dying wizard's face was nothing like anything he had seen on a mere beast, and he knew it would haunt his dreams.

And the air was alive with tension, a tension he could not immediately explain.

But then time sped up again, and the tension was released, and as storm winds whipped at him, though he was still in a closed room, as voices sang and screamed in his mind, as light flickered and blazed across the walls and ceiling, Breaker realized what was happening.

Many of the *ler* that had been confined by the Wizard Lord's spells, the natural forces he had trapped in charms and talismans, were released by his death, and were escaping back into their own world.

"No!" the Leader cried from where he lay. "No! All the magic!"

Breaker jerked his sword from the Wizard Lord's chest, and let the corpse fall heavily to the rough plank floor; bright blood dribbled from the wound and formed a spreading pool on the wood. Then Breaker stepped away from the stairs and turned to face the fallen Leader.

"He enchanted me!" the Leader said, looking up at Breaker's face. "I swear by my soul, he had me bound to him! He knew my true name, he *made* me betray you. . . ."

"Shut up," Breaker said, setting his lamp on the chair where the wizard's staff had rested.

"No, really, he had me in his spell! I know it's not supposed to work on the Chosen, but he'd found a way . . ."

"Shut up," Breaker repeated. "I'm not going to kill you—at least, not yet, not if you shut up. It's not my job—and what would be the point?"

"But I didn't . . ."

"Just shut up, will you? It doesn't matter anymore. He's dead—I killed the Wizard Lord. Our job's done. It's over."

The Leader blinked up at him, at the bloody blade of his sword, and fell silent.

"One thing, though," Breaker said. "You're going to pass on your talisman, first chance you get. You've had your turn, you'll say—you understand? There probably won't be another Dark Lord in our lifetimes anyway, but I'm not taking any chances—if you still have that talisman in a year's time, *then* I'll kill you. You understand me?"

The Leader nodded desperately.

"And the Thief, and the Seer—their time's up, too. You tell them that."

"Me?"

"You—you're the Leader. We aren't going to tell them what happened here—there's no reason to. You and I escaped the trap together, and we killed him. Why should we say anything else?"

"Yes, yes! Of course. We don't . . . I don't want any trouble . . ."

"One year," Breaker said. "No more. And sooner would be better."

Then he knelt and wiped the blood from his sword on the Wizard Lord's robe.

[34]

Breaker dragged the Wizard Lord's corpse down the stairs, to prove to the maids that he was dead; once they saw the remains, somewhat battered by the none-too-gentle descent, they were eager to cooperate. The Archer was freed, and an hour later the seven Chosen were reunited on the hillside by the wagon.

Breaker and Boss gave no details of what happened, merely said that the Leader had distracted the Wizard Lord and the Swordsman had then killed him.

The Beauty noticed how subdued the Leader was, and looked questioningly at Breaker.

"He saw something," Breaker said. "Something the Wizard Lord did before we killed him; I don't know exactly what."

"I can't believe it's over," the Archer said.

"It's not," the Scholar said. "Not quite. Now we need to find his talismans, and take them back to the Council of Immortals. We each carry our own talisman's mate—no one else can handle them safely."

"What about the Thief's?" Breaker asked.

"It stays here until the new Wizard Lord comes to claim it, I suppose. Just as the talisman would if one of us had died."

"The new Wizard Lord?"

"Yes, of course—the Council will choose a new one as soon as they know this one's dead."

"Why?"

A sudden silence fell as the other six all stared at Breaker.

"What do you mean, why?" the Seer asked.

"Why should we have a new Wizard Lord? You all saw how much damage a bad one can do—why should we help them set up another?"

"We don't have much choice," the Scholar said mildly. "They'll do it whether we want it or not."

"To control the weather and kill rogue wizards," the Beauty said.

"But there haven't *been* any rogue wizards in years—in *centuries*!" Breaker protested. "And the weather can manage itself."

"It's not our decision," the Scholar said. "It's up to the Council."

"But why?"

"That's just the way it's always been."

Breaker stared at him, baffled, then turned and stalked away.

A moment later, as he sat on a rock staring out across the hills, the Beauty came up and sat down beside him. She said nothing at first, but she pulled the scarf from her face, and flung back her hood.

He turned and looked at her fully and directly for the first time, at her heart-shaped face, her lush auburn hair shining in the late afternoon sun; she was unquestionably the most beautiful woman, the most beautiful creature, he had ever seen. He felt a stirring in his loins as her scent reached him—no perfume, but simply the smell of a clean, healthy woman.

"Was it bad?" she asked. "Killing him?"

"It was quick," Breaker replied. "That's not the problem, not really."

"He killed dozens of people—is that it?"

"Hundreds, maybe. Yes."

"But without a Wizard Lord, wild lightning might kill just as many—crops could fail, floods wash people away, storms sink fishing boats . . ."

"But . . . it's not the same. That's not deliberate. It's not *evil.*"

"The people would be just as dead."

"I suppose."

"We can tell the Council we think they should reconsider," she suggested.

"We can, yes," Breaker agreed. "We will." He hesitated, unsure what to say, not wanting to tell the truth, then rose. "Let's go find those talismans."

They did not find the talismans, but the maids did, as they cleaned the Wizard Lord's body—all eight were sewn onto a leather belt the dead man wore beneath his faded robe. No one had any difficulty in identifying which one to remove, as each matched the talisman one of the Chosen already carried. Breaker pulled the silver blade from the belt, ripping it loose without bothering to sever the threads that held it, and watched as the Archer took the golden arrow, the Beauty the silver mirror, the Seer the crystal orb.

The Leader hesitated, his hand hovering over the golden crown; he looked at Breaker.

"Take it," Breaker said, and Boss obeyed.

The wounded Babble had to be helped over to the cooling corpse to collect the vaguely tongue-shaped garnet, and the Scholar waited until last to retrieve the tiny rune-carved stone tablet.

That left an iron key, which clearly represented the Thief. Breaker prodded it experimentally, and found that his fingers could not close on it, and any touch left his fingertips bleeding from dozens of tiny cuts.

"She'll need to come and fetch it," he said, putting his bleeding fingers in his mouth.

The others nodded, and they left the Wizard Lord's body to his maids.

They stayed the night at the tower, the maids waiting on them as if they were mighty lords, and the next morning, as they were readying the wagon for departure and idly debating whether they should bother tearing off the lightning cage to lighten the oxen's burden, the wizards began to arrive.

The first came by air, of course—an old man Breaker had never seen before. The winds that carried him alerted the Chosen to his approach, as they suddenly howled and whistled from a clear sky; Breaker and the others looked up from where they stood to see the wizard sailing over the hills, and a moment later he stumbled to the snowy ground a dozen yards from the wagon.

No one moved to aid him. Breaker felt a twinge of shame at that, an old man on one knee in the snow and no one rushing to help him up, but on the other hand—this was a wizard. This was a member of the Council of Immortals that had sent them to kill the Wizard Lord, and had given them no assistance whatsoever. *No one* had given them much help, but the wizards least of all.

This man had magic that could carry him as fast as the wind, but he had let the Chosen struggle for weeks through endless seas of mud and slush. No wizards had offered to carry the Chosen to the Galbek Hills, nor to shield them from the Wizard Lord's storms.

Let the old man stand up on his own, Breaker thought.

The wizard righted himself, brushed the snow from his black robe, and called, "Congratulations!"

"You're welcome," Breaker said coldly.

The wizard blinked, then smiled. "Yes, of course, thank you! Thank you all for freeing us from that madman! Well done, well done!"

"Do you know what you're talking about?" the Archer asked. "Why do you call him a madman?"

The wizard was stepping gingerly toward them, holding the hem of his robe up out of the slush and wet snow; he looked up from his feet. "Wasn't he? From the damage he did to the towns along your route, I could scarcely think otherwise."

"He was mad," Breaker said. "As you say, he could scarcely be otherwise. And when did you first realize this?"

The wizard looked puzzled, and stopped walking. "Me? Oh, perhaps a fortnight back."

Breaker marveled to himself at that; their slow and miserable journey from Winterhome had taken over a month, but this wizard had noticed nothing wrong until two weeks ago.

"Yet you did nothing about it?"

"Well, *no,*" the wizard said. "That was *your* job—if *I* had opposed him, he would have killed me."

"Was there *nothing* you could have done to aid us, to ease our path, to hinder his plans?"

"Not without risking his anger, Swordsman—that's why the Council created the Chosen in the first place, all those centuries ago!"

"And what about *our* risks?"

"You agreed to those when you agreed to be Chosen!"

"I was told that we would be acting *with* the Council, not in its stead, if it ever became necessary to remove a Wizard Lord!"

"Oh. Well, that's not how it actually worked, was it? It's certainly not how *I* understood the situation. But in any case, it's over, and he's dead, and I'm sure we're all very proud of you. How did you know he was mad?"

"He murdered an entire town," the Seer said. "His own childhood home, a place called Stoneslope."

"Someone will need to go there and placate the dead," the Scholar said. "Take his head to show them, that should do it."

"Ah, and perhaps you . . ."

"*That* is not what we were chosen for," the Beauty snapped, pulling down the scarf that had covered her mouth, the better to shout. "You can fly—*you* do it."

"Ah—well, I'm sure something can be arranged, when the others get here."

"Others are coming, then?" Breaker asked.

"Oh, yes," the wizard said. "All of us, the entire Council." He pointed skyward. "Here's the next one, now."

And sure enough, a red speck was swooping nearer, one that Breaker soon recognized as the man the people of Mad Oak had called the Red Wizard—and he was carrying someone, a woman.

"That's very nice," Breaker said. "Enjoy your meeting. We'll be going now."

"No, no! You must stay—you must pass on the talismans to the new Wizard Lord."

Breaker exchanged glances with the others—though the Leader's gaze flicked away quickly, then fell to the ground.

"How long will this take?" the Scholar asked.

"Oh, not long. A day or two at most."

Breaker sighed.

"A day or two, then," he agreed.

Over the next few hours several more wizards arrived, and Breaker recognized six of them—he had seen four of them less than a year ago, when he dueled the Old Swordsman, and the other two had accompanied the old man when he first arrived in Mad Oak. Half a dozen of the wizards flew in, but some of those were carrying other, nonflying wizards. Two arrived on foot, one traveling at a normal pace, the other somehow walking so fast his legs were a blur of motion; one arrived on monsterback, and three on various more normal beasts of burden.

In all, nineteen wizards converged on the dead Wizard Lord's tower, there in the Galbek Hills, by nightfall.

Breaker watched them arrive, watched them greet each other, and stared at the ones he recognized from Mad Oak.

Had it really been less than a year since they saw him jab the Old Swordsman in the shoulder? It hardly seemed possible, but he knew it was—the duel had been late in the last winter, and this winter was still young.

During one of the lulls between arrivals Breaker became aware that the Leader was trying to get his attention; he turned and said, "What is it?"

"Could we speak in private, Sword?"

Breaker did not want to talk to the man, but he could see no graceful way to avoid it; he sighed, adjusted the sword on his belt, and accompanied the Leader for a walk, away from the tower and the wagon, up across the next hill. When they were out of sight of the others, both wizards and Chosen, Breaker stopped.

"What do you want?" he demanded.

"We need to discuss what happened. These wizards—they'll want details, and our stories must match."

Breaker stared at him for a moment, then asked, "How long did the two of you conspire together?"

Boss swallowed. "Five or six years," he said. "Ever since the massacre in Stoneslope."

"So you knew what he had done."

"Yes, I knew—though I didn't know it was as bad as you and the others say it was. The Seer told me there had been killing, and I came here and talked to the Wizard Lord, and he told me all about it, and asked what I was going to do, and I saw my opportunity."

"*Opportunity?* A hundred men, women, and children slaughtered, and you saw an *opportunity*?"

"Yes, I did! Go ahead and be self-righteous if you want, Sword, but those people were already dead, and I saw that I had a chance to do something new, to make us rich and powerful. Don't you see?"

"No. I don't."

"Look at it—the first Council was so frightened of power that they deliberately set up a system to prevent anyone from using it freely. The Wizard Lord restrains the Council, the Chosen restrain the Wizard Lord, and the Council restrains the Chosen, and *nothing gets done*—each little town goes on about its business in its own individual way, and Barokan stays a patchwork of priesthoods. But if two of the three sides were to join forces, think what we could accomplish!"

"What?"

Boss stammered, then said, "*Anything!* Don't you see?"

"No."

"Well, *I* do, and I did from the moment I became the Leader. I didn't find a way to bring it up with the old Wizard Lord in Spilled Basket, but this one—I got to know him a little, and then when he got his nasty little revenge I realized I had a hold on him, and something to offer him, and I agreed to lie to the Seer about the killings in exchange for his help. Together we would rule Barokan outright, not just in the limited way the Wizard Lord usually does—I would keep the rest of you from interfering with him, or if I couldn't I would help him capture you, and in exchange he would use his magic to help me get whatever I wanted. With my own magic, my persuasive powers, and his knowledge of true names, I could have anything I wanted. I have a *palace* back in Doublefall, Erren, a palace, with a dozen beautiful slave girls waiting on me hand and foot."

He paused, as if expecting Breaker to say something, but Breaker merely looked at him. Boss sighed.

"I tried to sound out the others about joining me—I talked to Lore about whether any of the Chosen were ever rich and powerful, and tried to hint that we could be the same, but he didn't see it. I didn't dare speak too openly, you understand. I think the Seer guessed what I was getting at, but she was too frightened to give it any real consideration. I couldn't *find* Stealth or Beauty—the Seer wouldn't help me—and I thought Babble had gone mad, with those voices of hers. And when I talked to Blade, before I could bring it up he started talking about how he didn't trust the Wizard Lord. So I gave up the idea of including the rest of you, and kept it just the two of us. Then when the Seer started collecting the Chosen I left home so you wouldn't see my palace and leap to any conclusions, and I headed to Winterhome to try to find the Beauty to convince her to back me up, but I couldn't locate her. I talked to the Wizard Lord, and we made some plans, but . . ."

"But I killed your partner. Fine, I see how it was, but it's over. You'll give up your talisman, and without your magic I suppose your slave girls will flee and you'll lose your palace. I don't care. I'm not going to kill you or tell anyone about it—though it wouldn't surprise me if Babble already knows what happened, or if the Seer guesses."

"But it doesn't have to be like that! When they choose the new Wizard Lord, we could talk to him . . ."

"No."

"But you could have anything you want . . . !"

"No. I swore an oath, and took a place among the Chosen, and I am not going to pervert that. And neither are you, not again. You're going to pass on the role of Leader."

"But . . ."

"No." His hand closed on the hilt of his sword.

Boss slumped.

"Have it your way, then," he said. "We still need to get our story straight."

Breaker frowned. "It's simple enough. After we agreed to go down to the cellars you heard a noise above, but you could not get my attention, or the Archer's, so you bravely and foolishly went to investigate by yourself, and found the Wizard Lord. You tried to use your persuasive powers to talk him into resigning peacefully, but he refused, and just then I came up the stairs, found you, heard his refusal, and killed him. How else could it have been?"

"How else?" The Leader sighed deeply. "Of course that's how it was."

"Shall we rejoin the others, then?"

"Of course."

And they did.

[35]

When the nineteenth wizard arrived, with the sun skimming the western horizon and the maids lighting torches, a tall woman in blue announced, "We are all gathered, then. Let the Council of Immortals be convened!"

"Out here in the cold?" a young wizard protested, but the others ignored him. Some had scattered across the hillside or wandered into the tower, but now they returned, and collected themselves in a rough circle around a campfire.

The Chosen were clustered around their wagon twenty yards away, watching this with varying degrees of interest. Breaker simply wanted them to get it over with, so that he could start the long walk home, but Lore was fascinated by the whole thing, the Seer was nervous about it . . .

The wizards had been speaking for only a few minutes when they all turned, as if called, to face the wagon.

"Will the Chosen please come forth, to tell us what befell them?" the blue-robed wizard called.

With varying degrees of enthusiasm the seven made their way to the Council's circle; the Speaker hobbling on a crutch the Scholar had improvised. The wizards parted to make way for them, and one quickly arranged a folding chair for the wounded Speaker.

"There are only seven," a wizard called. "Did Laquar kill one?"

"We kept the Thief in reserve," the Leader said. "We . . ."

"She refused to come," Breaker interrupted. "She should be replaced."

The other Chosen turned, startled, to look at him. "I thought we . . ." the Beauty began.

"I've had enough of deceit and evasion," Breaker said. "The Thief betrayed us and refused to come. The Seer, too, though she led us at first and came far, balked at the last moment, and should retire, as well."

"I would be *happy* to retire," the Seer said. "The Swordsman is right—my nerve failed me, and I am no longer fit for my role. I have seen too much as it is." She stepped toward the fire, and dropped two little orbs on the rocky ground near the flames.

"Pick up your talisman," the blue-robed wizard said. "If you want to retire, then so be it, but until a replacement is found you are still the Chosen Seer."

Reluctantly, the Seer stooped, retrieved the smaller of the two crystals, and stepped back.

Breaker turned a pointed gaze on the Leader, who took the hint.

"And I, too, feel I must resign," Boss said, tossing a golden talisman to the ground. "My plans were inadequate, and we only triumphed through good fortune and the Swordsman's skill. I will remain as Leader until my successor is found, but I trust that will be no longer than necessary." He threw Breaker a brief, venomous glare.

For a moment an awkward silence fell; then the blue-robed wizard asked, "Anyone else?"

"I feel I acquitted myself reasonably well," Lore said.

"I'm not ready to quit!" Bow snapped.

"Not *quite* yet," the Beauty added.

"I've only just accepted the role," Breaker said.

"The *ler*—no. I'm staying," Babble said.

"All right, then," the wizard said. "Tell us what happened."

For a moment no one spoke; then Breaker told the Seer, "You start. Five years ago."

The Seer nodded, and began.

The story, such as it was, took a little over an hour to tell; the Scholar took over from the Seer, the Speaker from the Scholar, the Leader from the Speaker, and finally the Swordsman from the Leader. The last two lied, telling the story they had agreed upon rather than the truth, but no one seemed to notice.

When the tale was done there was a brief silence; then a wizard called, "Very well, then, I think that was all in order, and we've agreed that three of the Chosen are to be replaced and the other five to continue. The next order of business, then, is to choose the new Wizard Lord."

"Wait," Breaker said. "Before you go any further, I must ask—do we still *need* a Wizard Lord?"

"Of course we do!" someone called, and a murmur of agreement ran through the little crowd.

"Why?" Breaker insisted. "There haven't been any rogue wizards in centuries!"

"But there *would* be, without a Wizard Lord," the Red Wizard replied. "Just as more Wizard Lords would become Dark Lords were it not for the Chosen."

"Would there? How many wizards are there? A few hundred? Surely . . ."

Breaker's planned speech was cut short by startled laughter. He blinked, and looked around, trying to see what was funny.

"A few *hundred*?" a wizard called. "Are you blind, Swordsman?"

"Perhaps he can't count that high," another suggested. "After all, you don't need numbers to use a blade."

"I don't understand," Breaker said.

"Swordsman, how many of us are here?"

"Nineteen. But this is the Council of Immortals . . ."

"The Council of Immortals is made up of all the wizards there are, Swordsman," the blue-robed leader explained gently. "This is all of us."

"But that's not . . ." Breaker looked for the female wizard who had accompanied the Old Swordsman to Mad Oak, and spotted her standing by one of the torches. "She said . . ."

She held up a hand. "I know, that's not what I told you. We were talking about centuries ago, though, when the Council was first formed, and back then it did *not* include every wizard. It's only in the past hundred and fifty years that we have all been members."

"But then—there are only nineteen wizards in all Barokan?"

"So far as we know, yes," the Red Wizard said. "It's the Wizard Lord's job to track down and kill any others."

"But they aren't *all* rogues . . . !"

"Yes, they are," another wizard said. "By definition. Our forefathers decided a century and a half back that it would be better for everyone if all wizards joined the Council, and with the Wizard Lord's aid, they did not make it optional."

"There are just *nineteen*?" the Archer said.

"You need a Wizard Lord to control *nineteen wizards*?" Breaker said.

"Well, there were hundreds when the system began," the old woman who had come to Mad Oak said. "But our numbers have dwindled."

"Then hasn't the need for a Wizard Lord dwindled, as well?" Breaker said. "Shouldn't we see what happens without one, rather than once again giving someone the power to kill entire towns and flood whole regions?"

There was a mutter among some of the wizards, but the blue-robed leader said firmly, "No. The system has worked for seven centuries, and I am not going to abandon it just because we happen to have had a ninth Dark Lord."

"But we don't need it, and another Dark Lord could be a disaster!"

"And how likely is it that we'll see another Dark Lord in our lifetimes? The system *works,* Swordsman—the Wizard Lord went mad, and the Chosen removed him, just as they were meant to. If there were no Wizard Lord, who knows how many people might have been killed or enslaved by wizards, or killed by storms or famines? We had more than a hundred years of peace and plenty—one small town and a few floods are not too high a price for that."

At the mention of enslavement Breaker glanced at Boss, who did not meet his gaze; then he turned back to the wizards.

"I think you're wrong," he said. "I think the Wizard Lords have outlived their purpose. I don't know why there are so few wizards now, compared to our ancestors' times, but whatever the reason, it makes a Wizard Lord an unnecessary danger!"

"It's because so many of the *ler* have been collected, or tamed by the priests, or softened by the mere presence of so many people nearby," a short, dark wizard in the back began. "There are fewer truly wild powers . . ."

"Never mind that," the blue-robed wizard snapped, holding up her hand. "It's none of his concern—he's merely the Swordsman. We have no obligation to answer to him."

"I just killed your Dark Lord!" Breaker protested.

"And that was your duty, your role," the wizard replied. "Thank you for performing it effectively—but it gives you no right to question us."

"I killed a man because your Council has propped up an ancient and unnecessary system . . ."

A sudden gust of wind whirled around him, unnaturally intense, snatching the breath from his mouth, and Breaker staggered back. His hand fell to the hilt of his sword.

"Stop it!" the Council's leader ordered over her shoulder. "He is the Chosen Swordsman, and entitled to our respect, if not our obedience. Release him!"

The wind stopped as abruptly as it had begun.

"You see why we need a Wizard Lord?" the blue-robed wizard said, more gently. "We can't be trusted. We know that. So we set one of us up to keep the others in check, and you eight are chosen to keep *him* in check. Thank you, Swordsman, for your service. Thank you all, O Chosen. Deliver now the Wizard Lord's talismans, and take your own with you, and go about your business."

"You'll exorcise the dead in Stoneslope?" Breaker demanded. "And see to it that the Seer, the Thief, and the Leader are replaced?"

The Council's leader sighed. "We will—and if you were not already the Swordsman, I'd make *you* the new Leader! You seem to take the role upon yourself."

"That's because . . . someone must, and Boss has—there are reasons he does not speak," Breaker said. He glanced around at his six companions.

"You're doing fine," the Archer said. "You killed the Dark Lord, so you get to speak for us here, so long as we agree with you—and so far, Sword, you haven't said a word I can't accept."

"There are things here I don't understand," the Beauty said, "and I have nothing more to say until I *do* understand them."

"I have no right to say anything," the Seer said. "We should have been here five years ago. I should have been at their side in the tower. Let the boy speak for us all."

"I am listening," the Speaker said. "My role is misnamed, for my task is always to listen, more than to speak."

"It's all too soon for me," the Scholar said. "Perhaps a year from now I'll know what to make of it."

"It's as he said," the Leader agreed, glancing at Breaker. "There are reasons I don't speak."

"It seems there may be more to the tale than you told us," the blue-robed wizard said.

"There's nothing more to tell you," Breaker said. "Anything we haven't said is private, and while you may choose us, you do not own us."

"That's rather the point, in fact," the Red Wizard agreed. "Let them go, Azal, and let us get on with choosing our new lord."

"Let them deliver the talismans," the Council's leader repeated.

"Swear you'll see that Stoneslope's ghosts are freed," Breaker said.

"*I* will swear it," the Red Wizard said. "I will go there myself, and bring whatever priests or others I find necessary to set the souls of the dead at peace. I swear by my own soul—is that good enough, Swordsman?"

"Thank you," Breaker said, with heartfelt gratitude. "And the three will be replaced? Then that's enough—I've had enough of all of this, and am eager to go home." He pulled out the little silver blade he had taken from the Wizard Lord's body and tossed it to the ground beside the orb and crown, then turned and walked away from the fire, the wizards, and the others, toward the waiting wagon.

The Seer and the Leader followed him, and the rest, in turn, added their captured talismans to the collection before leaving the Council of Immortals.

The Chosen spent another night in the Dark Lord's tower; the wizards' meeting ran late into the night, but did eventually end. In the morning Breaker arose to find the maids gossiping—some of the wizards had already departed, and others still slept in the catacombs beneath the tower, but the news had somehow been conveyed that the red-clad wizard, the man Breaker knew simply as the Red Wizard, was to be the new Wizard Lord.

The system would continue.

He ate a hearty breakfast from the dead Wizard Lord's pantries, bathed in a stone tub filled by the maids, and then dressed in his cleanest clothes—which were shabby and dingy, as he had been long upon the road. Still, he felt better than he had in some time. There would be a new Wizard Lord, yes, but the Red Wizard seemed a reasonable choice—Breaker remembered how polite he had been when he first arrived in Mad Oak, how he had deferred to the priestesses and tried not to trouble the *ler*.

Perhaps it *would* be another century before next the Chosen were called upon to remove a Dark Lord.

It was a new day, a new era—and he was free to go home to Mad Oak, or to go anywhere he chose. His job was done.

He was on the muddy, snowy hillside practicing his swordsmanship for the hour the *ler* still required of him when the Beauty emerged from the tower and headed toward him. Her face was wrapped in a black scarf, as always, but he could see her eyes, and he almost thought he could smell the subtle natural perfume of her hair. She watched solemnly as he slashed an imaginary opponent to ribbons, and when at last he stopped, stepped back, and began wiping the blade she approached.

"I wanted to say goodbye," she said. "I've talked one of the wizards into flying me back to Winterhome, so I won't be traveling with you."

"Oh," Breaker said.

He had been thinking of suggesting that she accompany him back to Mad Oak, but now that seemed overly bold. Instead he said, "Perhaps I could visit with you there."

"Erren," she said quietly, "I am twice your age."

"Oh," he said again.

She was right, he knew she was, but still, the sight of her eyes and the sound of her voice . . .

"It's not your fault," she said, "and if I were ever tempted by youth and vigor, believe me, you would receive very serious consideration—you are a fine young man. But I am *not* young."

He nodded; on some level he knew she was right, but his body, his heart, did not agree. His pulse had quickened just from her presence.

"Something happened in the tower, when you killed the Wizard Lord, that you haven't told us about," she said. It was not a question, and he did not answer.

For a moment they looked one another in the eye; then she asked, "Is it anything I should know?"

"You shouldn't need to," he said, "but ask me again a year from now."

She nodded.

The silence between them grew awkward after that, and at last, almost simultaneously, they turned and went their separate ways.

By midday the Chosen were scattered, each bound for his or her home, alone or in the company of wizards. Breaker turned down offers of magical aid and set out northward alone, on foot.

[36]

Breaker had passed through Redclay on his way south, and remembered the inn there as a convivial place. He looked around with a smile as he stepped inside, out of the snow.

"Hey, Swordsman!" someone called.

Breaker nodded an acknowledgment.

"Took you long enough to kill him," another voice called. "The whole town was almost washed away! And old Barga's house was burned to the ground by that lightning stuff."

Breaker's smile vanished. "We did the best we could," he said.

"Well, you should have done better."

"I didn't see *you* doing anything to help," Breaker retorted angrily.

"Why should I? It's *your* job, you and your magic sword! It's not like it's hard, killing a wizard when his magic can't hurt you!"

"I still had to *get* there, through all the storms," Breaker pointed out.

"You couldn't get some wizard to fly you there? Hire one as a guide?"

Breaker frowned. He ignored the question as he found a seat. He ignored other questions and comments as he ordered a mug of beer and drank it in silence.

Yes, it was his job—but he had done it as best he could, despite all the difficulties, despite storms and hardships and betrayal. He could have just gone home, like the Thief, but he hadn't.

And there was no way he could say that without sounding as if he were whining or boasting. His mood, so cheerful when he entered, had quickly become as sour as the local beer.

The innkeeper was friendly, at any rate, and when he ordered a second beer the man asked, "Staying in Redclay long?"

Breaker shook his head. "Just tonight. Then it's off northward—do you know a good guide heading north?"

"I thought the Chosen didn't need guides anymore."

"We don't really, but they can be helpful."

"Where are you going, then?"

"Mad Oak, up in Longvale."

"Ah. Never been there—is it nice?"

"I grew up there."

"So you'll be visiting family?"

Breaker smiled bitterly.

"No," he said. "I'm going home to stay."

"Really? They need a swordsman there, or a hero?"

"No. I've had enough of heroism. I'm going to grow barley."

"All done being the Chosen Swordsman, then?"

"I hope so," Breaker said, lifting his mug. He gulped beer. "By all the *ler,* I hope so!"

Spring was in full bloom by the time Breaker and the Greenwater Guide made their stooping dash past the mad oak and arrived at the familiar boundary shrine. The guide marched on past, but Breaker paused there and looked over the town.

It had not really changed, he knew, but it looked different to him now, all the same. It seemed smaller, for one thing. The oak and fieldstone construction looked rustic, almost crude. The pavilion built into the side of the ridge was almost exotic in the way it combined all the town's public buildings, from warehouse to dance hall, in a single structure, and the houses scattered along the slope below looked inefficient and almost random in how they were arranged, though he knew that it was actually the result of building them on the most level bits of land, because the *ler* here did not approve of digging out foundations.

Not all *ler* were so picky as these, he knew now.

And there below the town were the freshly planted fields, stretching down to the river, and there were the priestesses, walking through the fields talking to the *ler,* just as they always had, and shadows moved behind them as the *ler* flitted about in their peculiarly visible way.

"Is there a problem?" the guide asked.

Breaker shook his head. "No," he said, "just looking at the place."

"Hasn't changed much, has it?"

"No." Breaker knew that Mad Oak hadn't changed—but he had.

He walked on, and followed the guide to the pavilion. He knew he could have gone straight to his parents' home, but he preferred to take a little time to adjust to being back first.

Later, he was glad he had done so. Hearing the news from Digger in the pavilion and learning that he was not the only one who had changed was easier, he knew, than hearing it from his mother or sisters would have been.

His father was dead—a fever had taken him during the winter, despite Elder's best efforts. The *ler* insisted that Grumbler's time had come, and did not heed human entreaties.

Harp had married Smudge, as expected, but Little Weaver had married Brokenose, and Curly had married Joker, and Breaker had not expected either of those.

As news of his return circulated through Mad Oak, townspeople began to appear at the pavilion, ostensibly to welcome him home, but somehow Breaker did not find their reactions to his presence very welcoming.

Little Weaver and Brokenose arrived together, and her first words were "You didn't say how long you would be gone—I thought it might be *years*!"

"If the Dark Lord had had his way, it would have been forever," Breaker replied, looking at her and remembering the Beauty's face, knowing as he did that the comparison was horribly unfair—though in fact, Little Weaver fared better in the mental match than most women would have. "Congratulations on your marriage, both of you!"

Curly did not need to say anything to explain her marriage; her protruding belly was more than enough. Breaker gave her a kiss for old times' sake and wished her well.

Someone roused Brewer to roll out a keg of well-aged winter beer, and Digger gathered the village musicians, and by the time the sun was behind the ridge almost the entire village had collected in the pavilion, talking and laughing. A dozen couples danced to a brisk jig.

Breaker did not dance. He spoke quietly with his mother when she arrived, saying simply, "I'm sorry. I'm sorry I wasn't here. And I'm back, and I'll stay as long as I can."

She embraced him and said nothing; her eyes remained dry.

And when next the musicians took a break, Joker called, "Swordsman! Welcome home, congratulations on your survival, and thank you for ridding us of the Dark Lord of the Galbek Hills!"

Breaker nodded an acknowledgment. "I did what I had sworn to do," he said. "No more, and no less." And as he spoke he thought of the Thief, and the Seer, and the Leader, and the Wizard Lord himself, who could not truthfully have made even so modest a claim.

"Tell us about it!"

That elicited a chorus of echoes. "Tell us! Tell us!"

"What was it like?"

"Was his magic very fearsome?"

"Did he really throw lightning bolts at you?"

Breaker looked out at the eager faces of his townsmen, at their expectant smiles and ready ears, and felt a sudden surge of disgust—with them, and with himself, and with all the world, Chosen and wizards, priests and farmers, everyone and everything. They did not see the truth, that he was a hired killer, sent to dispose of another killer, that the Chosen and the Wizard Lord were just men and women no better than themselves.

This might be his home, but at the heart it was no better, no more understanding of what he had done, what he had been through, than Redclay or any of the other places he had stopped. They wanted a tale of heroism and glory, and he had nothing true to say to them that would serve.

"I'll leave that to the storytellers," he said. "I've said and done enough."

And he stood, and left the pavilion, walking back to his mother's house alone in the gathering dusk.